SWORD ART ONLINE phantom bullet

002

SWORD ART ONLINE phantom bullet

art: koutarou yamada
original story: reki kawahara
character design: abec

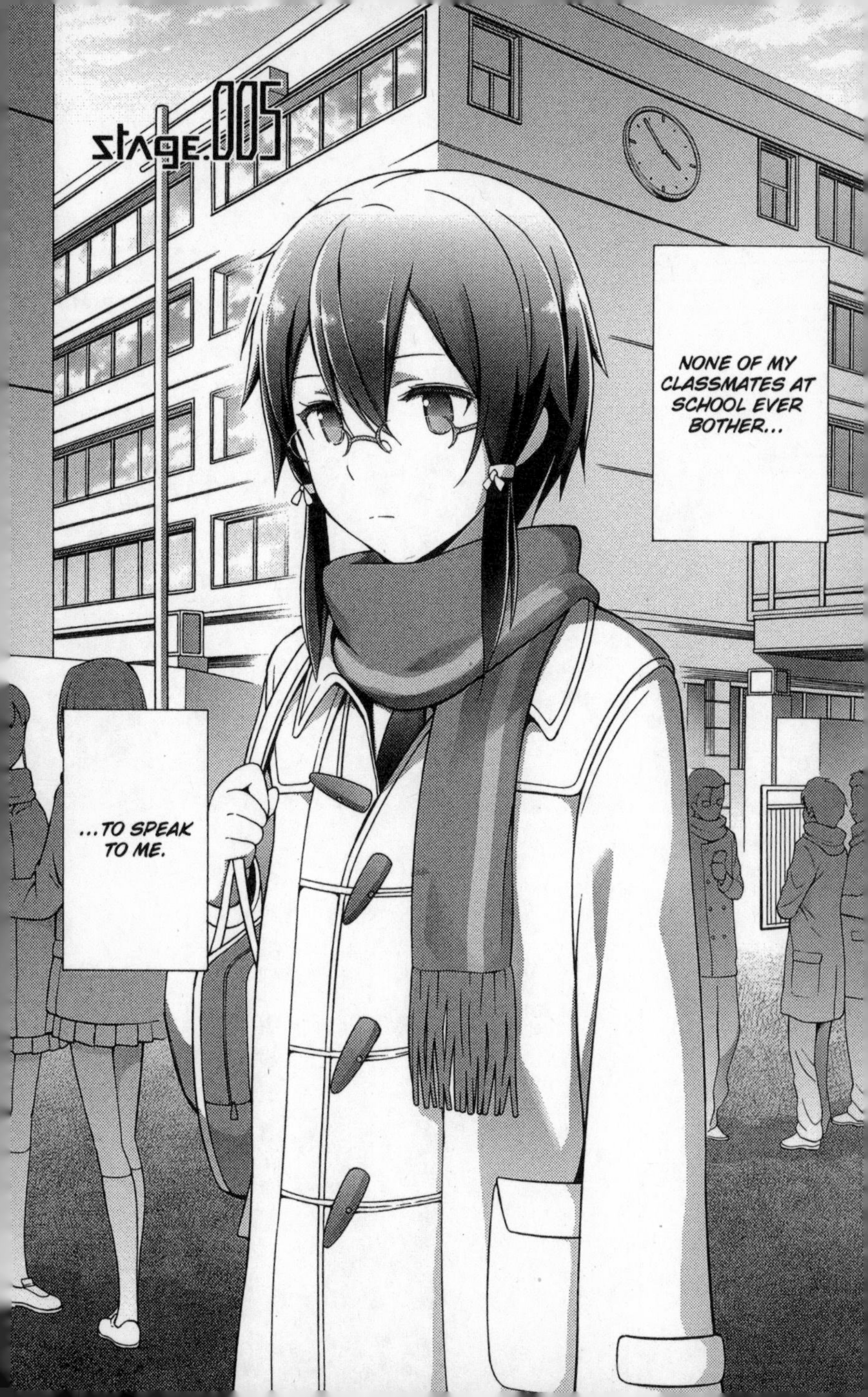
stage.005
NONE OF MY CLASSMATES AT SCHOOL EVER BOTHER...
...TO SPEAK TO ME.

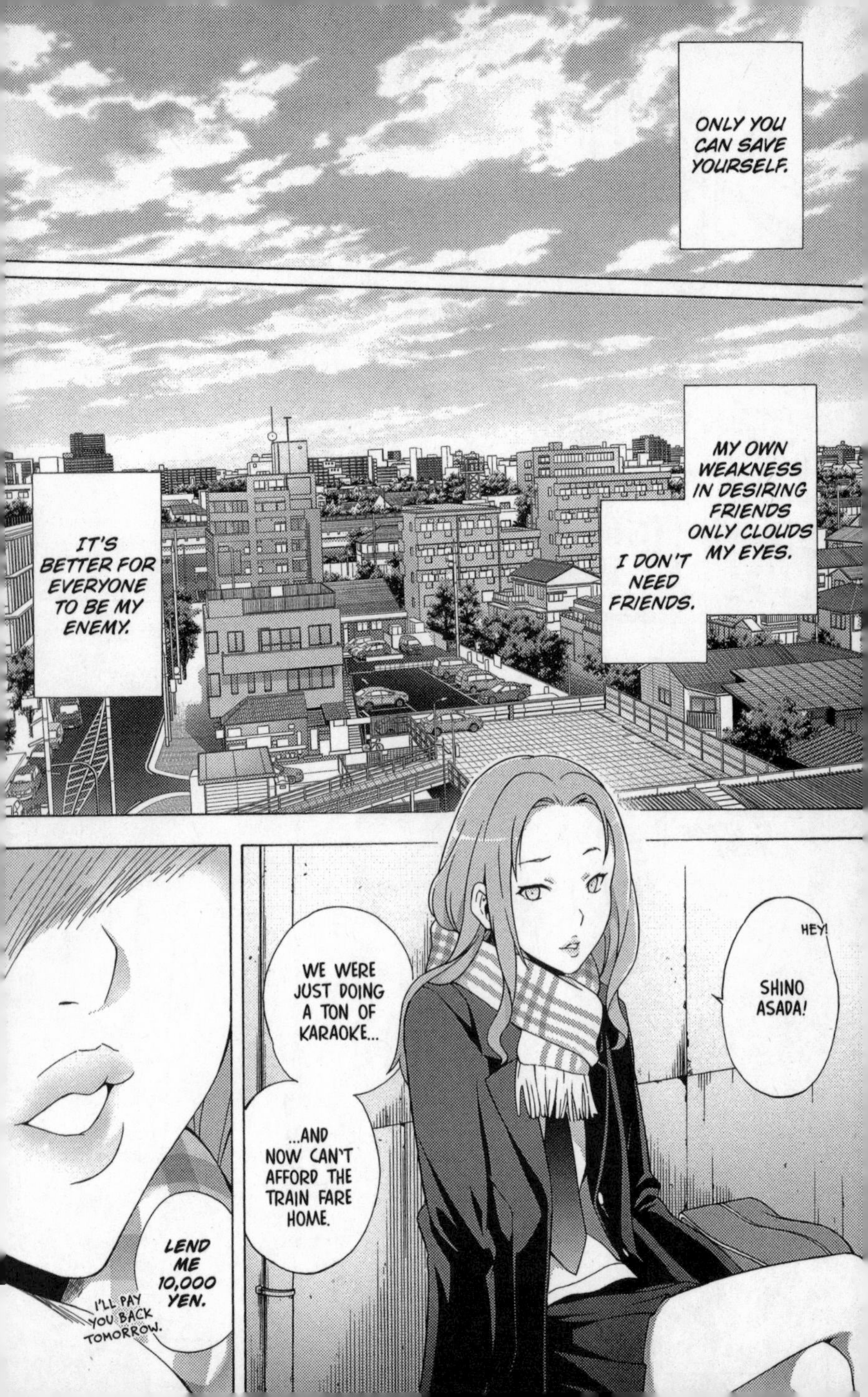
ONLY YOU CAN SAVE YOURSELF.
MY OWN WEAKNESS IN DESIRING FRIENDS ONLY CLOUDS MY EYES.
I DON'T NEED FRIENDS.
IT'S BETTER FOR EVERYONE TO BE MY ENEMY.
HEY!
SHINO ASADA!
WE WERE JUST DOING A TON OF KARAOKE...
...AND NOW CAN'T AFFORD THE TRAIN FARE HOME.
LEND ME 10,000 YEN.
I'LL PAY YOU BACK TOMORROW.

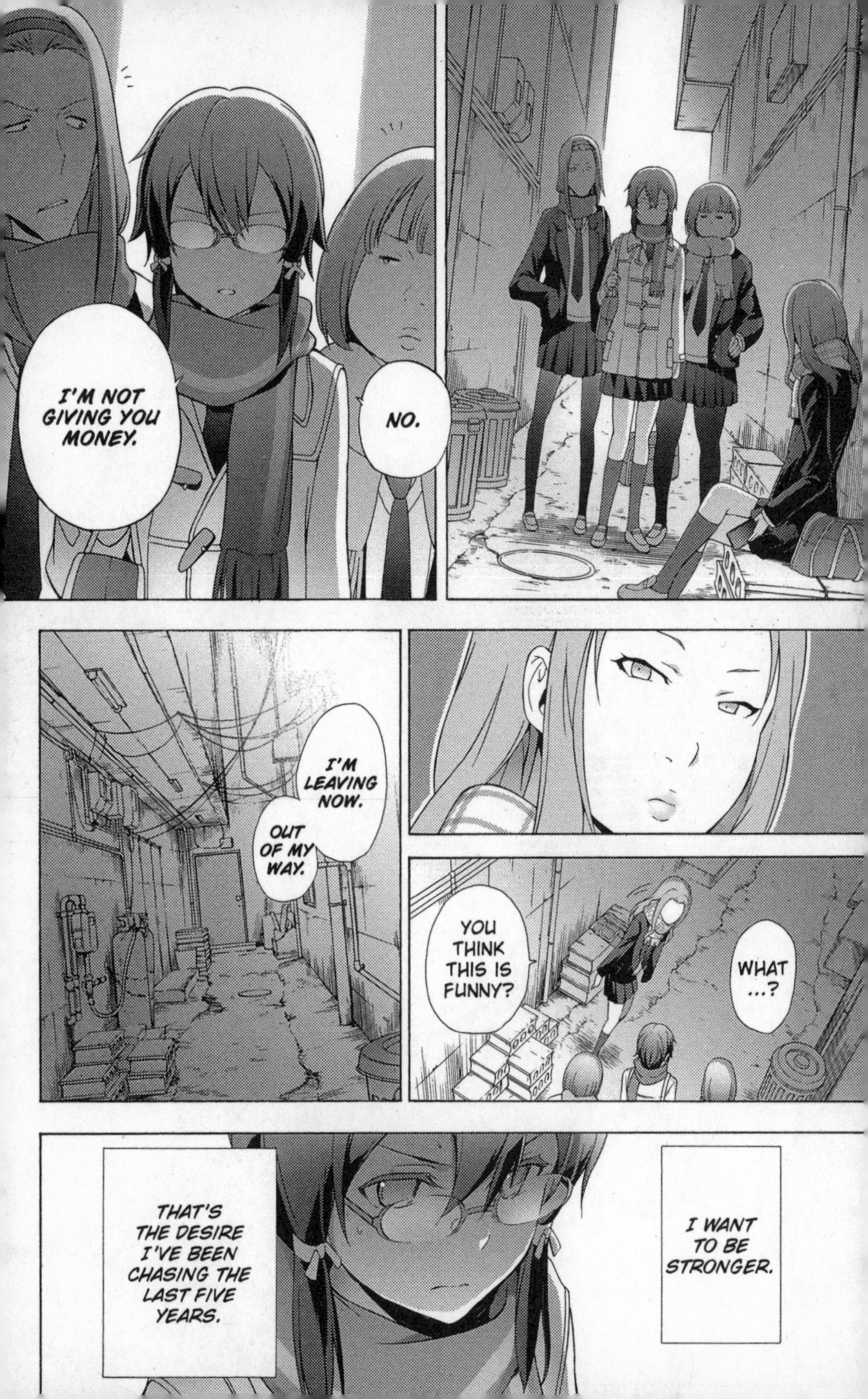
NO.
I'M NOT GIVING YOU MONEY.
WHAT ...?
YOU THINK THIS IS FUNNY?
I'M LEAVING NOW.
OUT OF MY WAY.
I WANT TO BE STRONGER.
THAT'S THE DESIRE I'VE BEEN CHASING THE LAST FIVE YEARS.

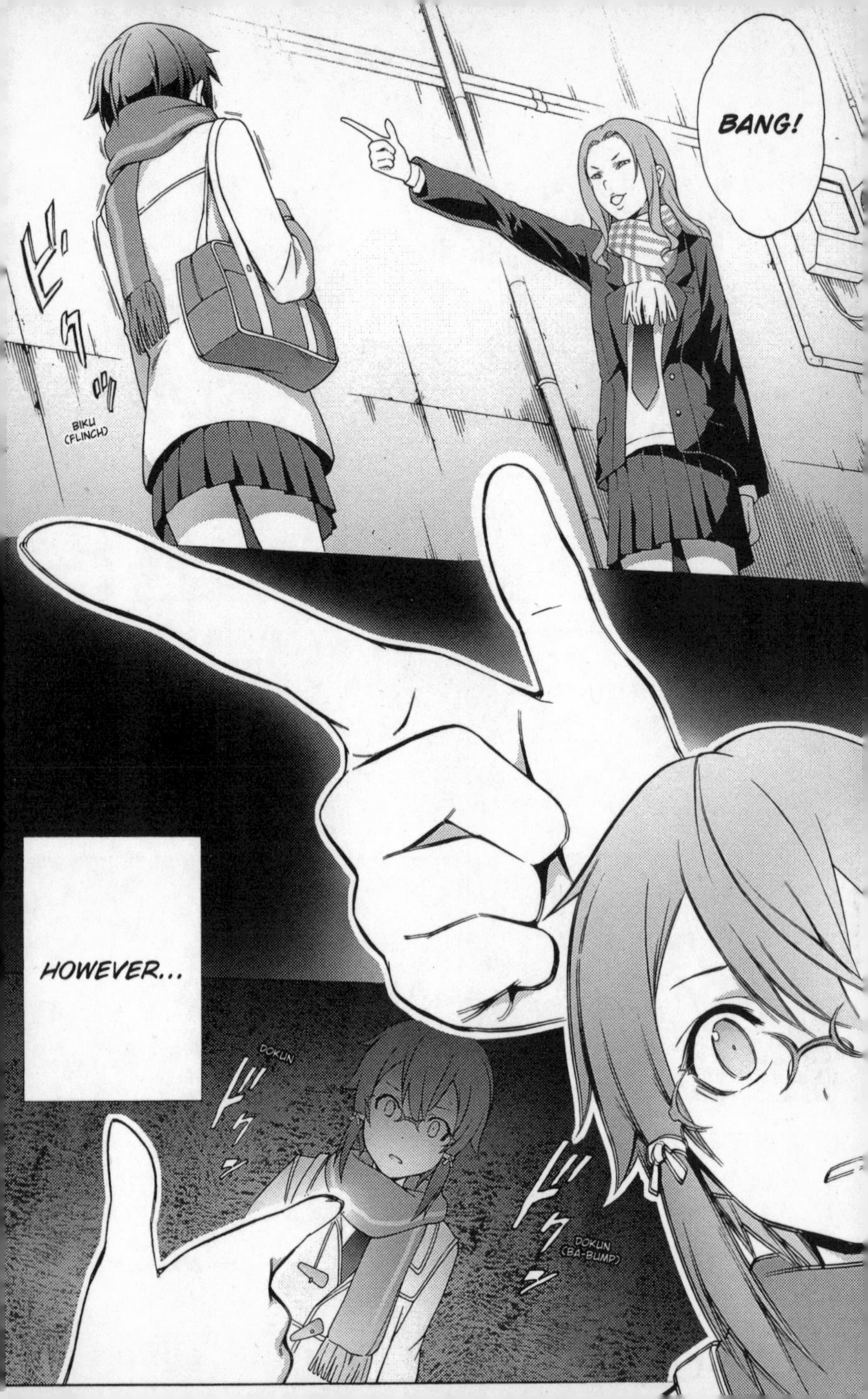
BANG!
BIKU (FLINCH)
HOWEVER...
DOKUN
DOKUN (BA-BUMP)

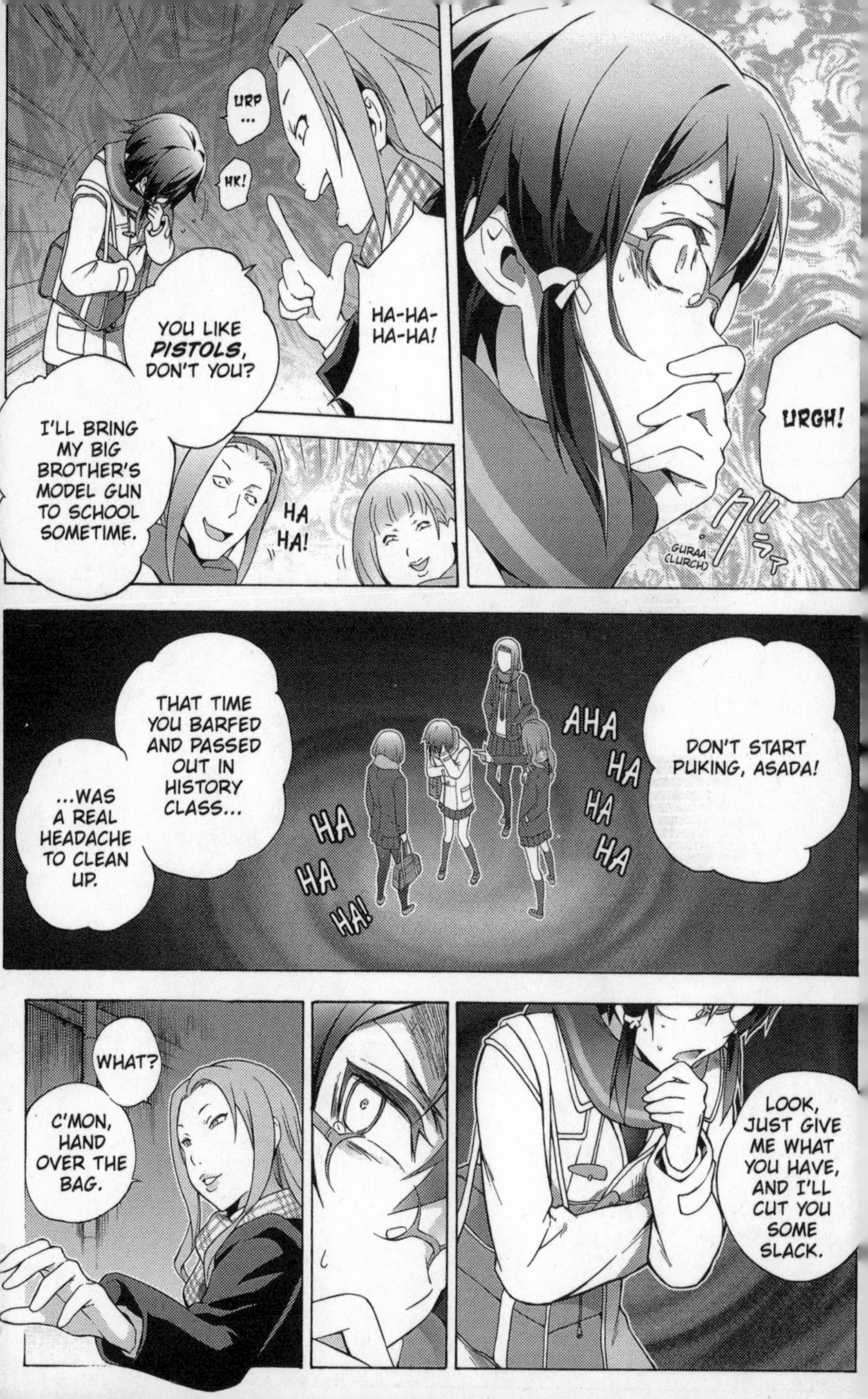
URGH!
GURAA (LURCH)
URP ...
HK!
HA-HA-HA-HA!
YOU LIKE PISTOLS, DON'T YOU?
I'LL BRING MY BIG BROTHER'S MODEL GUN TO SCHOOL SOMETIME.
HA HA!
DON'T START PUKING, ASADA!
AHA HA HA HA HA
THAT TIME YOU BARFED AND PASSED OUT IN HISTORY CLASS...
...WAS A REAL HEADACHE TO CLEAN UP.
HA HA HA!
LOOK, JUST GIVE ME WHAT YOU HAVE, AND I'LL CUT YOU SOME SLACK.
WHAT?
C'MON, HAND OVER THE BAG.

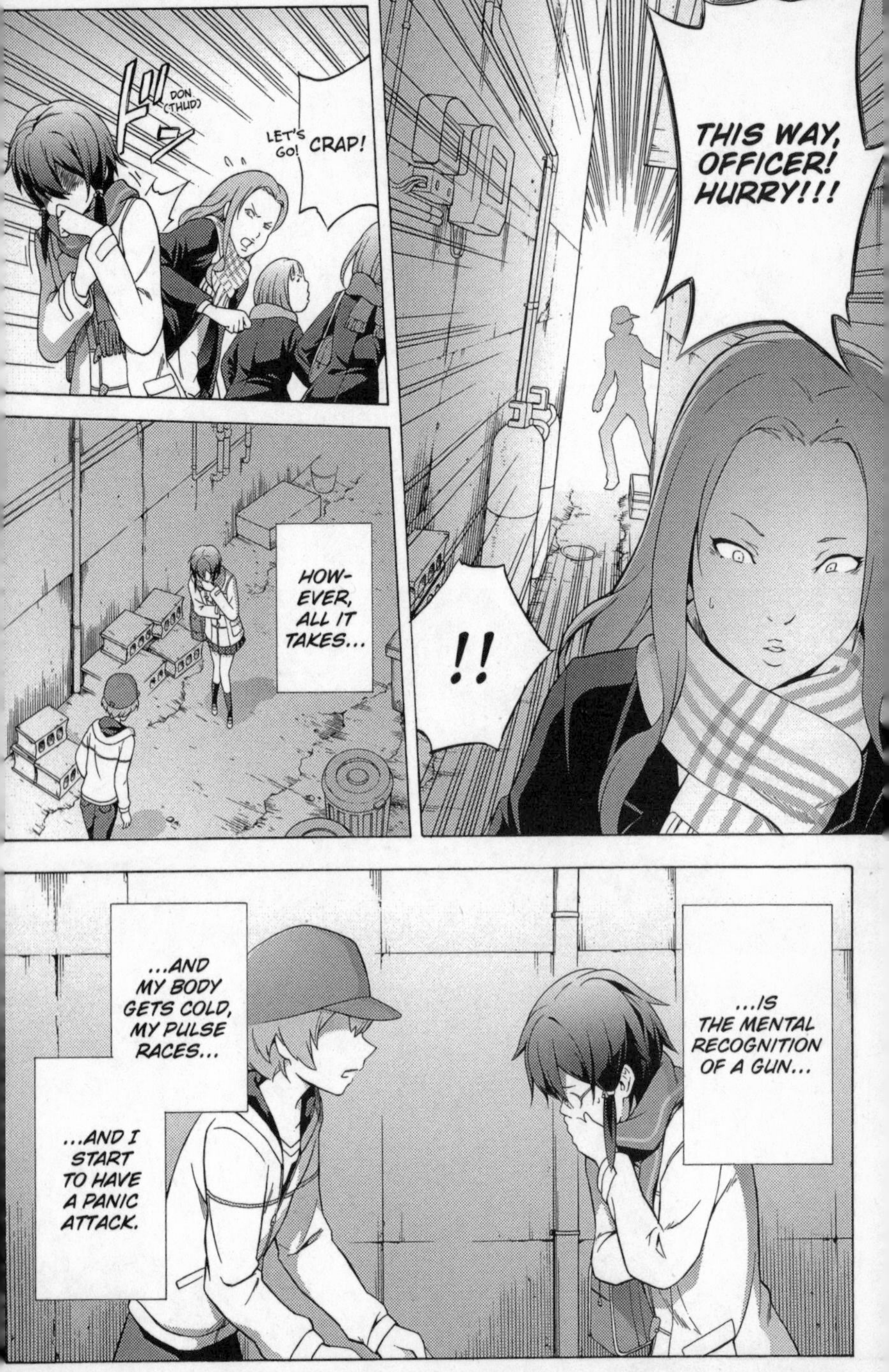
THIS WAY, OFFICER! HURRY!!!
!!
CRAP!
LET'S GO!
DON. (THUD)
HOW-EVER, ALL IT TAKES...
...IS THE MENTAL RECOGNITION OF A GUN...
...AND MY BODY GETS COLD, MY PULSE RACES...
...AND I START TO HAVE A PANIC ATTACK.

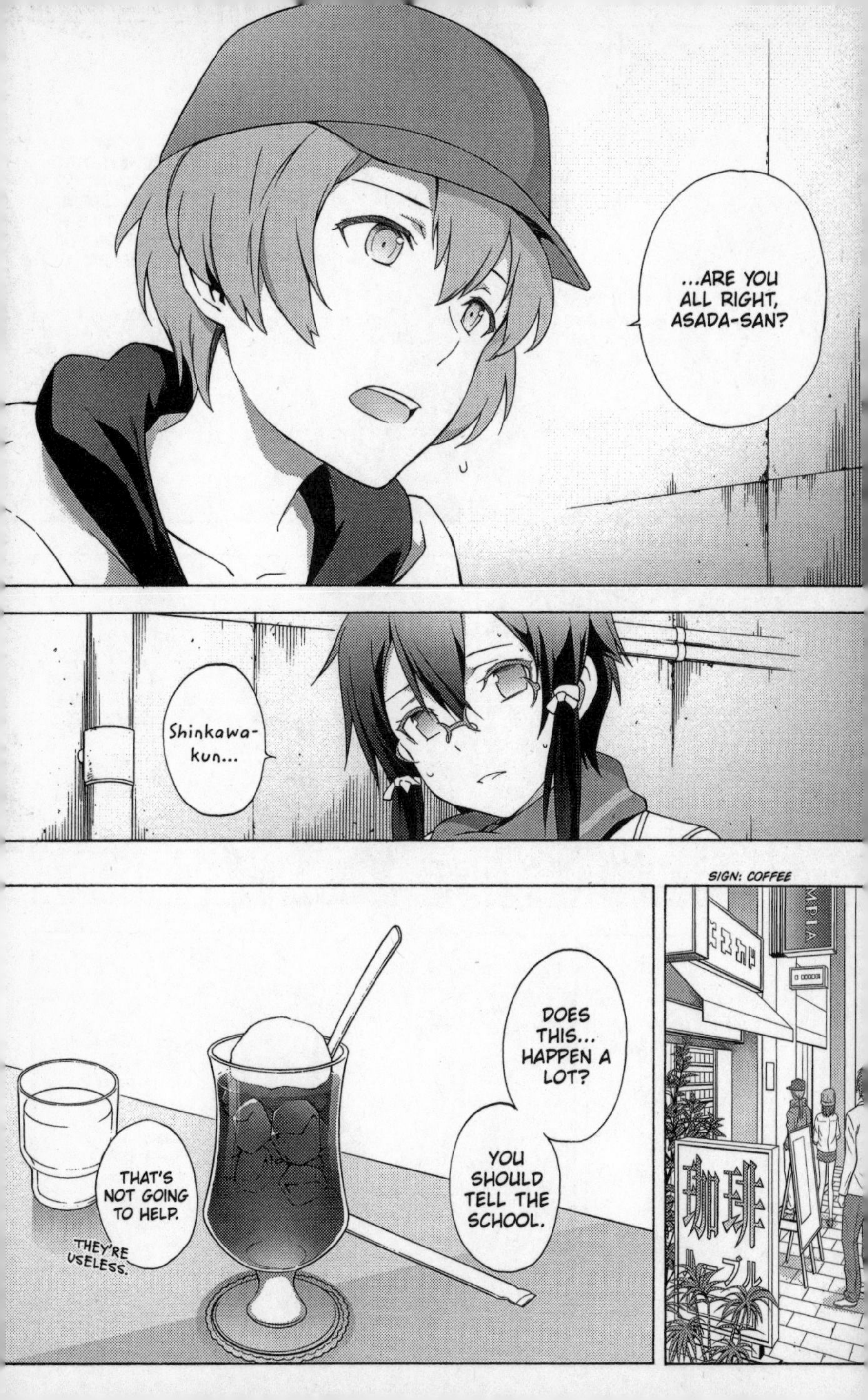
...ARE YOU ALL RIGHT, ASADA-SAN?
Shinkawa-kun...
SIGN: COFFEE
珈琲
DOES THIS... HAPPEN A LOT?
YOU SHOULD TELL THE SCHOOL.
THAT'S NOT GOING TO HELP.
THEY'RE USELESS.

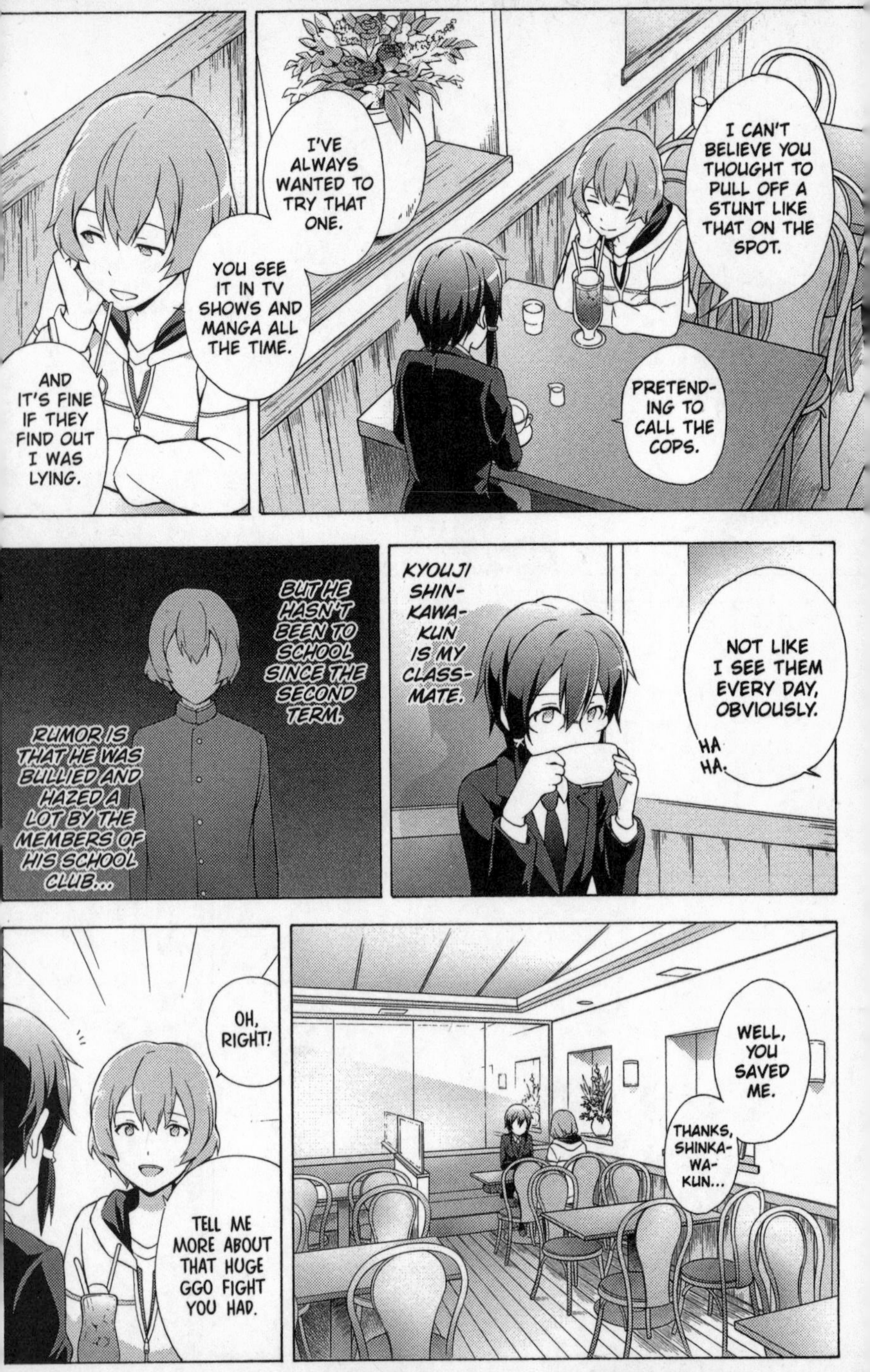
I CAN'T BELIEVE YOU THOUGHT TO PULL OFF A STUNT LIKE THAT ON THE SPOT.
PRETEND-ING TO CALL THE COPS.
I'VE ALWAYS WANTED TO TRY THAT ONE.
YOU SEE IT IN TV SHOWS AND MANGA ALL THE TIME.
AND IT'S FINE IF THEY FIND OUT I WAS LYING.
NOT LIKE I SEE THEM EVERY DAY, OBVIOUSLY.
HA HA.
KYOUJI SHIN-KAWA-KUN IS MY CLASS-MATE.
BUT HE HASN'T BEEN TO SCHOOL SINCE THE SECOND TERM.
RUMOR IS THAT HE WAS BULLIED AND HAZED A LOT BY THE MEMBERS OF HIS SCHOOL CLUB...
WELL, YOU SAVED ME.
THANKS, SHINKA-WA-KUN...
OH, RIGHT!
TELL ME MORE ABOUT THAT HUGE GGO FIGHT YOU HAD.

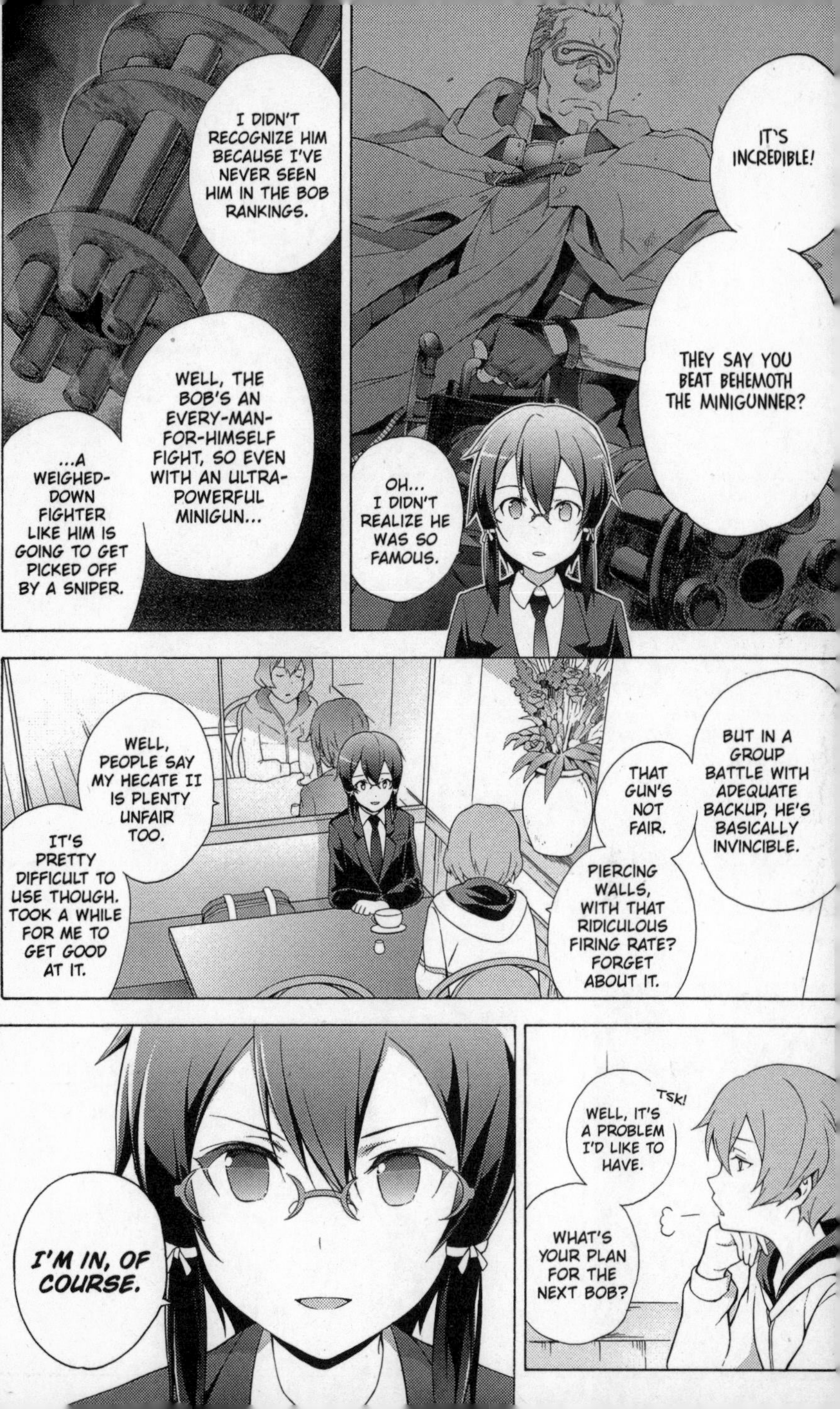
IT'S INCREDIBLE!
THEY SAY YOU BEAT BEHEMOTH THE MINIGUNNER?
OH... I DIDN'T REALIZE HE WAS SO FAMOUS.
I DIDN'T RECOGNIZE HIM BECAUSE I'VE NEVER SEEN HIM IN THE BOB RANKINGS.
WELL, THE BOB'S AN EVERY-MAN-FOR-HIMSELF FIGHT, SO EVEN WITH AN ULTRA-POWERFUL MINIGUN...
...A WEIGHED-DOWN FIGHTER LIKE HIM IS GOING TO GET PICKED OFF BY A SNIPER.
BUT IN A GROUP BATTLE WITH ADEQUATE BACKUP, HE'S BASICALLY INVINCIBLE.
THAT GUN'S NOT FAIR.
PIERCING WALLS, WITH THAT RIDICULOUS FIRING RATE? FORGET ABOUT IT.
WELL, PEOPLE SAY MY HECATE II IS PLENTY UNFAIR TOO.
IT'S PRETTY DIFFICULT TO USE THOUGH. TOOK A WHILE FOR ME TO GET GOOD AT IT.
TSK!
WELL, IT'S A PROBLEM I'D LIKE TO HAVE.
WHAT'S YOUR PLAN FOR THE NEXT BOB?
I'M IN, OF COURSE.

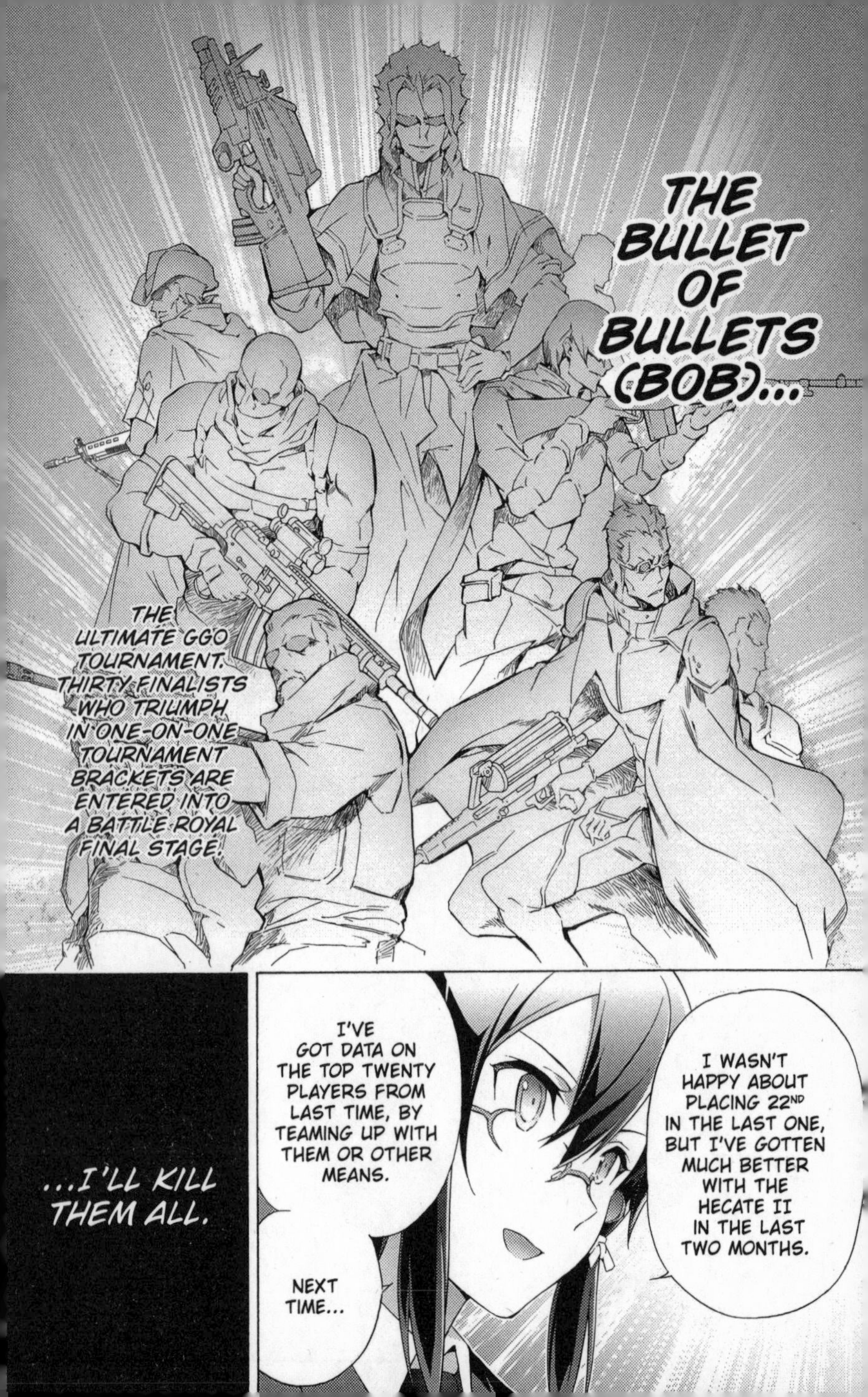
THE BULLET OF BULLETS (BOB)...
THE ULTIMATE GGO TOURNAMENT. THIRTY FINALISTS WHO TRIUMPH IN ONE-ON-ONE TOURNAMENT BRACKETS ARE ENTERED INTO A BATTLE ROYAL FINAL STAGE.
I WASN'T HAPPY ABOUT PLACING 22ND IN THE LAST ONE, BUT I'VE GOTTEN MUCH BETTER WITH THE HECATE II IN THE LAST TWO MONTHS.
I'VE GOT DATA ON THE TOP TWENTY PLAYERS FROM LAST TIME, BY TEAMING UP WITH THEM OR OTHER MEANS.
NEXT TIME...
...I'LL KILL THEM ALL.

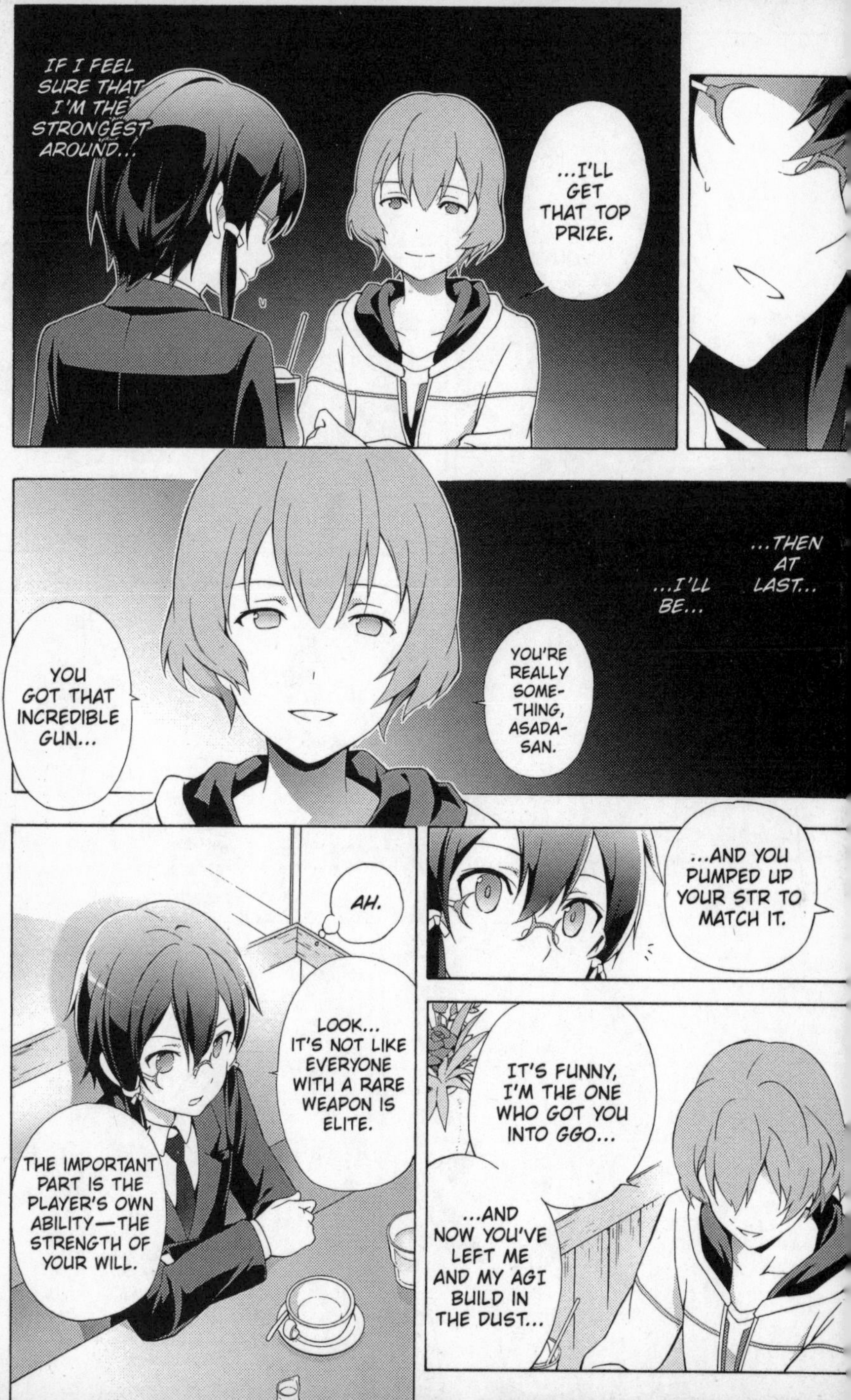
IF I FEEL SURE THAT I'M THE STRONGEST AROUND...
...I'LL GET THAT TOP PRIZE.
...THEN AT LAST...
...I'LL BE...
YOU'RE REALLY SOME-THING, ASADA-SAN.
YOU GOT THAT INCREDIBLE GUN...
...AND YOU PUMPED UP YOUR STR TO MATCH IT.
IT'S FUNNY, I'M THE ONE WHO GOT YOU INTO GGO...
...AND NOW YOU'VE LEFT ME AND MY AGI BUILD IN THE DUST...
AH.
LOOK... IT'S NOT LIKE EVERYONE WITH A RARE WEAPON IS ELITE.
THE IMPORTANT PART IS THE PLAYER'S OWN ABILITY—THE STRENGTH OF YOUR WILL.

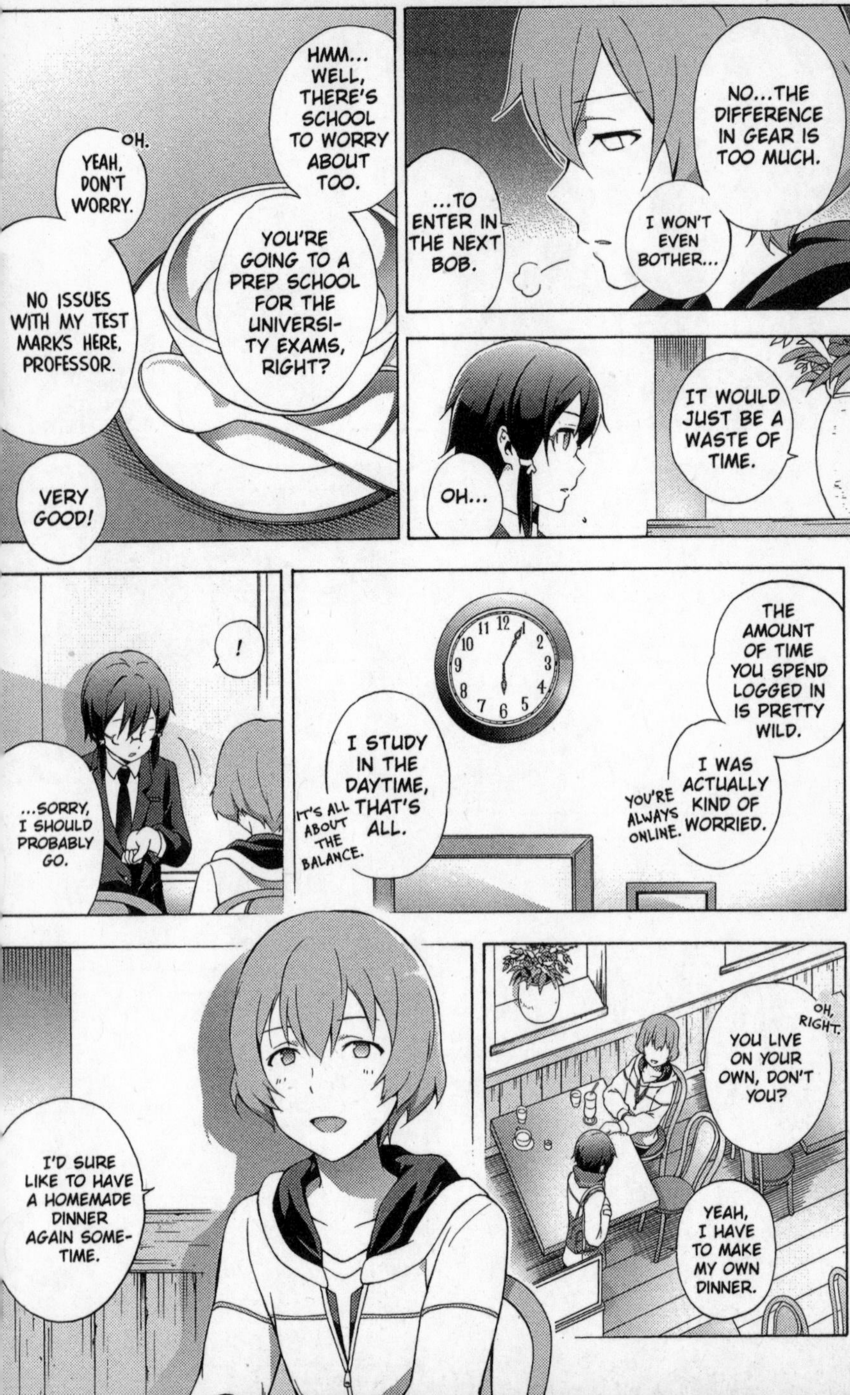
NO...THE DIFFERENCE IN GEAR IS TOO MUCH.
I WON'T EVEN BOTHER...
...TO ENTER IN THE NEXT BOB.
IT WOULD JUST BE A WASTE OF TIME.
OH...
HMM... WELL, THERE'S SCHOOL TO WORRY ABOUT TOO.
YOU'RE GOING TO A PREP SCHOOL FOR THE UNIVERSI-TY EXAMS, RIGHT?
OH.
YEAH, DON'T WORRY.
NO ISSUES WITH MY TEST MARKS HERE, PROFESSOR.
VERY GOOD!
THE AMOUNT OF TIME YOU SPEND LOGGED IN IS PRETTY WILD.
I WAS ACTUALLY KIND OF WORRIED.
YOU'RE ALWAYS ONLINE.
I STUDY IN THE DAYTIME, THAT'S ALL.
IT'S ALL ABOUT THE BALANCE.
!
...SORRY, I SHOULD PROBABLY GO.
OH, RIGHT.
YOU LIVE ON YOUR OWN, DON'T YOU?
YEAH, I HAVE TO MAKE MY OWN DINNER.
I'D SURE LIKE TO HAVE A HOMEMADE DINNER AGAIN SOME-TIME.

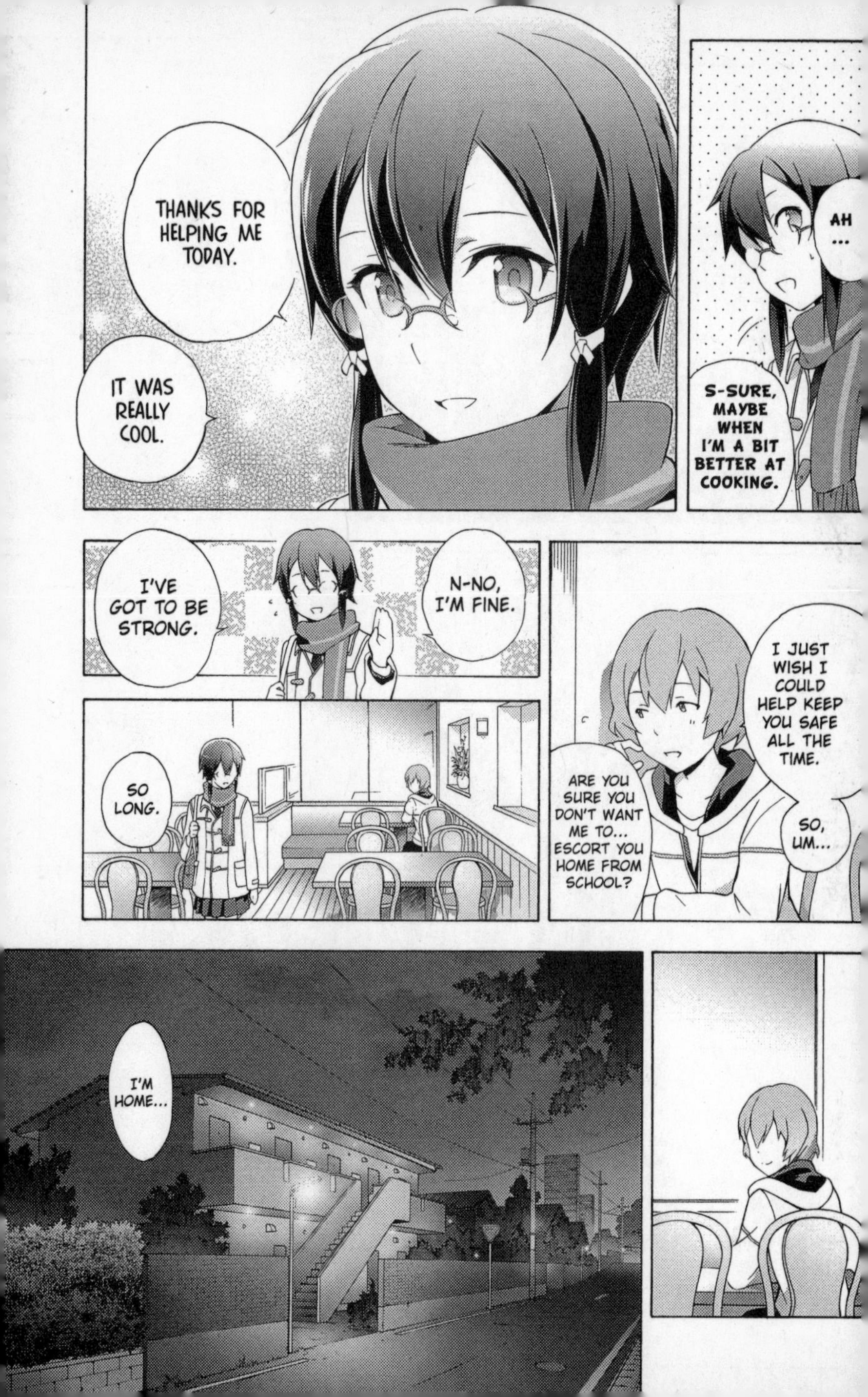
AH ...
S-SURE, MAYBE WHEN I'M A BIT BETTER AT COOKING.
THANKS FOR HELPING ME TODAY.
IT WAS REALLY COOL.
I JUST WISH I COULD HELP KEEP YOU SAFE ALL THE TIME.
SO, UM...
ARE YOU SURE YOU DON'T WANT ME TO... ESCORT YOU HOME FROM SCHOOL?
N-NO, I'M FINE.
I'VE GOT TO BE STRONG.
SO LONG.
I'M HOME...

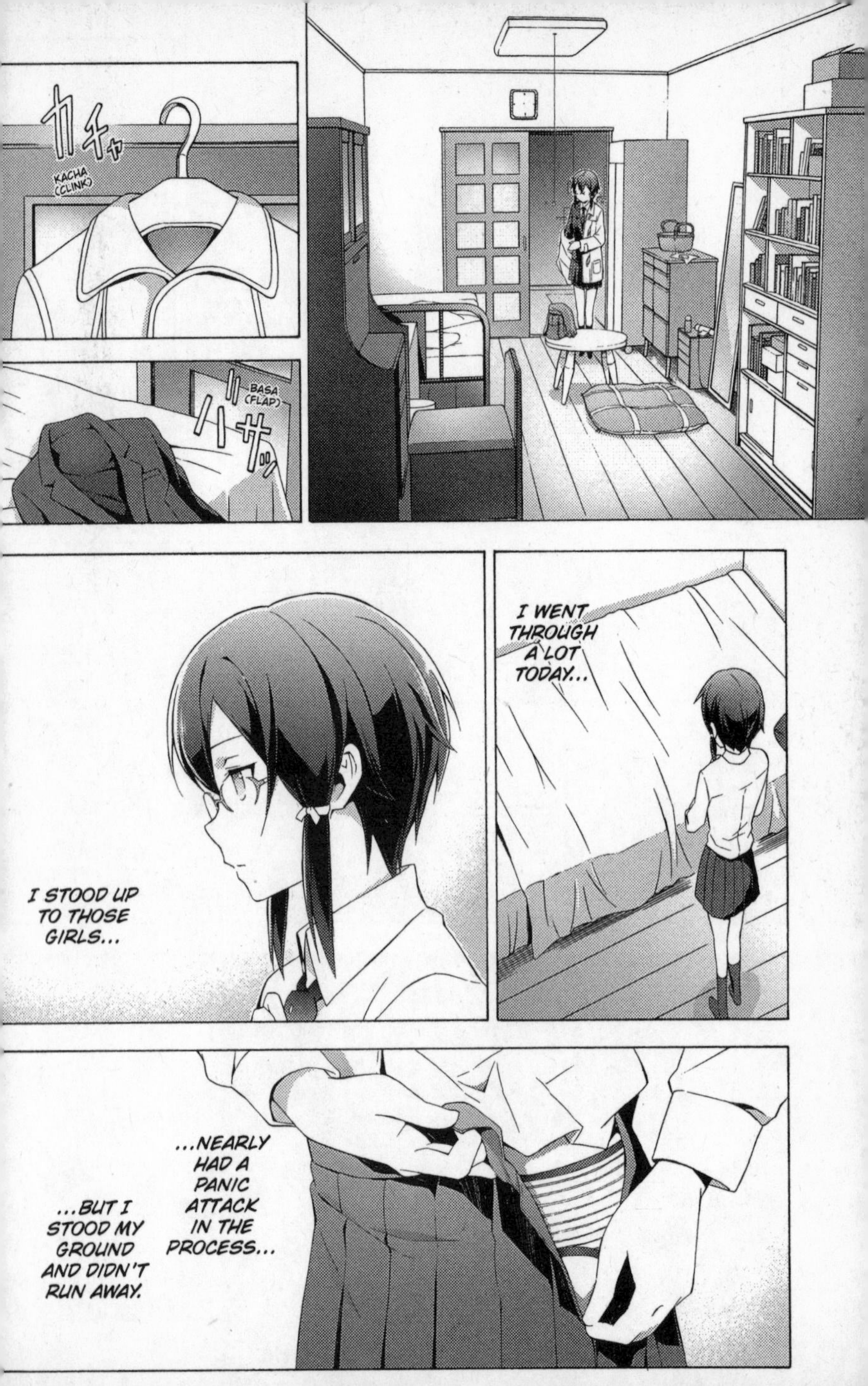
カチャ
KACHA (CLINK)
バサッ
BASA (FLAP)
I WENT THROUGH A LOT TODAY...
I STOOD UP TO THOSE GIRLS...
...NEARLY HAD A PANIC ATTACK IN THE PROCESS...
...BUT I STOOD MY GROUND AND DIDN'T RUN AWAY.

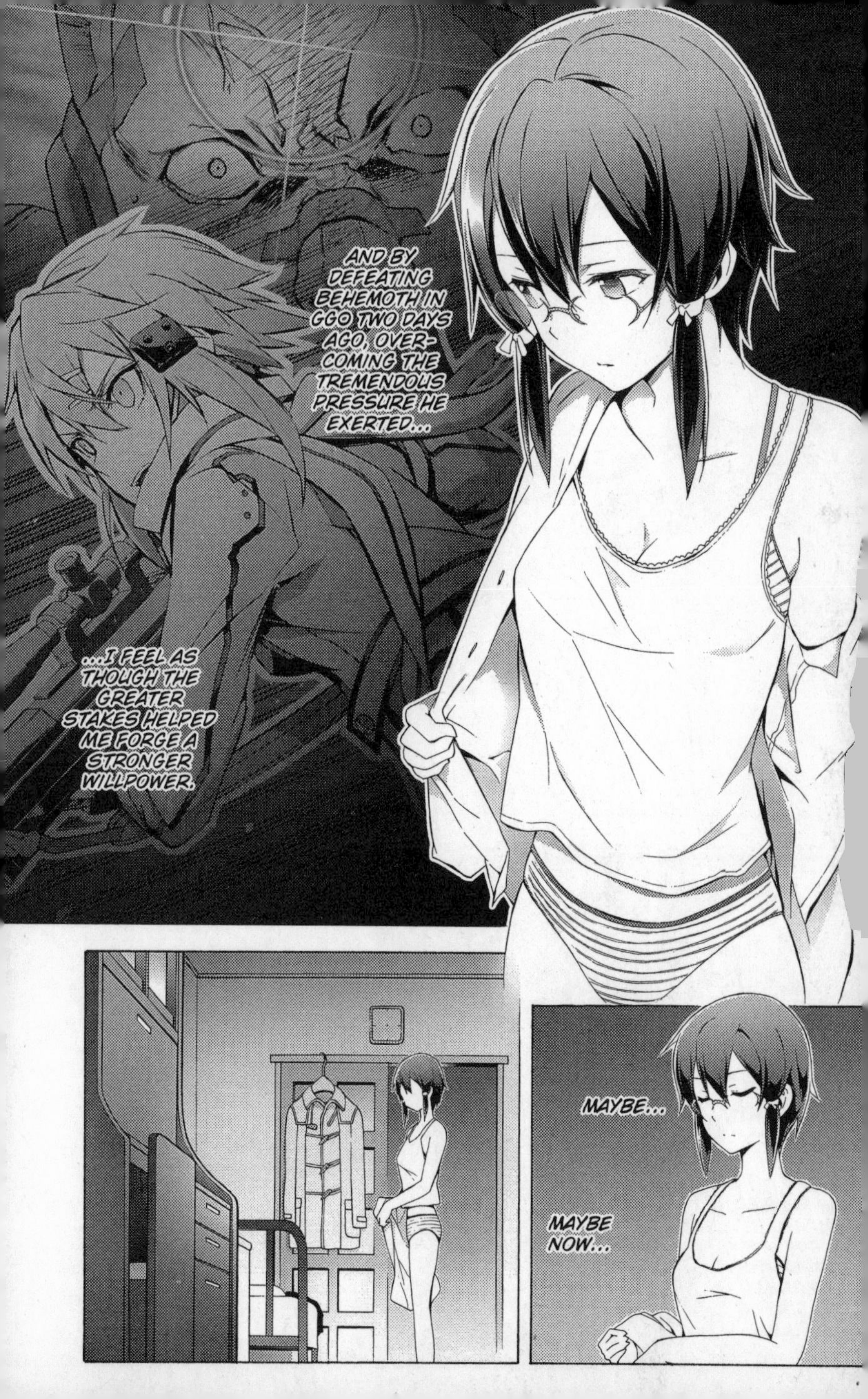
AND BY DEFEATING BEHEMOTH IN GGO TWO DAYS AGO, OVER-COMING THE TREMENDOUS PRESSURE HE EXERTED...
...I FEEL AS THOUGH THE GREATER STAKES HELPED ME FORGE A STRONGER WILLPOWER.
MAYBE...
MAYBE NOW...

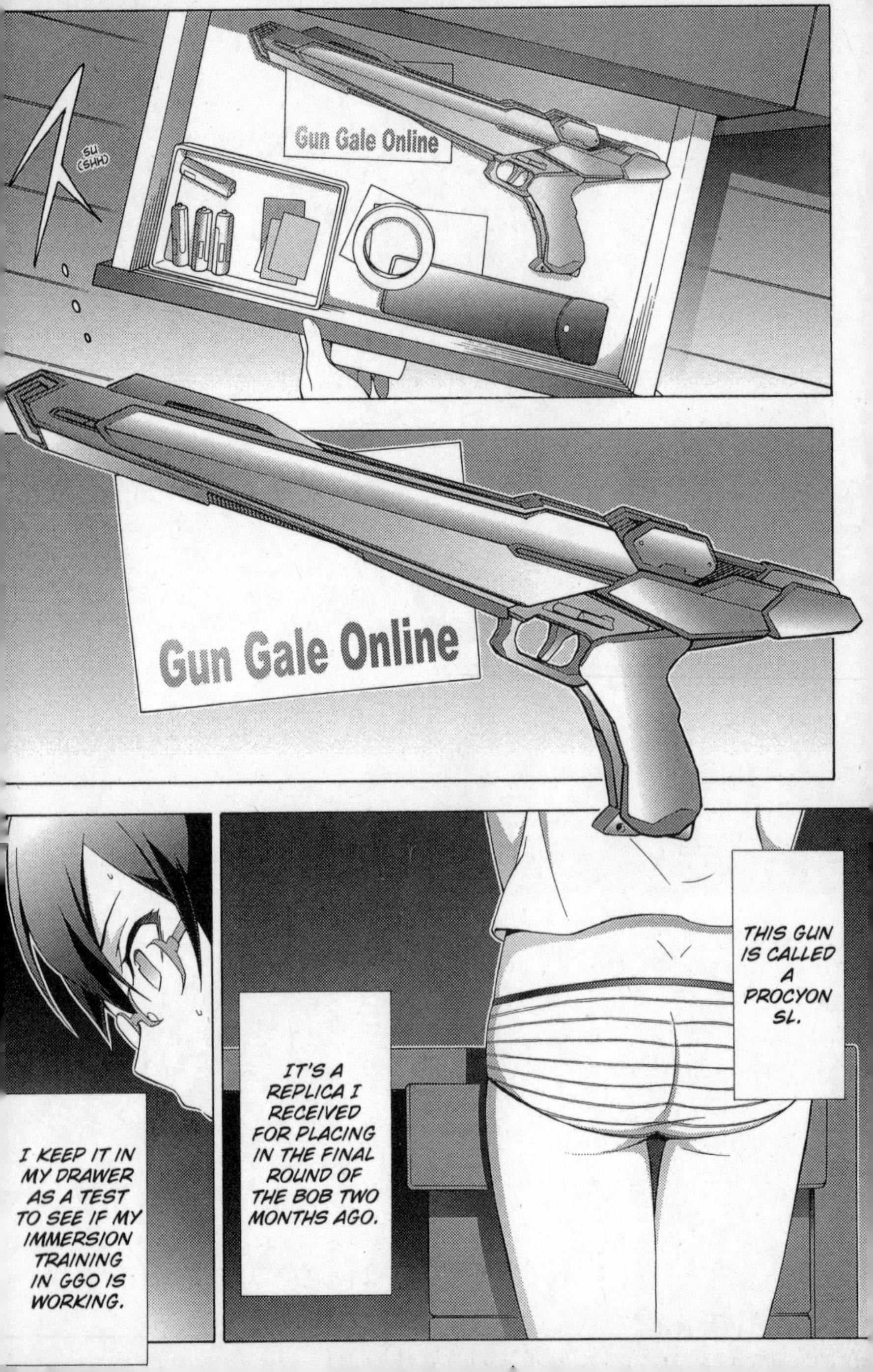
SU (SHH)
Gun Gale Online
Gun Gale Online
THIS GUN IS CALLED A PROCYON SL.
IT'S A REPLICA I RECEIVED FOR PLACING IN THE FINAL ROUND OF THE BOB TWO MONTHS AGO.
I KEEP IT IN MY DRAWER AS A TEST TO SEE IF MY IMMERSION TRAINING IN GGO IS WORKING.

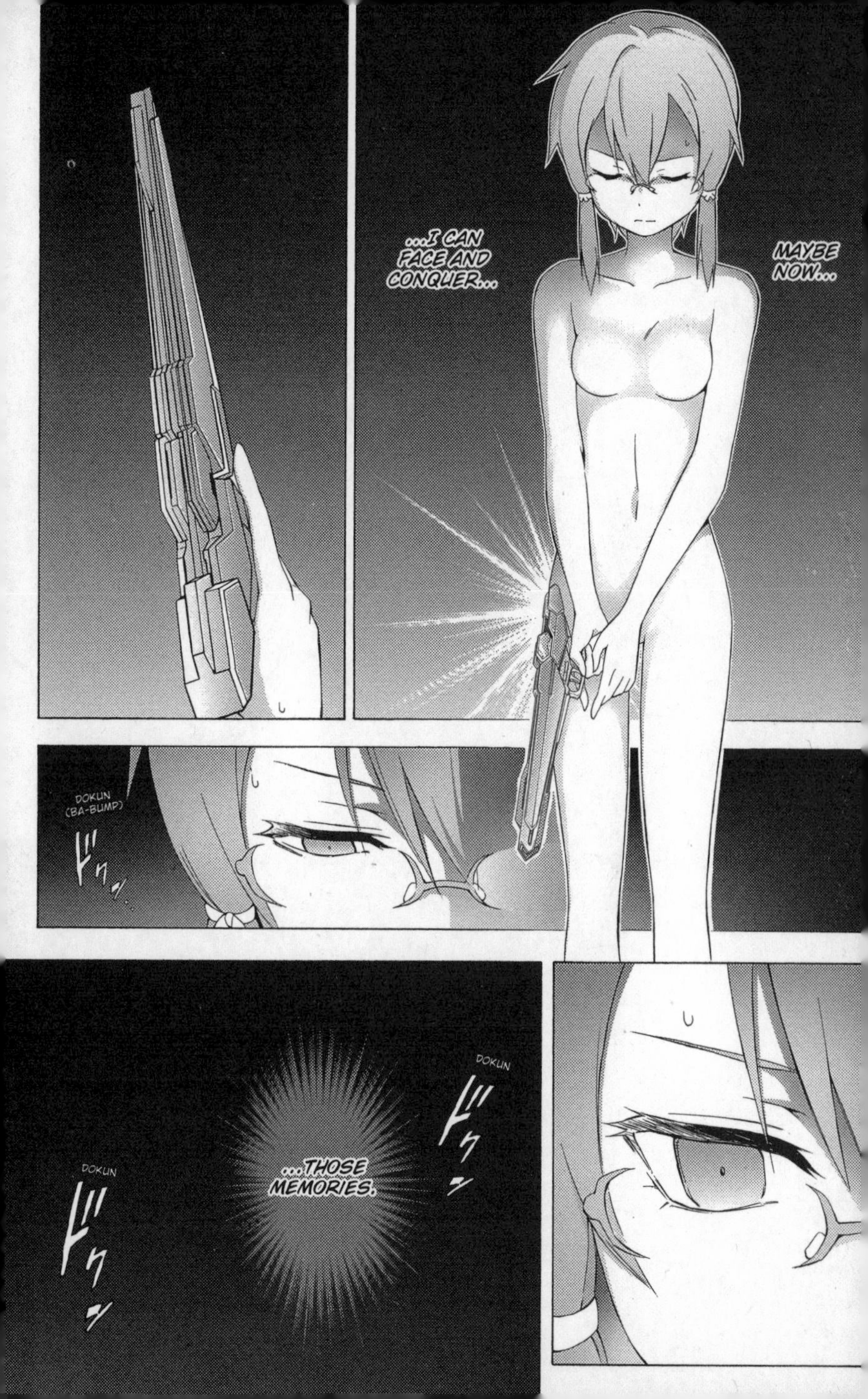
MAYBE NOW...
...I CAN FACE AND CONQUER...
DOKUN (BA-BUMP)
ドクッ...
DOKUN
ドクッ
...THOSE MEMORIES.
DOKUN
ドクッ

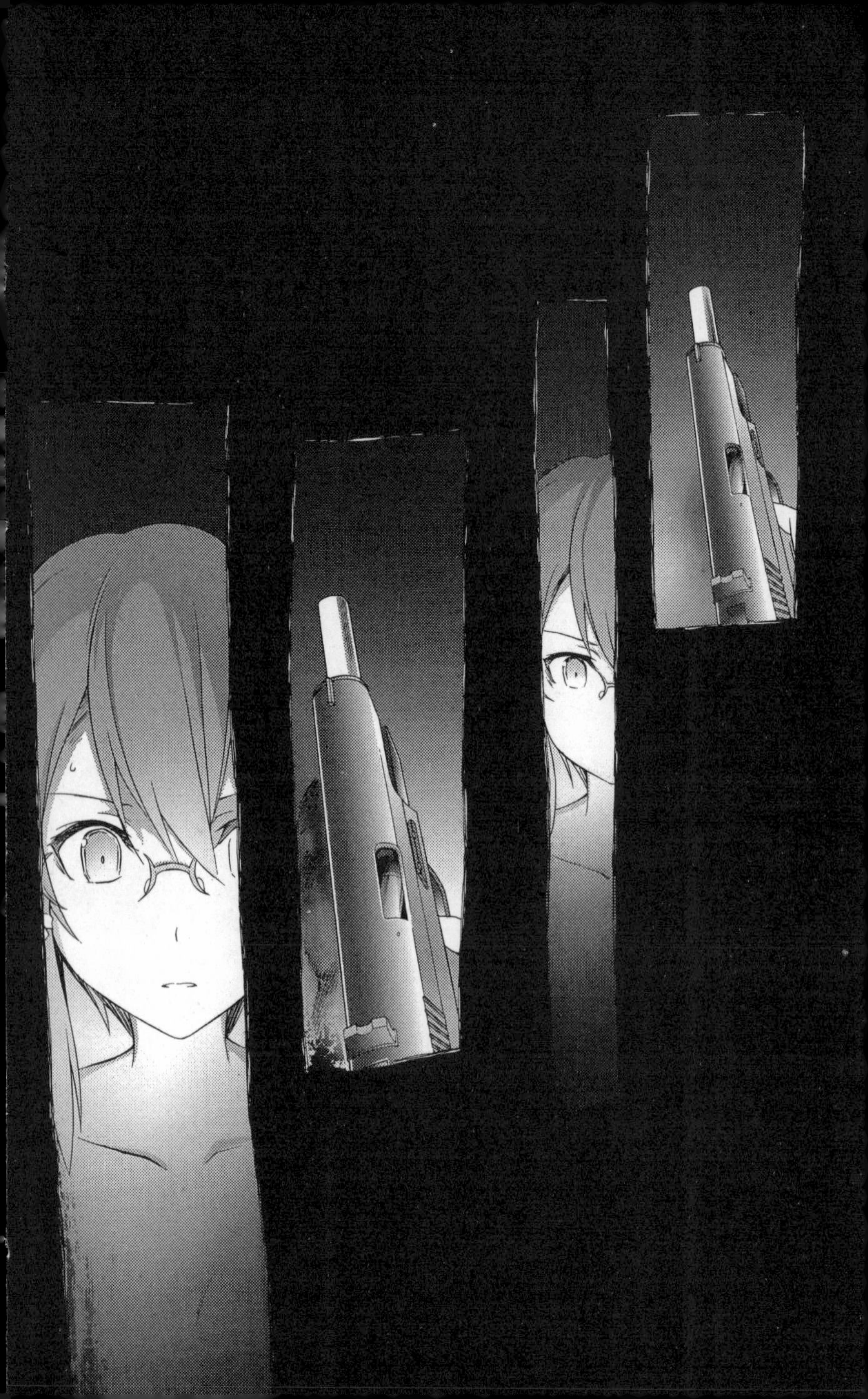

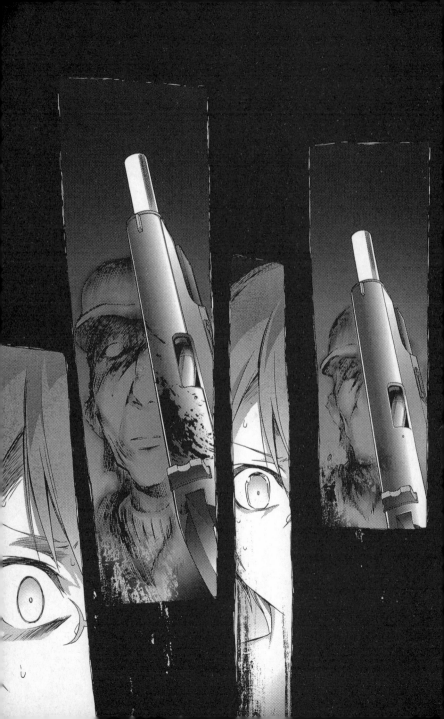

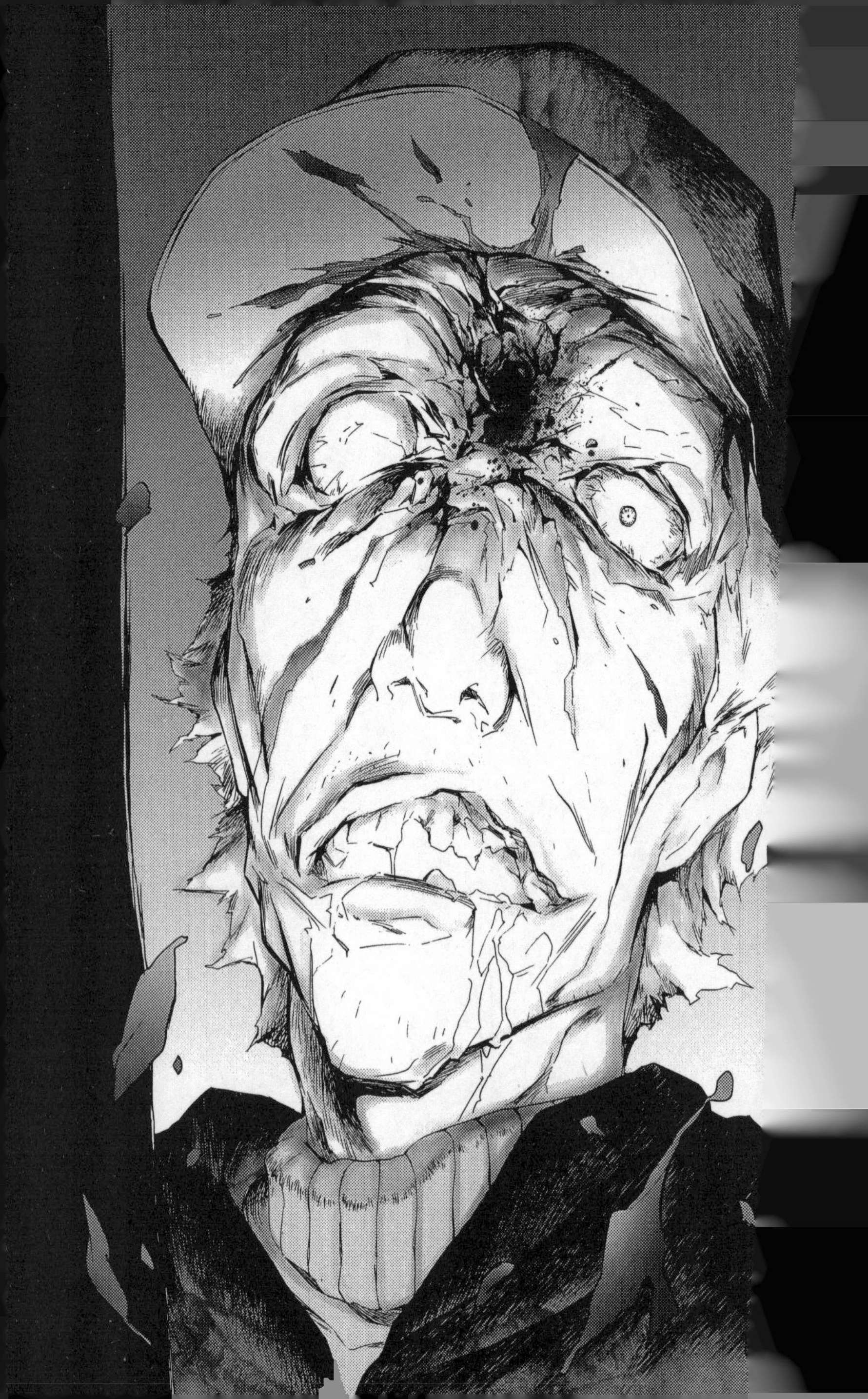

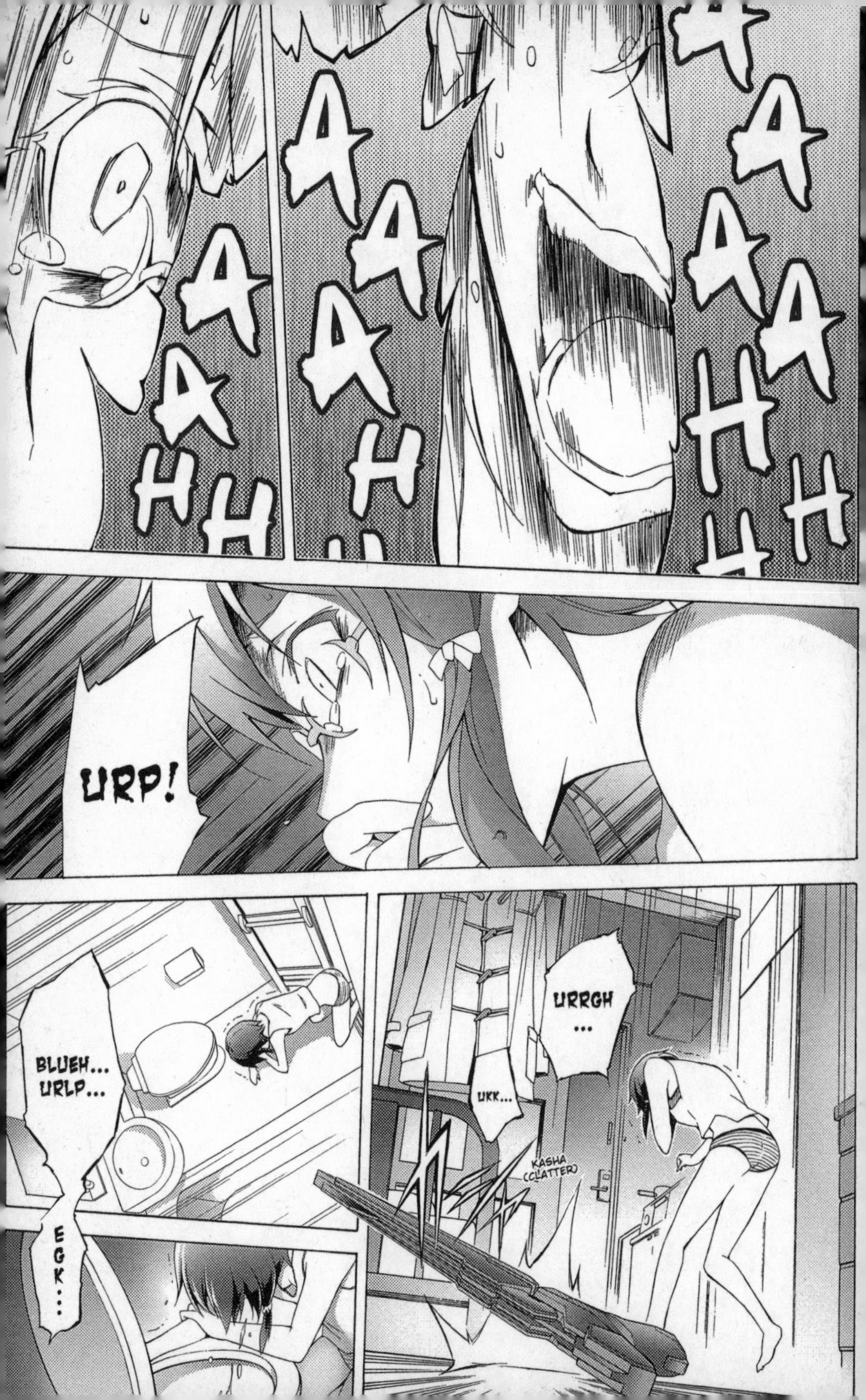
AAAAHHH
AAAHH
AAHH
URP!
URRGH ...
UKK...
KASHA (CLATTER)
BLUEH... URLP...
EGK...

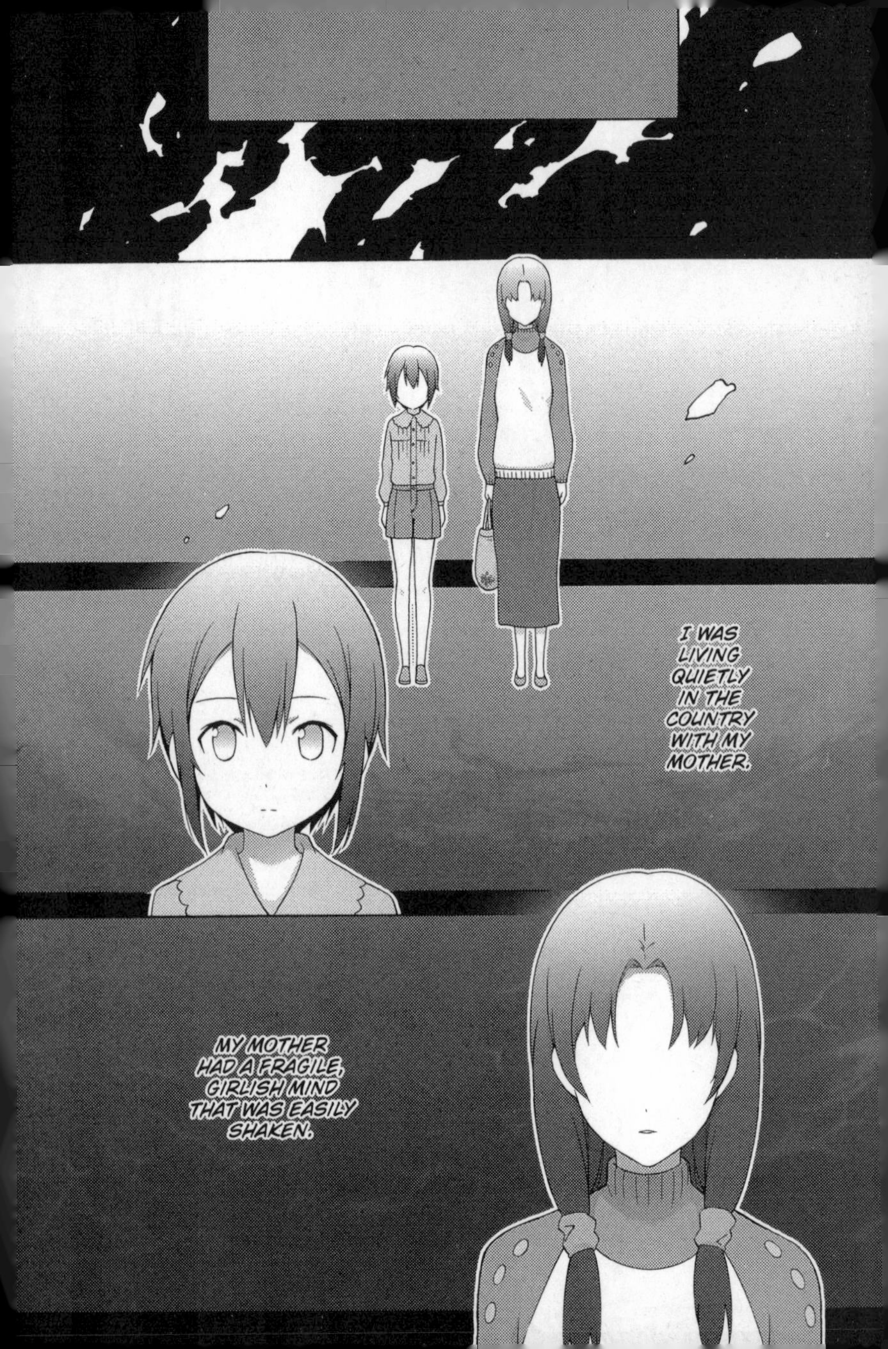
I WAS LIVING QUIETLY IN THE COUNTRY WITH MY MOTHER.
MY MOTHER HAD A FRAGILE, GIRLISH MIND THAT WAS EASILY SHAKEN.

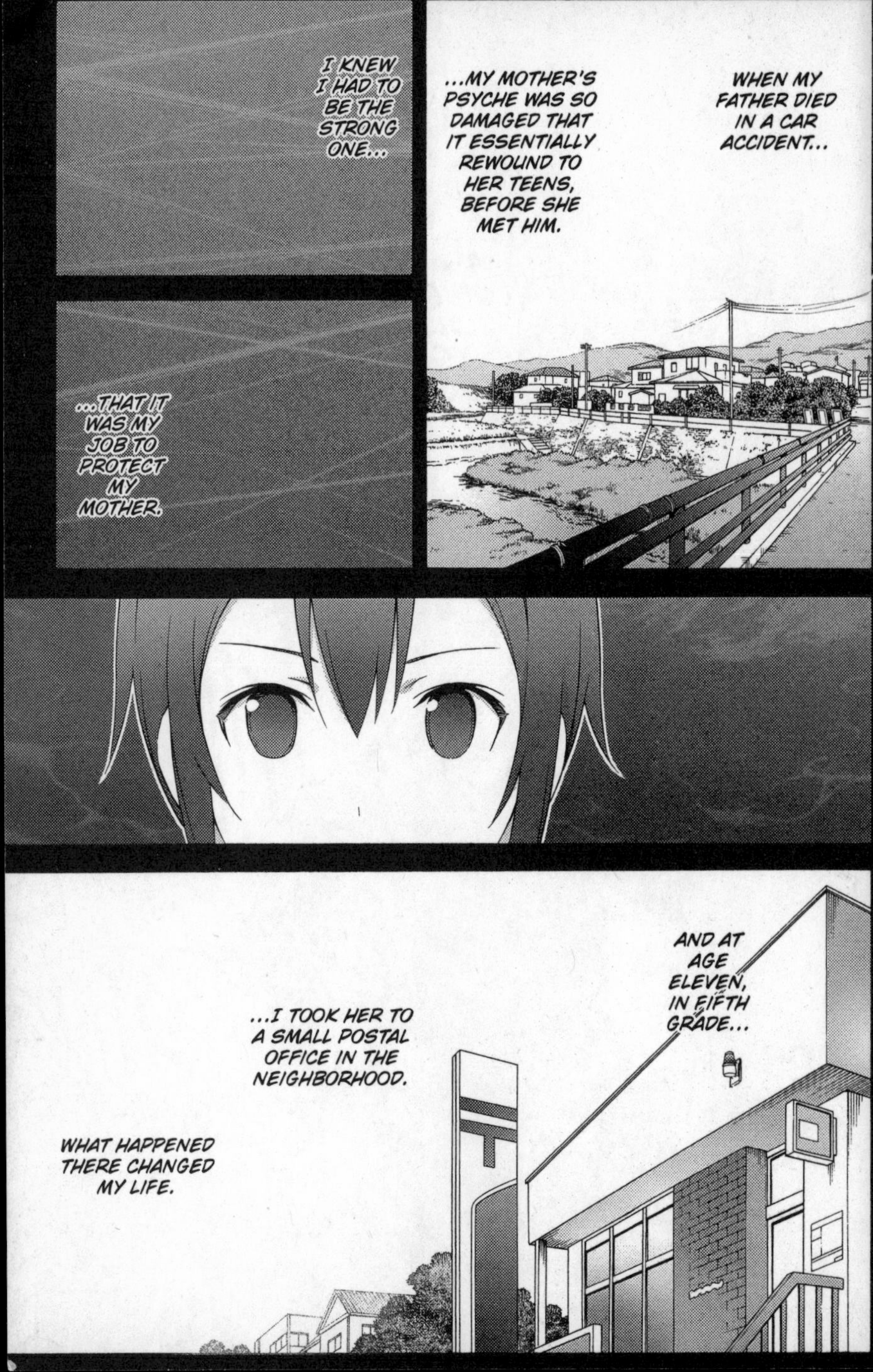
WHEN MY FATHER DIED IN A CAR ACCIDENT...
...MY MOTHER'S PSYCHE WAS SO DAMAGED THAT IT ESSENTIALLY REWOUND TO HER TEENS, BEFORE SHE MET HIM.
I KNEW I HAD TO BE THE STRONG ONE...
...THAT IT WAS MY JOB TO PROTECT MY MOTHER.
AND AT AGE ELEVEN, IN FIFTH GRADE...
...I TOOK HER TO A SMALL POSTAL OFFICE IN THE NEIGHBORHOOD.
WHAT HAPPENED THERE CHANGED MY LIFE.

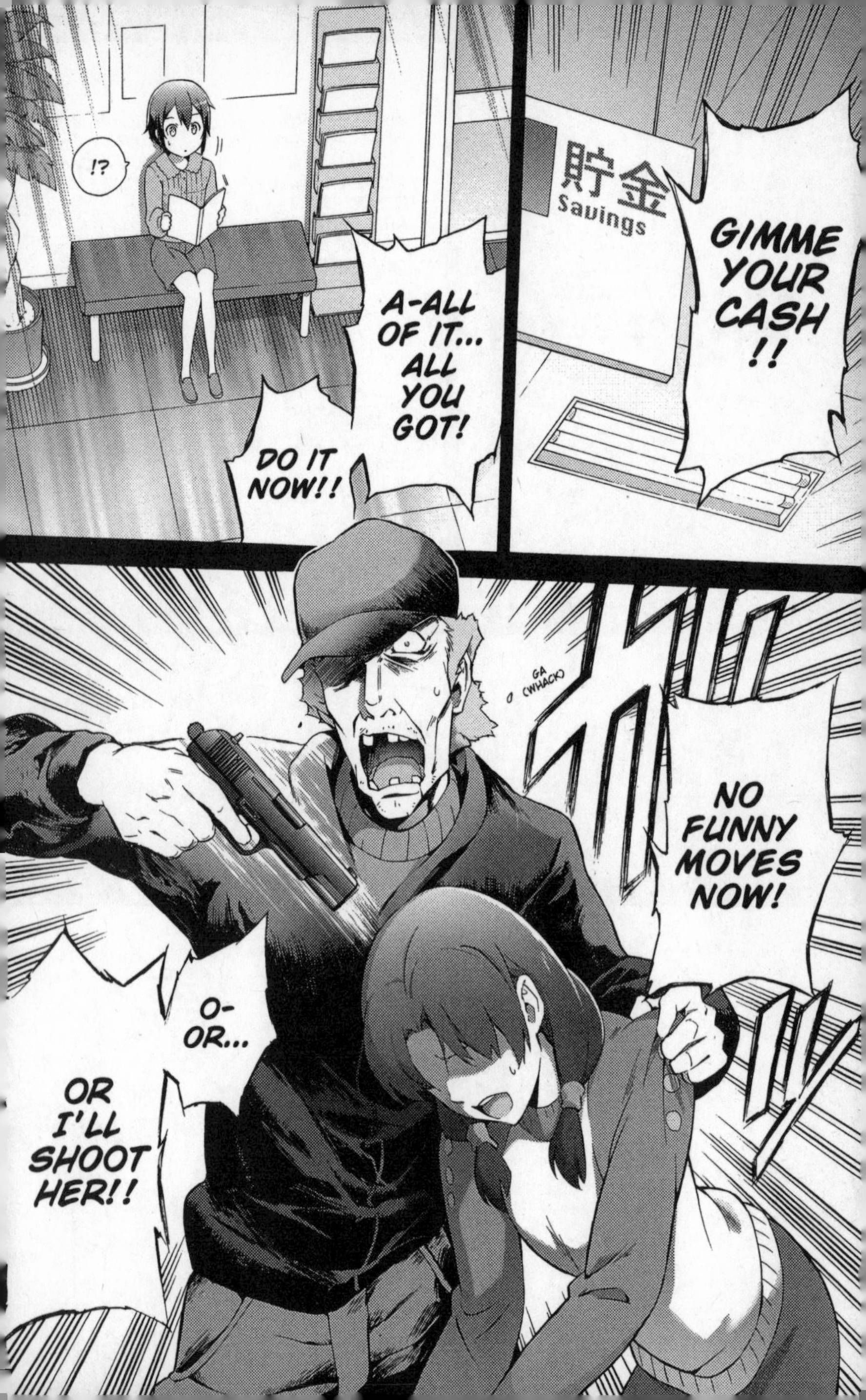
貯金
Savings
GIMME YOUR CASH!!
A-ALL OF IT... ALL YOU GOT!
DO IT NOW!!
!?
GA (WHACK)
NO FUNNY MOVES NOW!
O-OR...
OR I'LL SHOOT HER!!

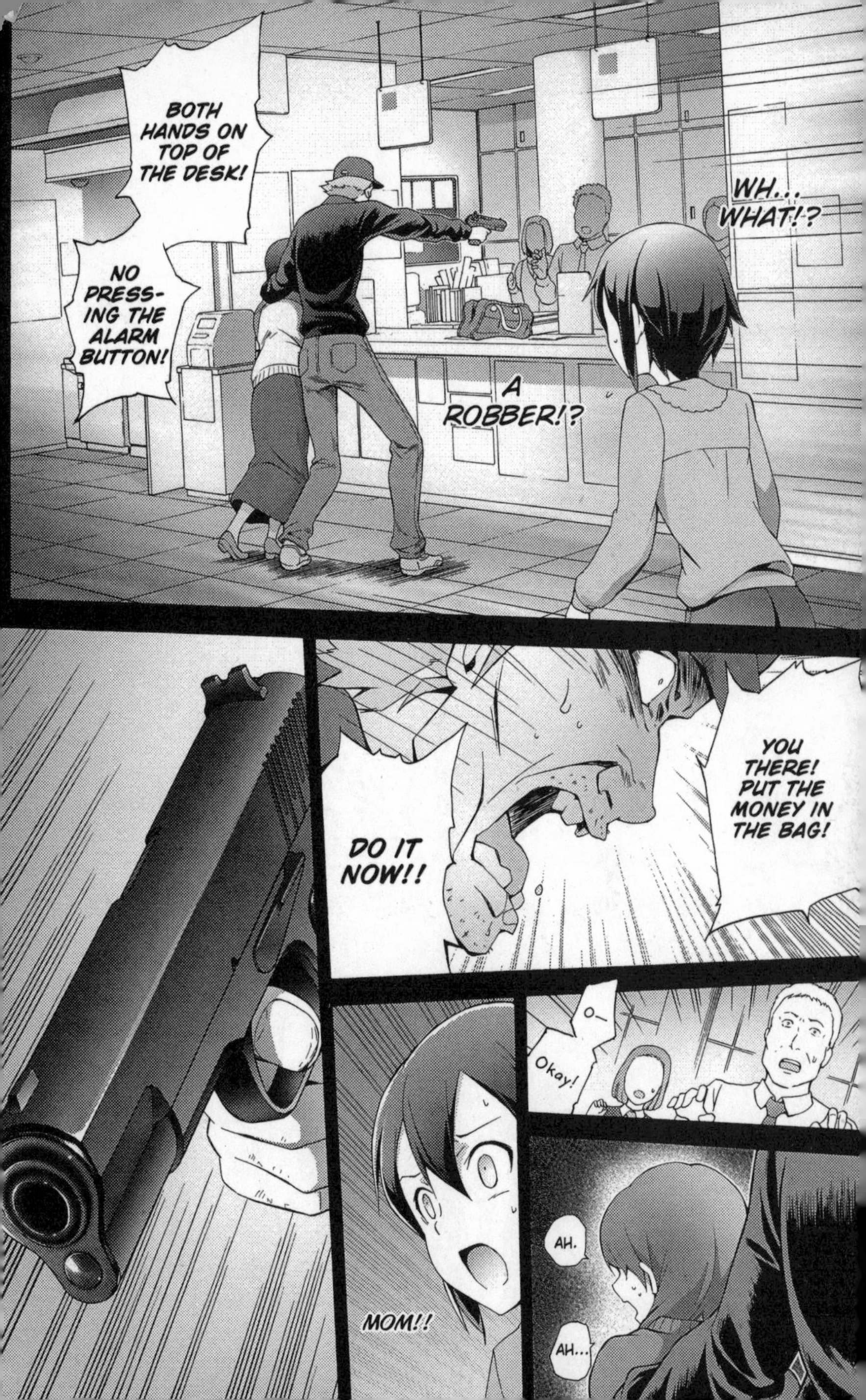
BOTH HANDS ON TOP OF THE DESK!
NO PRESSING THE ALARM BUTTON!
WH... WHAT!?
A ROBBER!?
YOU THERE! PUT THE MONEY IN THE BAG!
DO IT NOW!!
O–
Okay!
AH.
AH...
MOM!!

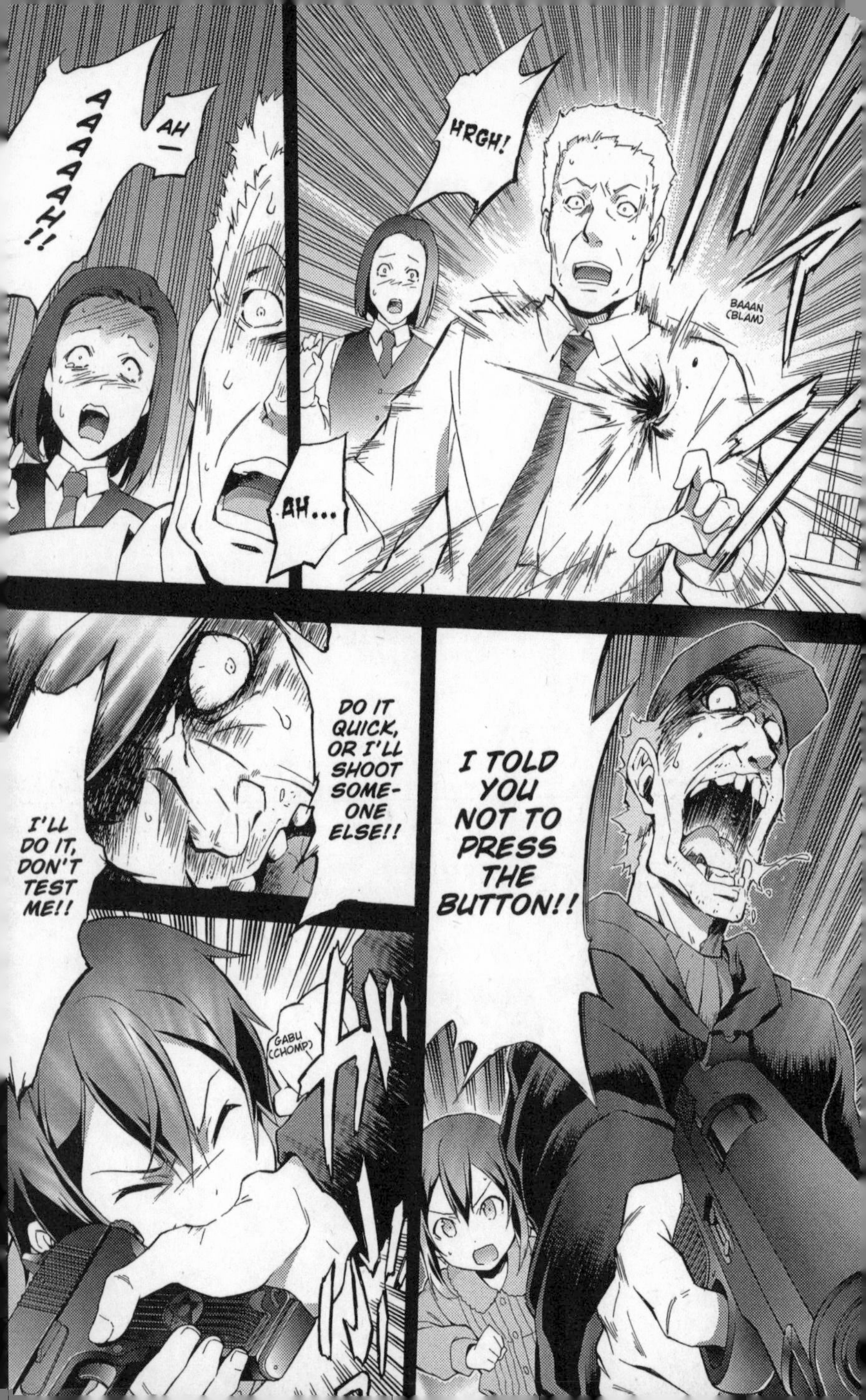
HRGH!
BAAAN (BLAM)
AH—
AAAAAAAH!!
AH...
I TOLD YOU NOT TO PRESS THE BUTTON!!
DO IT QUICK, OR I'LL SHOOT SOME-ONE ELSE!!
I'LL DO IT, DON'T TEST ME!!
GABU (CHOMP)

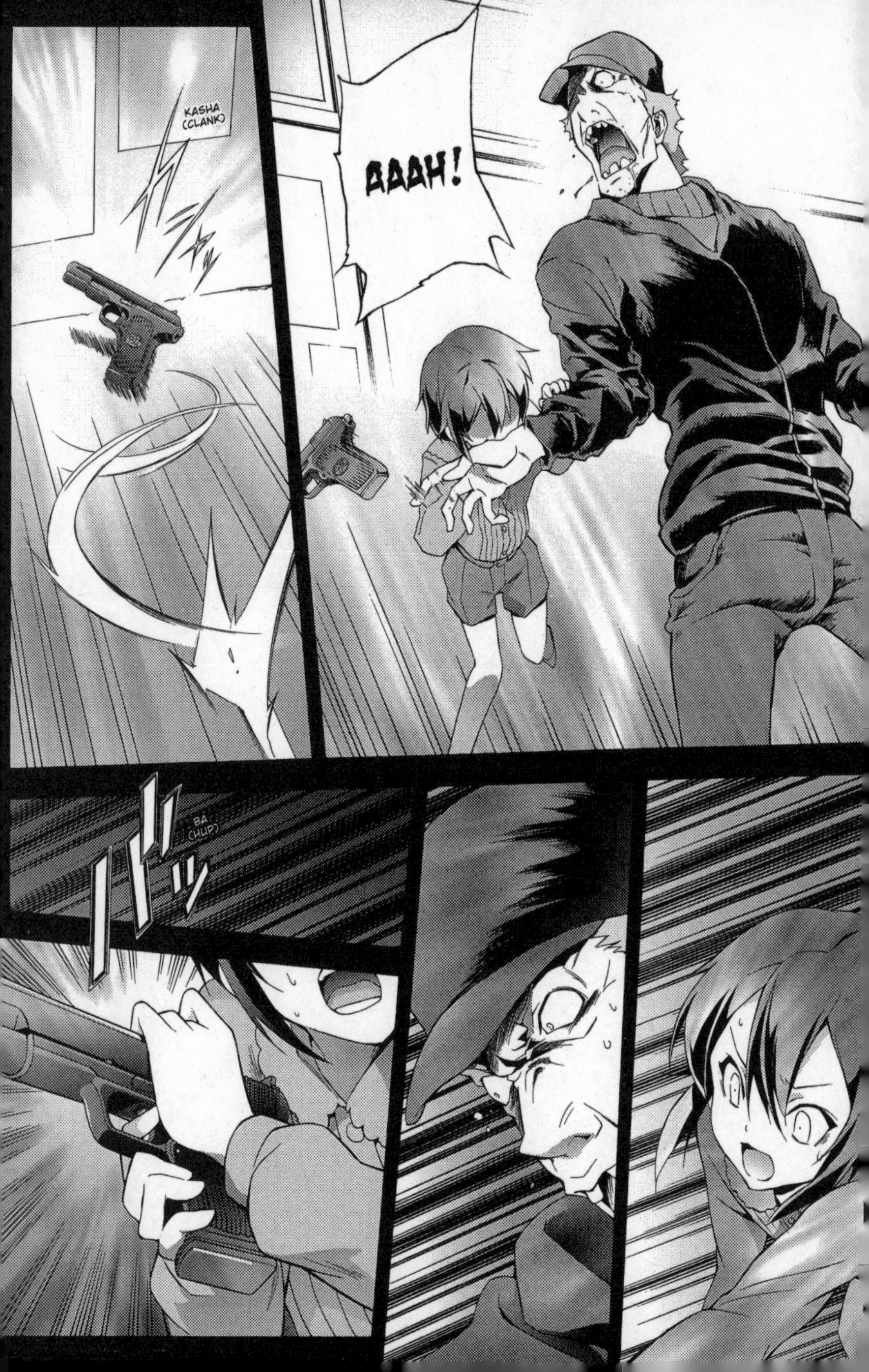
AAAH!
KASHA (CLANK)
BA (HUP)

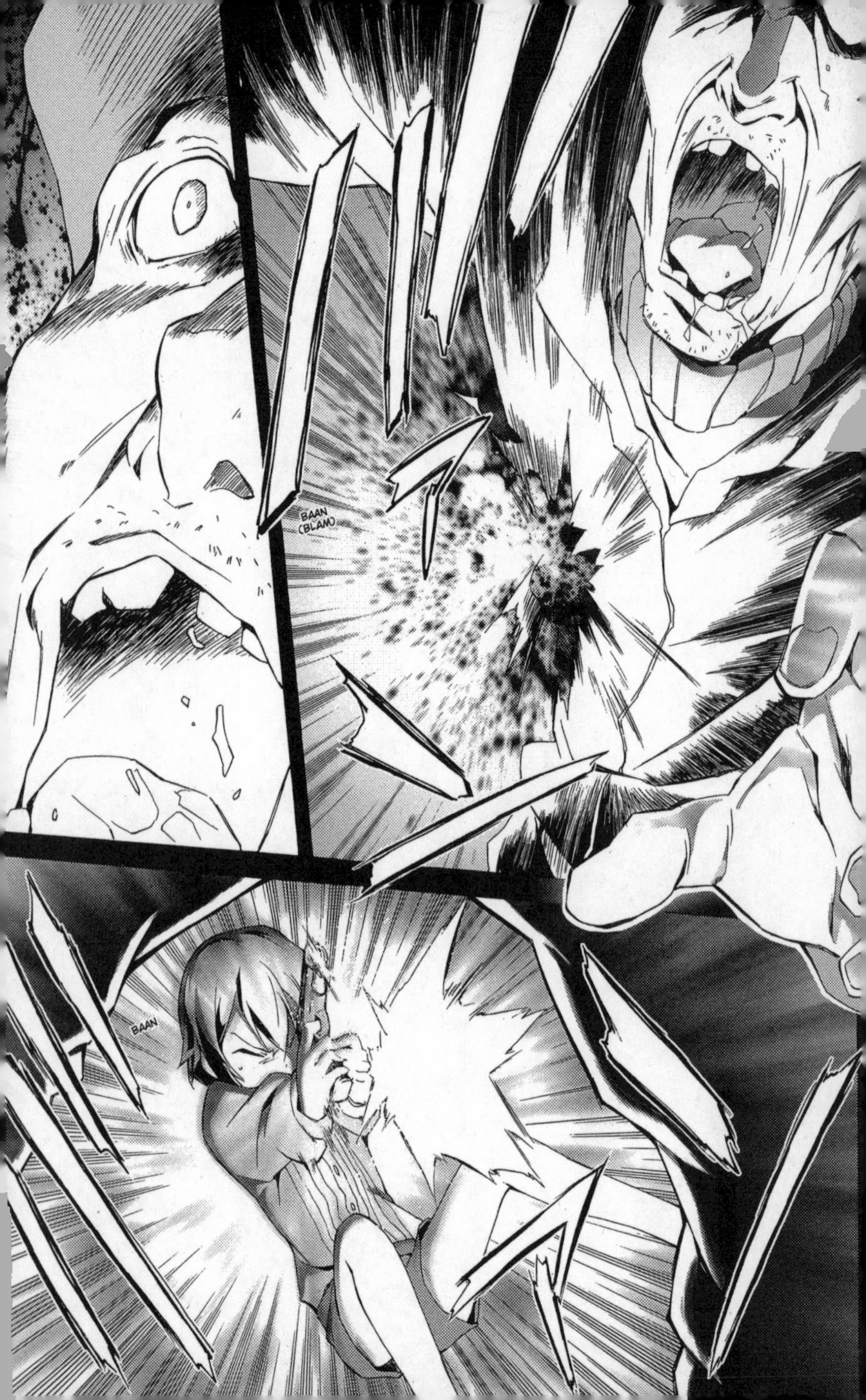
BAAN
(BLAM)
BAAN

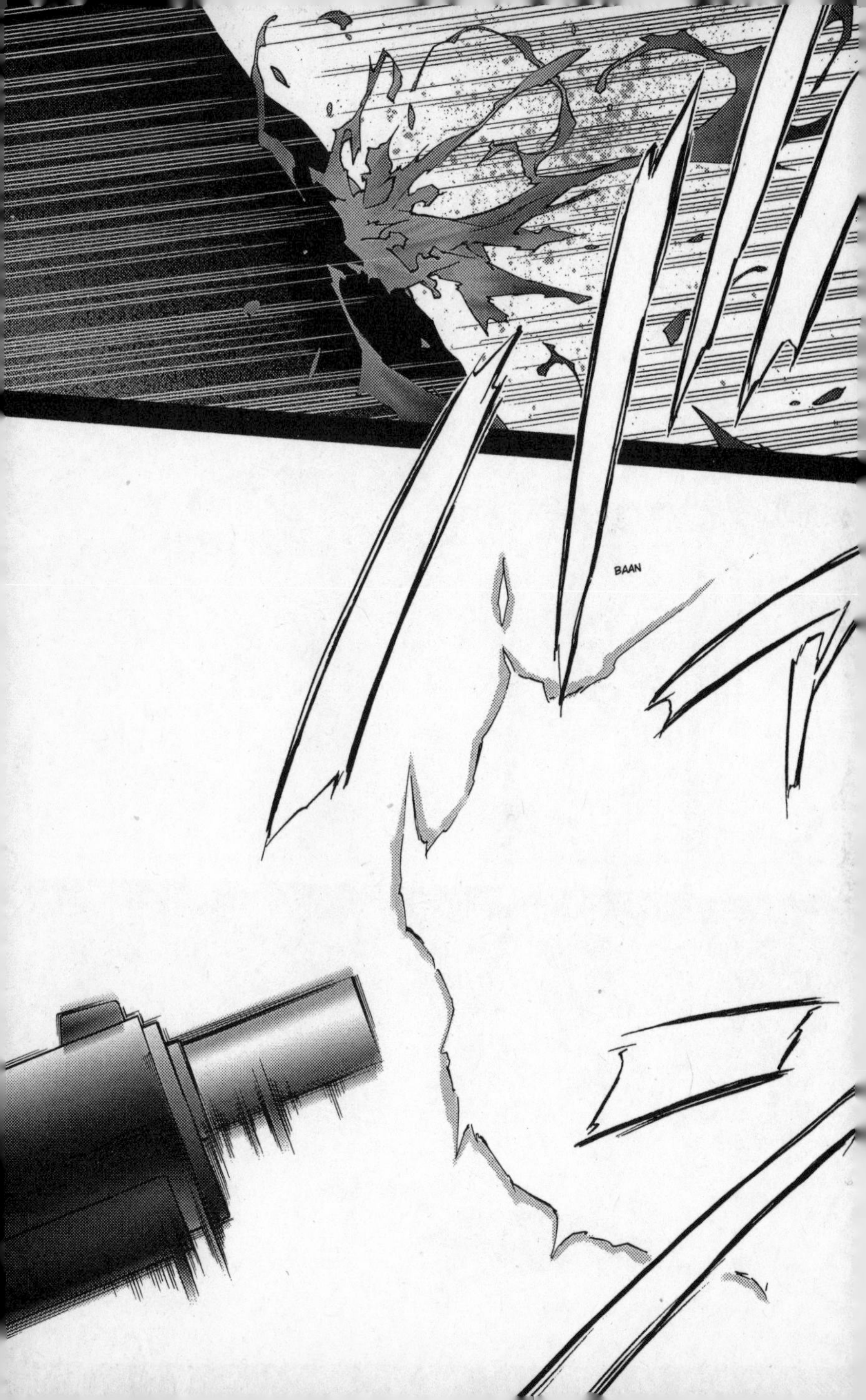
BAAN

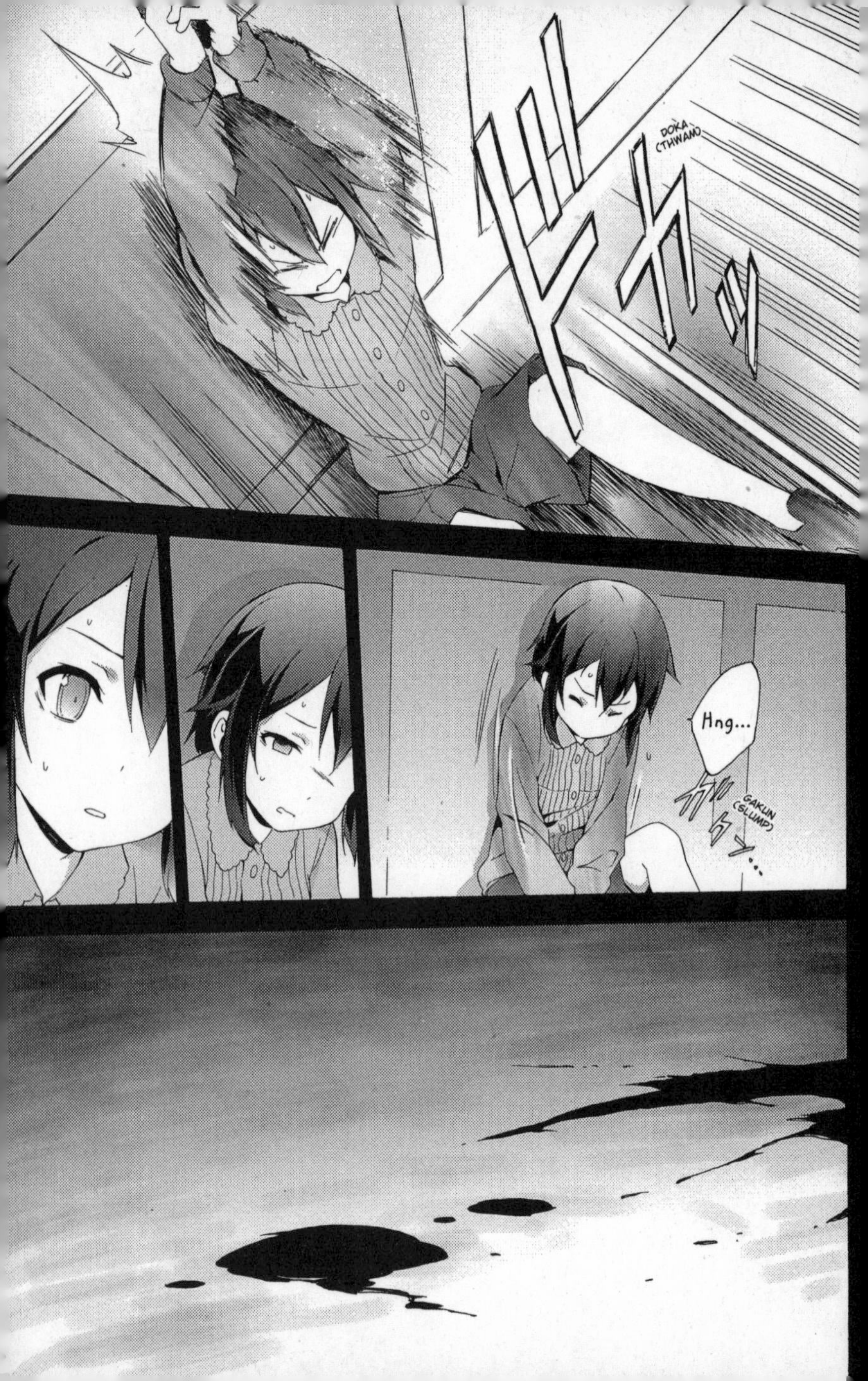
DOKA (THWAM)
ドカッ
Hng...
GAKUN (SLUMP)
ガクッ...

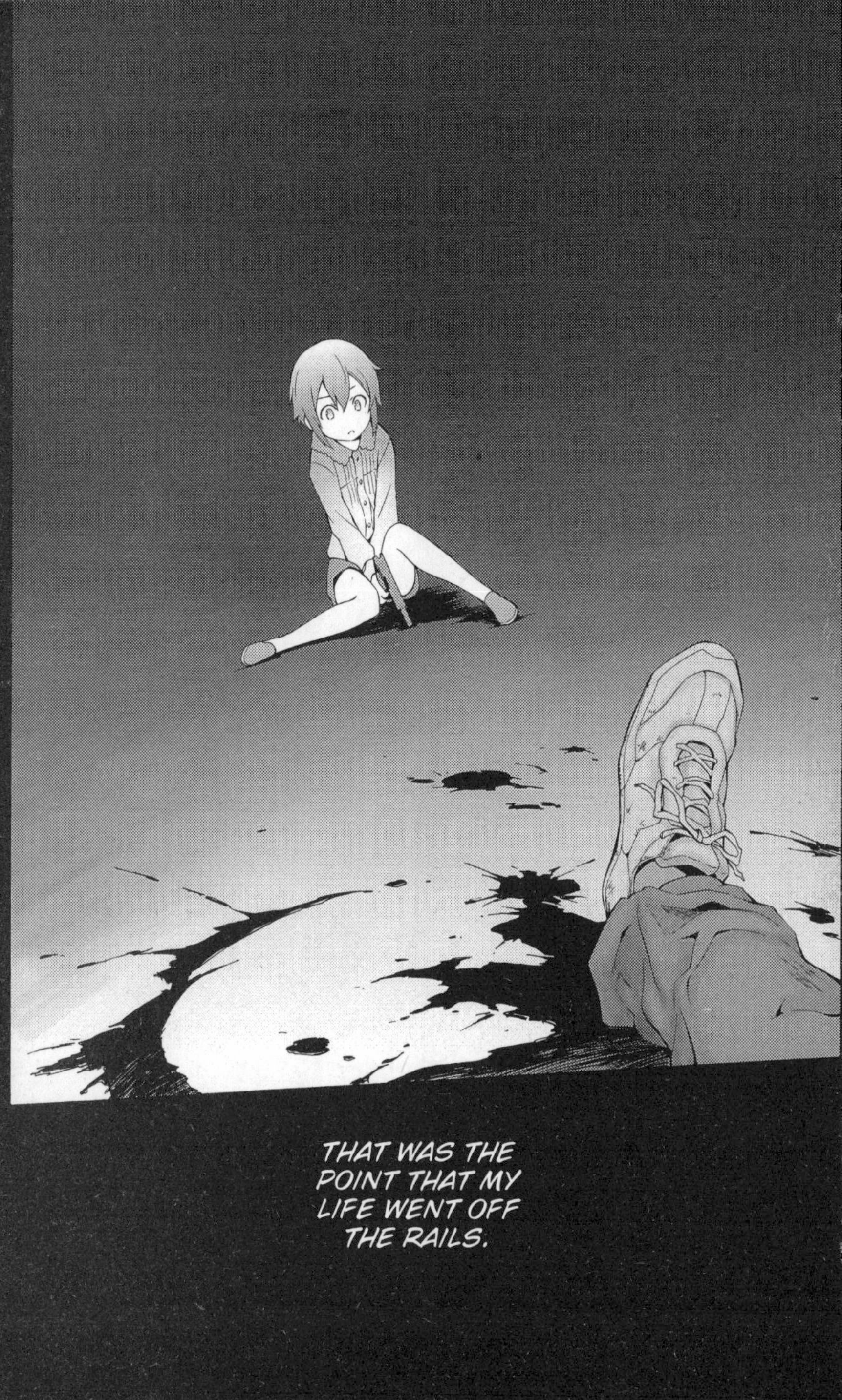
THAT WAS THE POINT THAT MY LIFE WENT OFF THE RAILS.

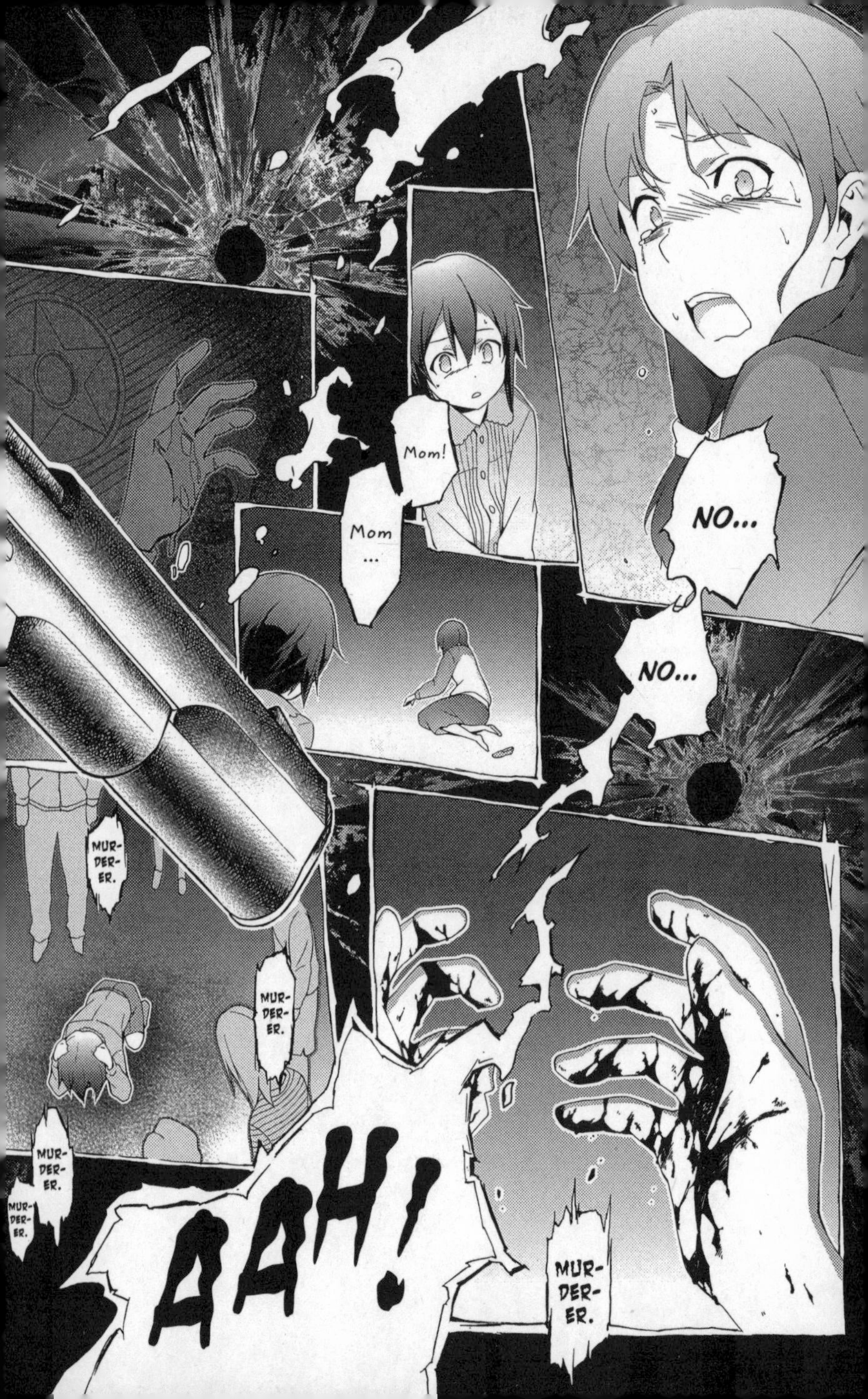
NO...
NO...
Mom!
Mom ...
MURDERER.
MURDERER.
MURDERER.
AAH!
MURDERER.
MURDERER.

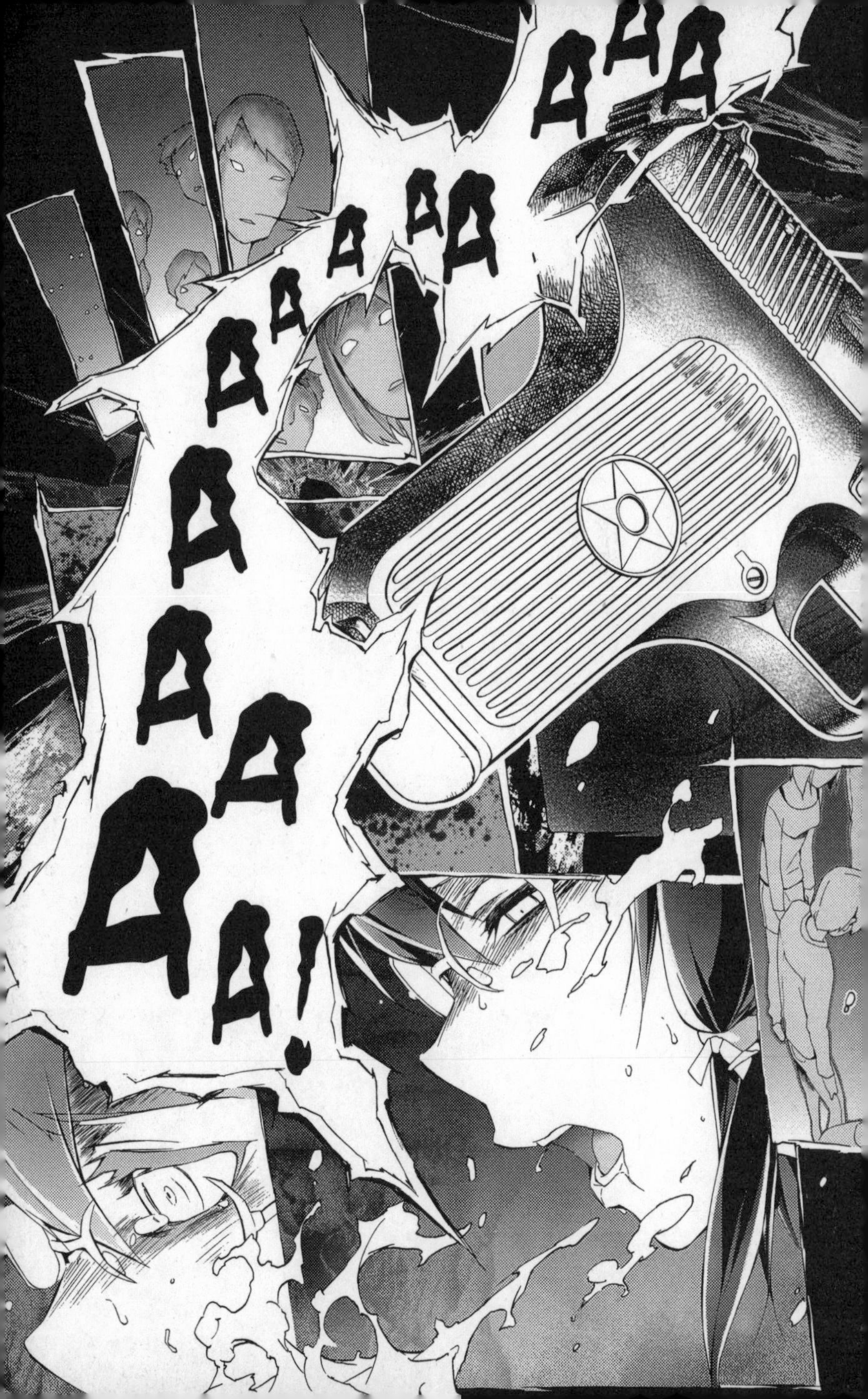
AAAAAAAAAAAAAAAA!

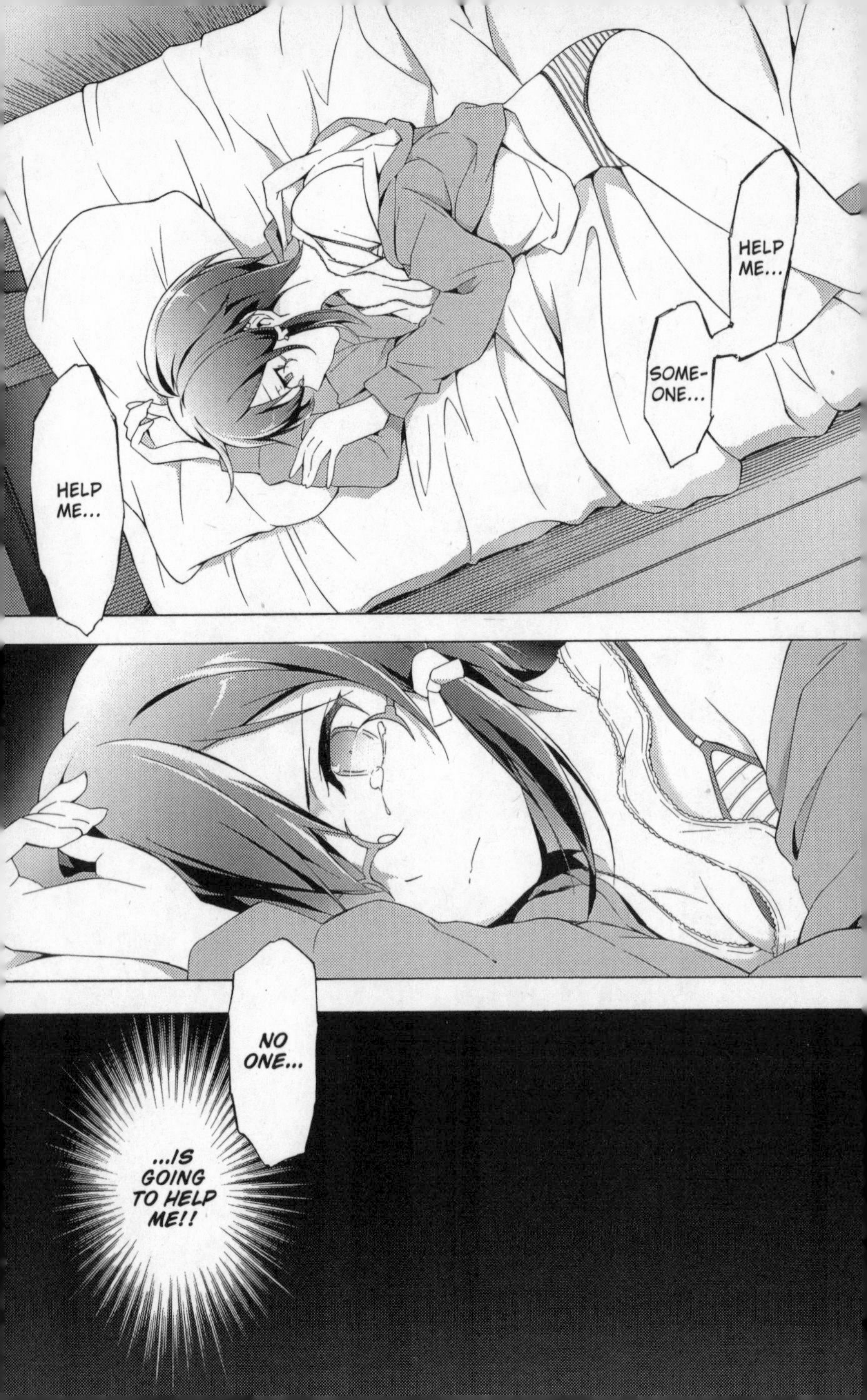
HELP ME...
SOME-ONE...
HELP ME...
NO ONE...
...IS GOING TO HELP ME!!

SWORD ART ONLINE
phantom bullet

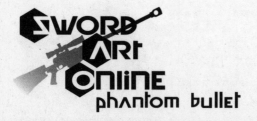

SWORD ART ONLINE
phantom bullet

check point! 001

KYOUJI SHINKAWA: WORLD

SHINO'S FORMER CLASSMATE. HE WAS BULLIED BY THE SOCCER CLUB HE JOINED AND HASN'T BEEN TO SCHOOL SINCE THE START OF THE SECOND TERM. HE TAUGHT SHINO ABOUT THE VRMMO *GUN GALE ONLINE* WHEN HE SPOTTED HER LOOKING AT A BOOK OF GUNS IN THE LIBRARY, HOPING TO CONQUER HER TRAUMA. HIS FATHER IS A DOCTOR WHO RUNS A FAIRLY LARGE HOSPITAL, A SOURCE OF PRESSURE HE IS NOT ABLE TO OVERCOME. HIS CHARACTER, SPIEGEL, IS AN AGI BUILD OF THE KIND THAT WAS PRESUMED TO BE THE BEST AT THE START OF GGO BUT IS RAPIDLY LOSING EFFECTIVENESS AS PATCHES AND UPDATES CHANGE THE GAME BALANCE. HE FEELS LIKE HE CAN'T KEEP UP WITH THE PRESENT GGO.

BLACK STAR (TYPE 54): ITEM

A CHINESE-PRODUCED PISTOL BASED ON THE WWII-ERA SOVIET TOKAREV TT-33. IT USES 7.62 X 25 MM BULLETS, WHICH ARE CONSIDERED LONG FOR A HANDGUN. THAT GIVES THEM GREAT PROJECTILE SPEED, AND THEIR TUNGSTEN CORE IS LIGHTER BUT HARDER THAN LEAD, GIVING THE GUN EXTREME PENETRATION. ONE OF ITS CHIEF FEATURES IS ALSO THE LACK OF A SAFETY, A PRODUCTION CHOICE MADE TO REDUCE PARTS AND MAKE IT EASIER TO MASS-PRODUCE. MANY OF THEM FOUND THEIR WAY INTO JAPAN OVER TIME, WHICH COMBINED WITH THE ABOVE FEATURES, MADE IT THE SYMBOL OF THE MENACE OF GUNS TO THE NATION.

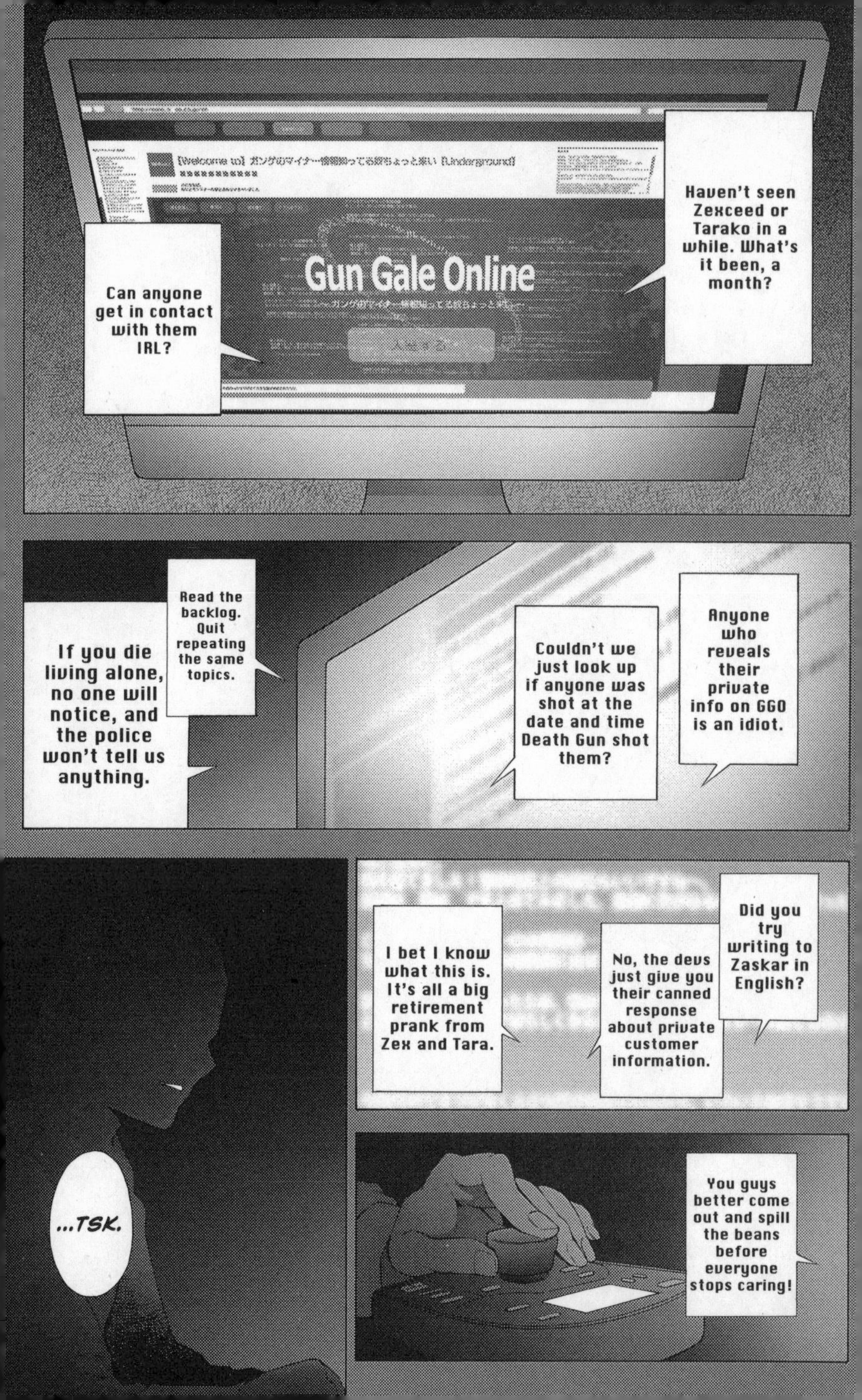
Gun Gale Online
Haven't seen Zexceed or Tarako in a while. What's it been, a month?
Can anyone get in contact with them IRL?
Anyone who reveals their private info on GGO is an idiot.
Couldn't we just look up if anyone was shot at the date and time Death Gun shot them?
Read the backlog. Quit repeating the same topics.
If you die living alone, no one will notice, and the police won't tell us anything.
Did you try writing to Zaskar in English?
No, the devs just give you their canned response about private customer information.
I bet I know what this is. It's all a big retirement prank from Zex and Tara.
You guys better come out and spill the beans before everyone stops caring!
...TSK.

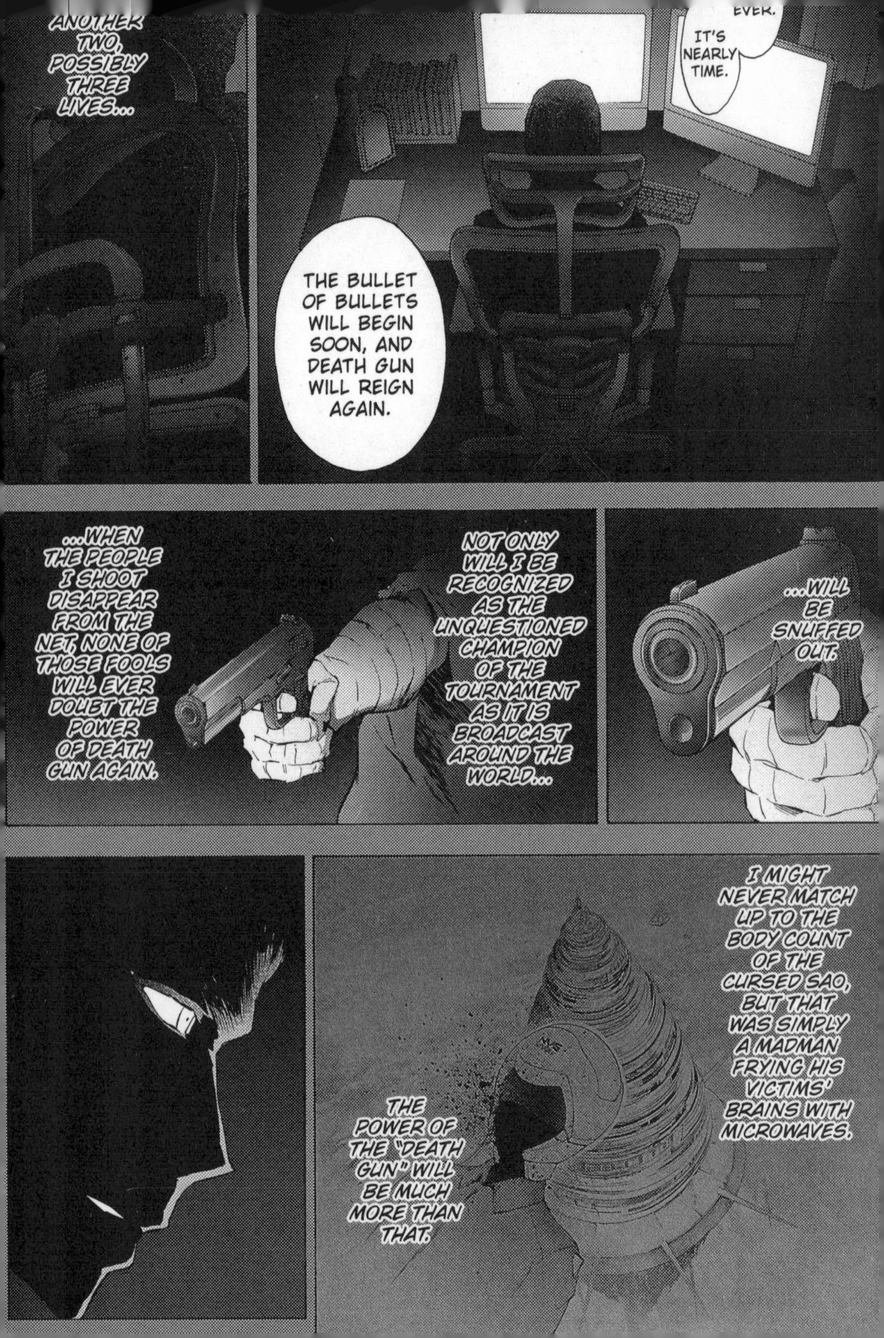
EVER.
IT'S NEARLY TIME.
THE BULLET OF BULLETS WILL BEGIN SOON, AND DEATH GUN WILL REIGN AGAIN.
ANOTHER TWO, POSSIBLY THREE LIVES...
...WILL BE SNUFFED OUT.
NOT ONLY WILL I BE RECOGNIZED AS THE UNQUESTIONED CHAMPION OF THE TOURNAMENT AS IT IS BROADCAST AROUND THE WORLD...
...WHEN THE PEOPLE I SHOOT DISAPPEAR FROM THE NET, NONE OF THOSE FOOLS WILL EVER DOUBT THE POWER OF DEATH GUN AGAIN.
I MIGHT NEVER MATCH UP TO THE BODY COUNT OF THE CURSED SAO, BUT THAT WAS SIMPLY A MADMAN FRYING HIS VICTIMS' BRAINS WITH MICROWAVES.
THE POWER OF THE "DEATH GUN" WILL BE MUCH MORE THAN THAT.

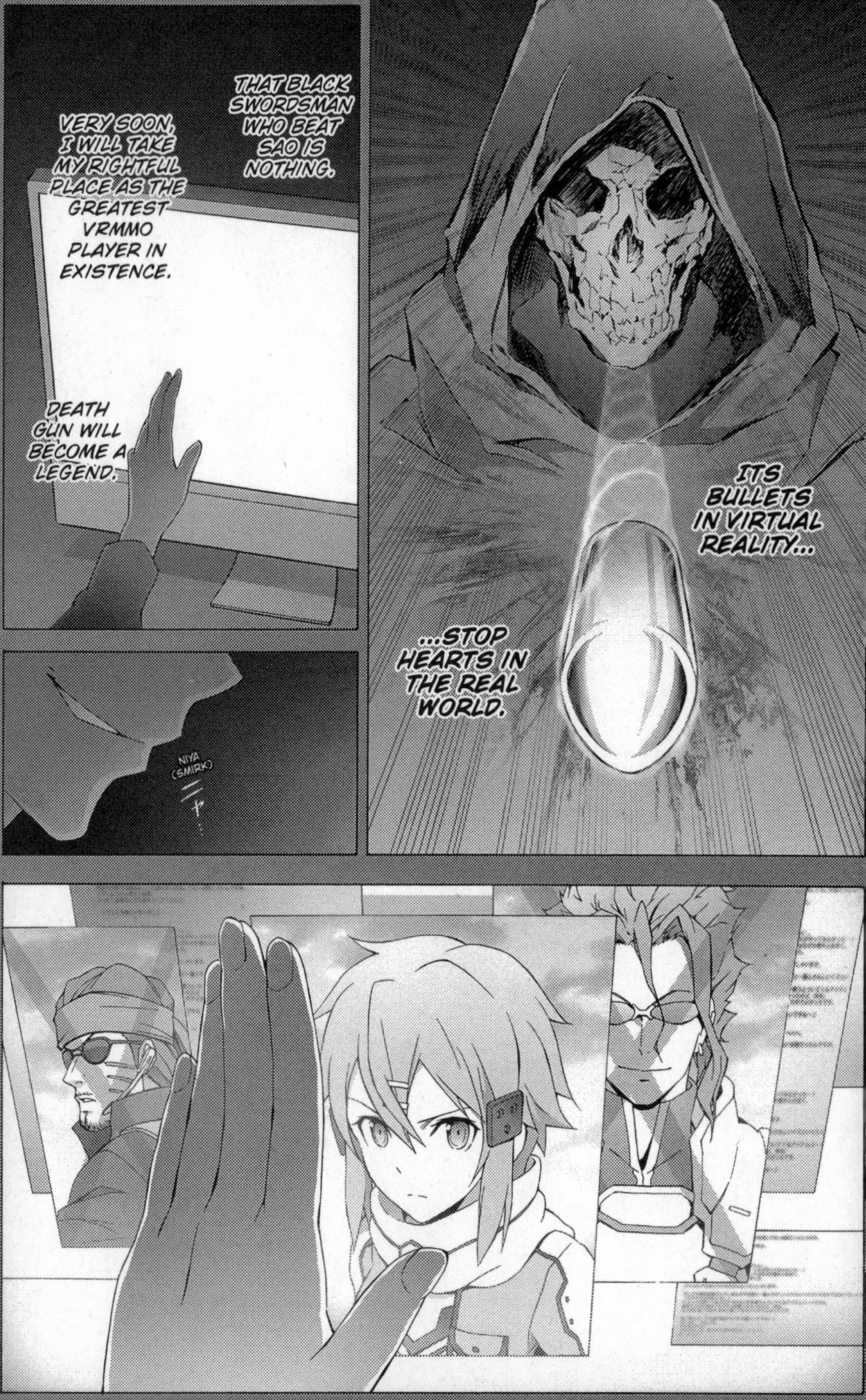
ITS BULLETS IN VIRTUAL REALITY...
...STOP HEARTS IN THE REAL WORLD.
THAT BLACK SWORDSMAN WHO BEAT SAO IS NOTHING.
VERY SOON, I WILL TAKE MY RIGHTFUL PLACE AS THE GREATEST VRMMO PLAYER IN EXISTENCE.
DEATH GUN WILL BECOME A LEGEND.
NIYA (SMIRK)

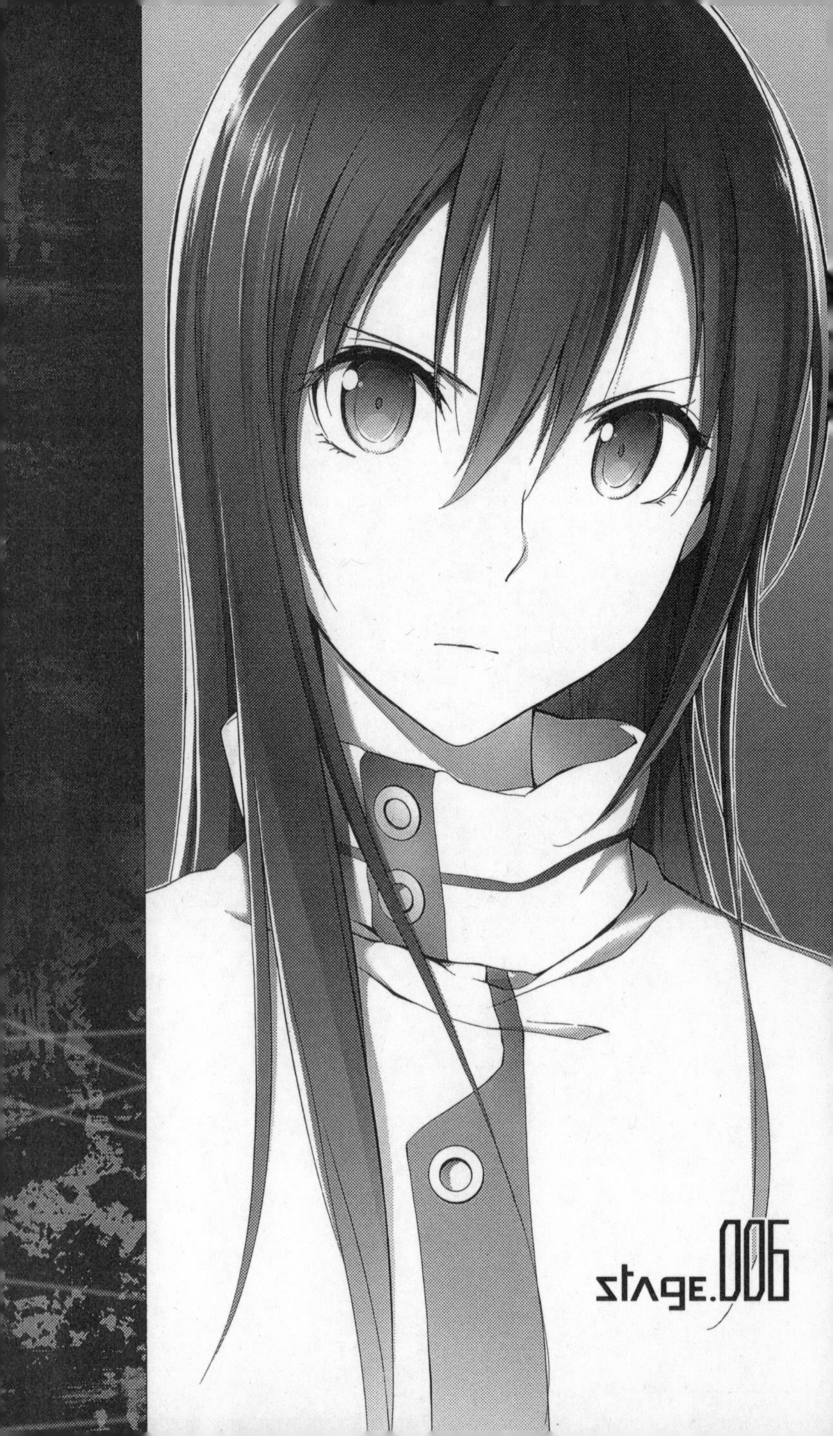
stage.006

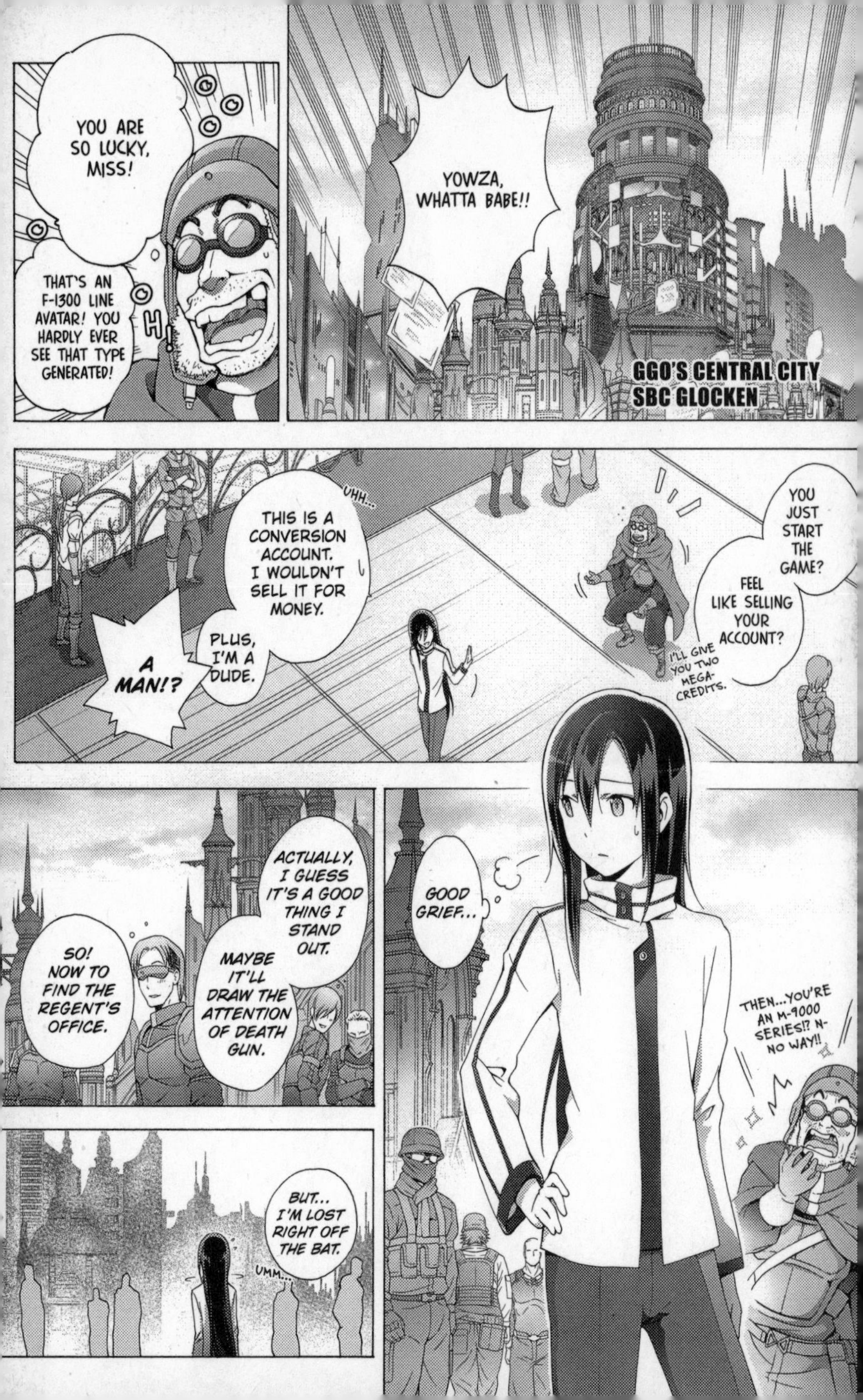
YOWZA, WHATTA BABE!!
GGO'S CENTRAL CITY SBC GLOCKEN
YOU ARE SO LUCKY, MISS!
THAT'S AN F-1300 LINE AVATAR! YOU HARDLY EVER SEE THAT TYPE GENERATED!
H!
YOU JUST START THE GAME?
FEEL LIKE SELLING YOUR ACCOUNT?
I'LL GIVE YOU TWO MEGA-CREDITS.
UHH...
THIS IS A CONVERSION ACCOUNT. I WOULDN'T SELL IT FOR MONEY.
PLUS, I'M A DUDE.
A MAN!?
THEN...YOU'RE AN M-9000 SERIES!? N-NO WAY!!
GOOD GRIEF...
ACTUALLY, I GUESS IT'S A GOOD THING I STAND OUT.
MAYBE IT'LL DRAW THE ATTENTION OF DEATH GUN.
SO! NOW TO FIND THE REGENT'S OFFICE.
BUT... I'M LOST RIGHT OFF THE BAT.
UMM...

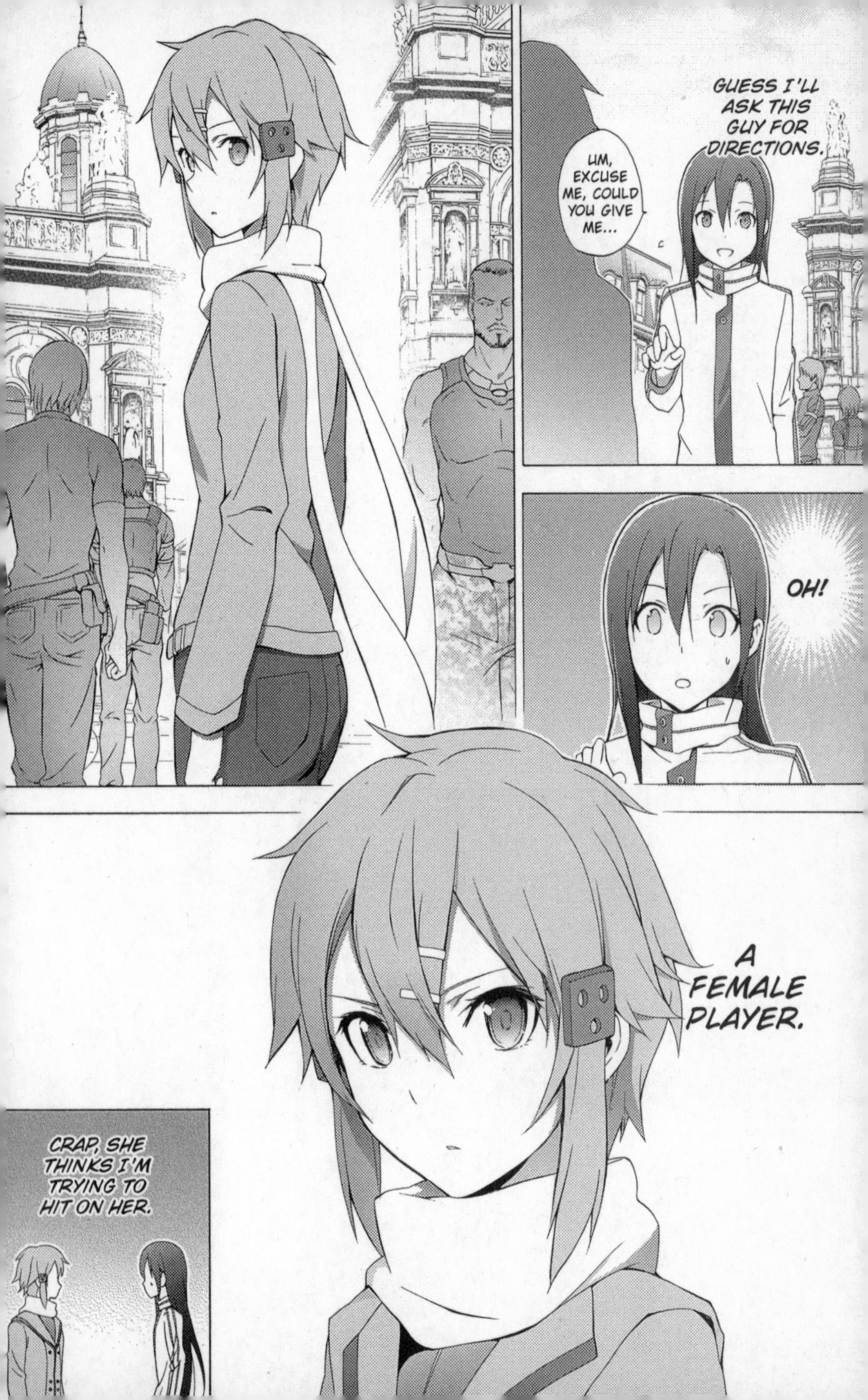
GUESS I'LL ASK THIS GUY FOR DIRECTIONS.
UM, EXCUSE ME, COULD YOU GIVE ME...
OH!
A FEMALE PLAYER.
CRAP, SHE THINKS I'M TRYING TO HIT ON HER.

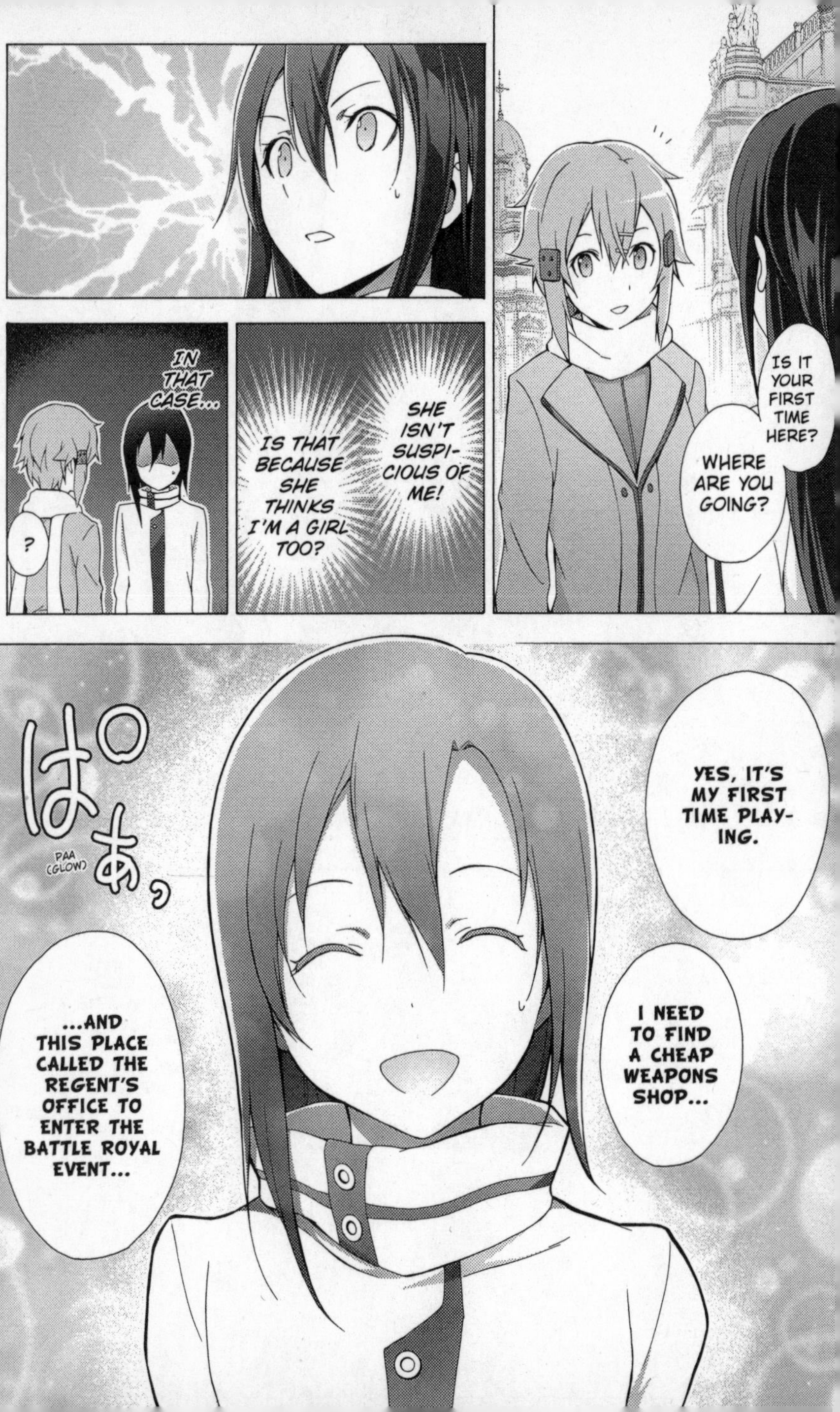
IS IT YOUR FIRST TIME HERE?
WHERE ARE YOU GOING?
SHE ISN'T SUSPICIOUS OF ME!
IS THAT BECAUSE SHE THINKS I'M A GIRL TOO?
IN THAT CASE...
?
YES, IT'S MY FIRST TIME PLAYING.
I NEED TO FIND A CHEAP WEAPONS SHOP...
はぁっ
PAA (GLOW)
...AND THIS PLACE CALLED THE REGENT'S OFFICE TO ENTER THE BATTLE ROYAL EVENT...

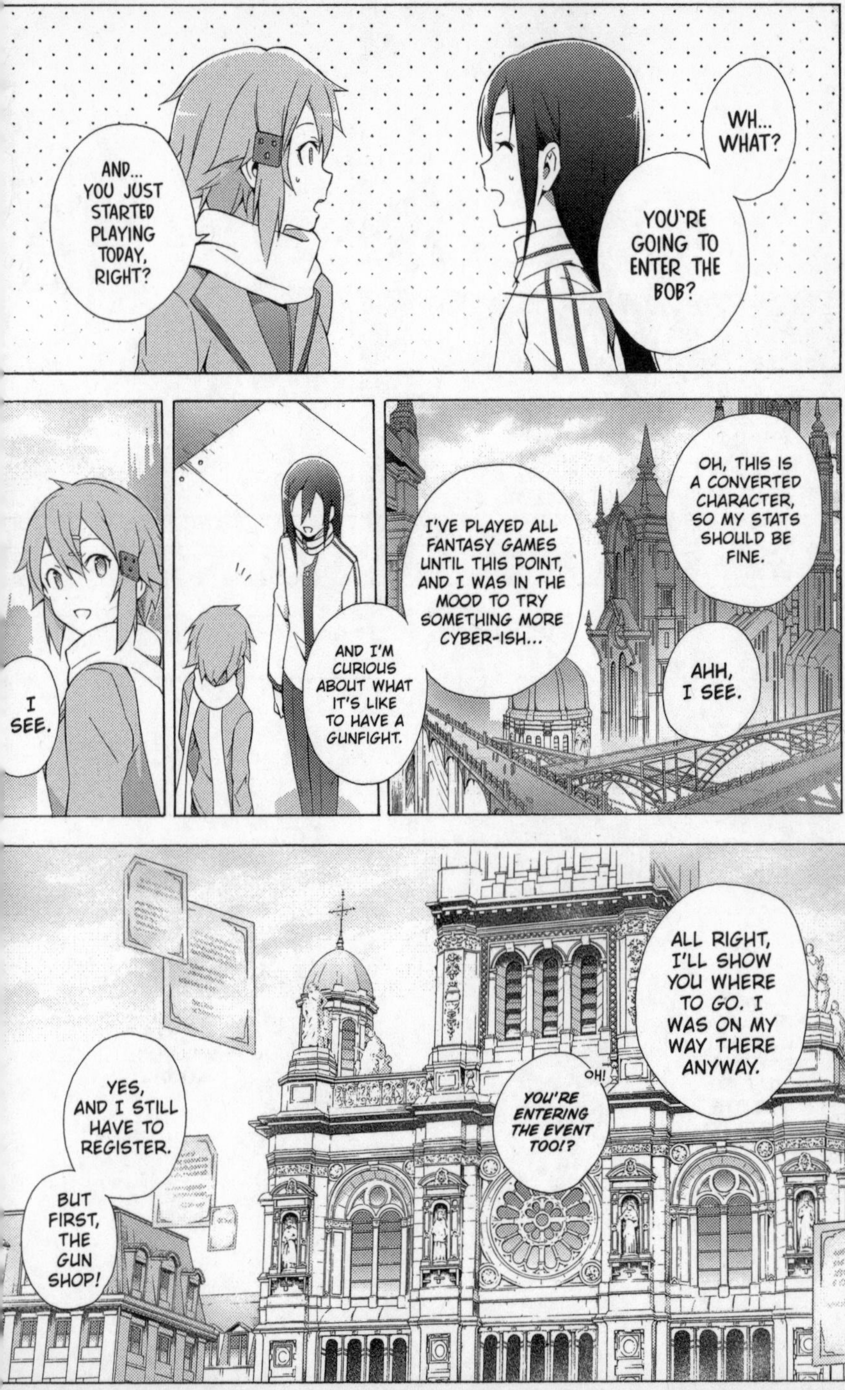
WH... WHAT?
YOU'RE GOING TO ENTER THE BOB?
AND... YOU JUST STARTED PLAYING TODAY, RIGHT?
OH, THIS IS A CONVERTED CHARACTER, SO MY STATS SHOULD BE FINE.
AHH, I SEE.
I'VE PLAYED ALL FANTASY GAMES UNTIL THIS POINT, AND I WAS IN THE MOOD TO TRY SOMETHING MORE CYBER-ISH...
AND I'M CURIOUS ABOUT WHAT IT'S LIKE TO HAVE A GUNFIGHT.
I SEE.
ALL RIGHT, I'LL SHOW YOU WHERE TO GO. I WAS ON MY WAY THERE ANYWAY.
OH!
YOU'RE ENTERING THE EVENT TOO!?
YES, AND I STILL HAVE TO REGISTER.
BUT FIRST, THE GUN SHOP!

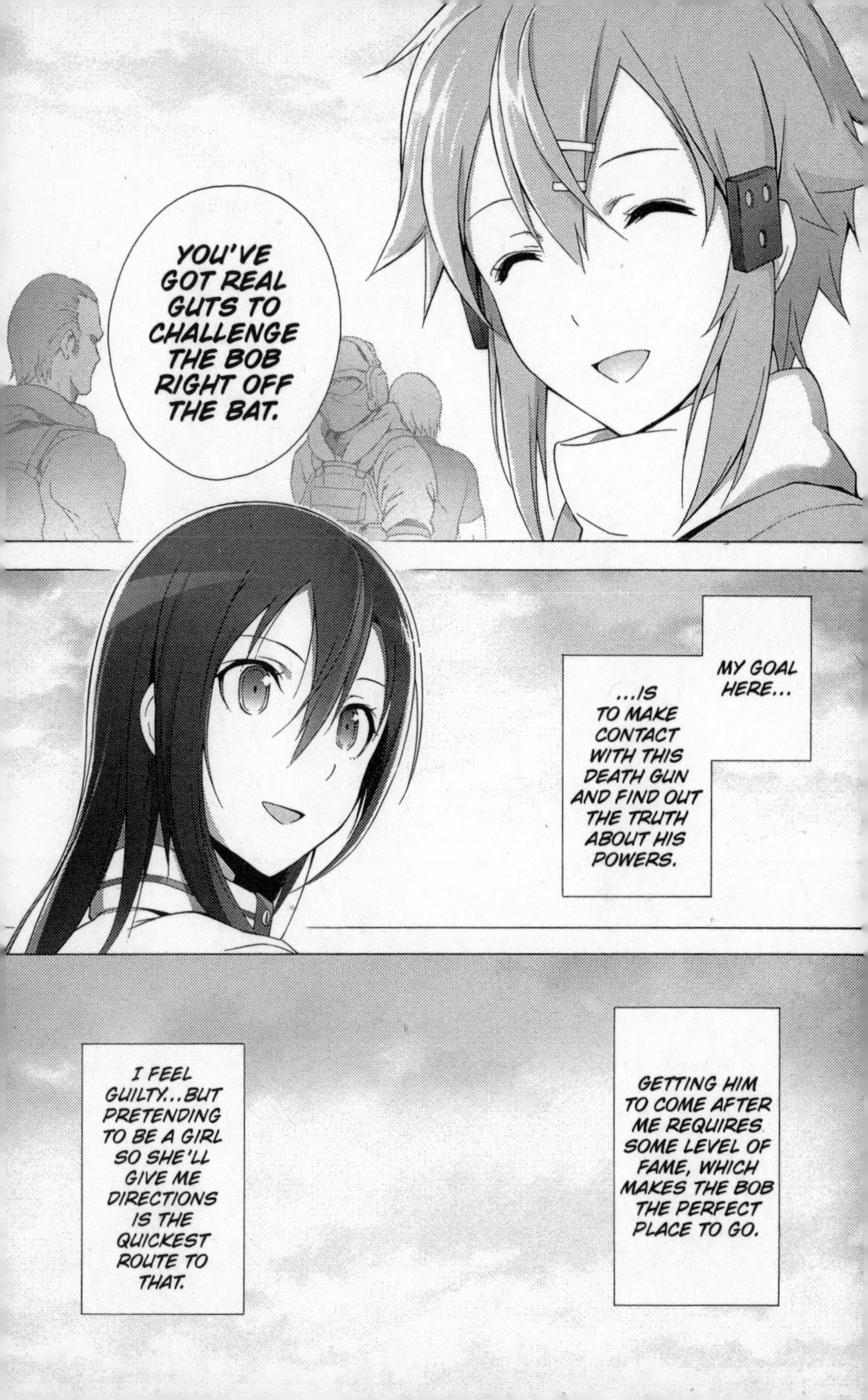
YOU'VE GOT REAL GUTS TO CHALLENGE THE BOB RIGHT OFF THE BAT.
MY GOAL HERE...
...IS TO MAKE CONTACT WITH THIS DEATH GUN AND FIND OUT THE TRUTH ABOUT HIS POWERS.
GETTING HIM TO COME AFTER ME REQUIRES SOME LEVEL OF FAME, WHICH MAKES THE BOB THE PERFECT PLACE TO GO.
I FEEL GUILTY...BUT PRETENDING TO BE A GIRL SO SHE'LL GIVE ME DIRECTIONS IS THE QUICKEST ROUTE TO THAT.

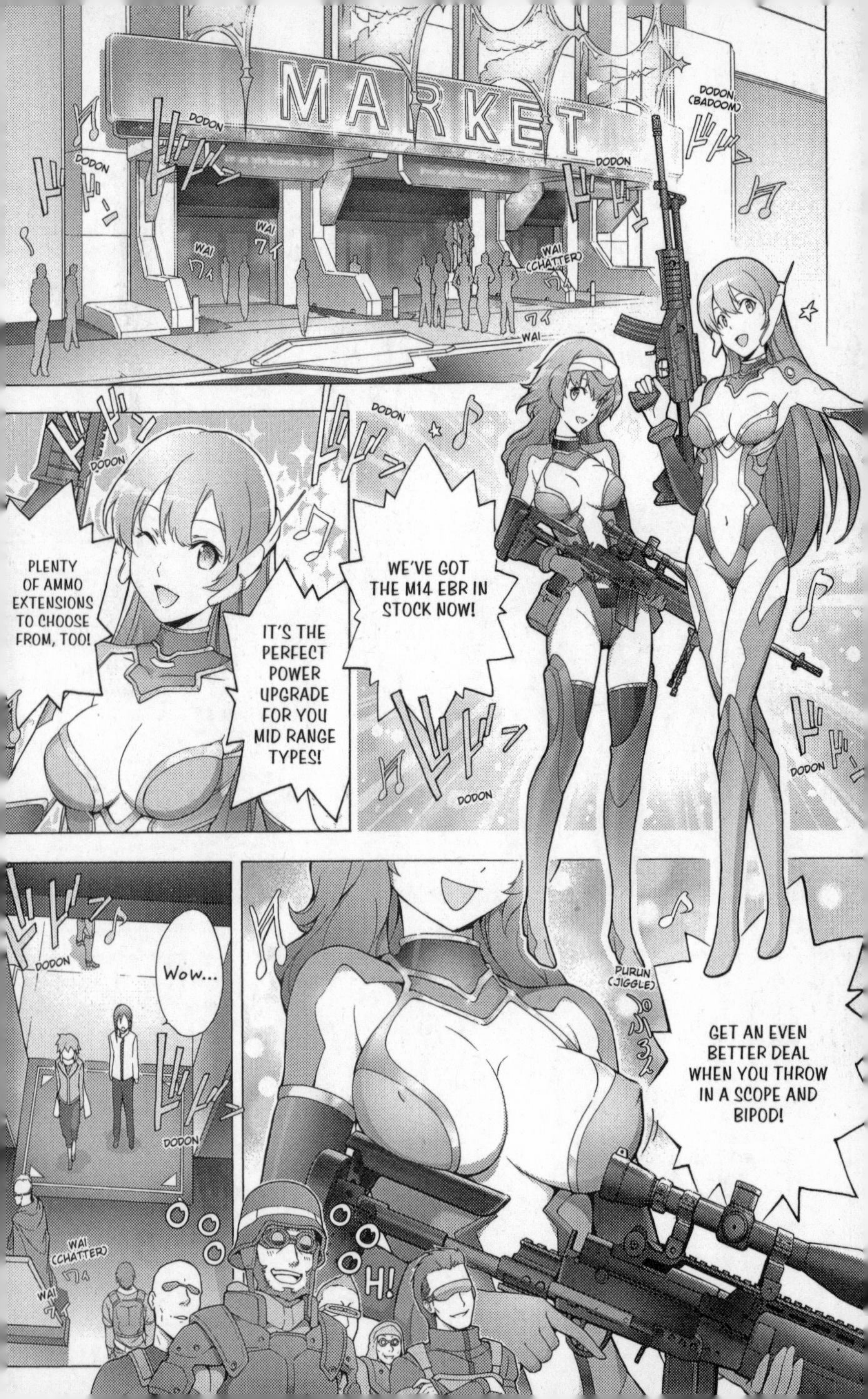
MARKET
DODON (BADOOM)
DODON
WAI (CHATTER)
WAI
WAI
WAI
DODON
DODON
DODON
DODON
WE'VE GOT THE M14 EBR IN STOCK NOW!
DODON
DODON
IT'S THE PERFECT POWER UPGRADE FOR YOU MID RANGE TYPES!
PLENTY OF AMMO EXTENSIONS TO CHOOSE FROM, TOO!
PURUN (JIGGLE)
GET AN EVEN BETTER DEAL WHEN YOU THROW IN A SCOPE AND BIPOD!
OOOOOOH!
Wow...
DODON
DODON
WAI (CHATTER)
WAI

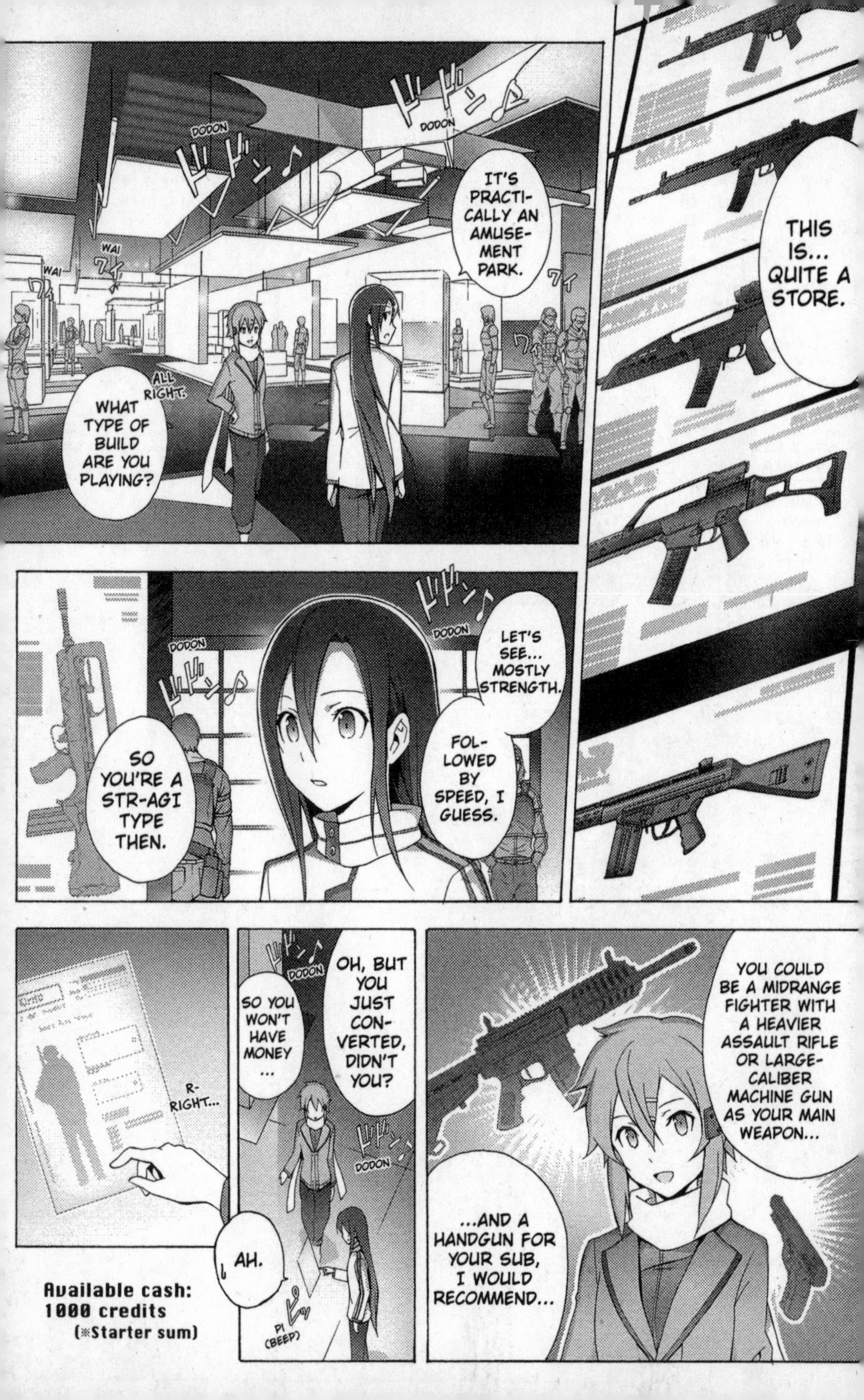
THIS IS... QUITE A STORE.
DODON
DODON
IT'S PRACTICALLY AN AMUSEMENT PARK.
WAI
WAI
ALL RIGHT.
WHAT TYPE OF BUILD ARE YOU PLAYING?
DODON
LET'S SEE... MOSTLY STRENGTH.
FOLLOWED BY SPEED, I GUESS.
DODON
SO YOU'RE A STR-AGI TYPE THEN.
YOU COULD BE A MIDRANGE FIGHTER WITH A HEAVIER ASSAULT RIFLE OR LARGE-CALIBER MACHINE GUN AS YOUR MAIN WEAPON...
...AND A HANDGUN FOR YOUR SUB, I WOULD RECOMMEND...
DODON
OH, BUT YOU JUST CONVERTED, DIDN'T YOU?
SO YOU WON'T HAVE MONEY...
DODON
AH.
PI (BEEP)
R-RIGHT...
Available cash: 1000 credits
(※Starter sum)

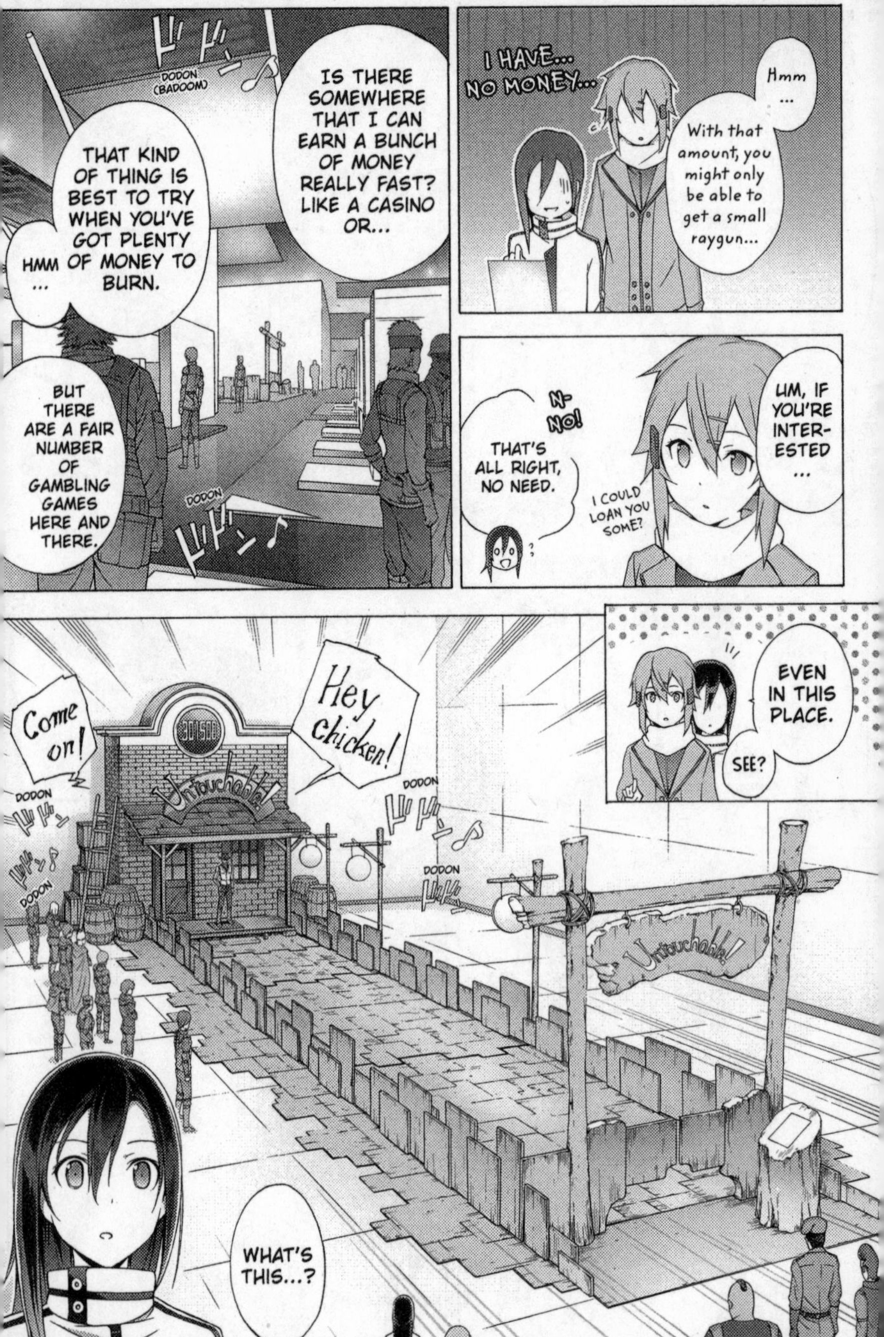
Hmm ...
I HAVE... NO MONEY...
With that amount, you might only be able to get a small raygun...
UM, IF YOU'RE INTERESTED ...
I COULD LOAN YOU SOME?
N-NO!
THAT'S ALL RIGHT, NO NEED.
DODON (BADOOM)
IS THERE SOMEWHERE THAT I CAN EARN A BUNCH OF MONEY REALLY FAST? LIKE A CASINO OR...
THAT KIND OF THING IS BEST TO TRY WHEN YOU'VE GOT PLENTY OF MONEY TO BURN.
HMM ...
BUT THERE ARE A FAIR NUMBER OF GAMBLING GAMES HERE AND THERE.
DODON
EVEN IN THIS PLACE.
SEE?
Hey chicken!
DODON
Come on!
DODON
DODON
DODON
Untouchable!
Untouchable!
WHAT'S THIS...?

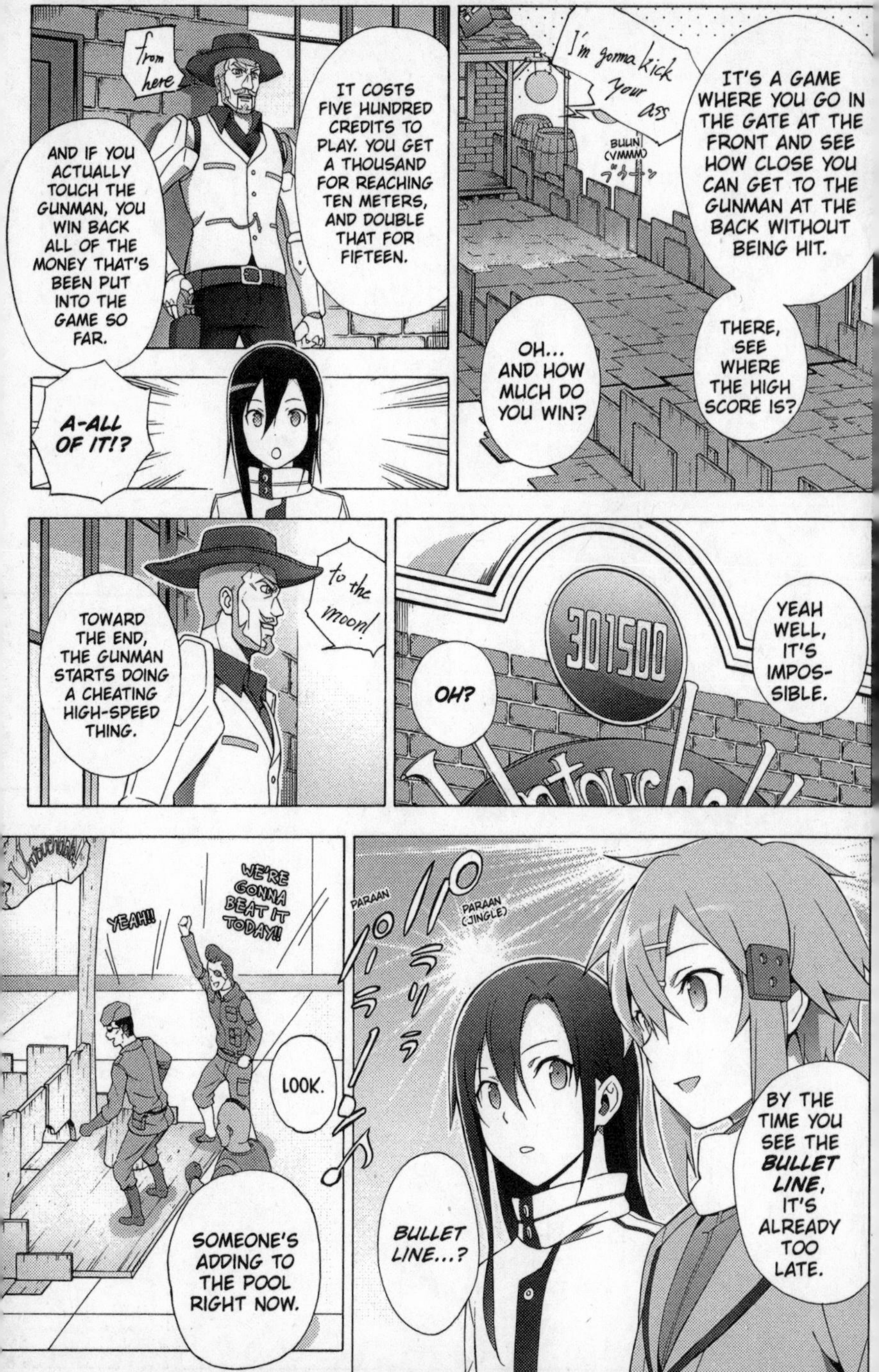
IT'S A GAME WHERE YOU GO IN THE GATE AT THE FRONT AND SEE HOW CLOSE YOU CAN GET TO THE GUNMAN AT THE BACK WITHOUT BEING HIT.
I'm gonna kick your ass
BUUN (VMMM)
THERE, SEE WHERE THE HIGH SCORE IS?
OH... AND HOW MUCH DO YOU WIN?
IT COSTS FIVE HUNDRED CREDITS TO PLAY. YOU GET A THOUSAND FOR REACHING TEN METERS, AND DOUBLE THAT FOR FIFTEEN.
from here
AND IF YOU ACTUALLY TOUCH THE GUNMAN, YOU WIN BACK ALL OF THE MONEY THAT'S BEEN PUT INTO THE GAME SO FAR.
A-ALL OF IT!?
301500
YEAH WELL, IT'S IMPOSSIBLE.
OH?
to the moon!
TOWARD THE END, THE GUNMAN STARTS DOING A CHEATING HIGH-SPEED THING.
BY THE TIME YOU SEE THE *BULLET LINE*, IT'S ALREADY TOO LATE.
PARAAN (JINGLE)
PARAAN
BULLET LINE...?
WE'RE GONNA BEAT IT TODAY!!
YEAH!!
LOOK.
SOMEONE'S ADDING TO THE POOL RIGHT NOW.

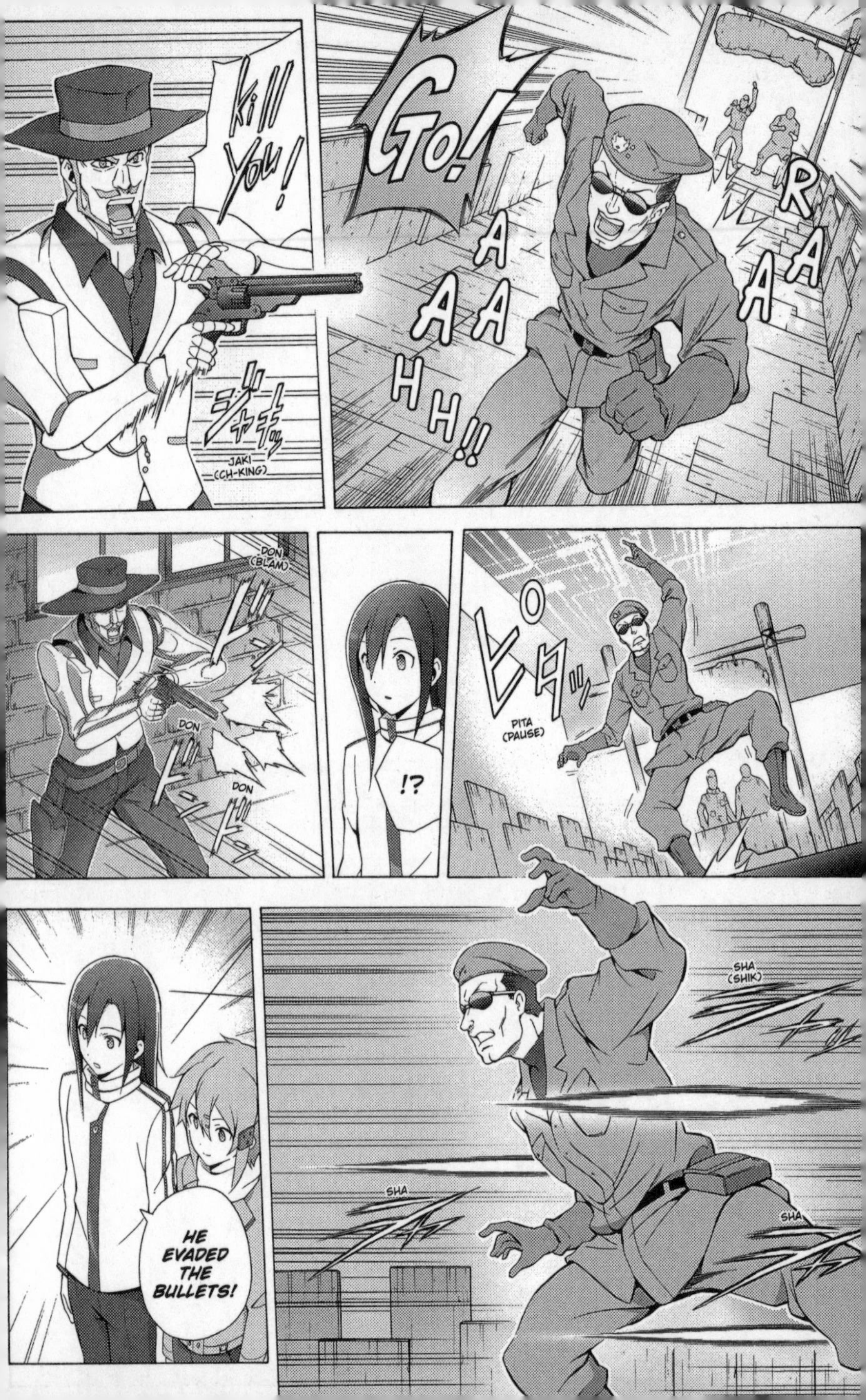
GO!
RAAA
AAAAHH!!
KILL YOU!
JAKI (CH-KING)
PITA (PAUSE)
!?
DON (BLAM)
DON
DON
SHA (SHIK)
SHA
SHA
HE EVADED THE BULLETS!

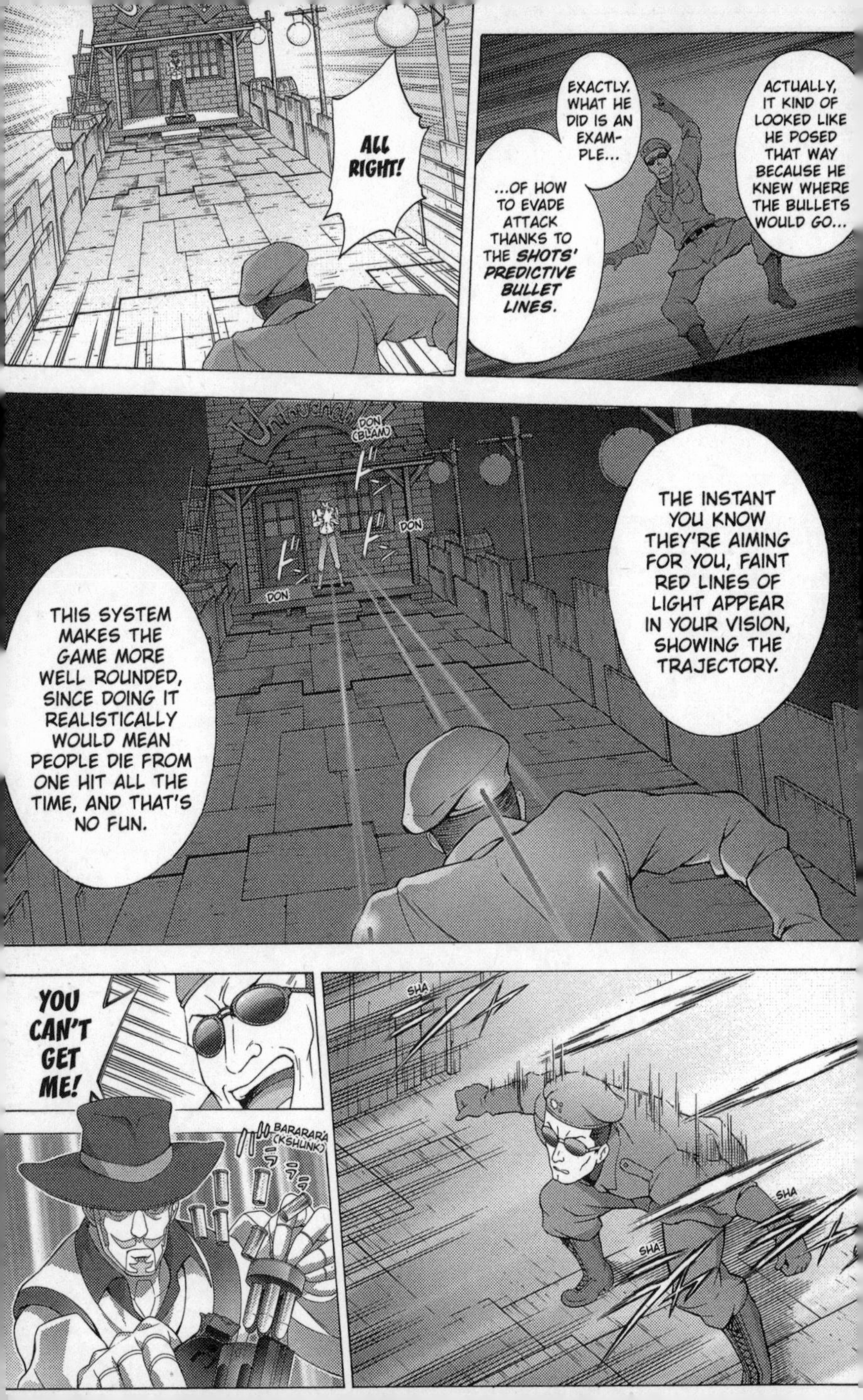
ACTUALLY, IT KIND OF LOOKED LIKE HE POSED THAT WAY BECAUSE HE KNEW WHERE THE BULLETS WOULD GO...
EXACTLY. WHAT HE DID IS AN EXAMPLE...
...OF HOW TO EVADE ATTACK THANKS TO THE *SHOTS' PREDICTIVE BULLET LINES.*
ALL RIGHT!
DON (BLAM)
DON
DON
THE INSTANT YOU KNOW THEY'RE AIMING FOR YOU, FAINT RED LINES OF LIGHT APPEAR IN YOUR VISION, SHOWING THE TRAJECTORY.
THIS SYSTEM MAKES THE GAME MORE WELL ROUNDED, SINCE DOING IT REALISTICALLY WOULD MEAN PEOPLE DIE FROM ONE HIT ALL THE TIME, AND THAT'S NO FUN.
SHA
SHA
SHA
YOU CAN'T GET ME!
BARARARA (KSHUNK)

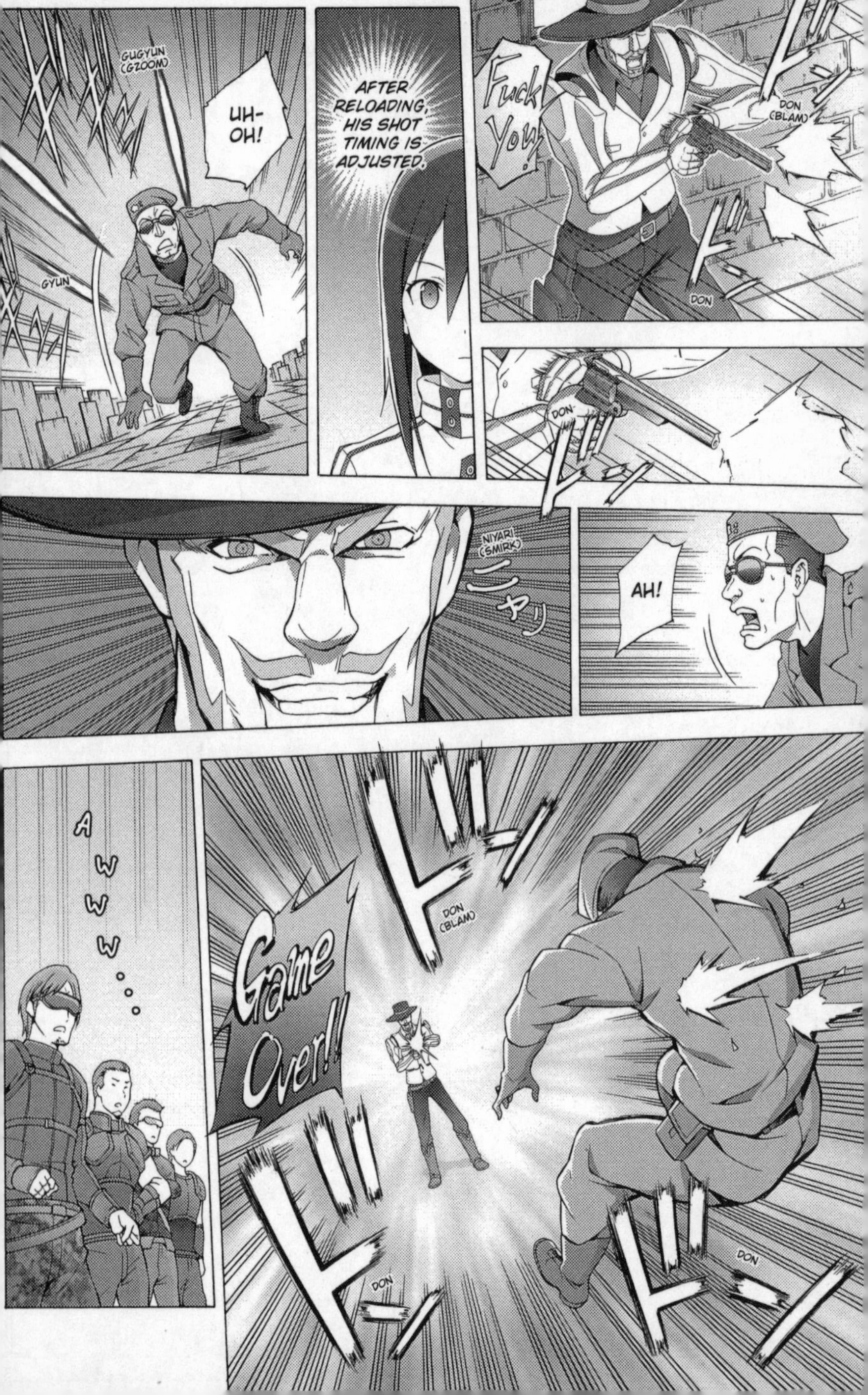
Fuck You!
DON (BLAM)
DON
DON
AFTER RELOADING, HIS SHOT TIMING IS ADJUSTED.
GUGYUN (GZOOM)
UH-OH!
GYUN
AH!
NIYARI (SMIRK)
DON (BLAM)
Game Over!!
DON
DON
AWWW...

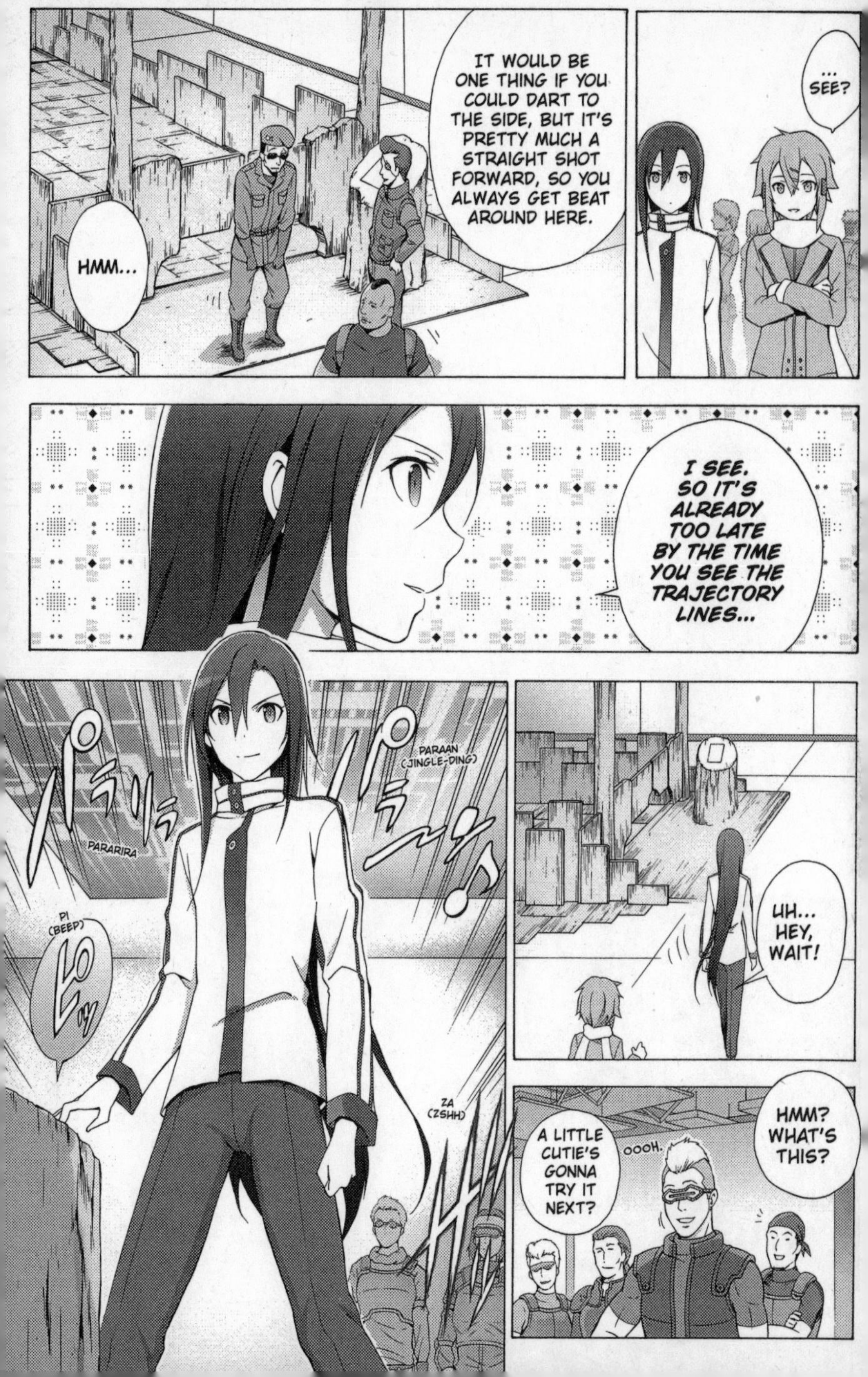

... SEE?
IT WOULD BE ONE THING IF YOU COULD DART TO THE SIDE, BUT IT'S PRETTY MUCH A STRAIGHT SHOT FORWARD, SO YOU ALWAYS GET BEAT AROUND HERE.
HMM...
I SEE. SO IT'S ALREADY TOO LATE BY THE TIME YOU SEE THE TRAJECTORY LINES...
UH... HEY, WAIT!
HMM? WHAT'S THIS?
OOOH.
A LITTLE CUTIE'S GONNA TRY IT NEXT?
PARAAN (JINGLE-DING)
PARARIRA
PI (BEEP)
ZA (ZSHH)

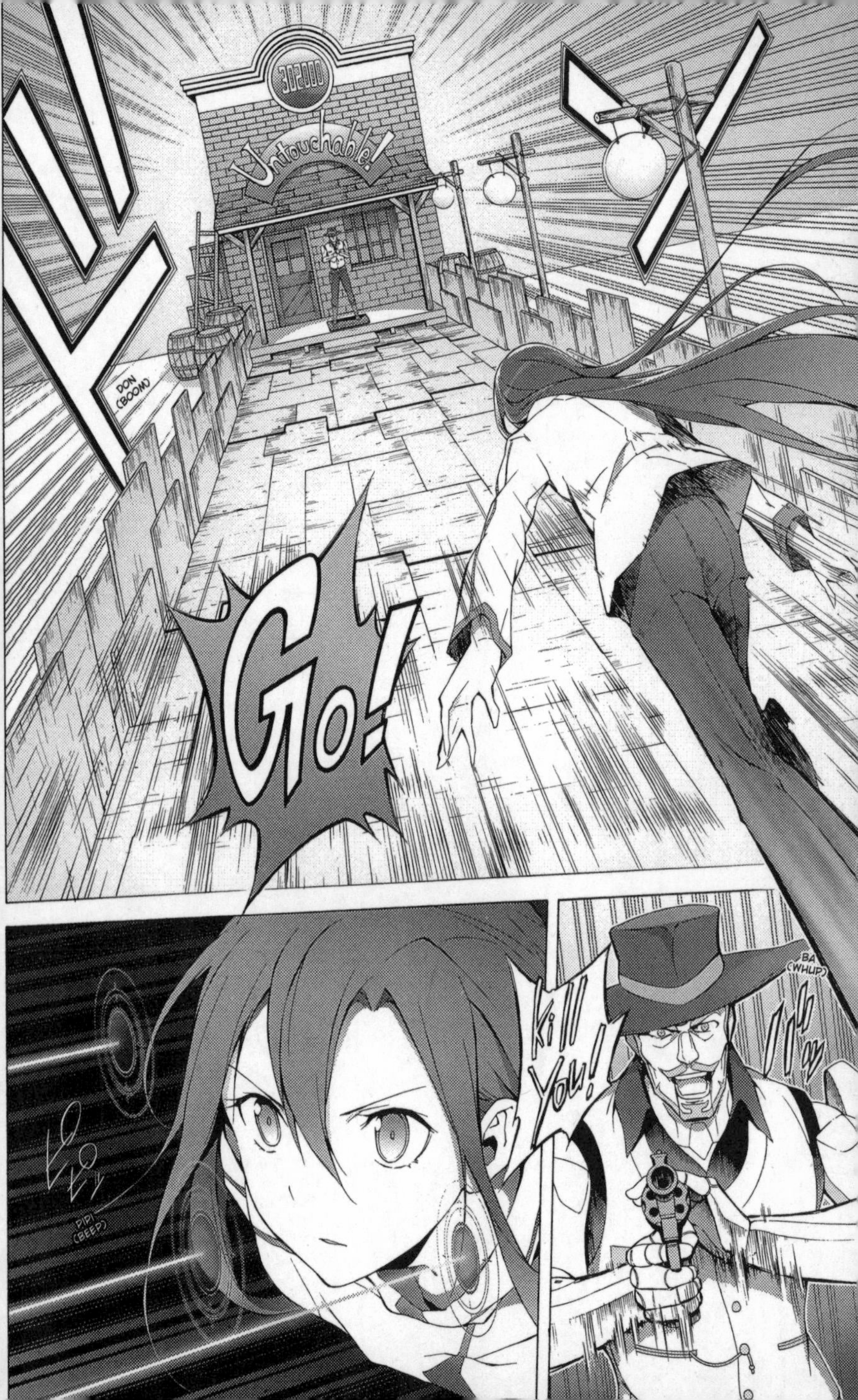
302000
Untouchable!
DON (BOOM)
GO!
BA (WHUP)
Kill You!
PIPI (BEEP)

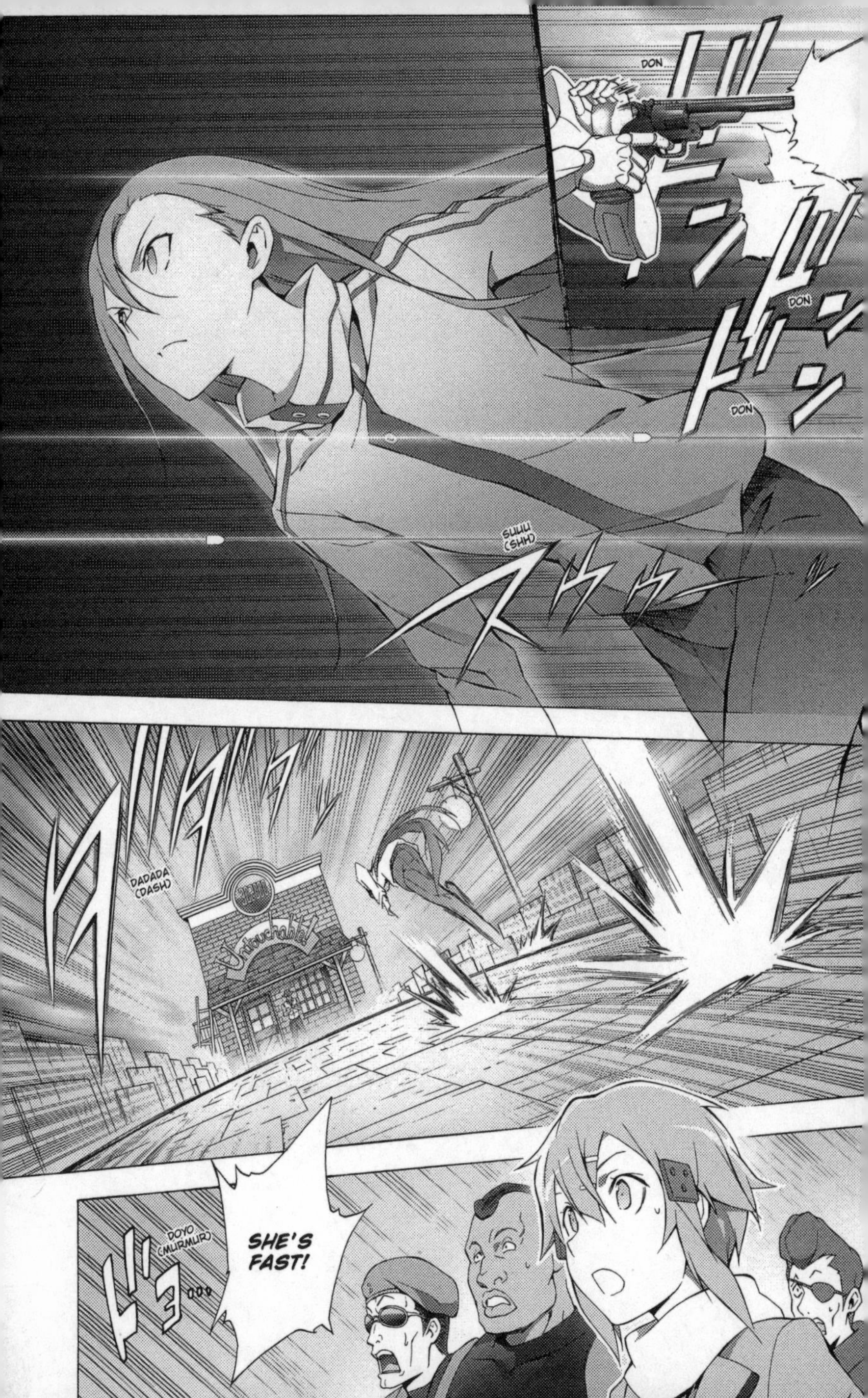
DON
DON
DON
SUUU (SHH)
DADADA (DASH)
SHE'S FAST!
DOYO (MURMUR)

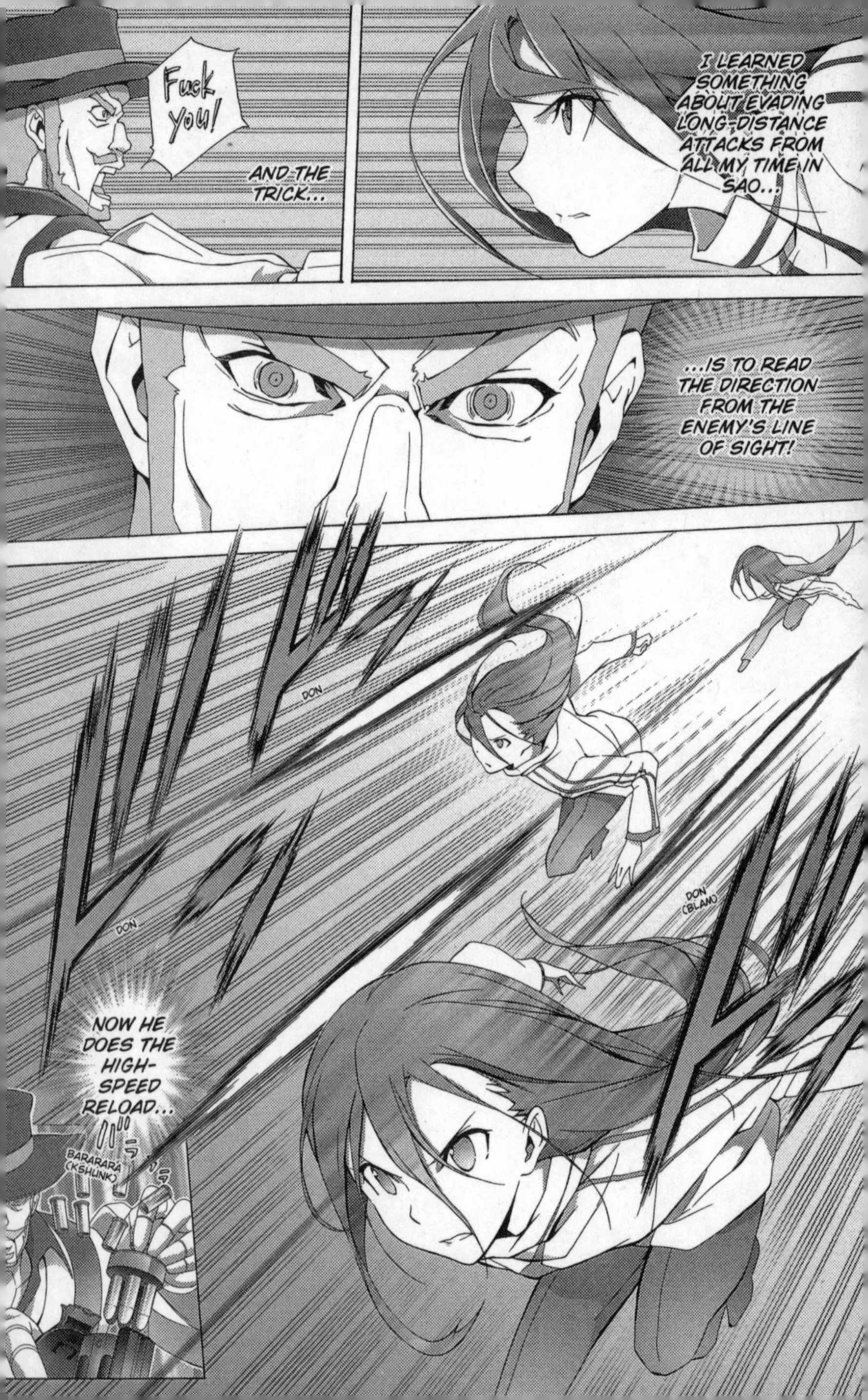
I LEARNED SOMETHING ABOUT EVADING LONG-DISTANCE ATTACKS FROM ALL MY TIME IN SAO...
AND THE TRICK...
Fuck you!
...IS TO READ THE DIRECTION FROM THE ENEMY'S LINE OF SIGHT!
DON
DON (BLAM)
DON
NOW HE DOES THE HIGH-SPEED RELOAD...
BARARARA (KSHUNK)

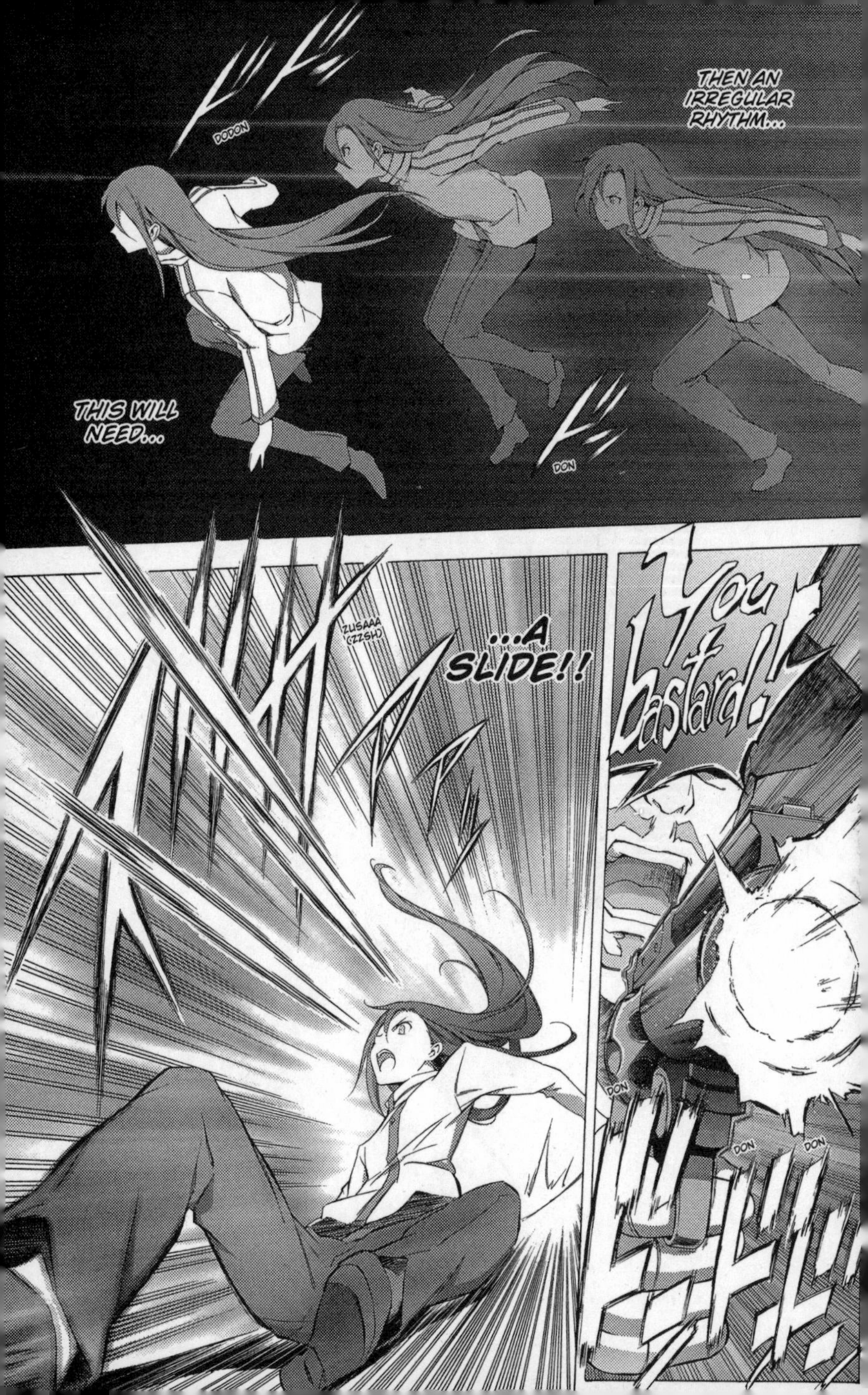
THEN AN IRREGULAR RHYTHM...
DODON
THIS WILL NEED...
DON
You bastard!!
DON
DON
DON
ZUSAAA (ZZSH)
...A SLIDE!!

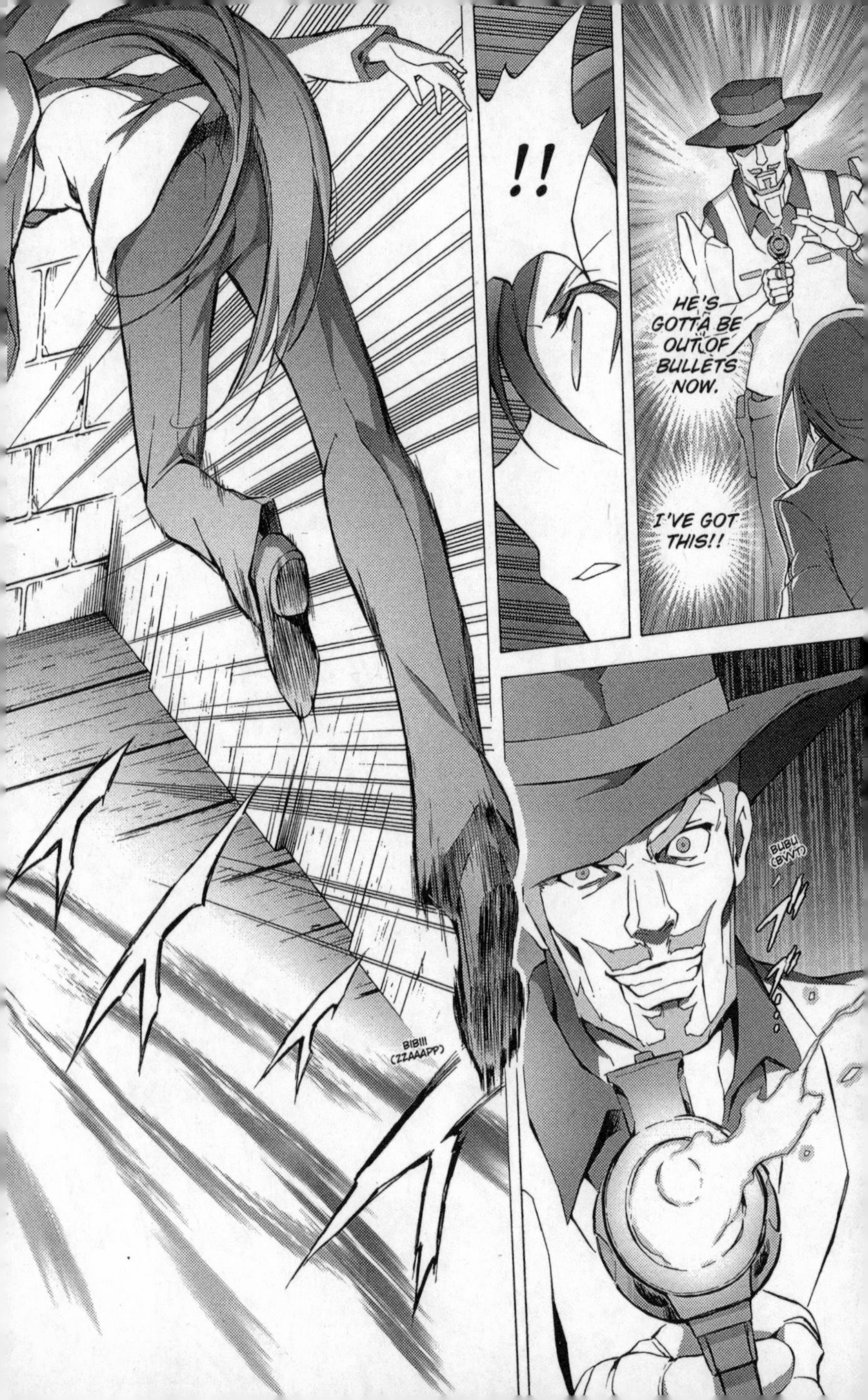
HE'S GOTTA BE OUT OF BULLETS NOW.
I'VE GOT THIS!!
!!
BUBU (BVVT)
BIBIII (ZZAAAPP)

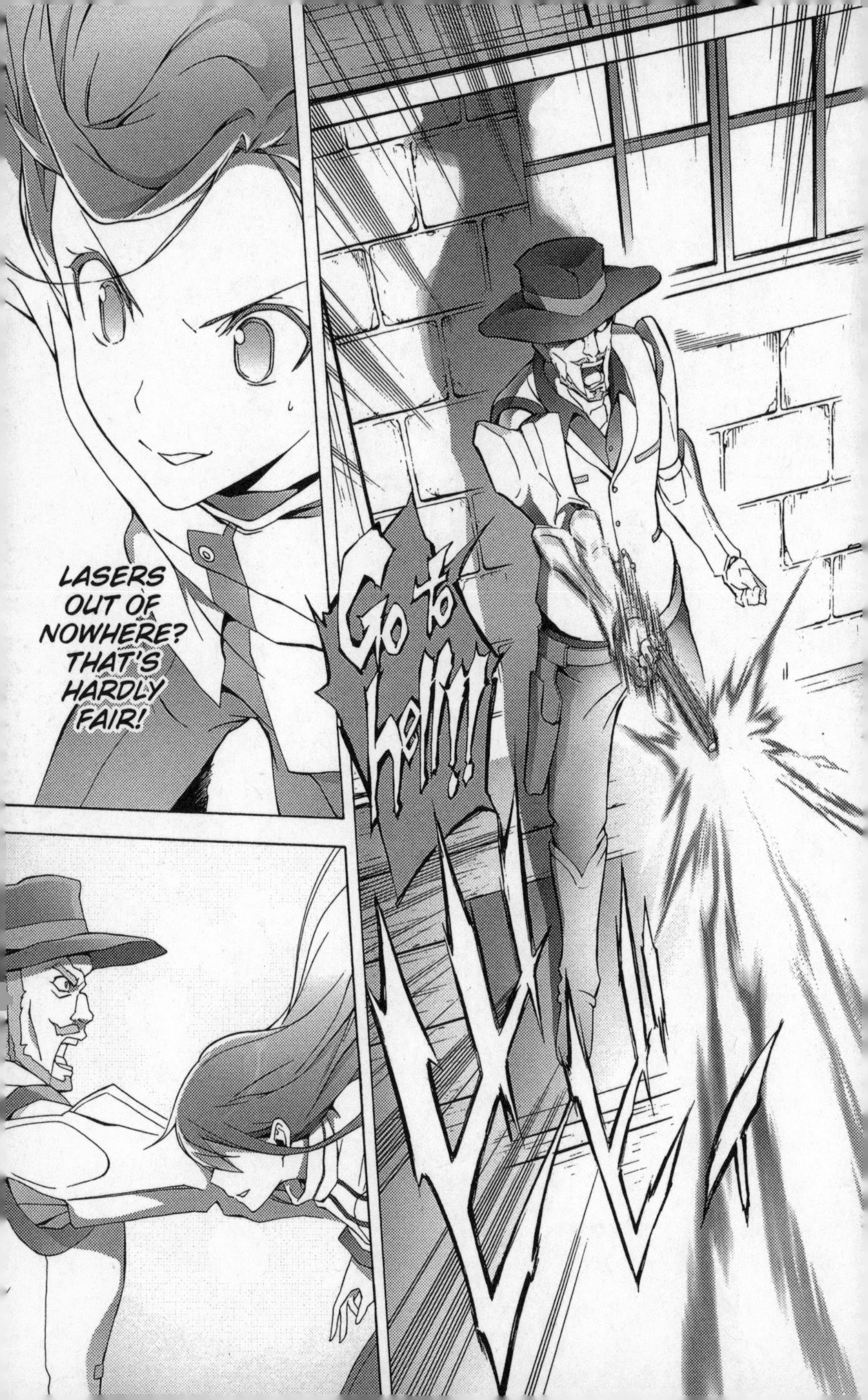
Go to hell!!
LASERS OUT OF NOWHERE? THAT'S HARDLY FAIR!

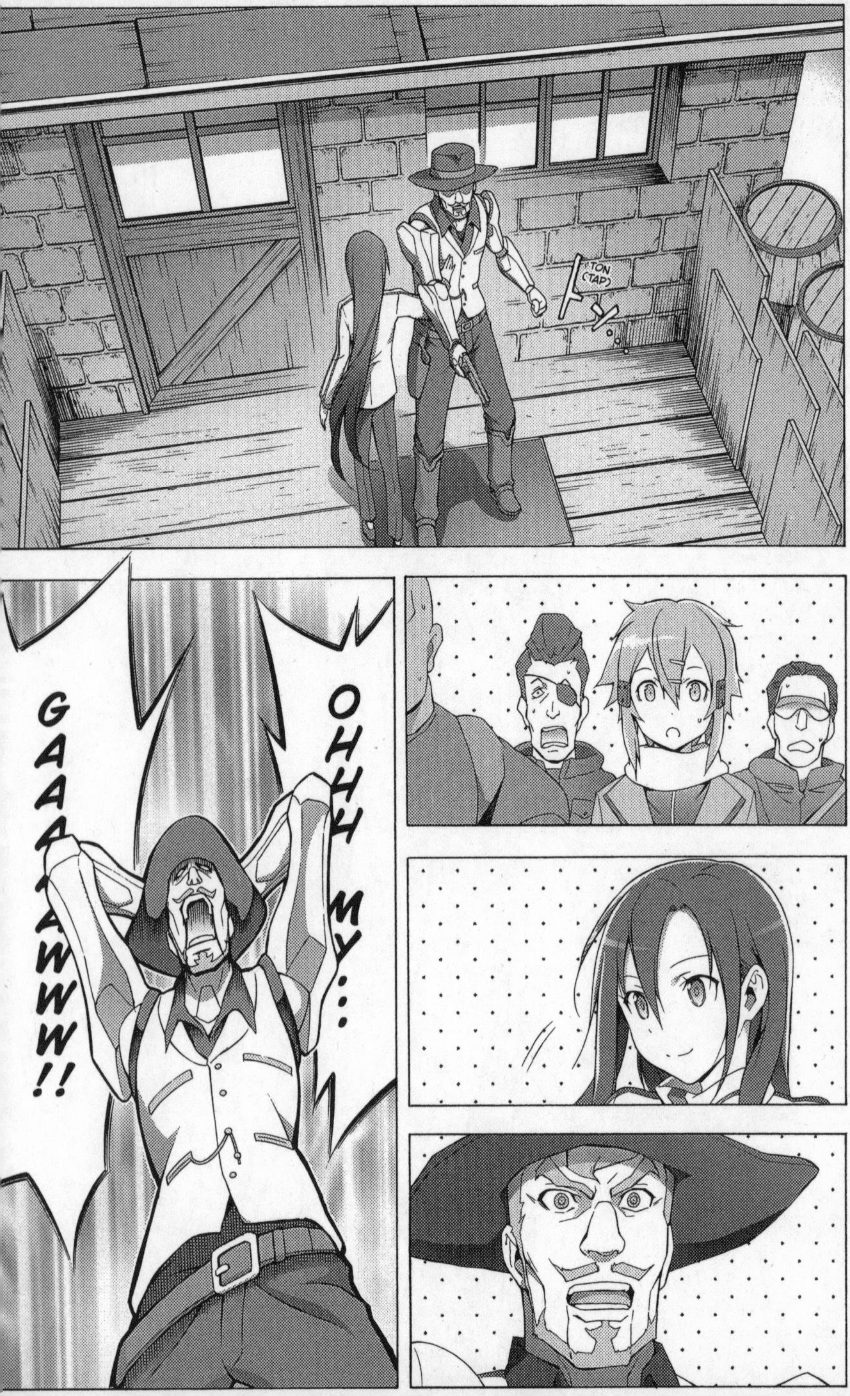
TON (TAP)
OHHH MY...
GAAAAAWWW!!

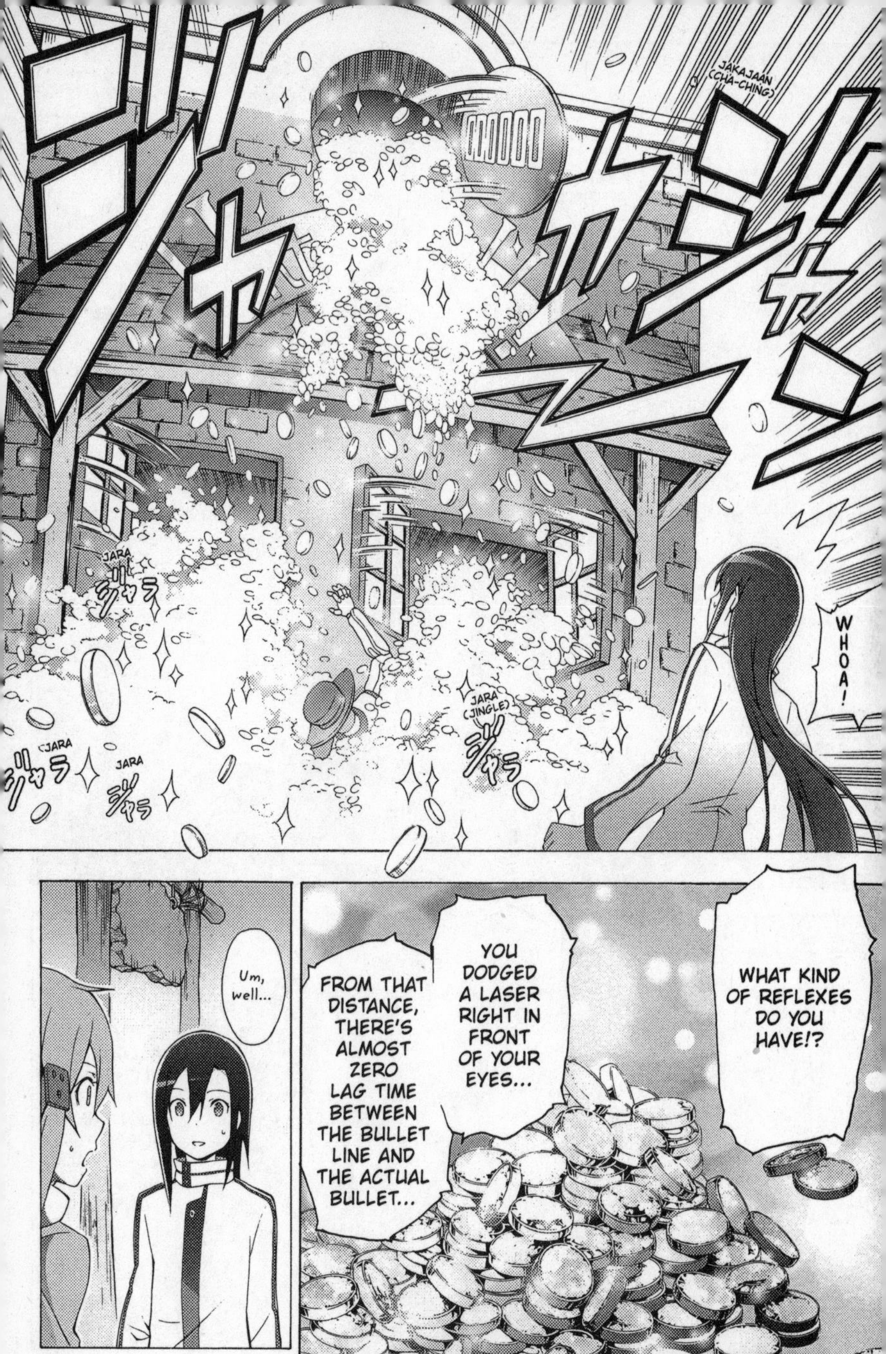
JAKAJAAN (CHA-CHING)
WHOA!
JARA (JINGLE)
JARA
JARA
JARA
WHAT KIND OF REFLEXES DO YOU HAVE!?
YOU DODGED A LASER RIGHT IN FRONT OF YOUR EYES...
FROM THAT DISTANCE, THERE'S ALMOST ZERO LAG TIME BETWEEN THE BULLET LINE AND THE ACTUAL BULLET...
Um, well...

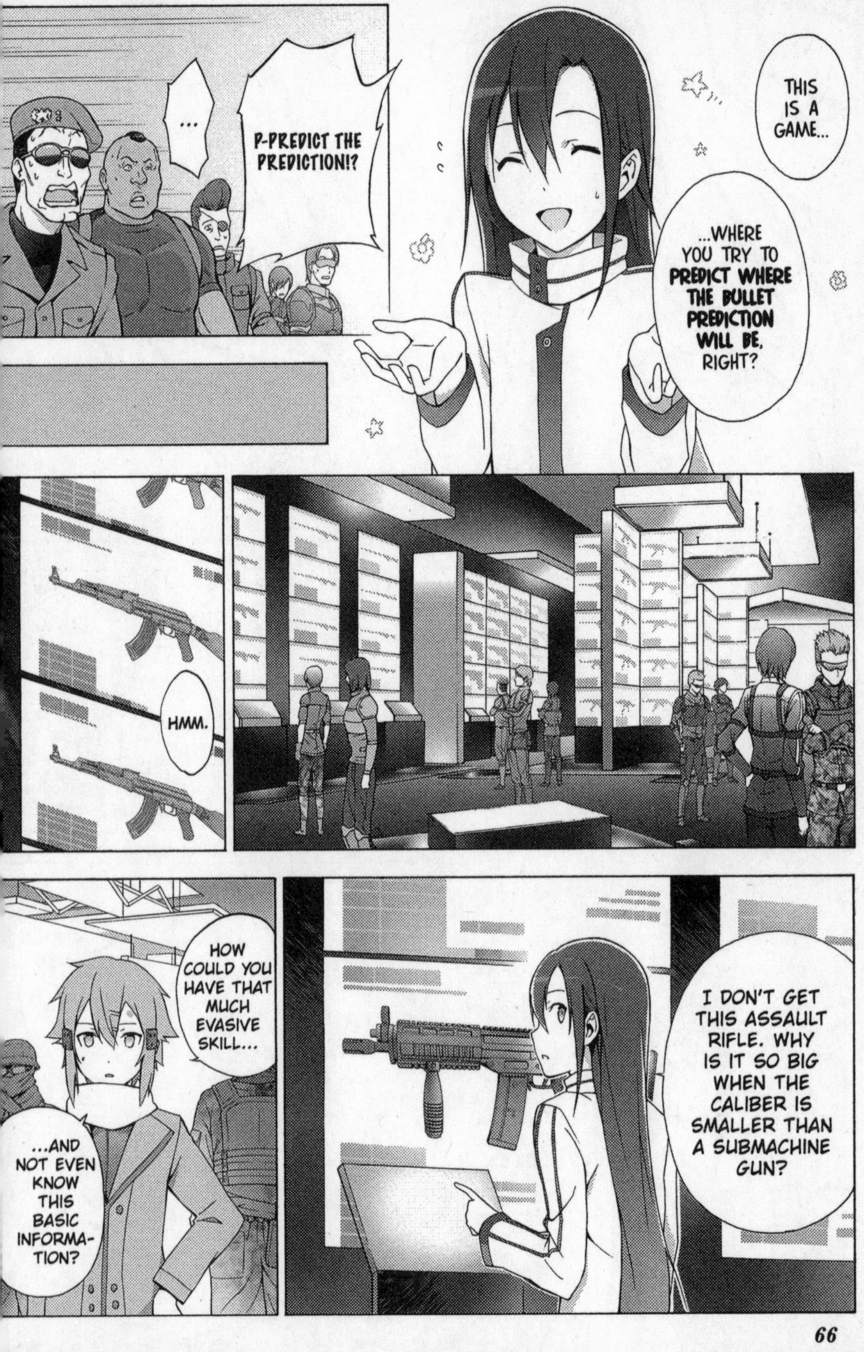

THIS IS A GAME...
...WHERE YOU TRY TO PREDICT WHERE THE BULLET PREDICTION WILL BE, RIGHT?
P-PREDICT THE PREDICTION!?
...
HMM.
I DON'T GET THIS ASSAULT RIFLE. WHY IS IT SO BIG WHEN THE CALIBER IS SMALLER THAN A SUBMACHINE GUN?
HOW COULD YOU HAVE THAT MUCH EVASIVE SKILL...
...AND NOT EVEN KNOW THIS BASIC INFORMATION?

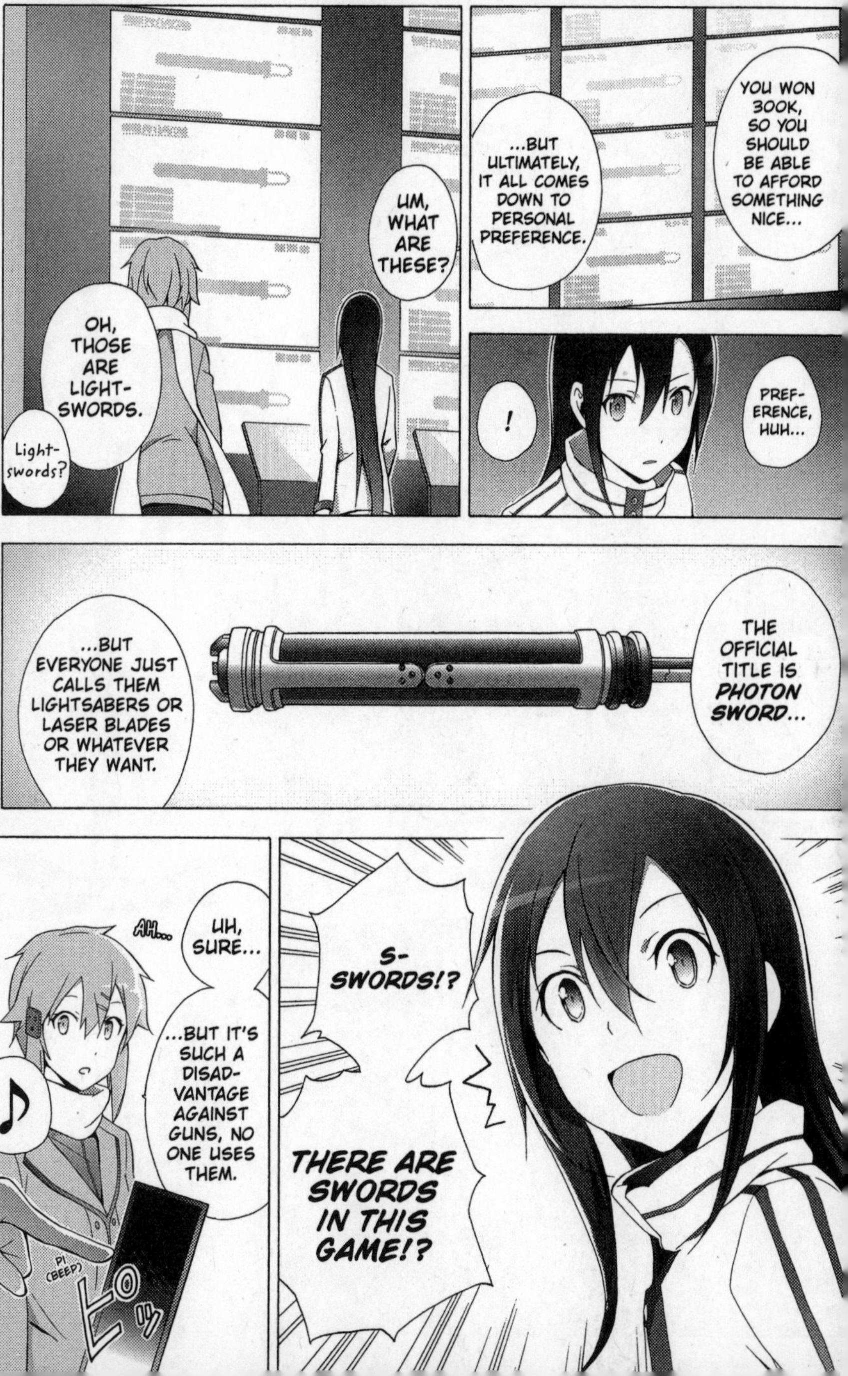
YOU WON 300K, SO YOU SHOULD BE ABLE TO AFFORD SOMETHING NICE...
...BUT ULTIMATELY, IT ALL COMES DOWN TO PERSONAL PREFERENCE.
PREFERENCE, HUH...
!
UM, WHAT ARE THESE?
OH, THOSE ARE LIGHT-SWORDS.
Light-swords?
THE OFFICIAL TITLE IS *PHOTON SWORD*...
...BUT EVERYONE JUST CALLS THEM LIGHTSABERS OR LASER BLADES OR WHATEVER THEY WANT.
S-SWORDS!?
THERE ARE SWORDS IN THIS GAME!?
UH, SURE...
AH...
...BUT IT'S SUCH A DISADVANTAGE AGAINST GUNS, NO ONE USES THEM.
♪
PI (BEEP)
ピッ

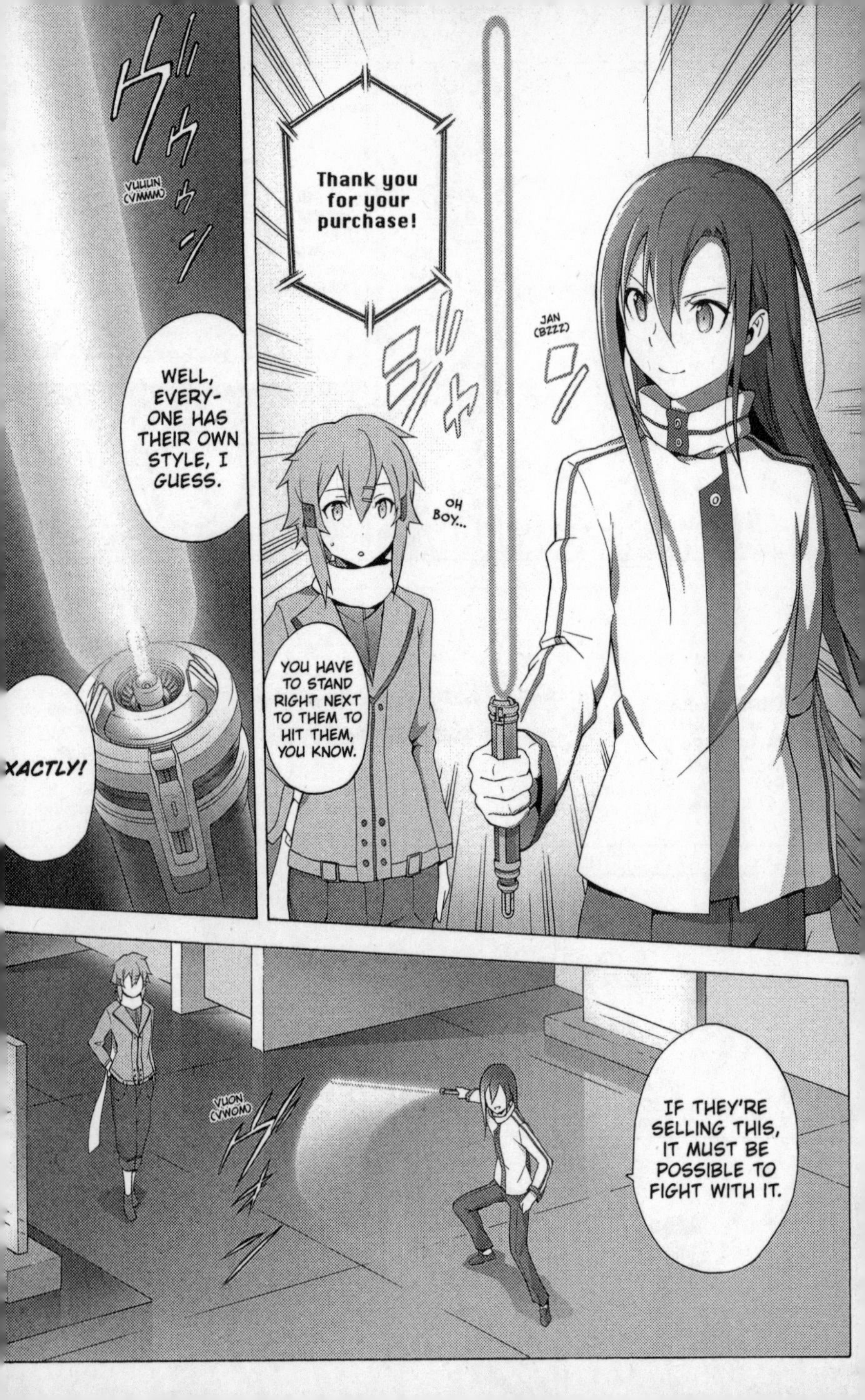

Thank you for your purchase!
JAN (BZZZ)
OH BOY...
YOU HAVE TO STAND RIGHT NEXT TO THEM TO HIT THEM, YOU KNOW.
VUUUN (VMMM)
WELL, EVERY-ONE HAS THEIR OWN STYLE, I GUESS.
XACTLY!
IF THEY'RE SELLING THIS, IT MUST BE POSSIBLE TO FIGHT WITH IT.
VUON (VWOM)

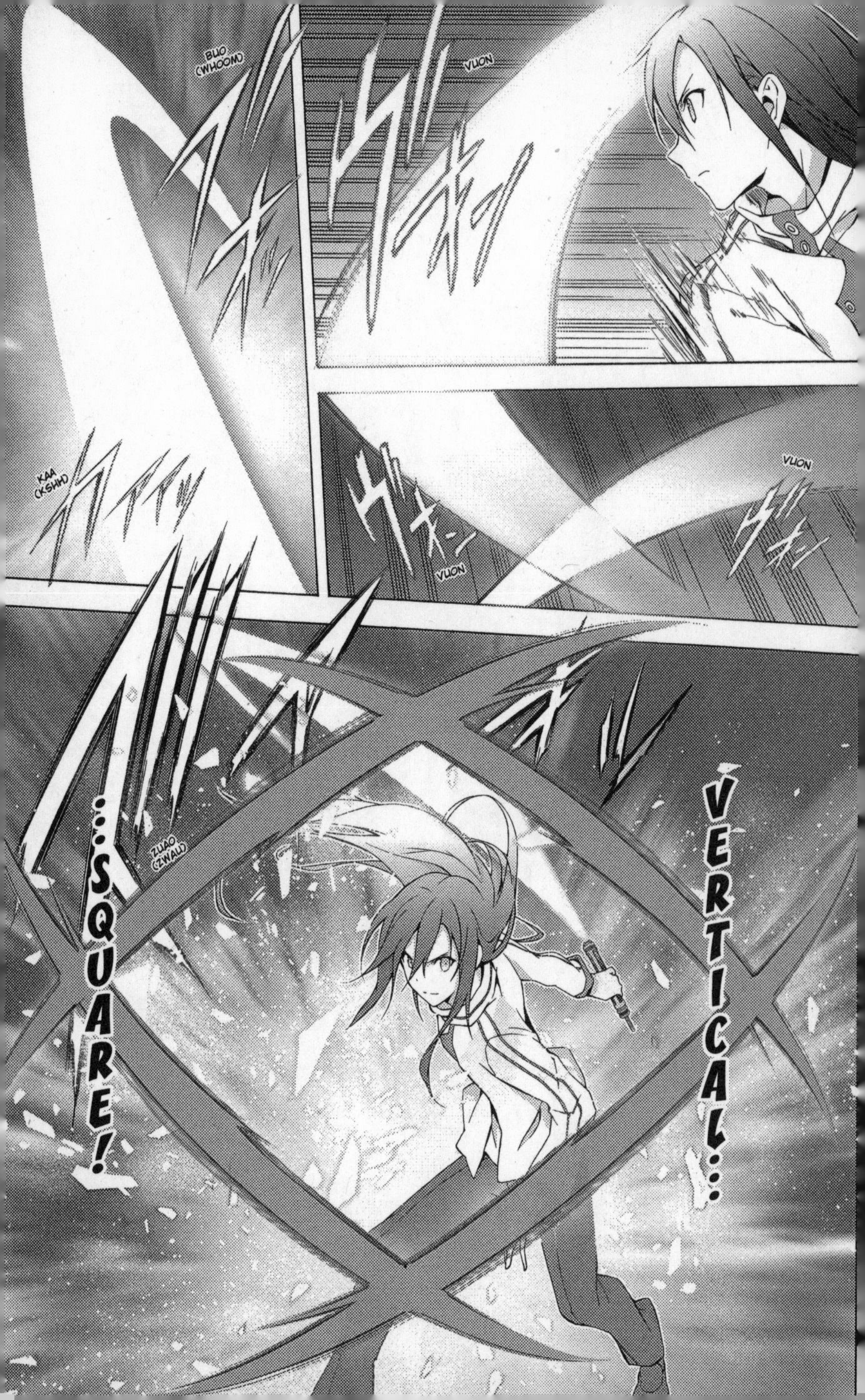

VUON
VUON
VUON
BUO (WHOOM)
KAA (KSHH)
VERTICAL...
ZUAO (ZWAU)
...SQUARE!

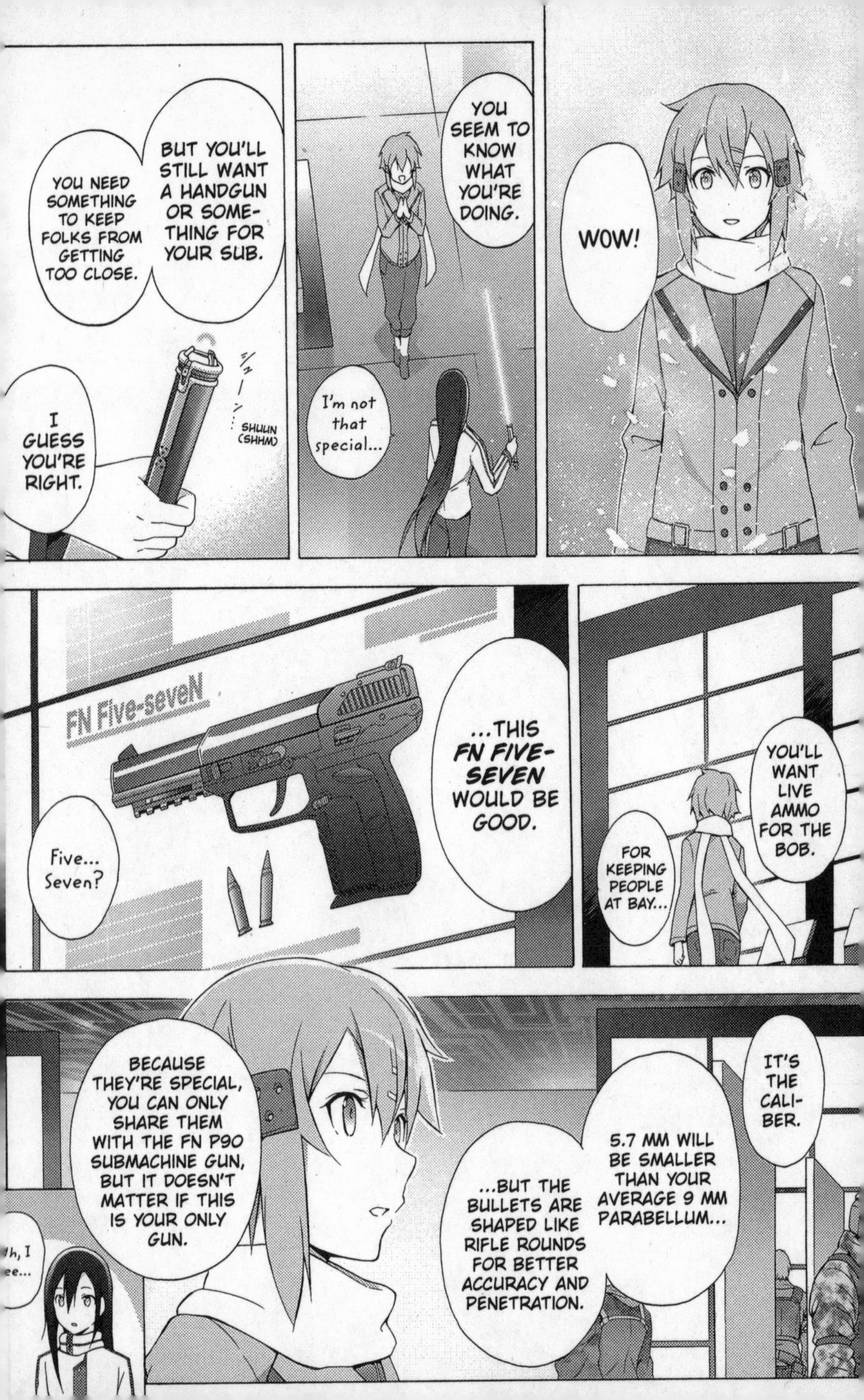
WOW!
YOU SEEM TO KNOW WHAT YOU'RE DOING.
I'm not that special...
BUT YOU'LL STILL WANT A HANDGUN OR SOME-THING FOR YOUR SUB.
YOU NEED SOMETHING TO KEEP FOLKS FROM GETTING TOO CLOSE.
SHUUN (SHHM)
I GUESS YOU'RE RIGHT.
YOU'LL WANT LIVE AMMO FOR THE BOB.
FOR KEEPING PEOPLE AT BAY...
...THIS FN FIVE-SEVEN WOULD BE GOOD.
FN Five-seveN
Five... Seven?
IT'S THE CALI-BER.
5.7 MM WILL BE SMALLER THAN YOUR AVERAGE 9 MM PARABELLUM...
...BUT THE BULLETS ARE SHAPED LIKE RIFLE ROUNDS FOR BETTER ACCURACY AND PENETRATION.
BECAUSE THEY'RE SPECIAL, YOU CAN ONLY SHARE THEM WITH THE FN P90 SUBMACHINE GUN, BUT IT DOESN'T MATTER IF THIS IS YOUR ONLY GUN.
h, I ee...

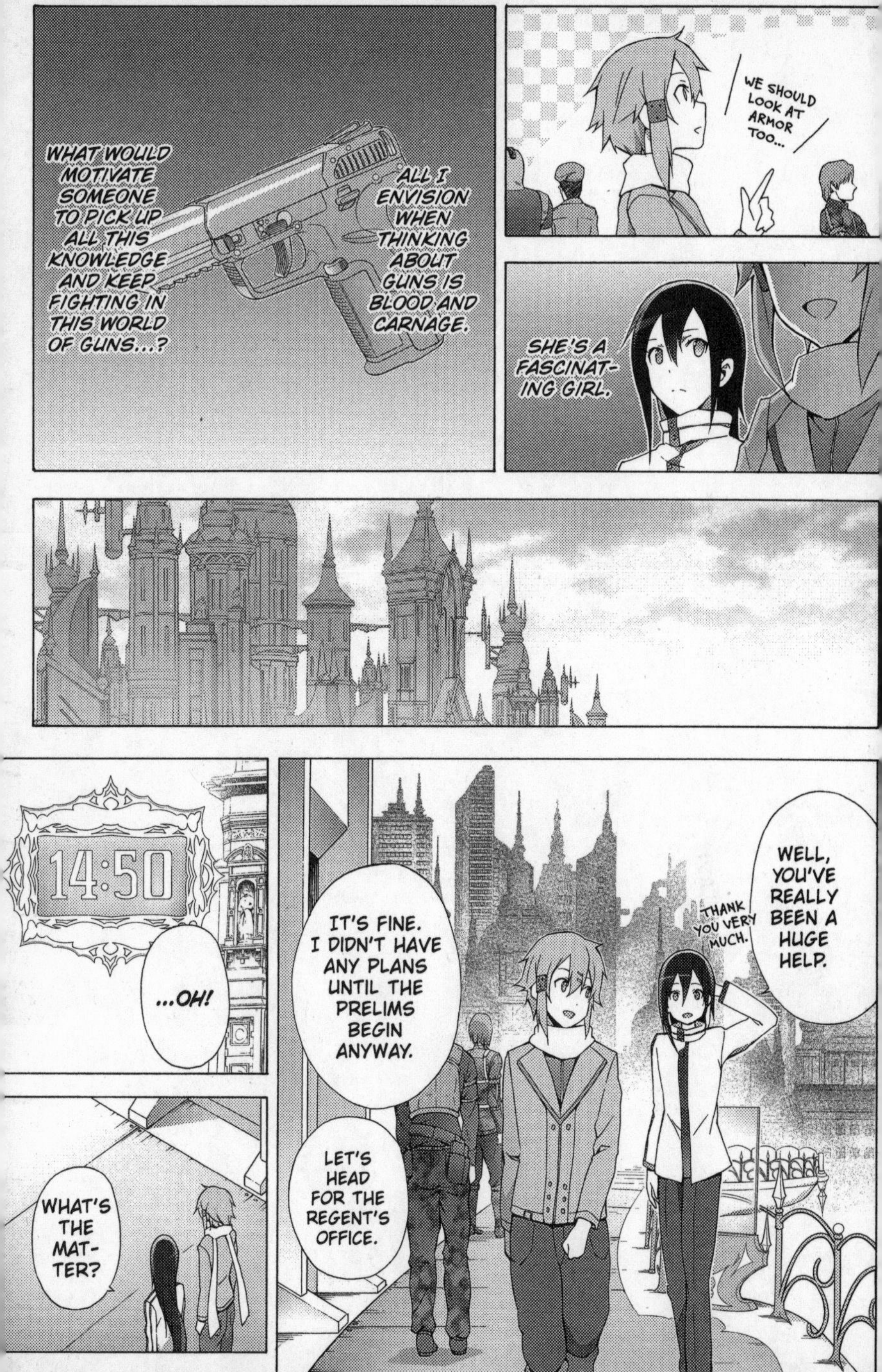
WE SHOULD LOOK AT ARMOR TOO...
SHE'S A FASCINATING GIRL.
ALL I ENVISION WHEN THINKING ABOUT GUNS IS BLOOD AND CARNAGE.
WHAT WOULD MOTIVATE SOMEONE TO PICK UP ALL THIS KNOWLEDGE AND KEEP FIGHTING IN THIS WORLD OF GUNS...?
WELL, YOU'VE REALLY BEEN A HUGE HELP.
THANK YOU VERY MUCH.
IT'S FINE. I DIDN'T HAVE ANY PLANS UNTIL THE PRELIMS BEGIN ANYWAY.
LET'S HEAD FOR THE REGENT'S OFFICE.
14:50
...OH!
WHAT'S THE MATTER?

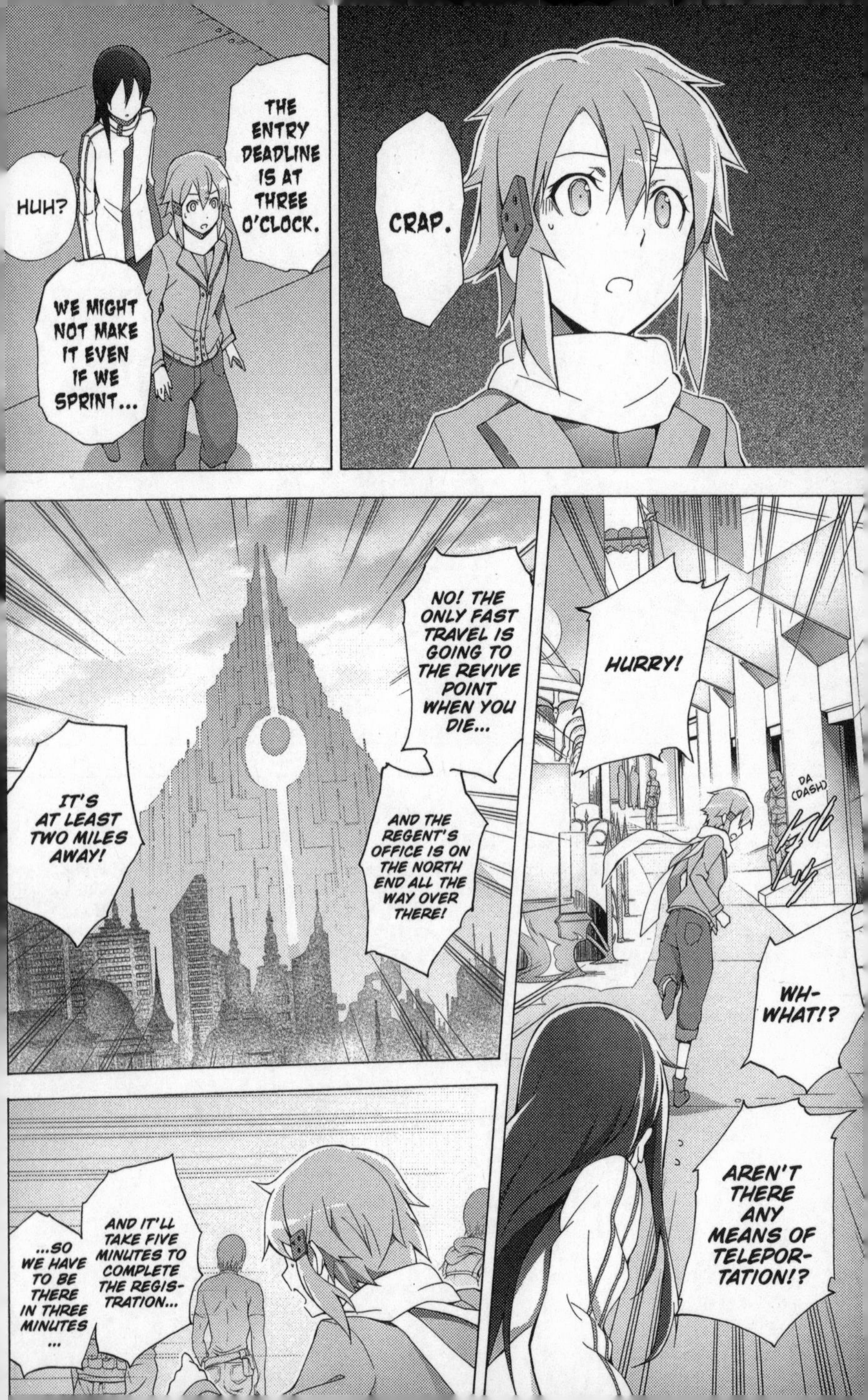
CRAP.
THE ENTRY DEADLINE IS AT THREE O'CLOCK.
HUH?
WE MIGHT NOT MAKE IT EVEN IF WE SPRINT...
HURRY!
DA (DASH)
WH- WHAT!?
AREN'T THERE ANY MEANS OF TELEPOR- TATION!?
NO! THE ONLY FAST TRAVEL IS GOING TO THE REVIVE POINT WHEN YOU DIE...
AND THE REGENT'S OFFICE IS ON THE NORTH END ALL THE WAY OVER THERE!
IT'S AT LEAST TWO MILES AWAY!
AND IT'LL TAKE FIVE MINUTES TO COMPLETE THE REGIS- TRATION...
...SO WE HAVE TO BE THERE IN THREE MINUTES ...

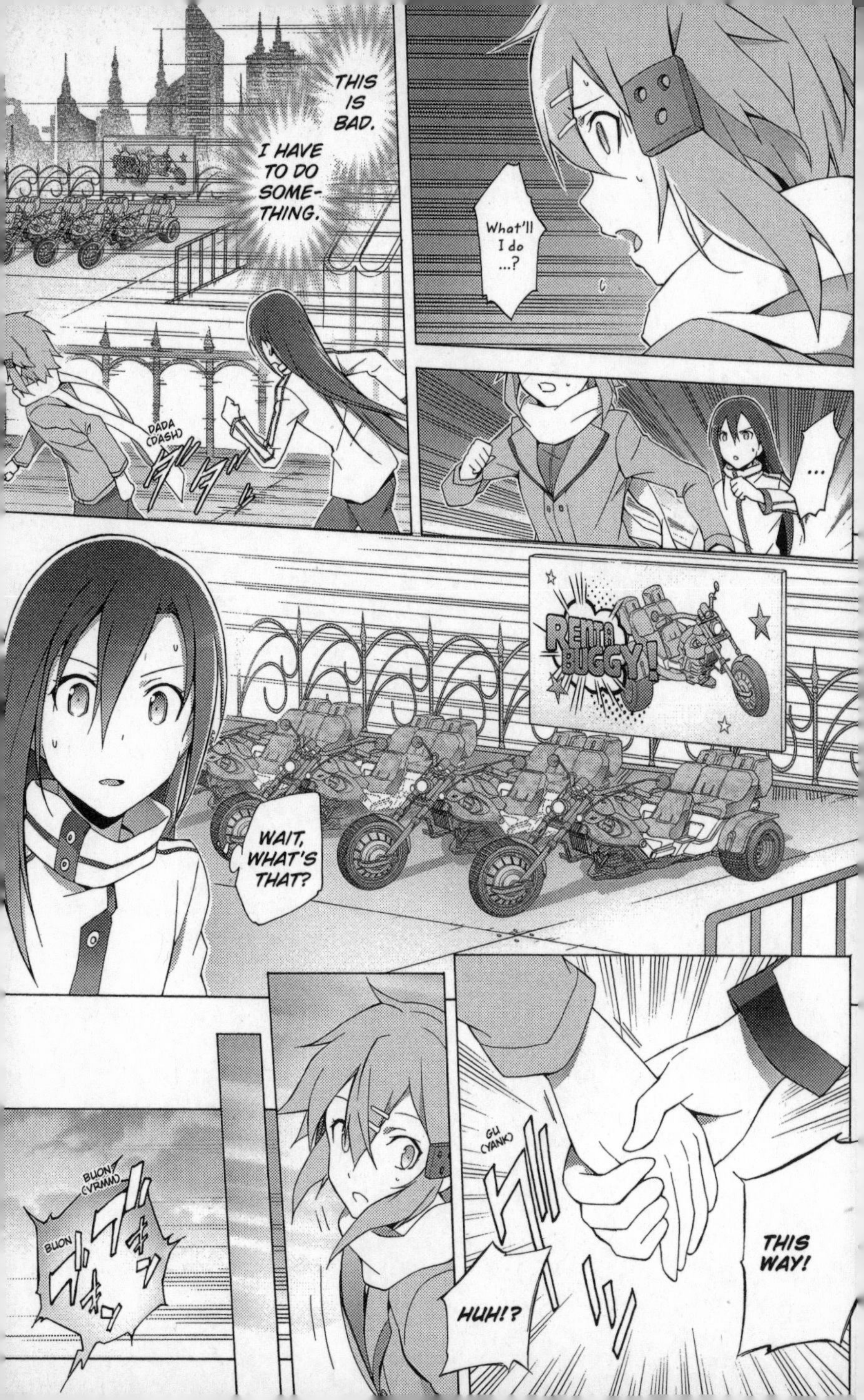

What'll I do ...?
...
THIS IS BAD.
I HAVE TO DO SOMETHING.
DADA (DASH)
RENTA BUGGY!
WAIT, WHAT'S THAT?
GU (YANK)
THIS WAY!
HUH!?
BUON (VRMM)
BUON

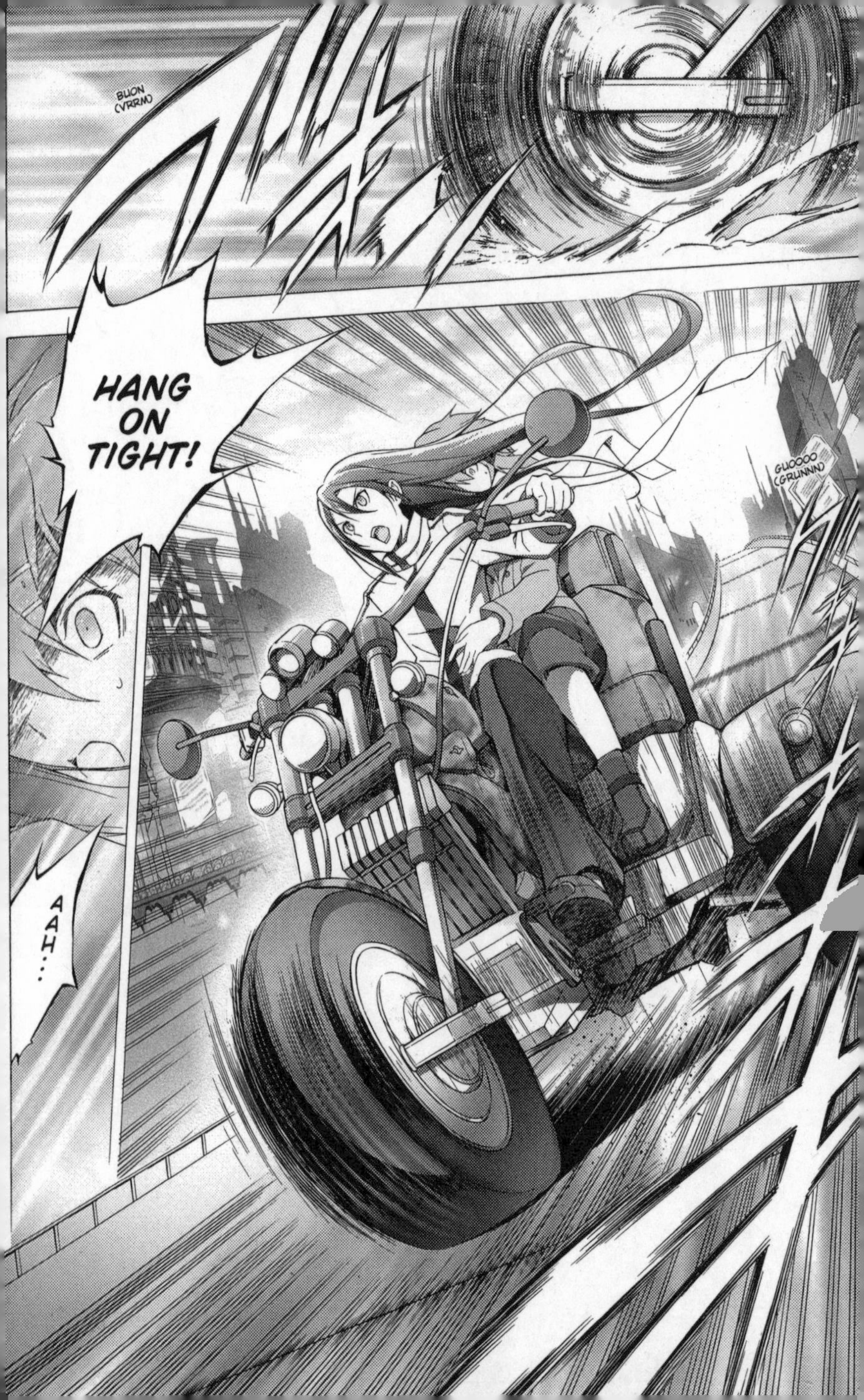
BUON (VRRM)
GUOOOO (GRUNNN)
HANG ON TIGHT!
AAH...

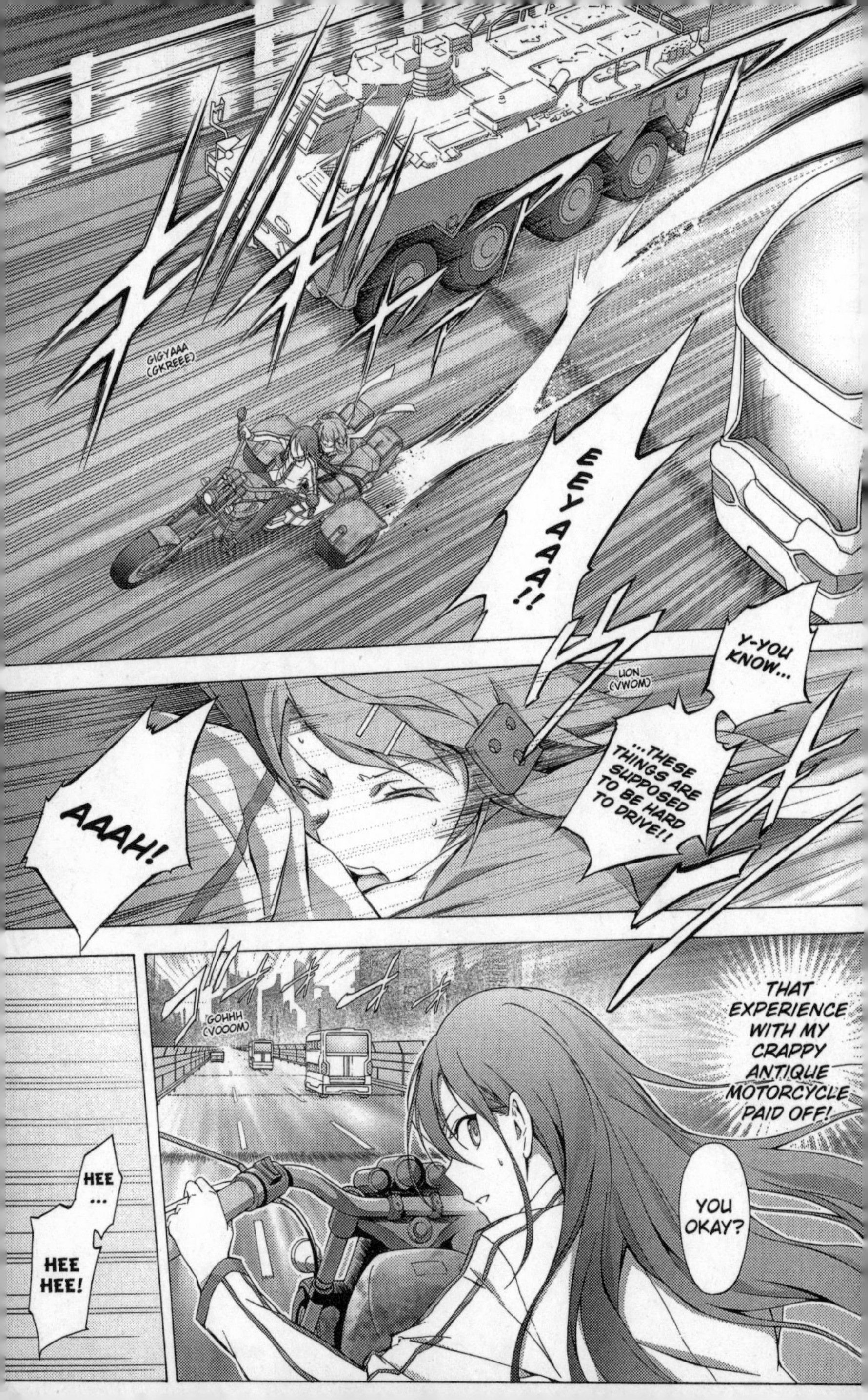
EEYAAAA!!
GIGYAAA (GKREEE)
Y-YOU KNOW...
...THESE THINGS ARE SUPPOSED TO BE HARD TO DRIVE!!
UON (VWOM)
AAAH!
THAT EXPERIENCE WITH MY CRAPPY ANTIQUE MOTORCYCLE PAID OFF!
GOHHH (VOOOM)
YOU OKAY?
HEE ... HEE HEE!

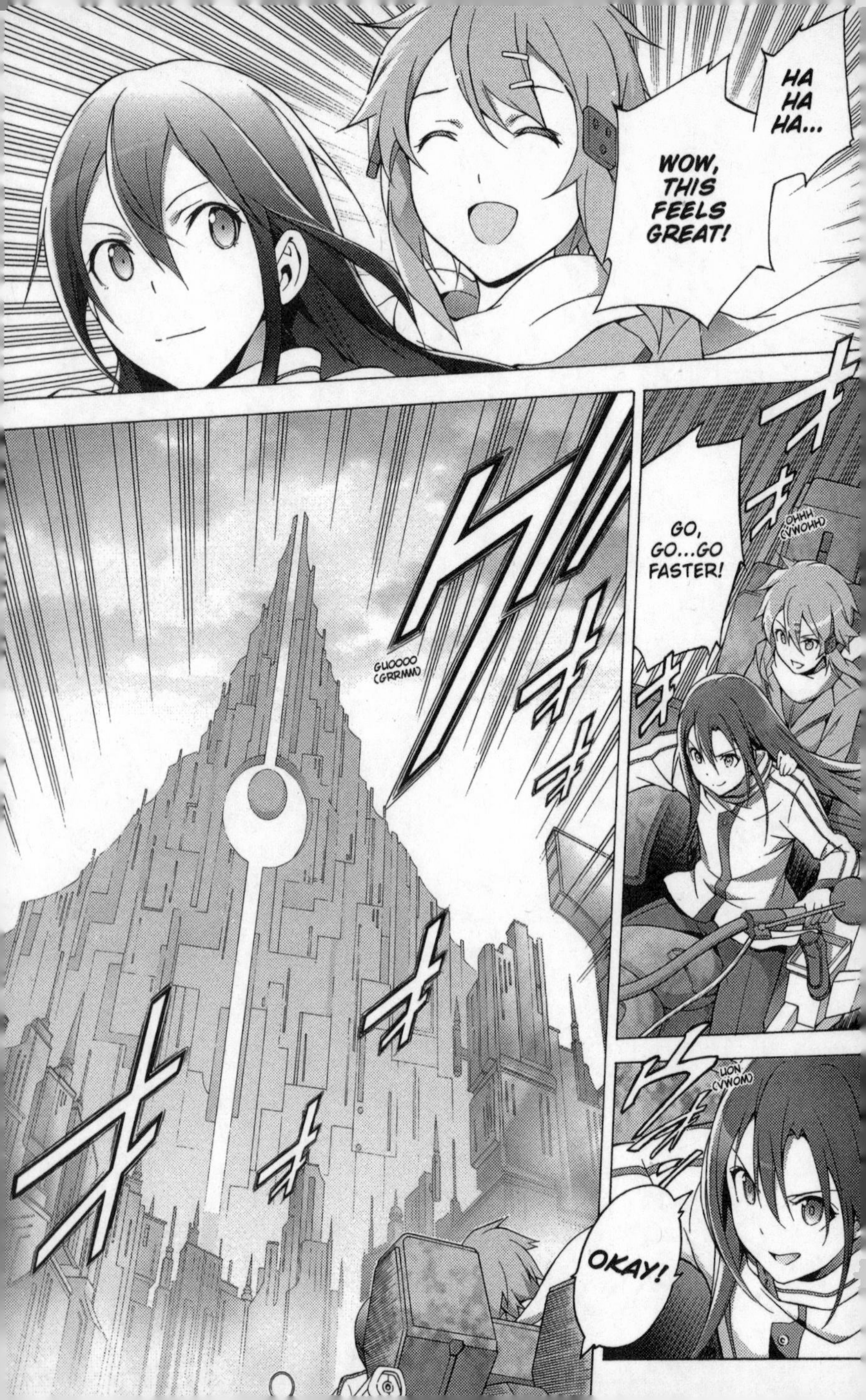
HA HA HA...
WOW, THIS FEELS GREAT!
OHHH (VWOHH)
GO, GO...GO FASTER!
GUOOOO (GRRMM)
UON (VWOM)
OKAY!

SWORD ART ONLINE
phantom bullet

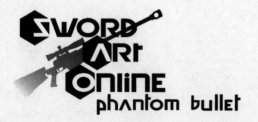

SWORD ART ONLINE
phantom bullet

check point! 002

KIRITO'S AVATAR: WORLD

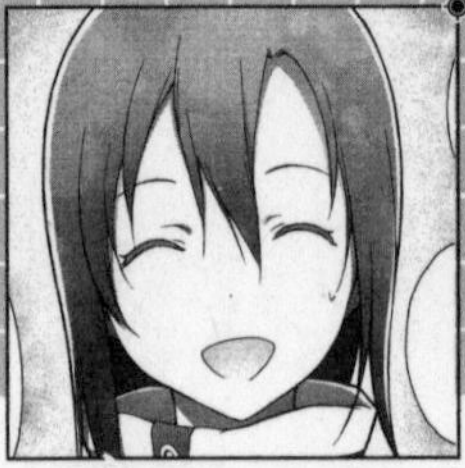

KIRITO'S GIRLISH AVATAR HAS FOUND CONSIDERABLE POPULARITY(?) FROM A SUBSET OF FANS. THE REASON HE WOUND UP WITH THIS LOOK IS A COMBINATION OF *GGO*'S RANDOM CHARACTER GENERATION UPON CONVERSION AND THE INCREASED LIKELIHOOD TO GET RARER AVATARS THE MORE GAME TIME YOU HAVE LOGGED. THANKS TO KIRITO'S LONG-TERM STAY IN *SAO*, HE WOUND UP WITH A VERY VALUABLE LOOK INDEED. IT'S A GENERAL RULE IN VRMMOS THAT PLAYERS CANNOT PLAY THE OPPOSITE SEX, DUE TO VERIFIED ADVERSE EFFECTS UPON THE PLAYER'S MENTAL AND PHYSICAL HEALTH.

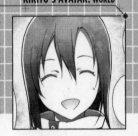

FN FIVE-SEVEN: ITEM

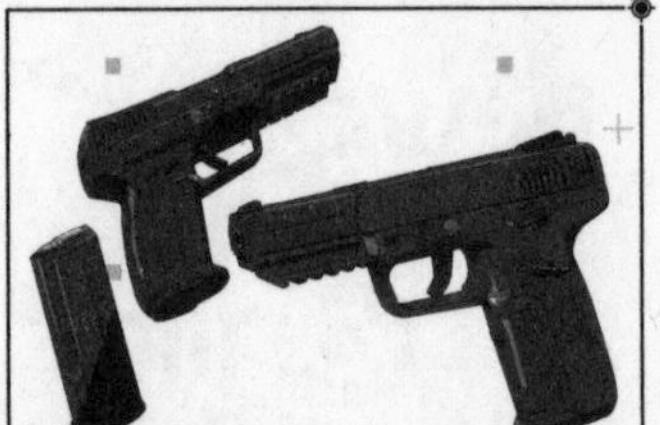

KIRITO'S HANDGUN, MADE WITH A POLYMER FRAME (REINFORCED PLASTIC). IT USES LONG, SKINNY 5.7 X 28 MM BULLETS WITH HIGH PENETRATING POWER. IT'S A GUN WITH SIMILAR FEATURES TO DEATH GUN'S BLACK STAR PISTOL, AS IF TO SUGGEST A CONNECTION BETWEEN THE TWO. IT'S INTERESTING TO NOTE THAT UNLIKE THE FORMER, THIS GUN HAS A SAFETY. IT WAS MANUFACTURED IN A SET WITH FN'S P90 SMG, SO AS SINON SAID, THEY SHARE THE SAME AMMO. THE P90 IS THE PREFERRED WEAPON OF LLENN, THE HEROINE OF KEIICHI SIGSAWA'S SPIN-OFF NOVEL SERIES, *SAO ALTERNATIVE: GUN GALE ONLINE*.

COURTESY OF: A-1 PICTURES

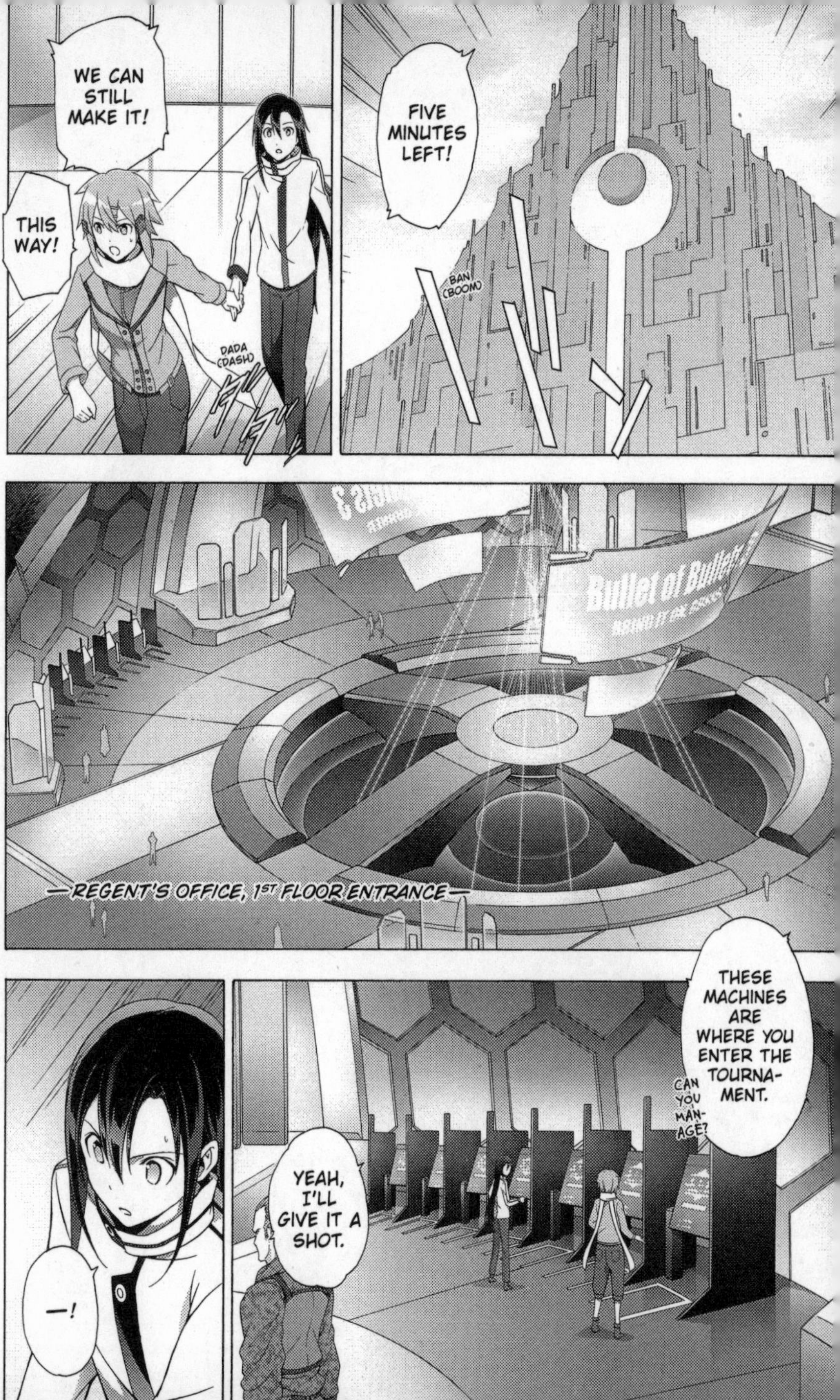
FIVE MINUTES LEFT!
BAN (BOOM)
WE CAN STILL MAKE IT!
THIS WAY!
DADA (DASH)
—REGENT'S OFFICE, 1ST FLOOR ENTRANCE—
THESE MACHINES ARE WHERE YOU ENTER THE TOURNAMENT.
CAN YOU MANAGE?
YEAH, I'LL GIVE IT A SHOT.
—!

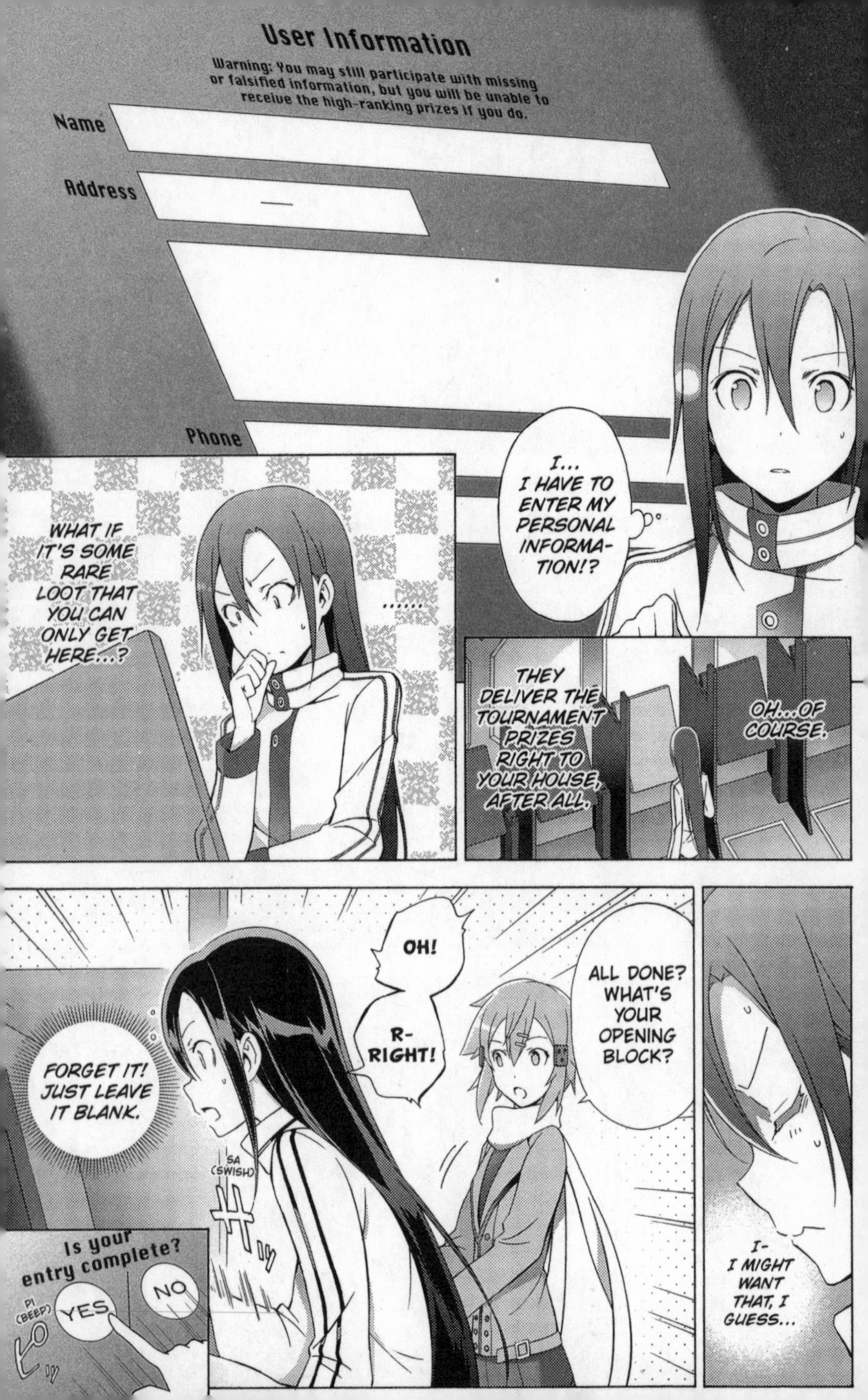
User Information
Warning: You may still participate with missing or falsified information, but you will be unable to receive the high-ranking prizes if you do.
Name
Address
Phone
I... I HAVE TO ENTER MY PERSONAL INFORMATION!?
THEY DELIVER THE TOURNAMENT PRIZES RIGHT TO YOUR HOUSE, AFTER ALL.
OH...OF COURSE.
......
WHAT IF IT'S SOME RARE LOOT THAT YOU CAN ONLY GET HERE...?
I- I MIGHT WANT THAT, I GUESS...
ALL DONE? WHAT'S YOUR OPENING BLOCK?
OH!
R-RIGHT!
FORGET IT! JUST LEAVE IT BLANK.
SA (SWISH)
Is your entry complete?
NO
YES
PI (BEEP)

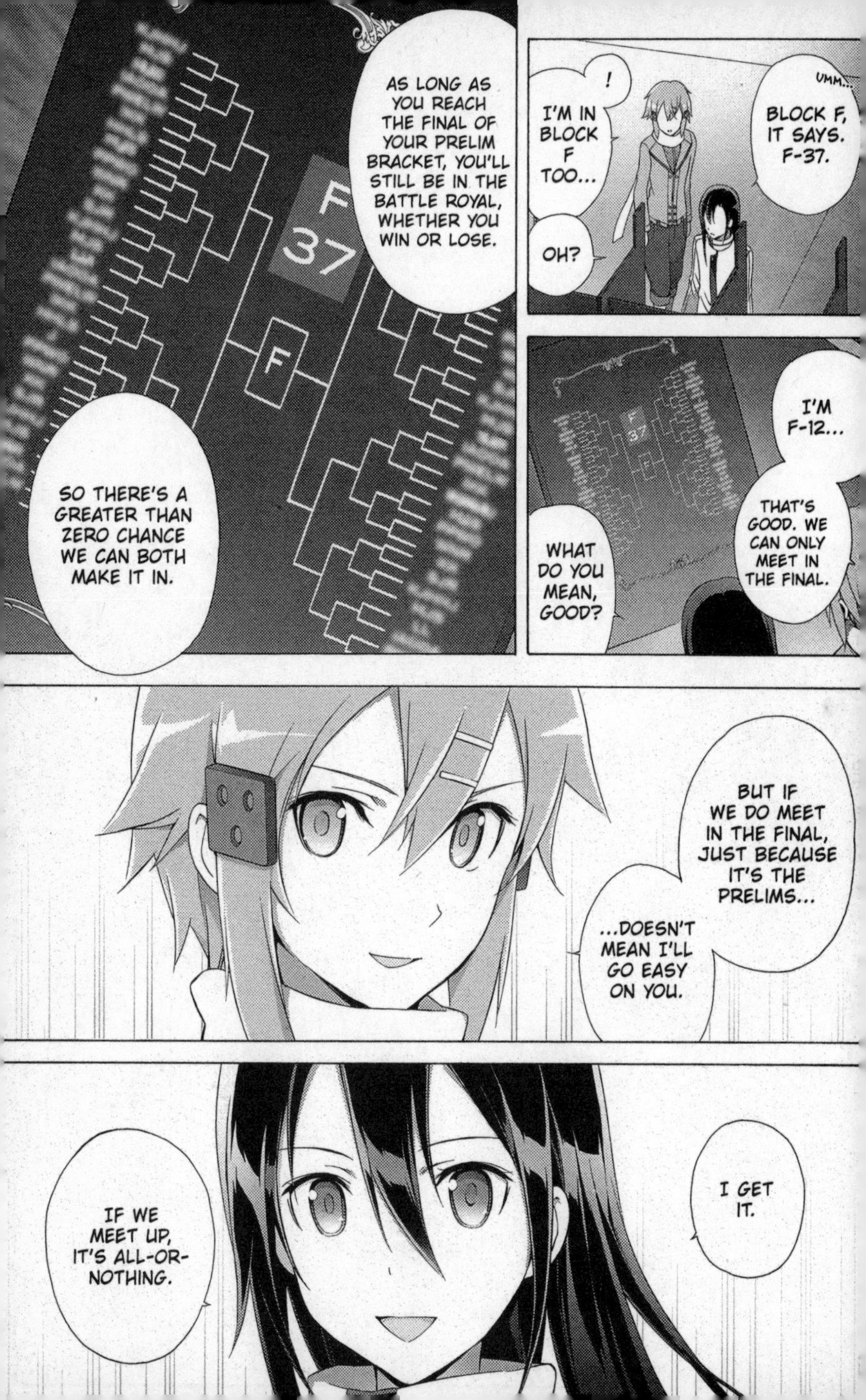
UMM...
BLOCK F, IT SAYS. F-37.
!
I'M IN BLOCK F TOO...
OH?
I'M F-12...
THAT'S GOOD. WE CAN ONLY MEET IN THE FINAL.
WHAT DO YOU MEAN, GOOD?
AS LONG AS YOU REACH THE FINAL OF YOUR PRELIM BRACKET, YOU'LL STILL BE IN THE BATTLE ROYAL, WHETHER YOU WIN OR LOSE.
F 37
F
SO THERE'S A GREATER THAN ZERO CHANCE WE CAN BOTH MAKE IT IN.
BUT IF WE DO MEET IN THE FINAL, JUST BECAUSE IT'S THE PRELIMS...
...DOESN'T MEAN I'LL GO EASY ON YOU.
I GET IT.
IF WE MEET UP, IT'S ALL-OR-NOTHING.

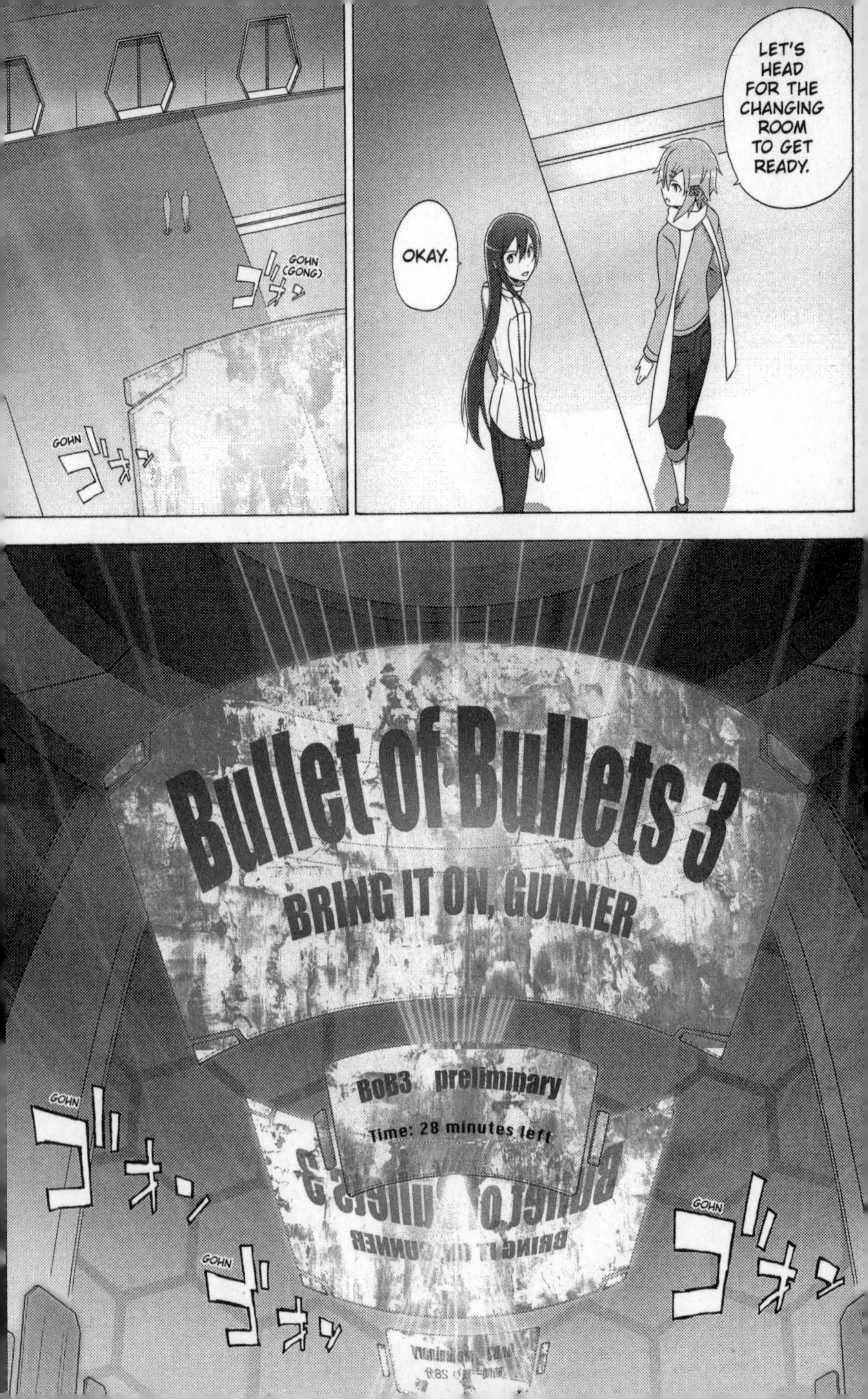
LET'S HEAD FOR THE CHANGING ROOM TO GET READY.
OKAY.
GOHN (GONG)
ゴォッ
GOHN
ゴォッ
Bullet of Bullets 3
BRING IT ON, GUNNER
BoB3 preliminary
Time: 28 minutes left
GOHN
ゴォン
GOHN
ゴォン
GOHN
ゴォッ

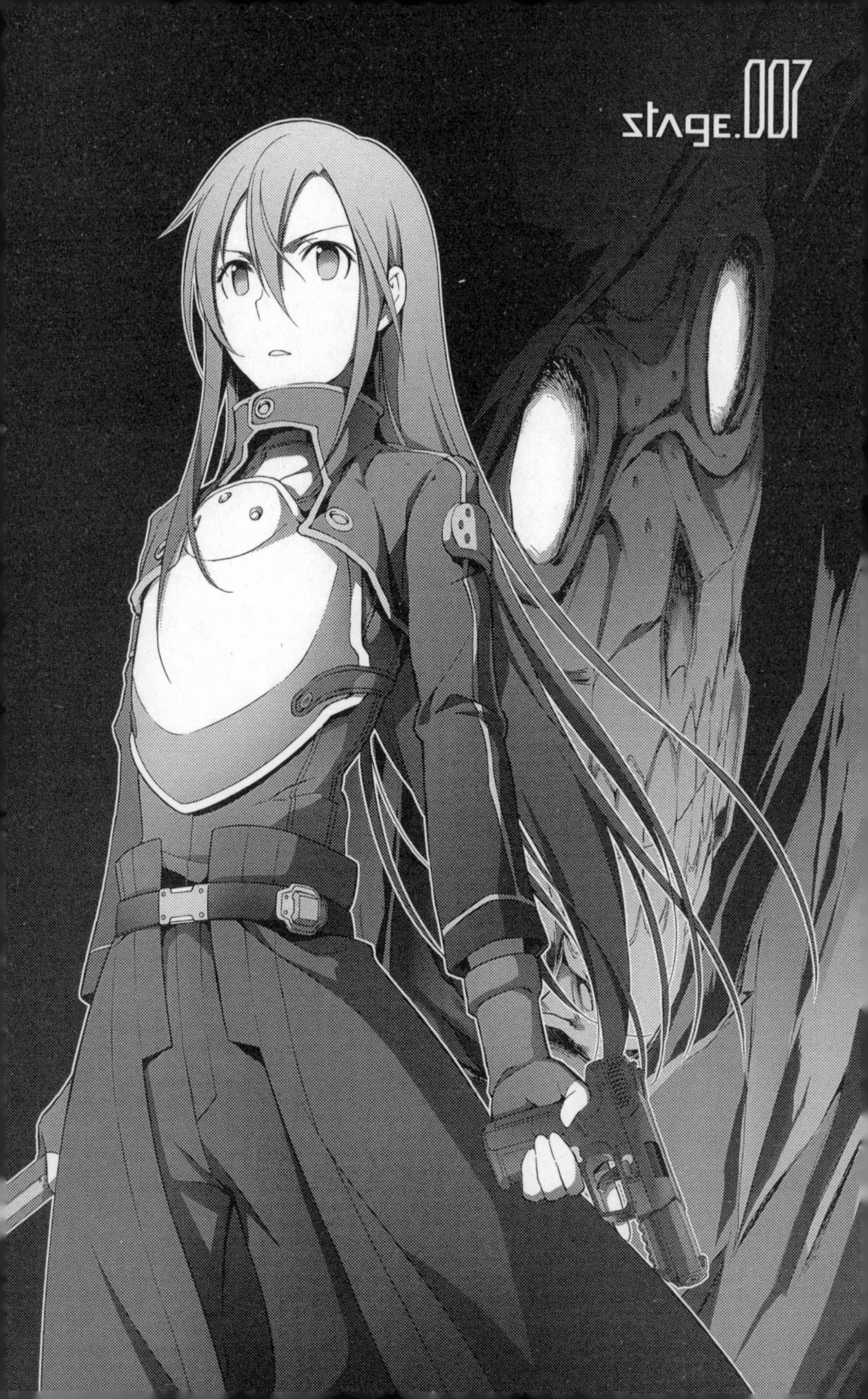
stage.007

ZAWA

ZAWA

ZAWA
(MURMUR)

—WAITING AREA—

THESE GRUBBY BASTARDS ARE ALL TRIED-AND-TRUE PVPERS.

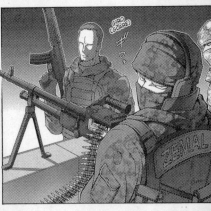

GIRO
(GLARE)

ZBMAL

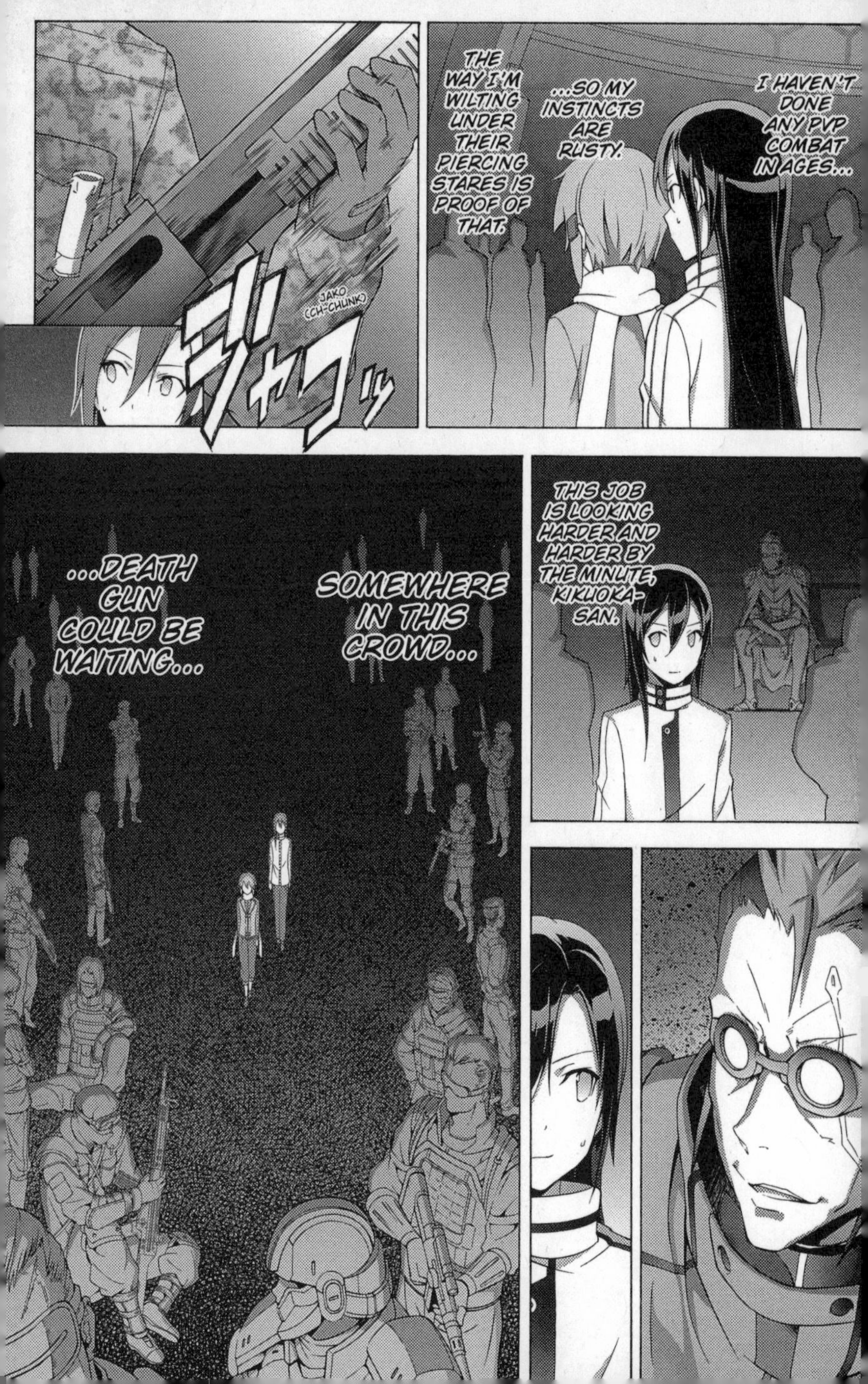
I HAVEN'T DONE ANY PVP COMBAT IN AGES...
...SO MY INSTINCTS ARE RUSTY.
THE WAY I'M WILTING UNDER THEIR PIERCING STARES IS PROOF OF THAT.
ジャコッ
JAKO (CH-CHUNK)
THIS JOB IS LOOKING HARDER AND HARDER BY THE MINUTE, KIKUOKA-SAN.
SOMEWHERE IN THIS CROWD...
...DEATH GUN COULD BE WAITING...

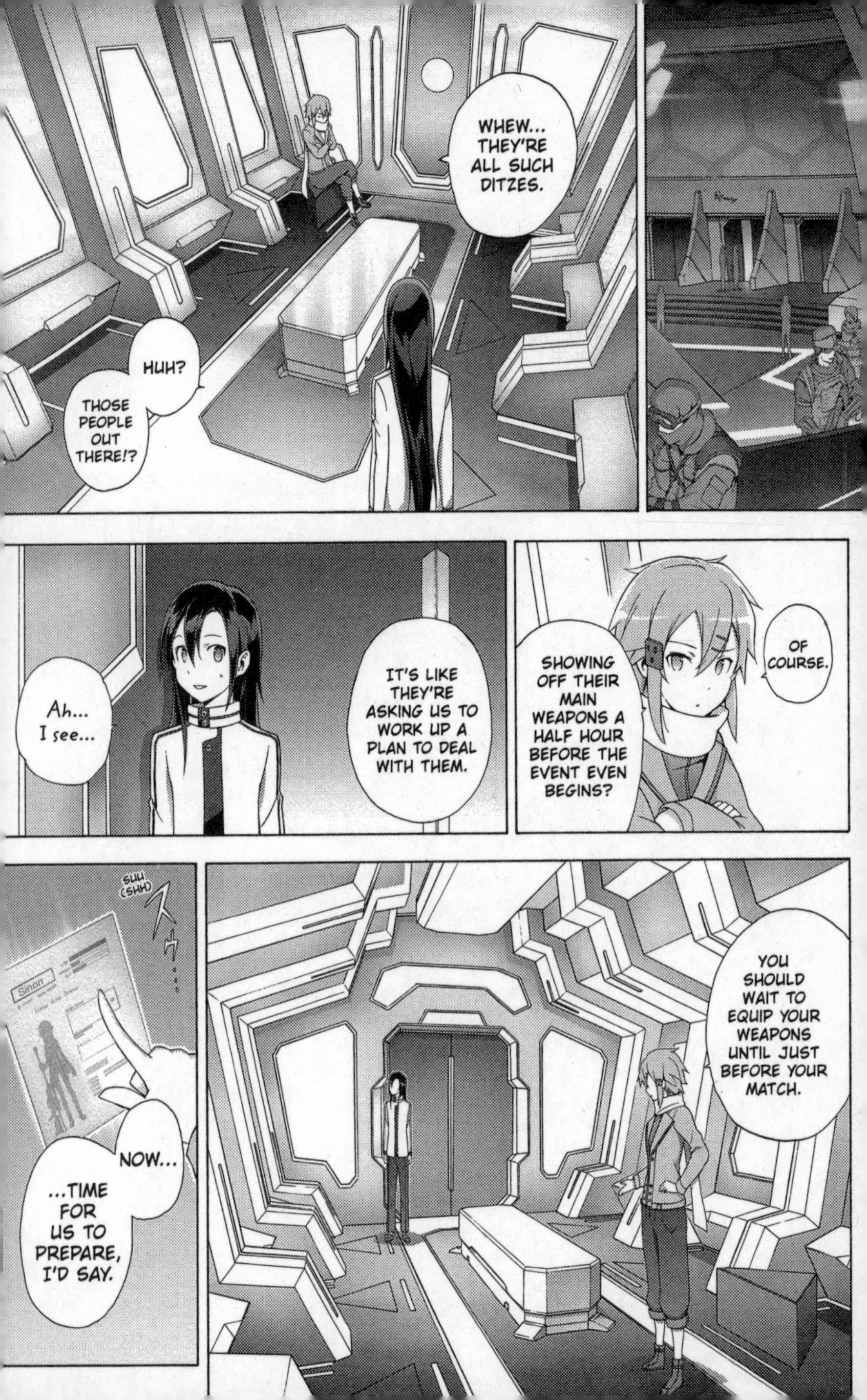
WHEW... THEY'RE ALL SUCH DITZES.
HUH?
THOSE PEOPLE OUT THERE!?
OF COURSE.
SHOWING OFF THEIR MAIN WEAPONS A HALF HOUR BEFORE THE EVENT EVEN BEGINS?
IT'S LIKE THEY'RE ASKING US TO WORK UP A PLAN TO DEAL WITH THEM.
Ah... I see...
YOU SHOULD WAIT TO EQUIP YOUR WEAPONS UNTIL JUST BEFORE YOUR MATCH.
SUU (SHH)
Sinon
NOW...
...TIME FOR US TO PREPARE, I'D SAY.

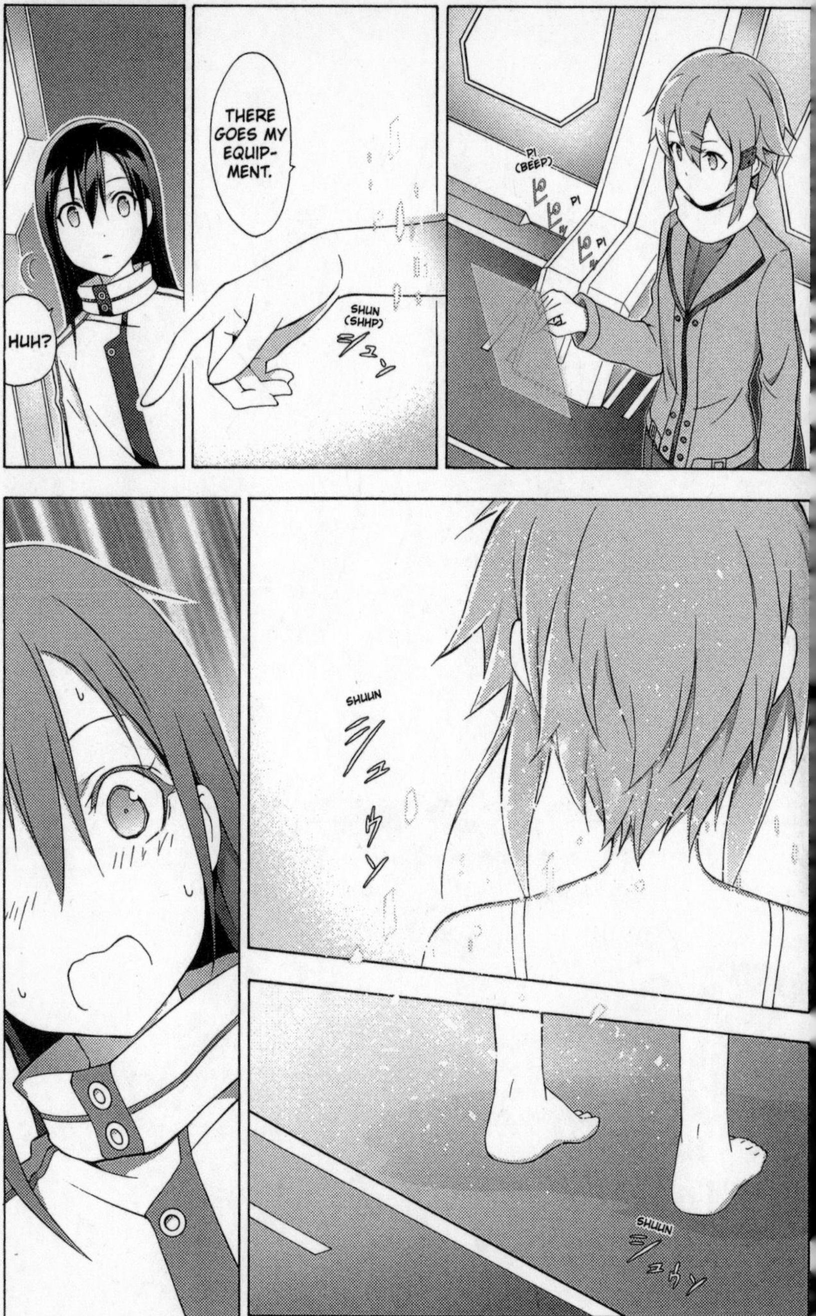
PI (BEEP)
PI
PI
THERE GOES MY EQUIP-MENT.
SHUN (SHHP)
HUH?
SHUUN
SHUUN

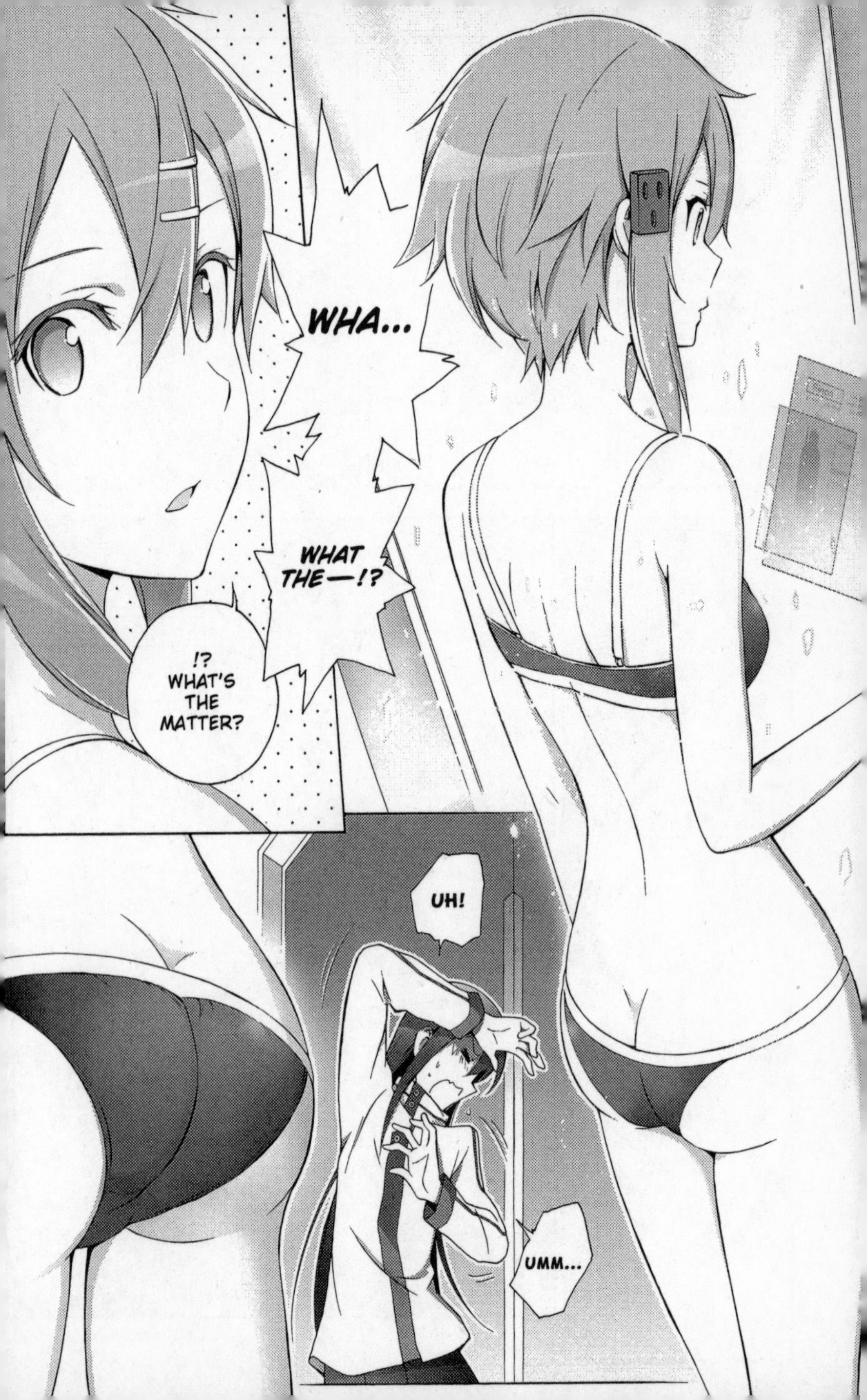
WHA...
WHAT THE—!?
!? WHAT'S THE MATTER?
UH!
UMM...

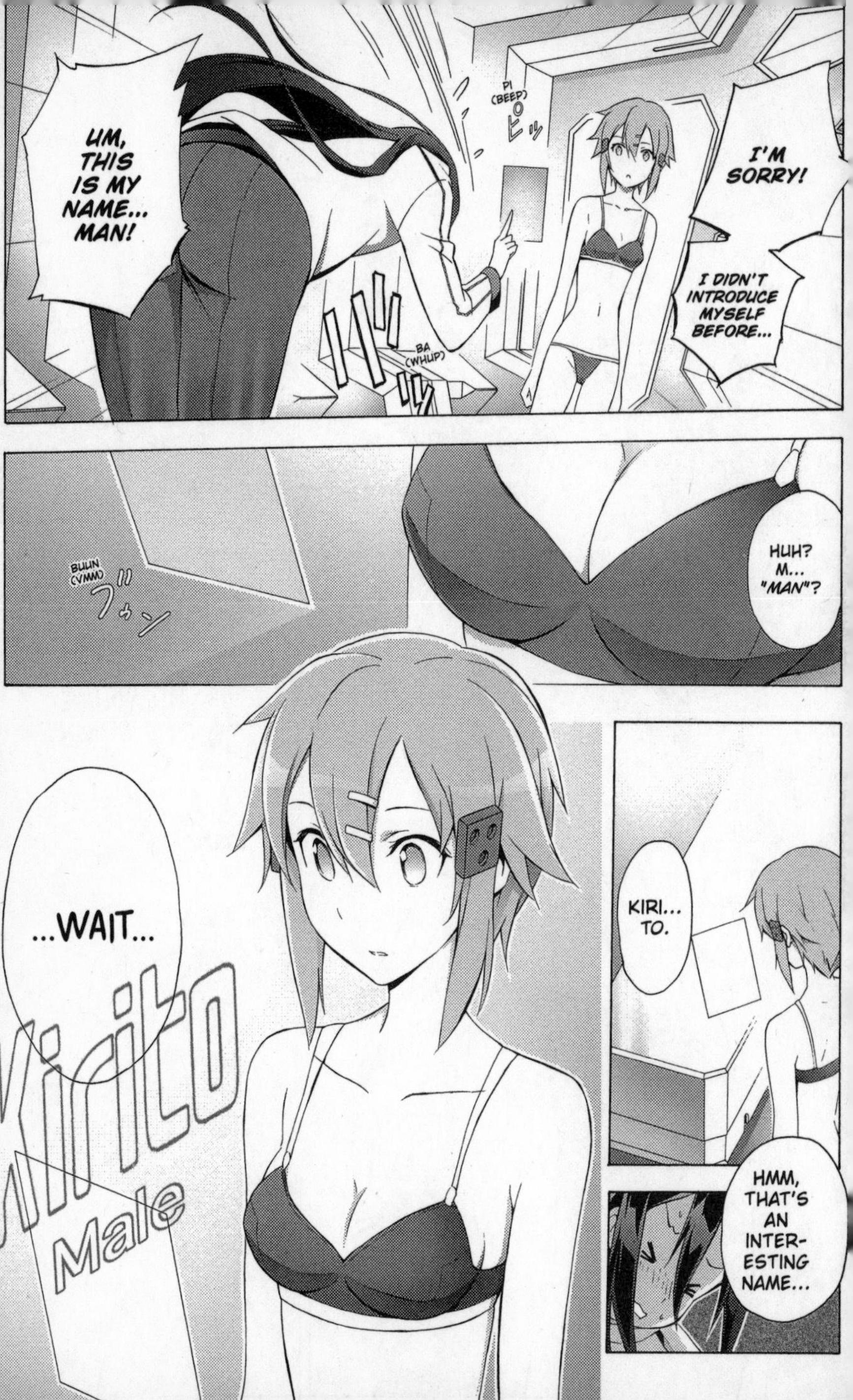
I'M SORRY!
I DIDN'T INTRODUCE MYSELF BEFORE...
PI (BEEP) ピッ
UM, THIS IS MY NAME... MAN!
BA (WHUP)
HUH? M... "MAN"?
BULN (VMM) ブォン
KIRI... TO.
HMM, THAT'S AN INTER-ESTING NAME...
...WAIT...
Kirito
Male

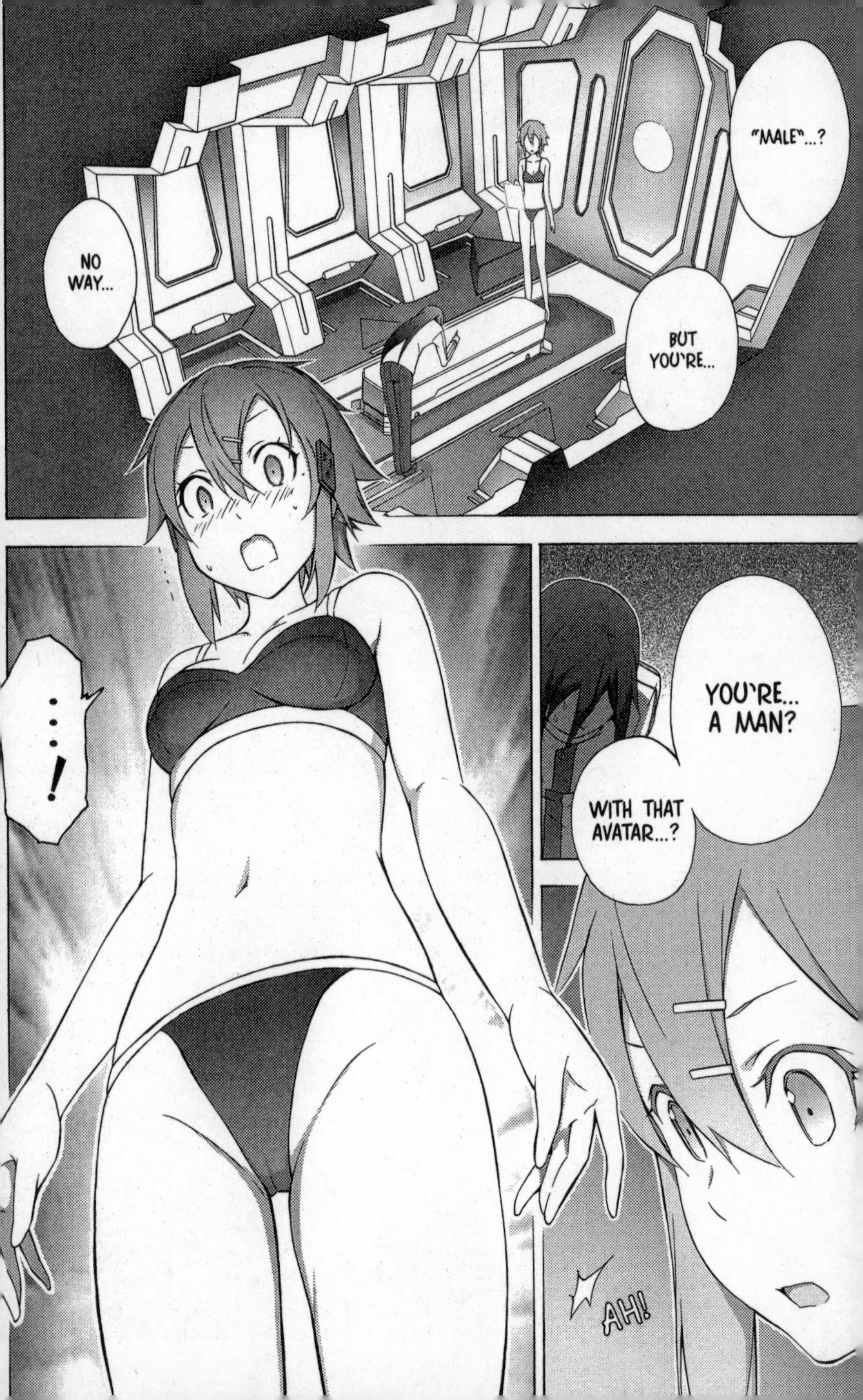
"MALE"...?
BUT YOU'RE...
NO WAY...
YOU'RE... A MAN?
WITH THAT AVATAR...?
AH!
...!

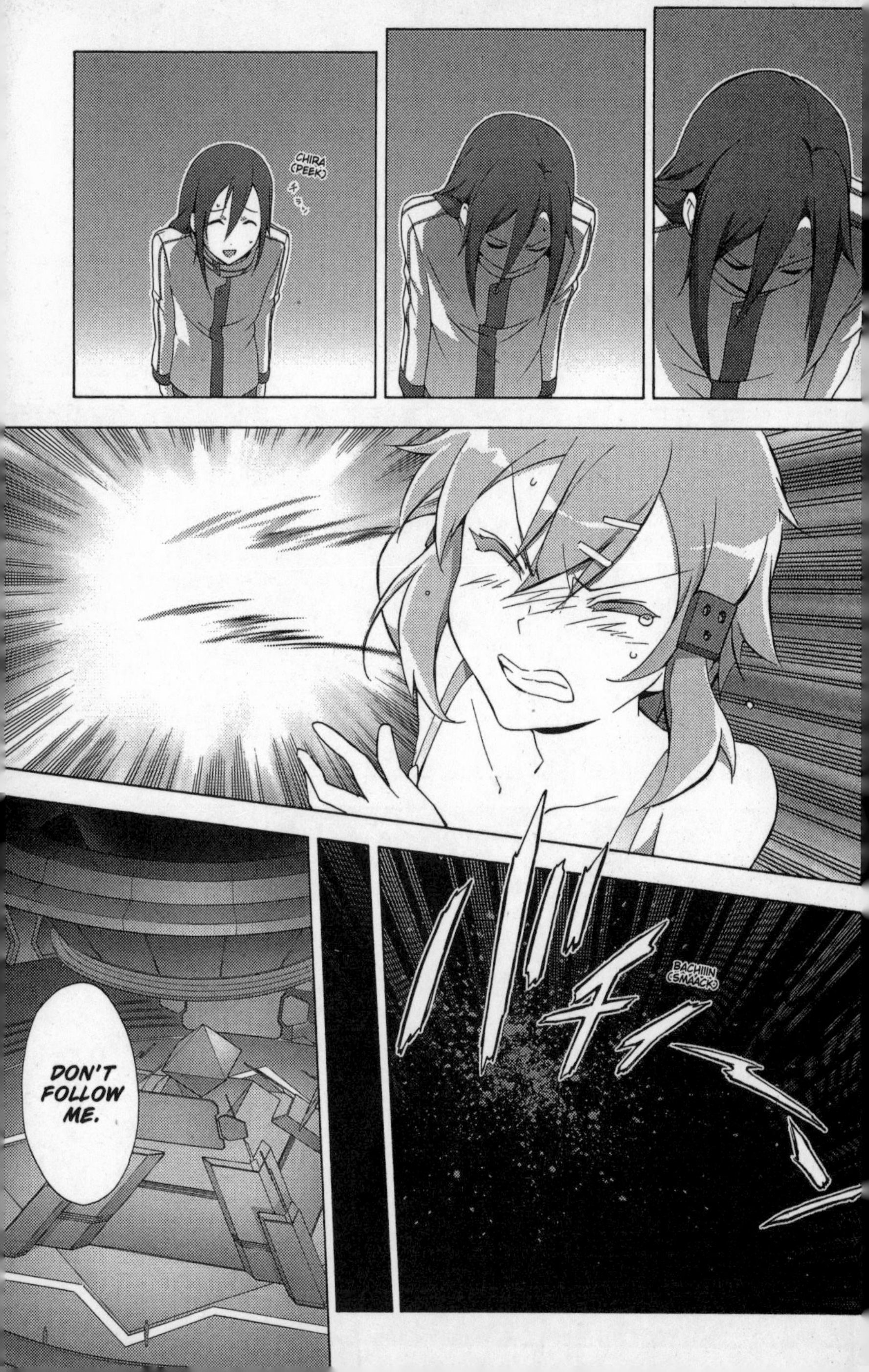
CHIRA (PEEK)
BACHIIIN (SMAACK)
DON'T FOLLOW ME.

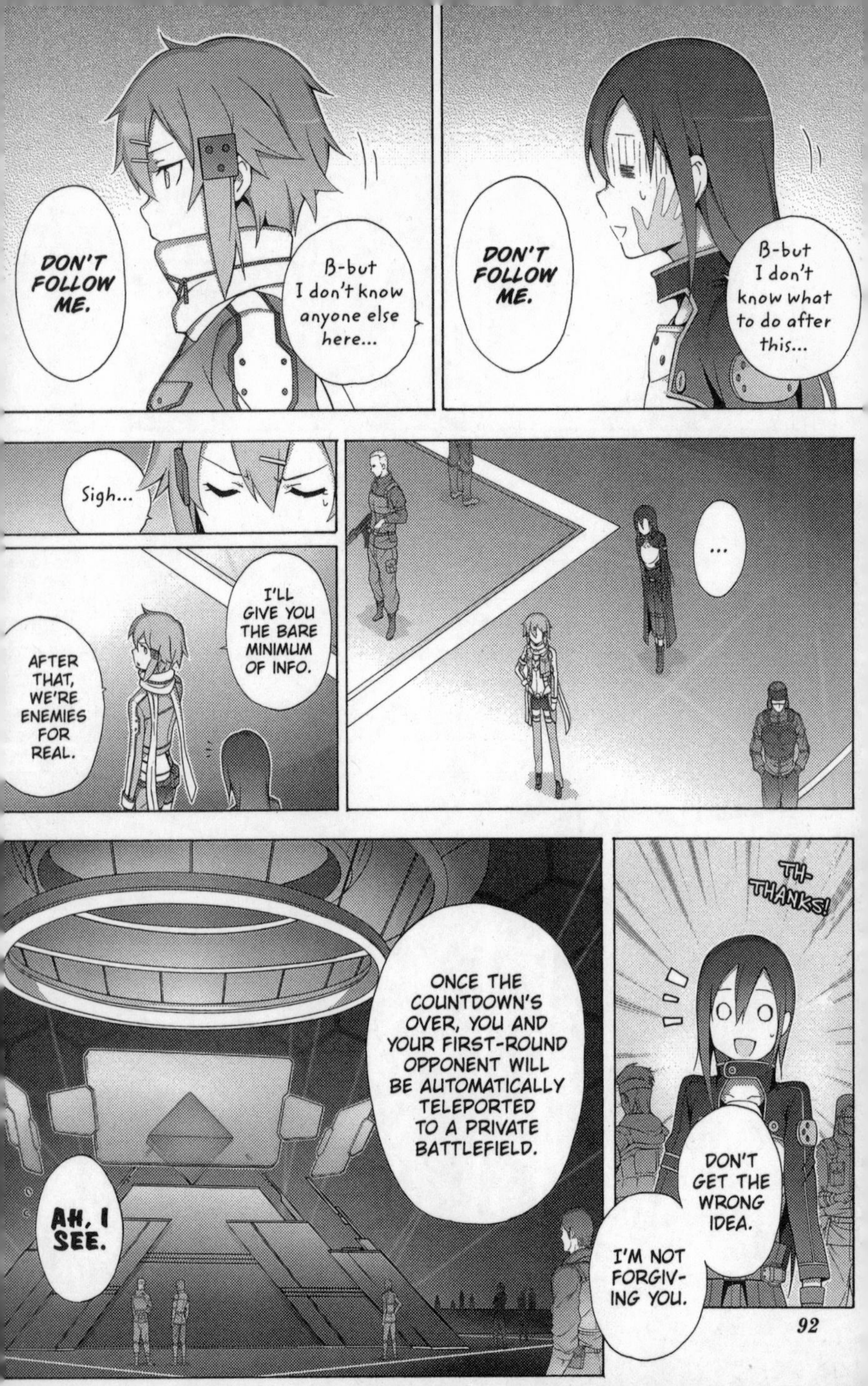
B-but I don't know what to do after this...
DON'T FOLLOW ME.
B-but I don't know anyone else here...
DON'T FOLLOW ME.
...
Sigh...
I'LL GIVE YOU THE BARE MINIMUM OF INFO.
AFTER THAT, WE'RE ENEMIES FOR REAL.
TH-THANKS!
DON'T GET THE WRONG IDEA.
I'M NOT FORGIV-ING YOU.
ONCE THE COUNTDOWN'S OVER, YOU AND YOUR FIRST-ROUND OPPONENT WILL BE AUTOMATICALLY TELEPORTED TO A PRIVATE BATTLEFIELD.
AH, I SEE.

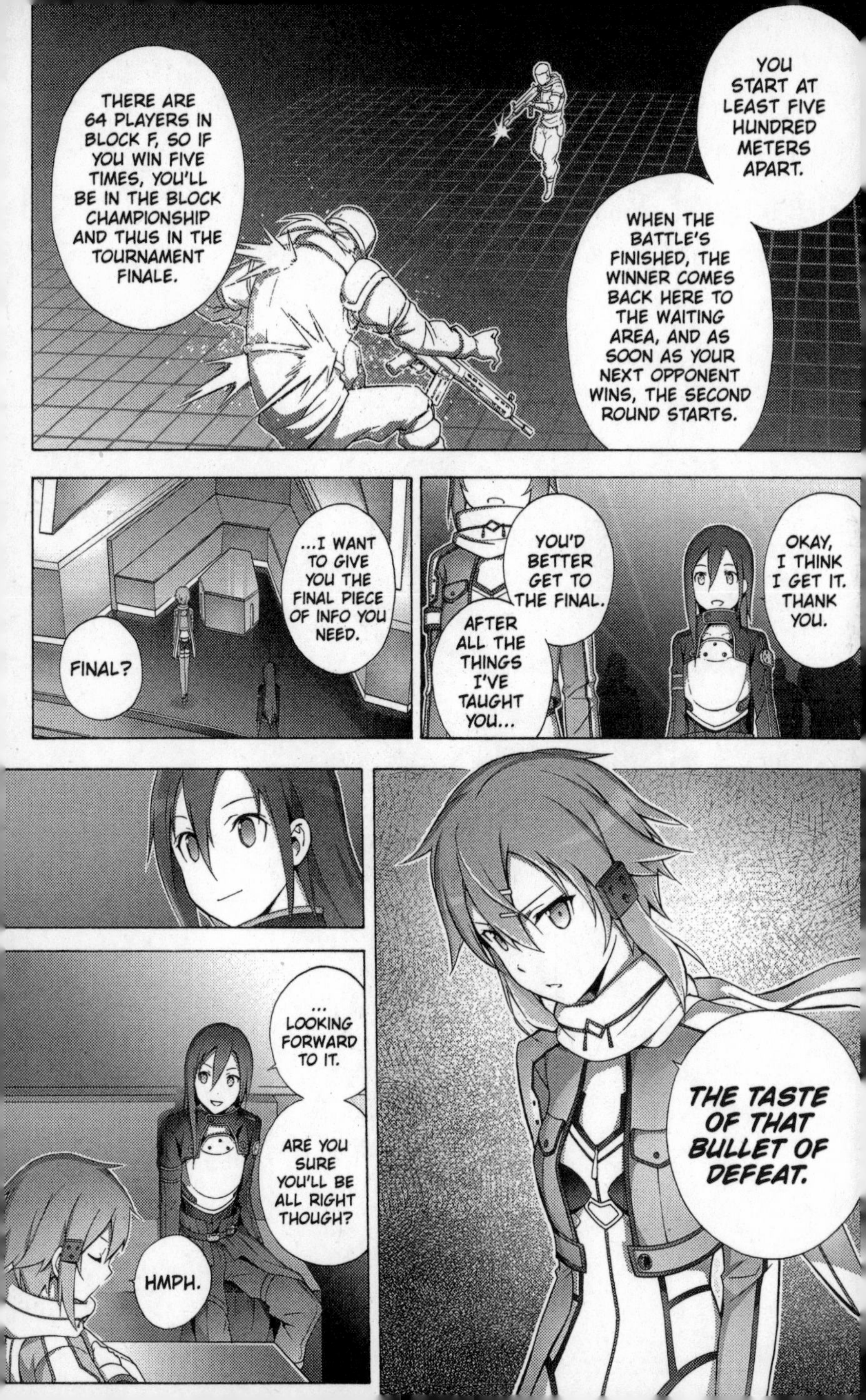
YOU START AT LEAST FIVE HUNDRED METERS APART.
WHEN THE BATTLE'S FINISHED, THE WINNER COMES BACK HERE TO THE WAITING AREA, AND AS SOON AS YOUR NEXT OPPONENT WINS, THE SECOND ROUND STARTS.
THERE ARE 64 PLAYERS IN BLOCK F, SO IF YOU WIN FIVE TIMES, YOU'LL BE IN THE BLOCK CHAMPIONSHIP AND THUS IN THE TOURNAMENT FINALE.
OKAY, I THINK I GET IT. THANK YOU.
YOU'D BETTER GET TO THE FINAL.
AFTER ALL THE THINGS I'VE TAUGHT YOU...
...I WANT TO GIVE YOU THE FINAL PIECE OF INFO YOU NEED.
FINAL?
THE TASTE OF THAT BULLET OF DEFEAT.
...LOOKING FORWARD TO IT.
ARE YOU SURE YOU'LL BE ALL RIGHT THOUGH?
HMPH.

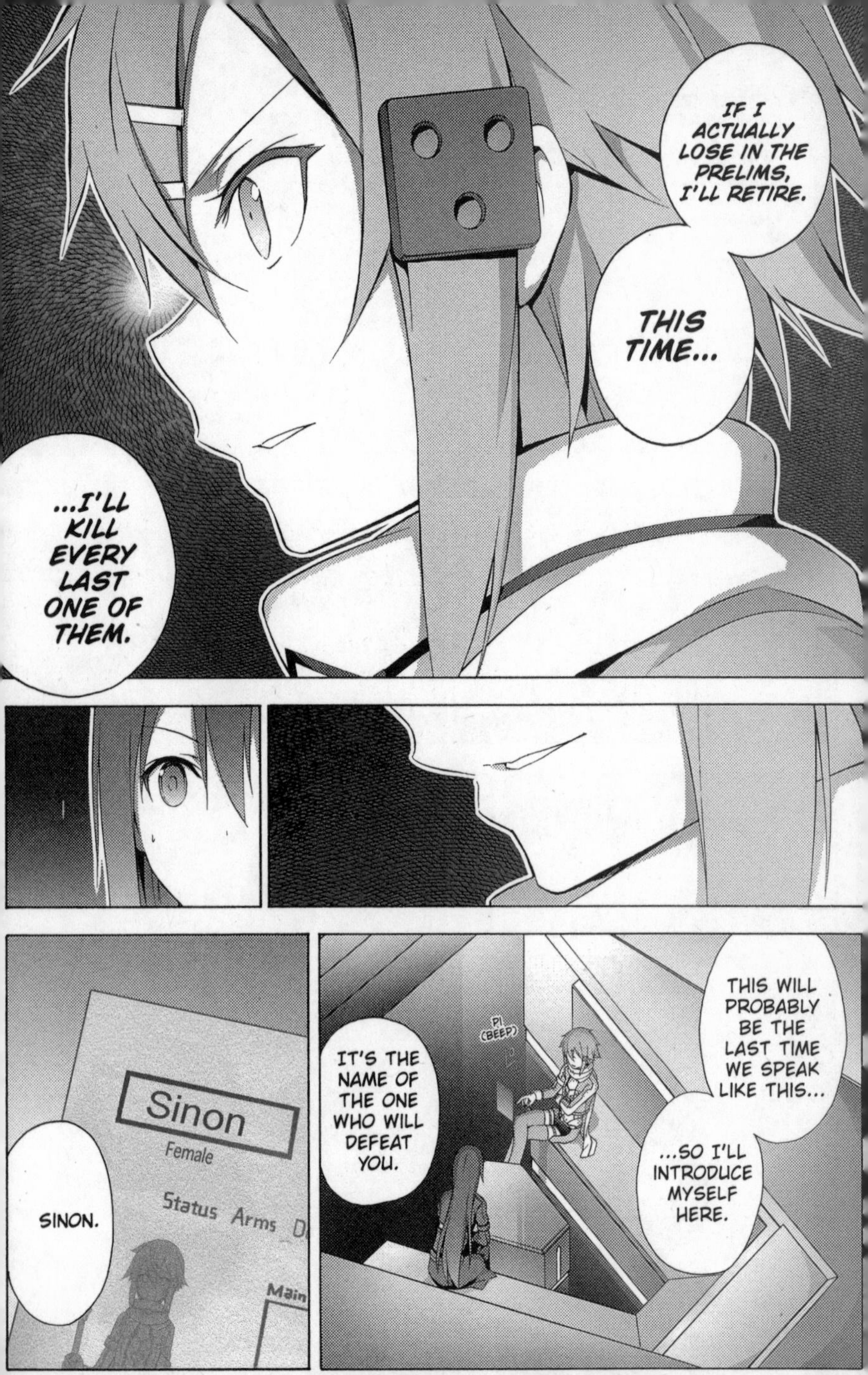
IF I ACTUALLY LOSE IN THE PRELIMS, I'LL RETIRE.
THIS TIME...
...I'LL KILL EVERY LAST ONE OF THEM.
THIS WILL PROBABLY BE THE LAST TIME WE SPEAK LIKE THIS...
...SO I'LL INTRODUCE MYSELF HERE.
PI (BEEP)
IT'S THE NAME OF THE ONE WHO WILL DEFEAT YOU.
Sinon
Female
Status Arms
Main
SINON.

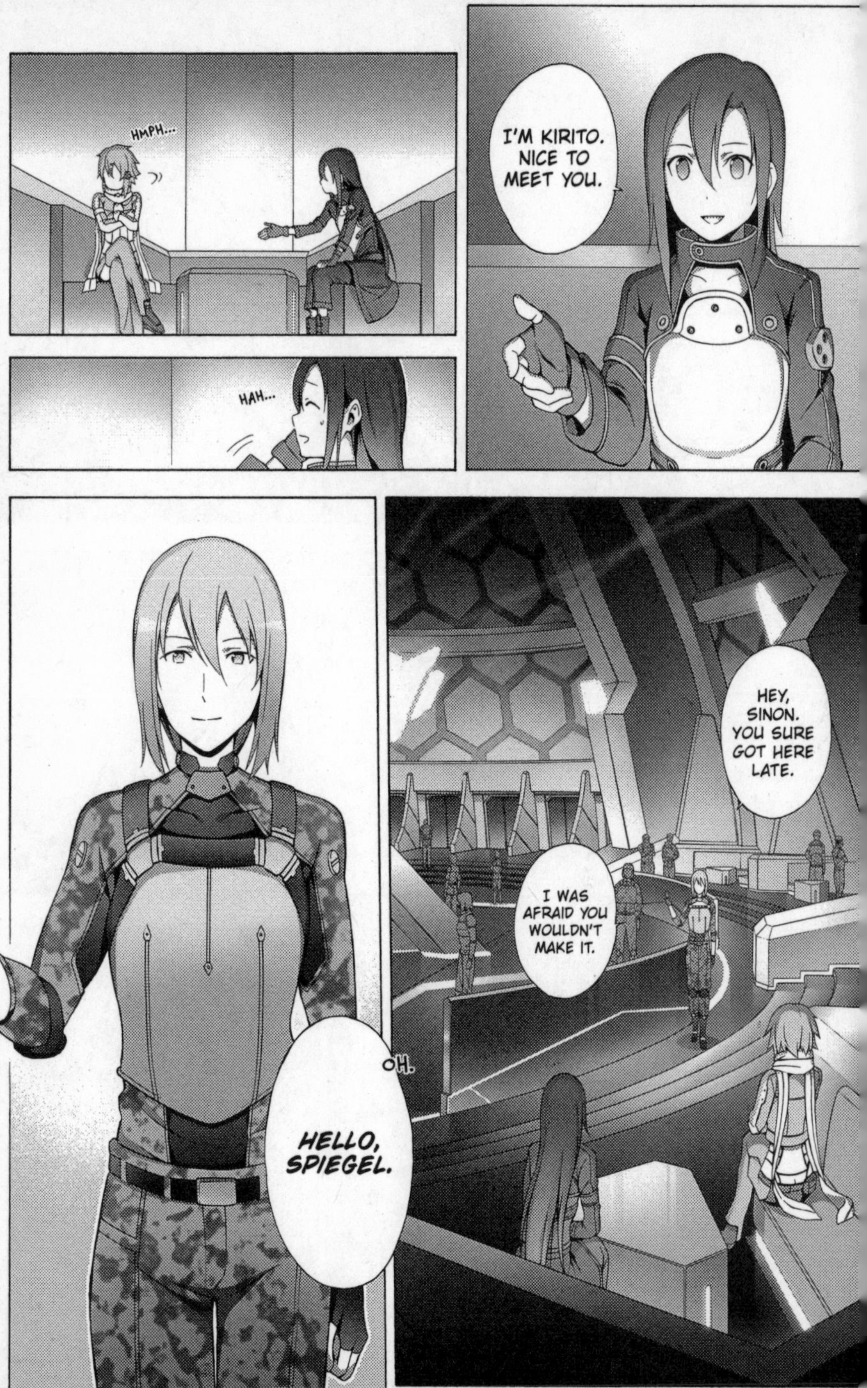
I'M KIRITO. NICE TO MEET YOU.
HMPH...
HAH...
HEY, SINON. YOU SURE GOT HERE LATE.
I WAS AFRAID YOU WOULDN'T MAKE IT.
OH.
HELLO, SPIEGEL.

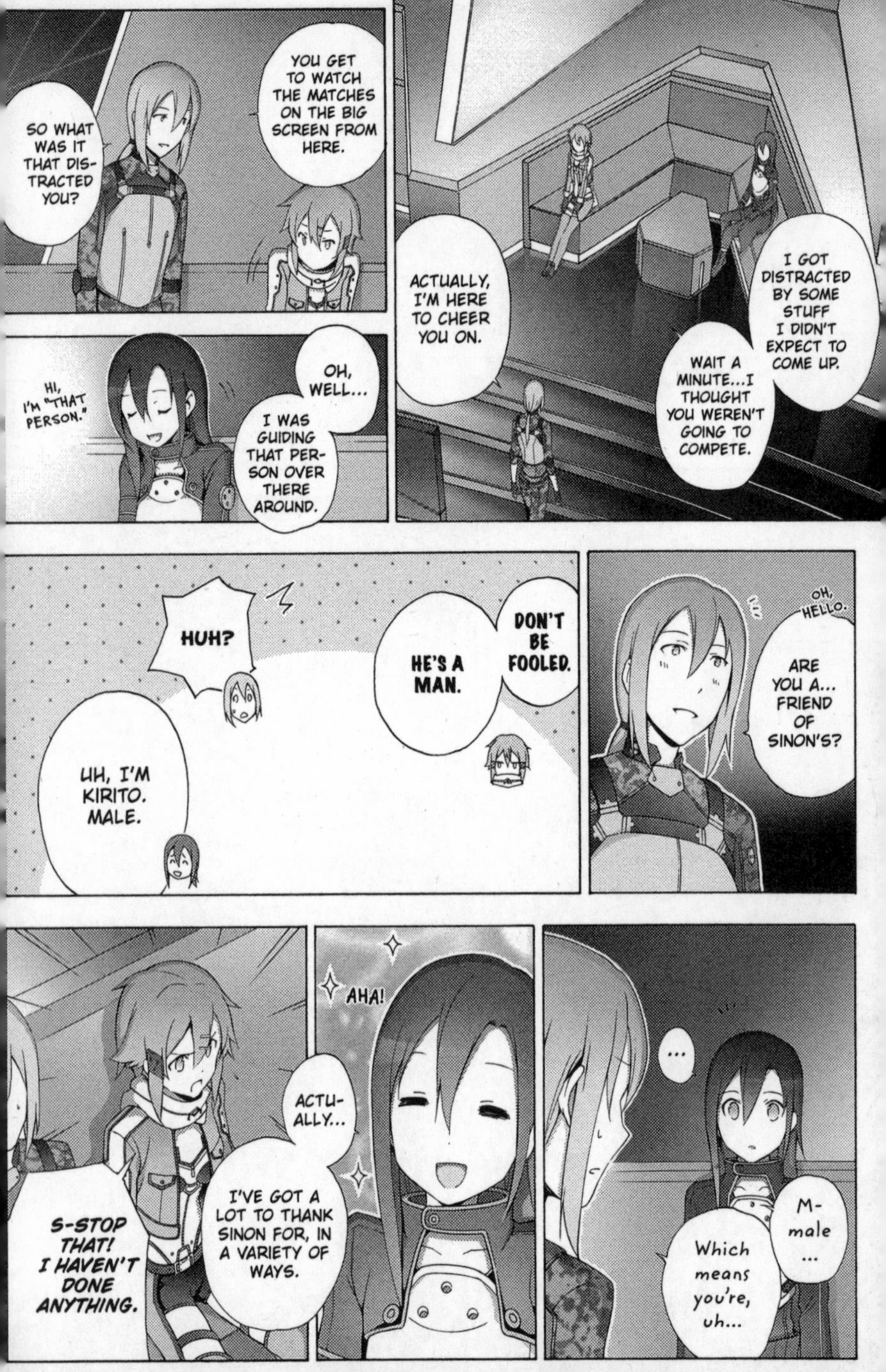
I GOT DISTRACTED BY SOME STUFF I DIDN'T EXPECT TO COME UP.
WAIT A MINUTE...I THOUGHT YOU WEREN'T GOING TO COMPETE.
ACTUALLY, I'M HERE TO CHEER YOU ON.
YOU GET TO WATCH THE MATCHES ON THE BIG SCREEN FROM HERE.
SO WHAT WAS IT THAT DISTRACTED YOU?
OH, WELL...
I WAS GUIDING THAT PERSON OVER THERE AROUND.
HI, I'M "THAT PERSON."
OH, HELLO.
ARE YOU A... FRIEND OF SINON'S?
DON'T BE FOOLED.
HE'S A MAN.
HUH?
UH, I'M KIRITO. MALE.
...
M-male...
Which means you're, uh...
AHA!
ACTUALLY...
I'VE GOT A LOT TO THANK SINON FOR, IN A VARIETY OF WAYS.
S-STOP THAT! I HAVEN'T DONE ANYTHING.

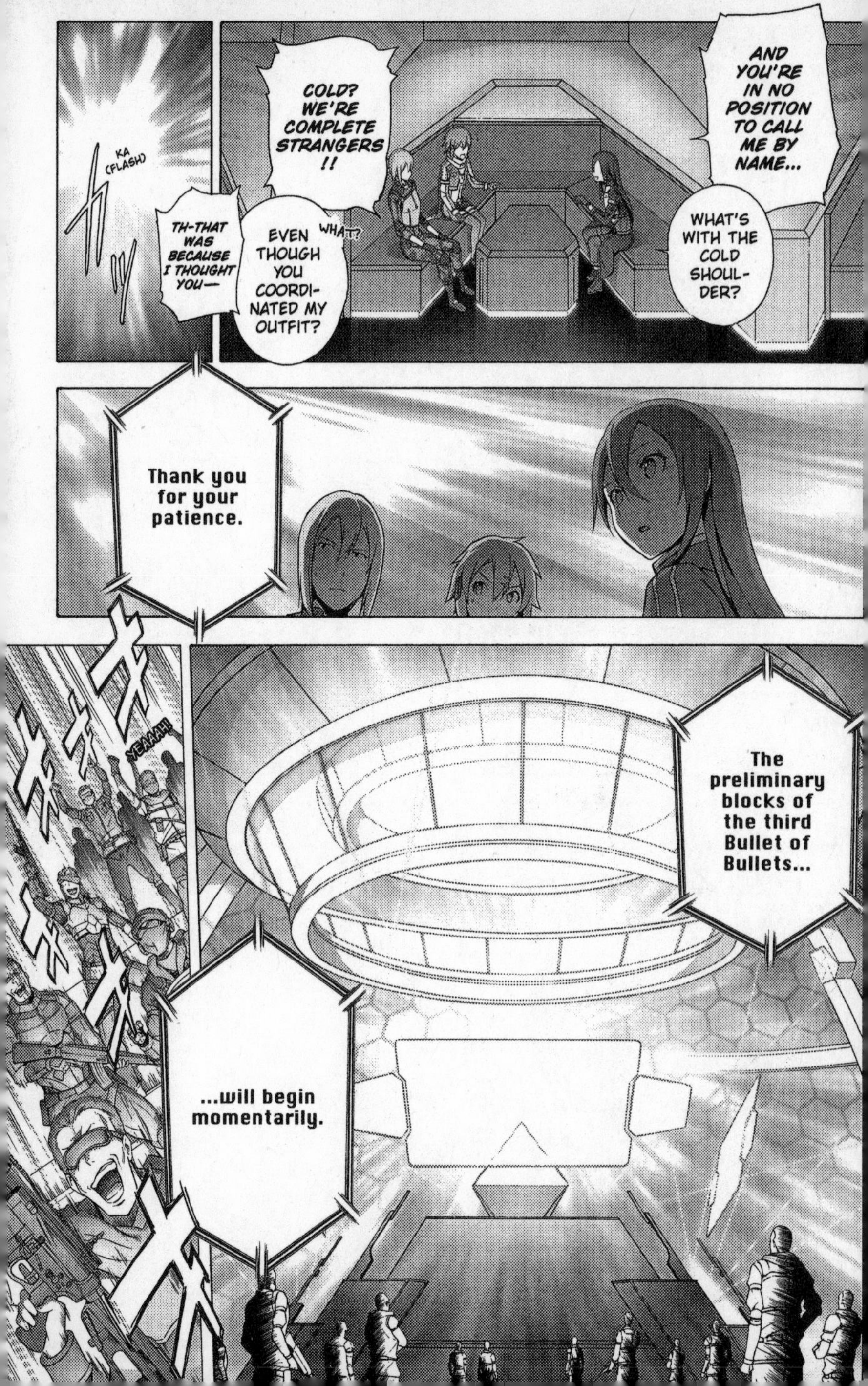
WHAT'S WITH THE COLD SHOULDER?
COLD? WE'RE COMPLETE STRANGERS!!
AND YOU'RE IN NO POSITION TO CALL ME BY NAME...
WHAT?
EVEN THOUGH YOU COORDINATED MY OUTFIT?
KA (FLASH)
TH-THAT WAS BECAUSE I THOUGHT YOU—
Thank you for your patience.
The preliminary blocks of the third Bullet of Bullets...
...will begin momentarily.
YEAAAH!

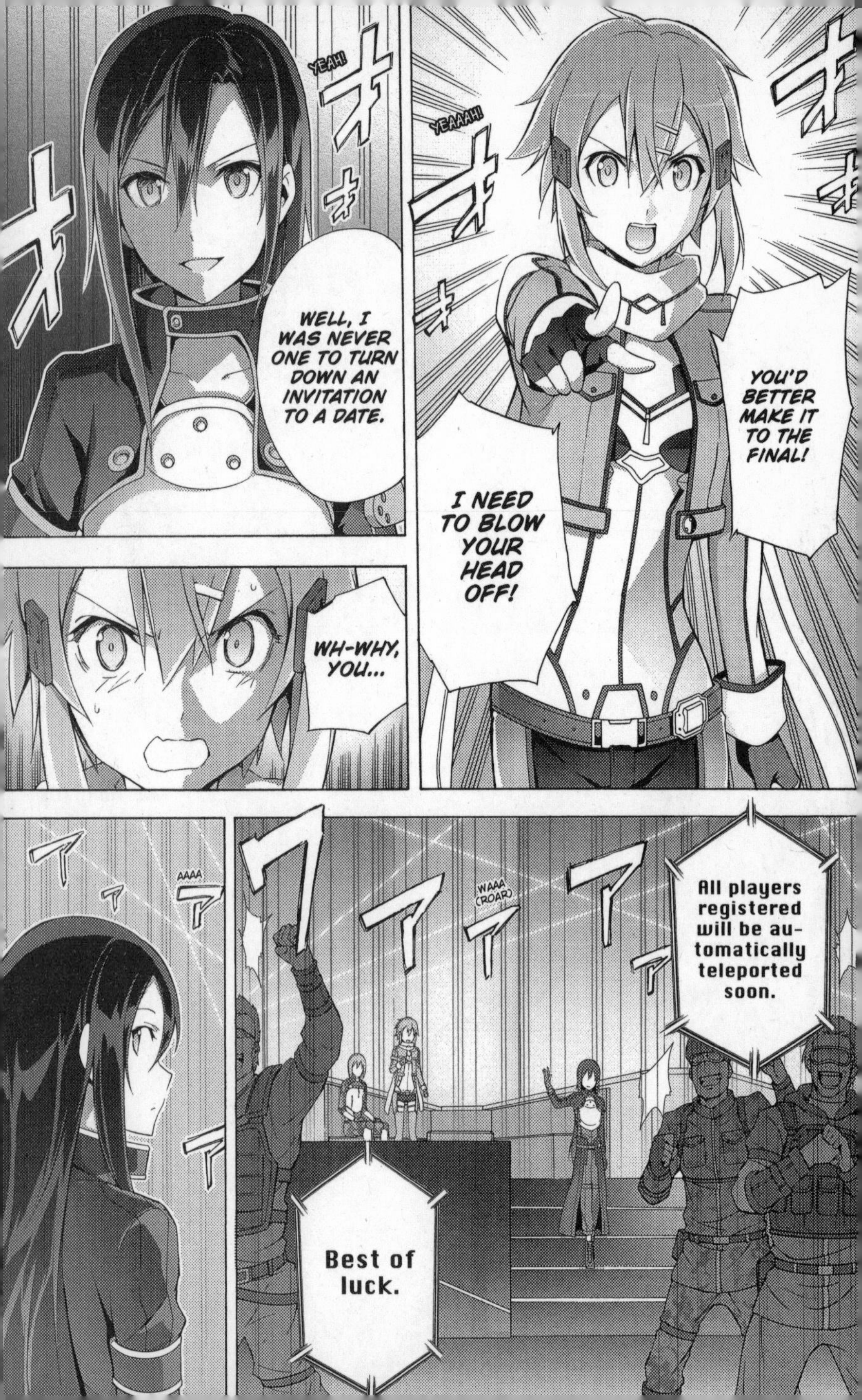
YEAAAH!
YOU'D BETTER MAKE IT TO THE FINAL!
I NEED TO BLOW YOUR HEAD OFF!
YEAH!
WELL, I WAS NEVER ONE TO TURN DOWN AN INVITATION TO A DATE.
WH-WHY, YOU...
All players registered will be au-tomatically teleported soon.
WAAA (ROAR)
Best of luck.
AAAA

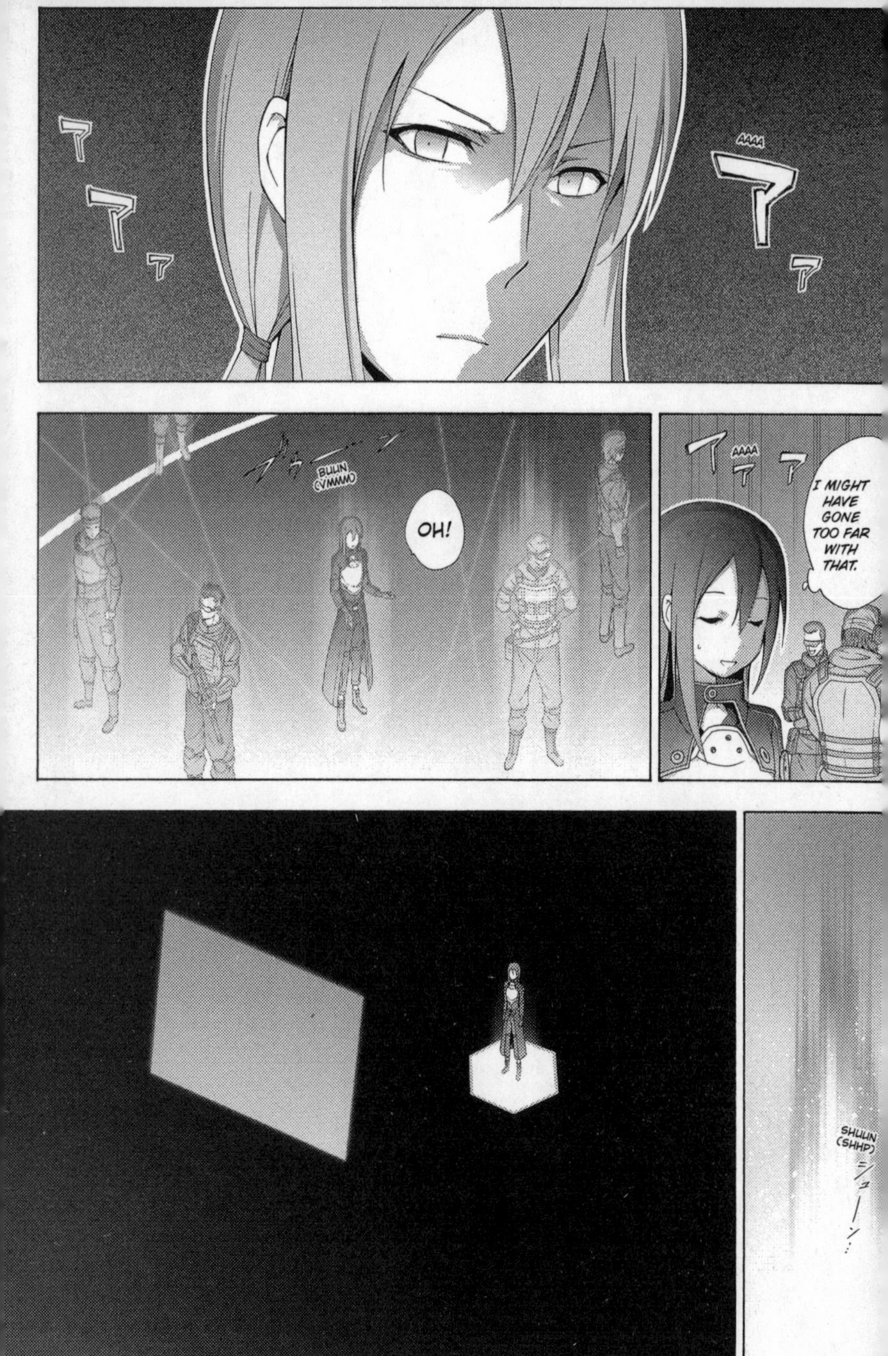
AAAA
AAAA
I MIGHT HAVE GONE TOO FAR WITH THAT.
BUUN (VMMM)
OH!
SHUUN (SHHP)

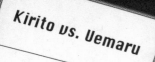

Kirito vs. Uemaru

Preparation Time: 56 secs
Field: Lost Ancient Temple

MY PRIMARY IS THE "KAGE-MITSU G4" PHOTON SWORD.

BULIN (VNIN)

PI (BEEP)

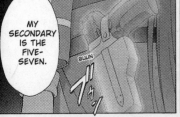

MY SECONDARY IS THE FIVE-SEVEN.

BULIN

"THIS TIME I'LL KILL EVERY LAST ONE OF THEM," SHE SAID.

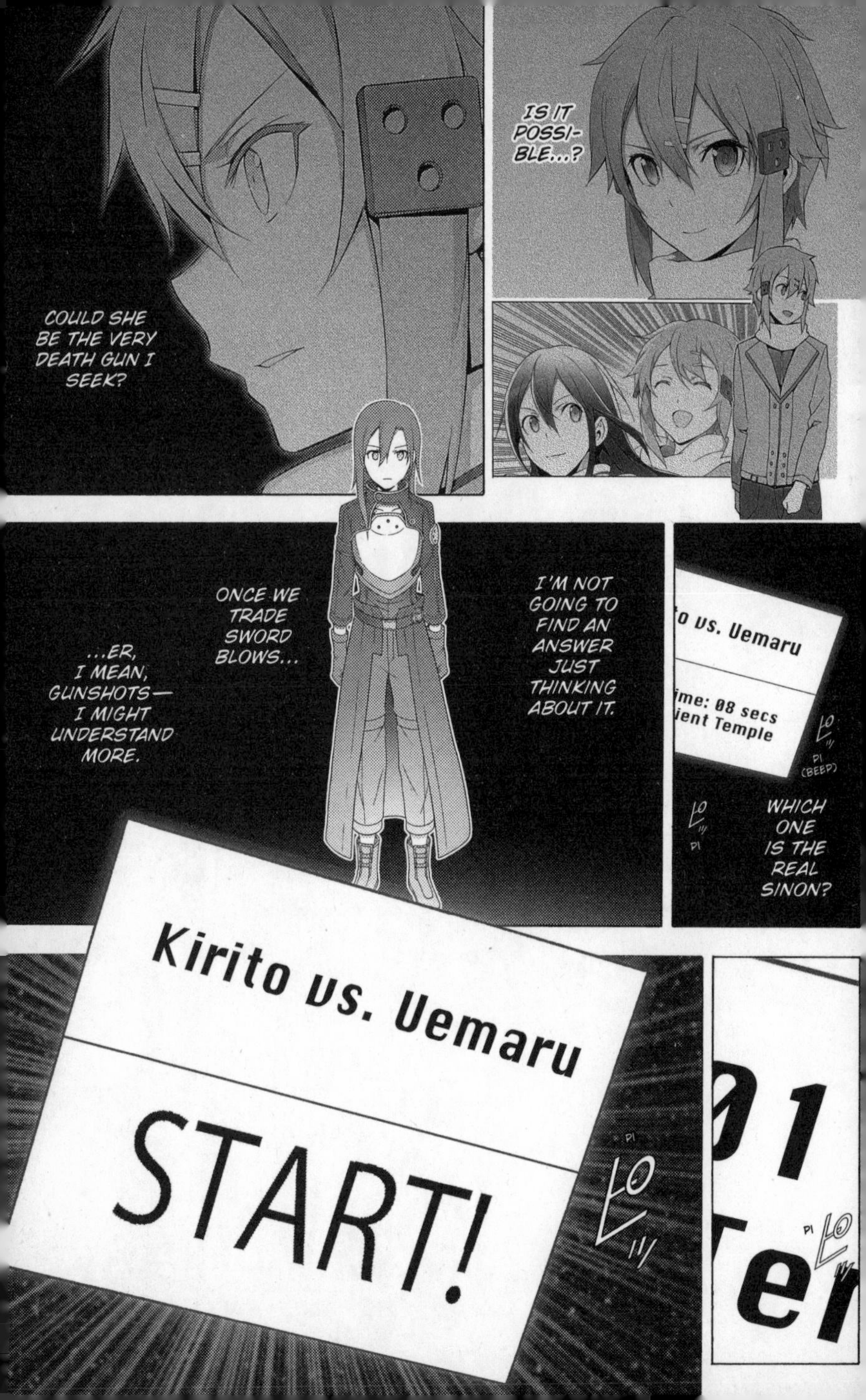
IS IT POSSI-BLE...?
COULD SHE BE THE VERY DEATH GUN I SEEK?
o vs. Uemaru
ime: 08 secs
ient Temple
PI (BEEP)
PI
WHICH ONE IS THE REAL SINON?
I'M NOT GOING TO FIND AN ANSWER JUST THINKING ABOUT IT.
ONCE WE TRADE SWORD BLOWS...
...ER, I MEAN, GUNSHOTS— I MIGHT UNDERSTAND MORE.
01
Ter
PI
Kirito vs. Uemaru
START!
PI

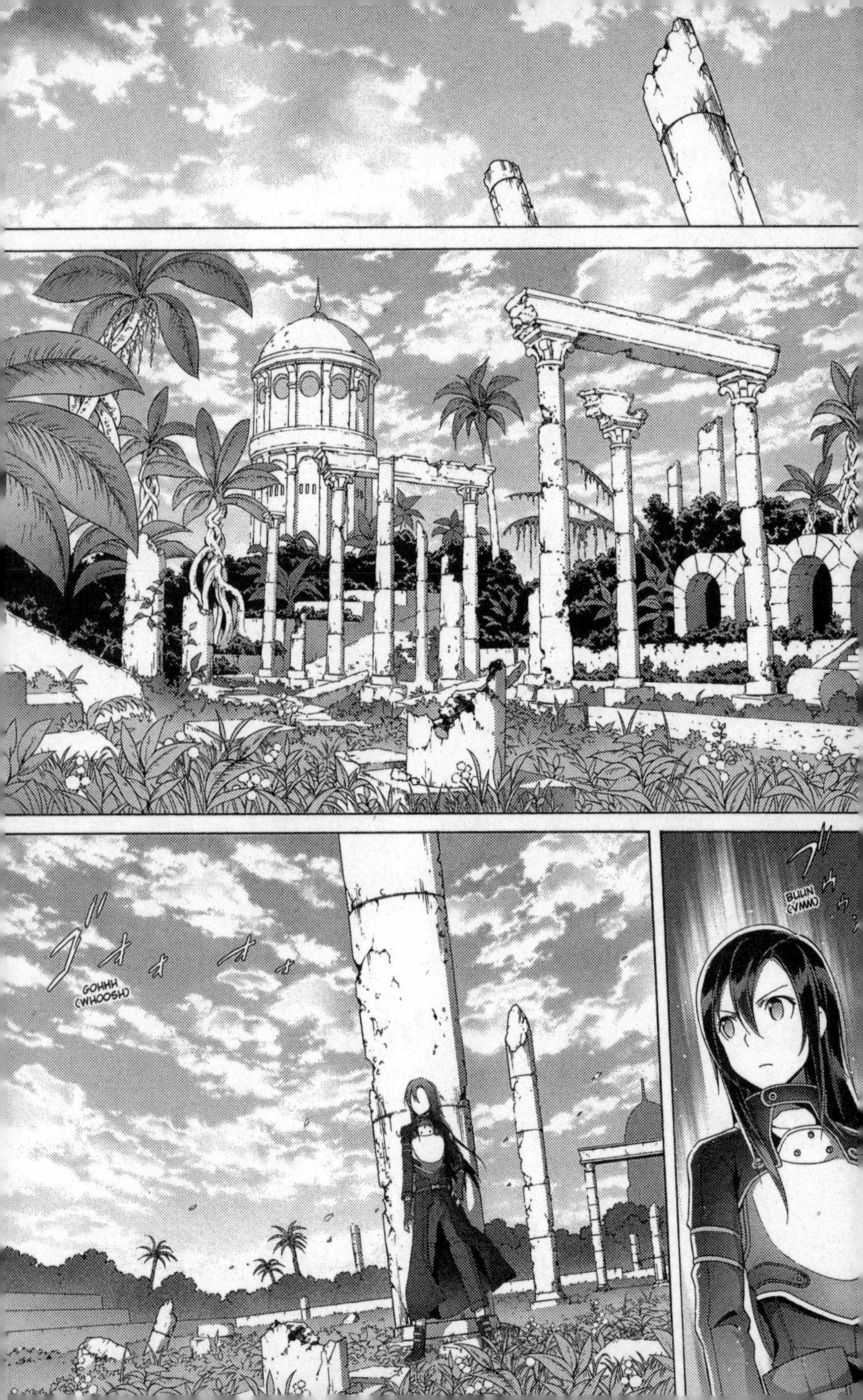
BULIN (VMM)
GOHHH (WHOOSH)

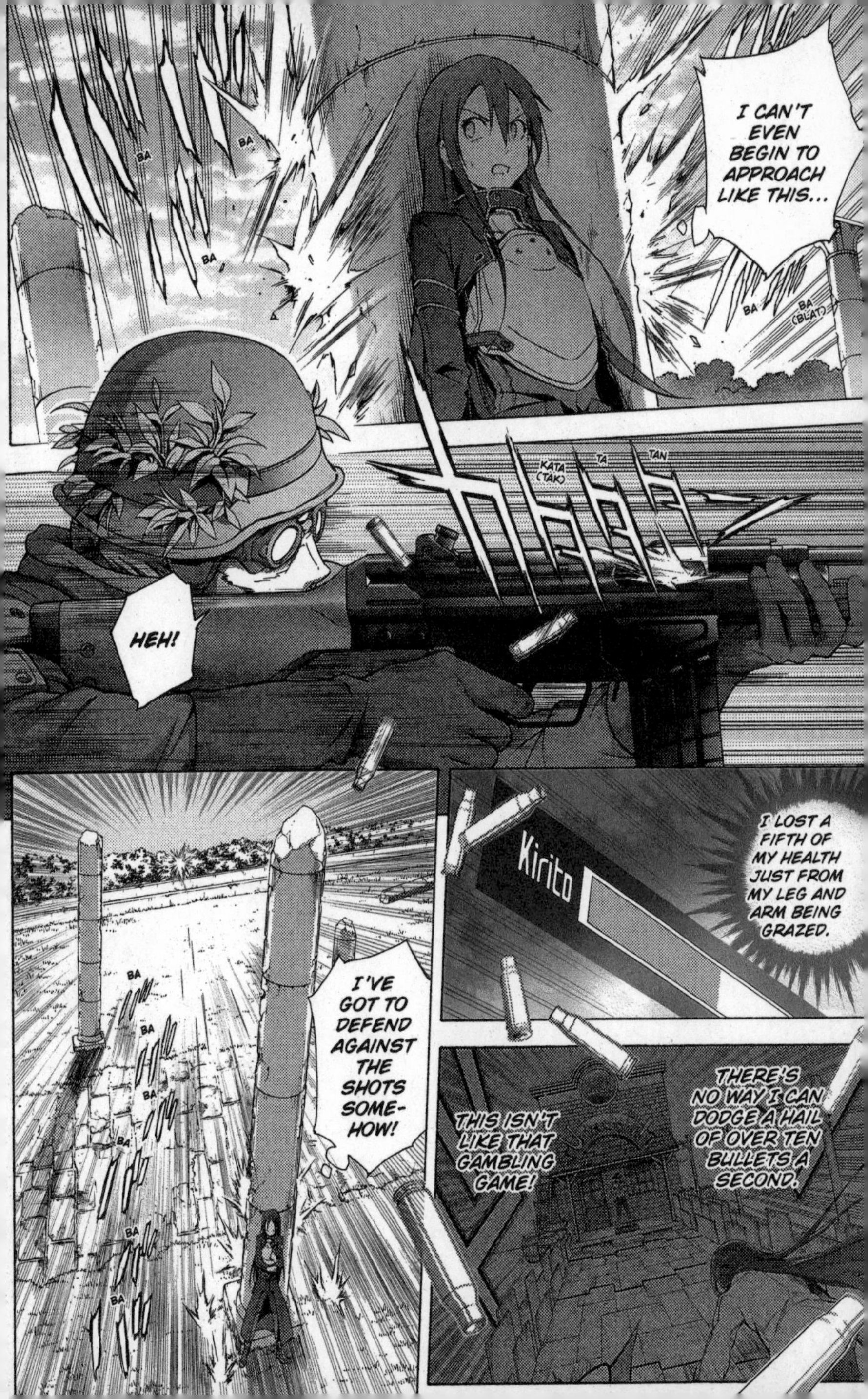
I CAN'T EVEN BEGIN TO APPROACH LIKE THIS...
BA
BA (BLAT)
BA
BA
BA
KATA (TAK)
TA
TAN
HEH!
Kirito
I LOST A FIFTH OF MY HEALTH JUST FROM MY LEG AND ARM BEING GRAZED.
THERE'S NO WAY I CAN DODGE A HAIL OF OVER TEN BULLETS A SECOND.
THIS ISN'T LIKE THAT GAMBLING GAME!
I'VE GOT TO DEFEND AGAINST THE SHOTS SOME-HOW!
BA
BA
BA
BA
BA
BA

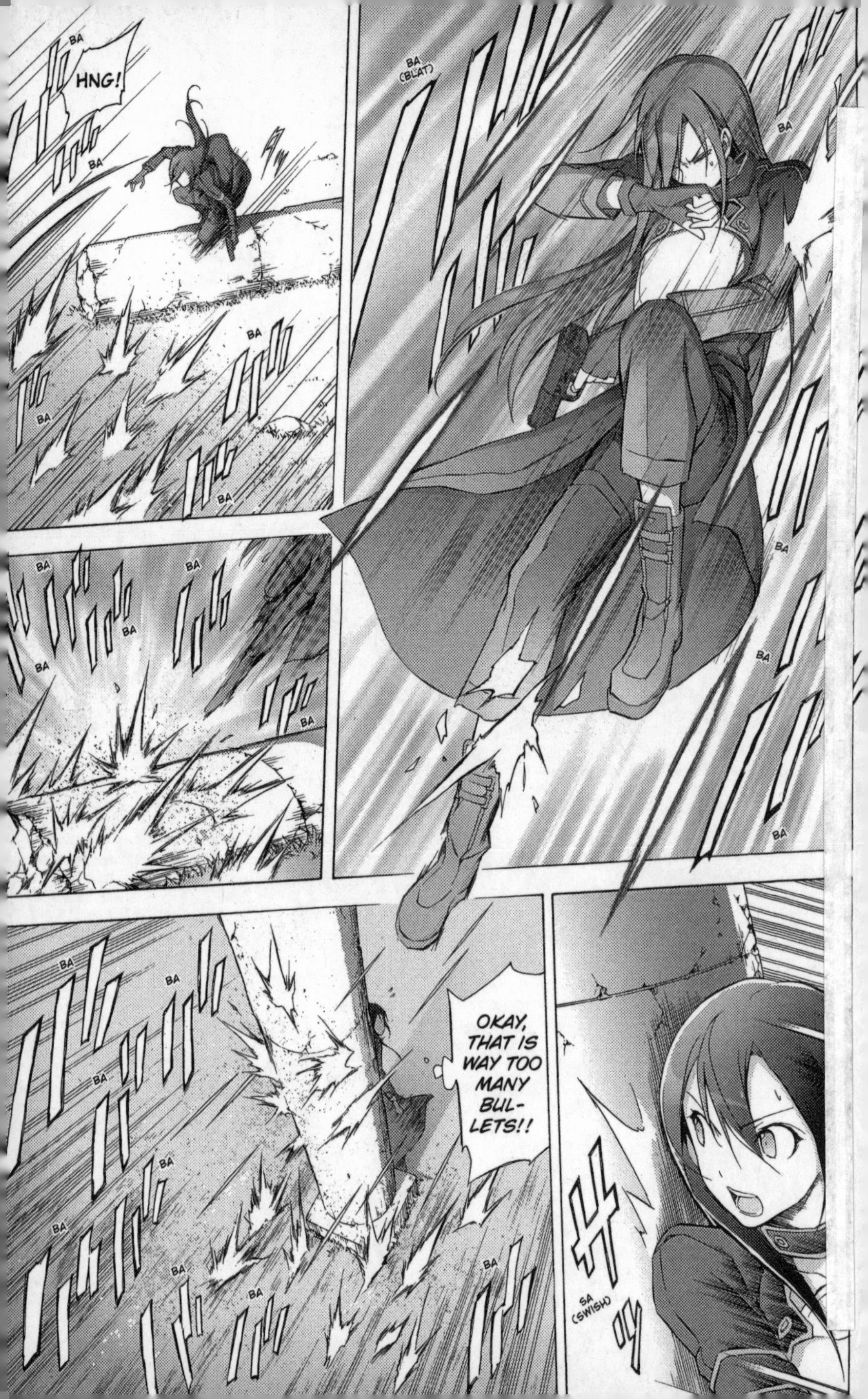
BA
(BLAT)
BA
BA
BA
BA
BA
BA
HNG!
BA
BA
BA
BA
BA
BA
BA
BA
BA
BA
OKAY, THAT IS WAY TOO MANY BUL- LETS!!
SA
(SWISH)
BA
BA
BA
BA
BA
BA
BA
BA

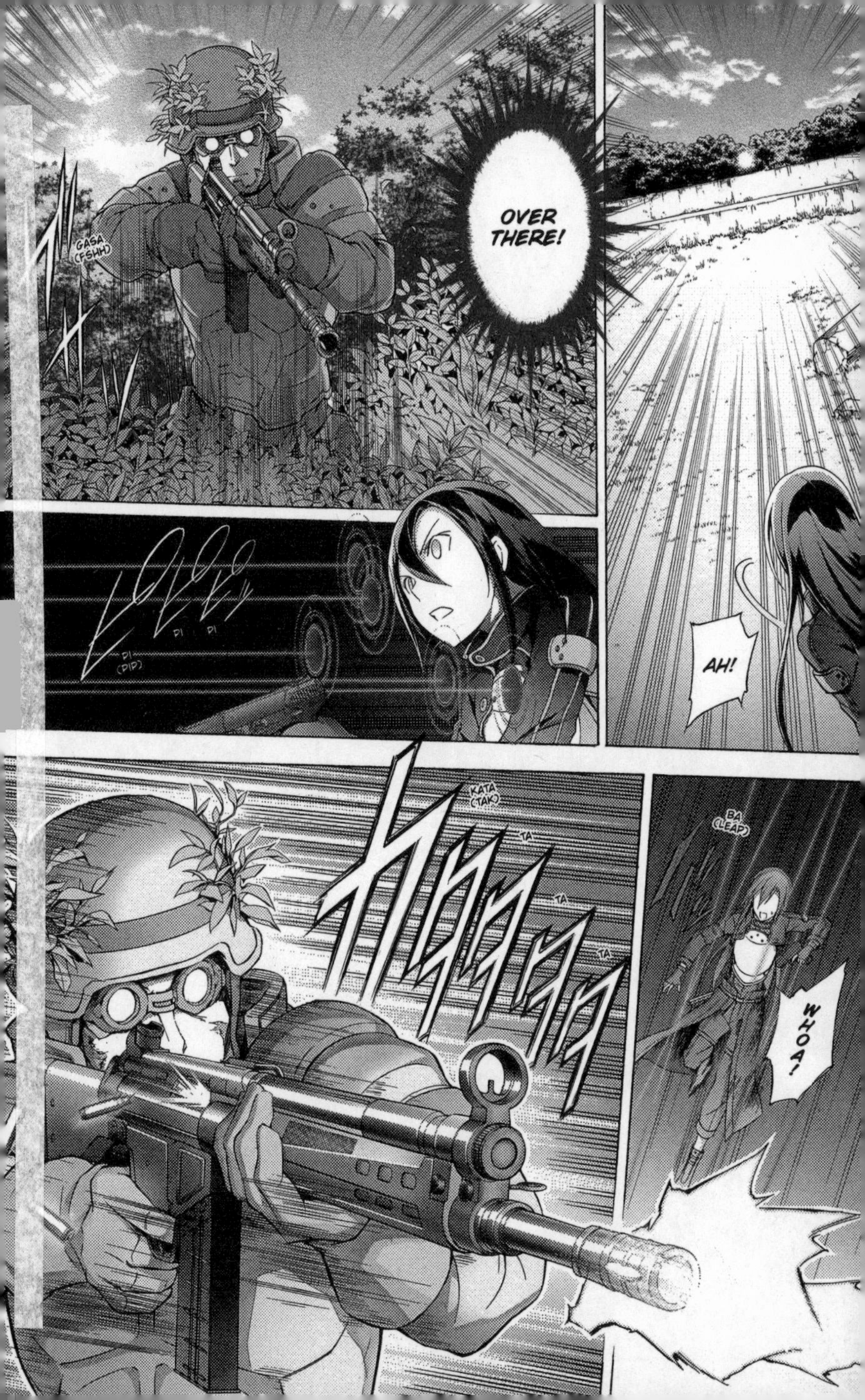
OVER THERE!
GASA (FSHH)
PI PI PI (PIP)
AH!
BA (LEAP)
WHOA!
KATA (TAK)
TA
TA
TA

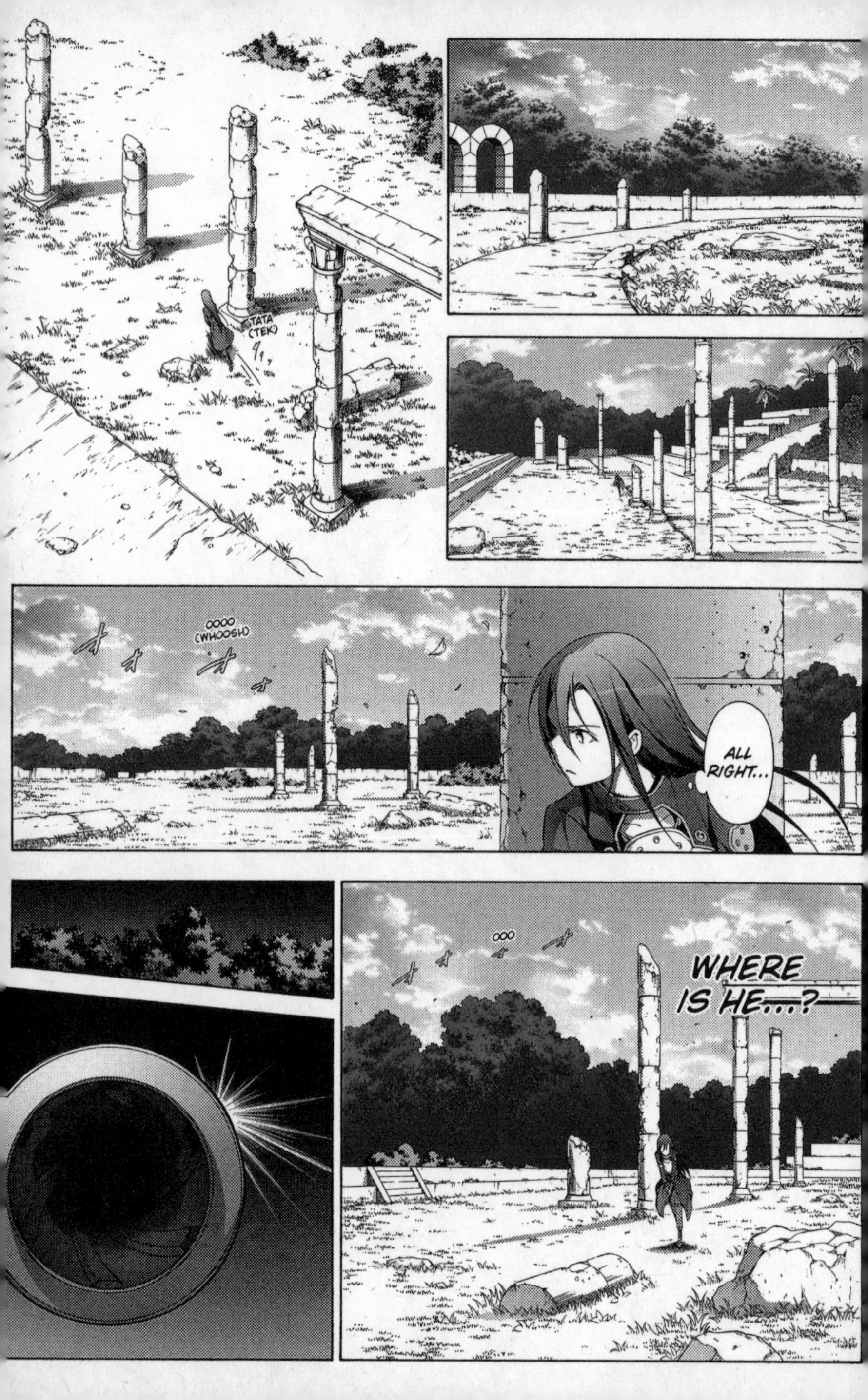
TATA
(TEK)
OOOO
(WHOOSH)
ALL RIGHT...
OOO
WHERE IS HE...?

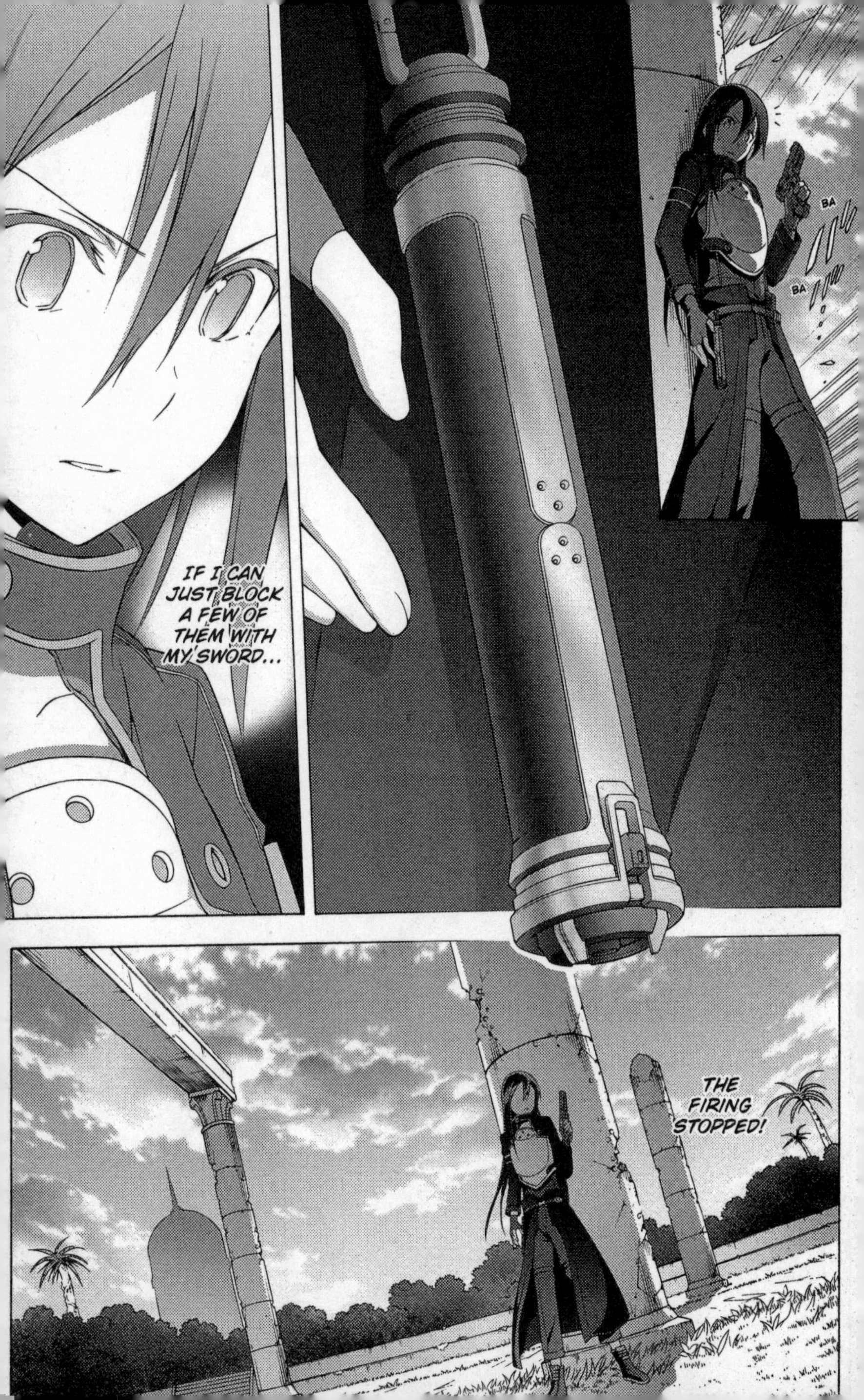
BA
BA
IF I CAN JUST BLOCK A FEW OF THEM WITH MY SWORD...
THE FIRING STOPPED!

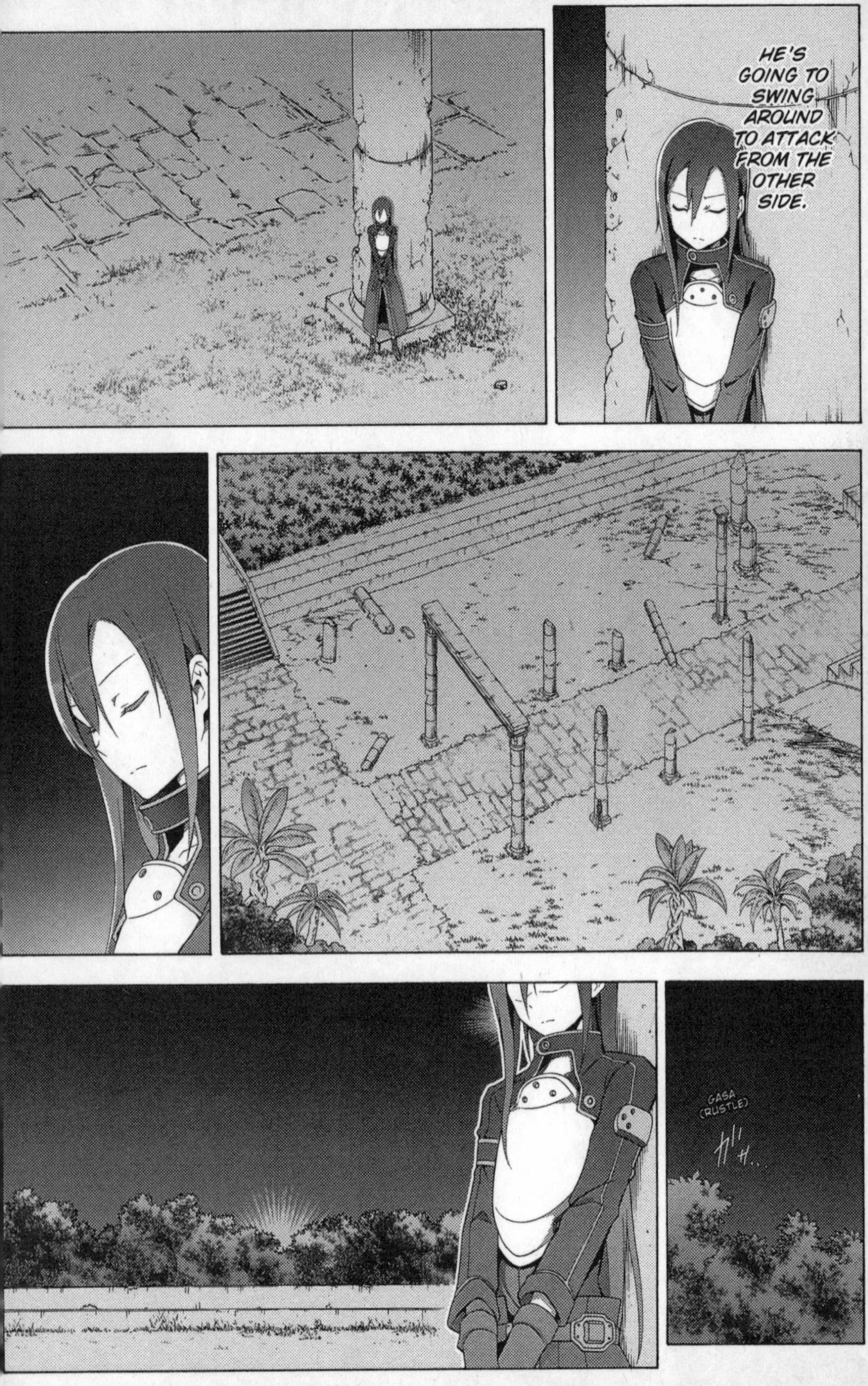
HE'S GOING TO SWING AROUND TO ATTACK FROM THE OTHER SIDE.
GASA (RUSTLE)
ガサ…

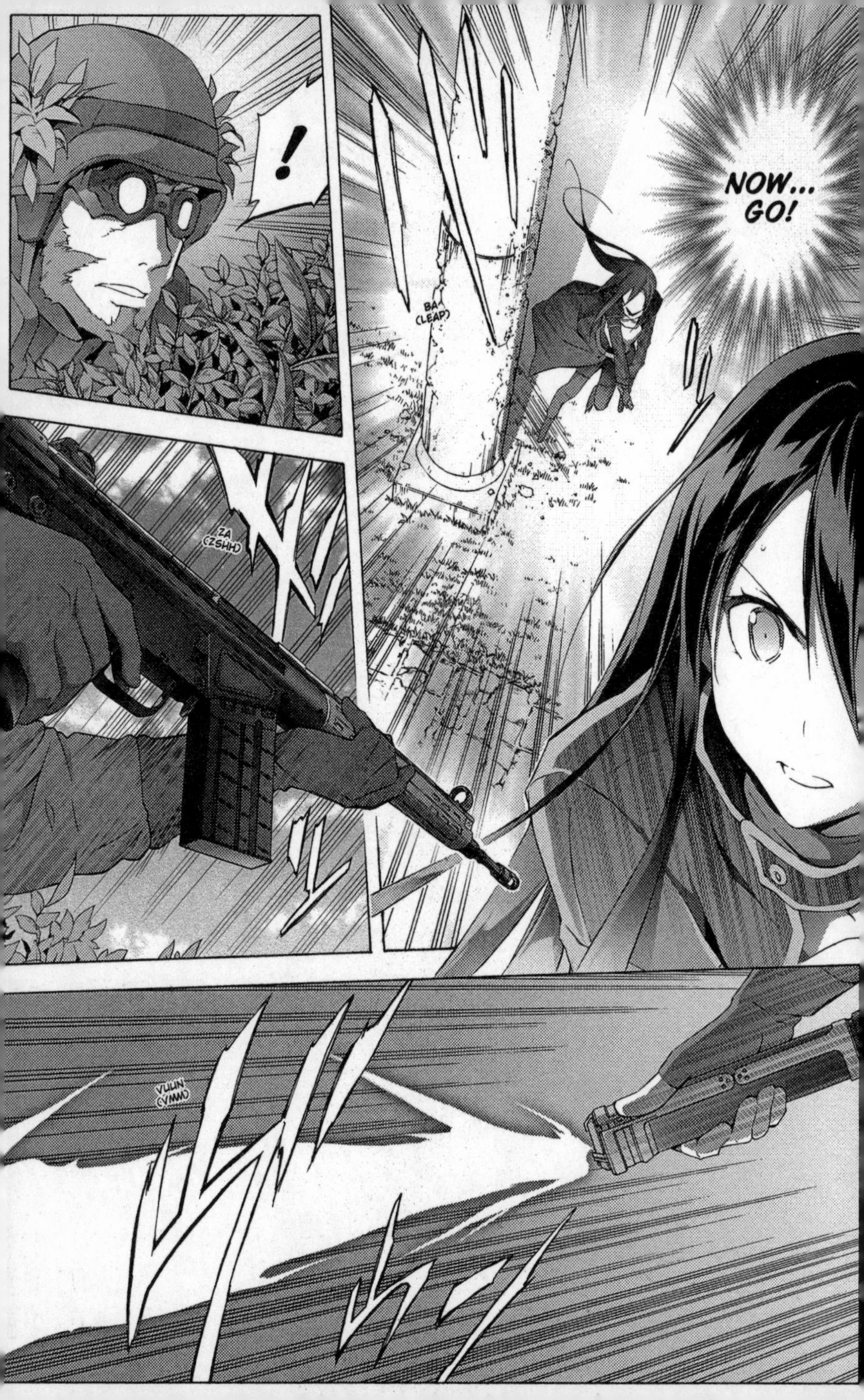
NOW... GO!
BA (LEAP)
!
ZA (ZSHH)
VUUN (VMM)

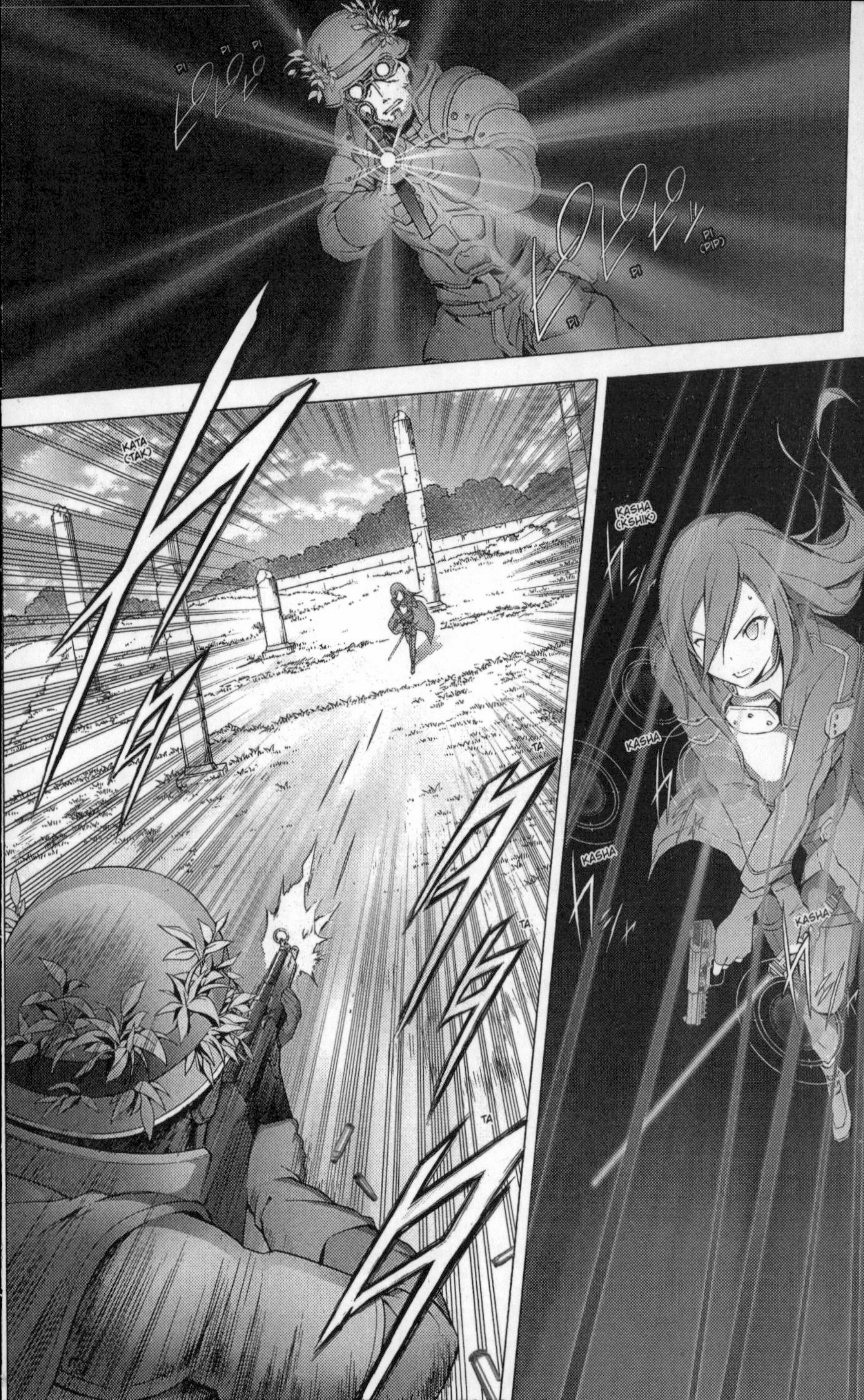
PI
PI
PI
PI
(PIP)
PI
PI
KASHA
(KSHIK)
KASHA
KASHA
KASHA
KATA
(TAK)
TA
TA
TA

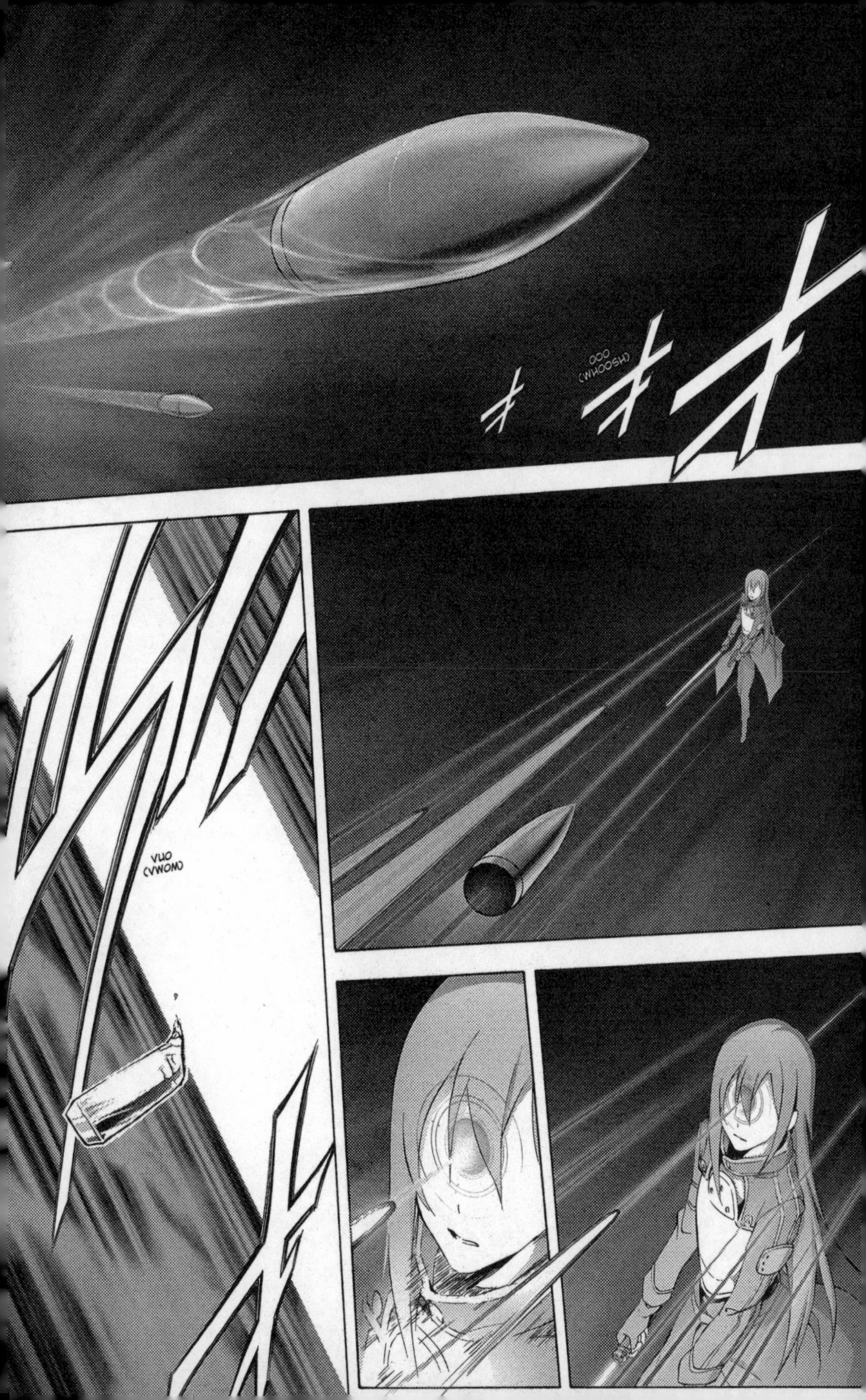
OOO
(WHOOSH)
VUO
(VWOM)

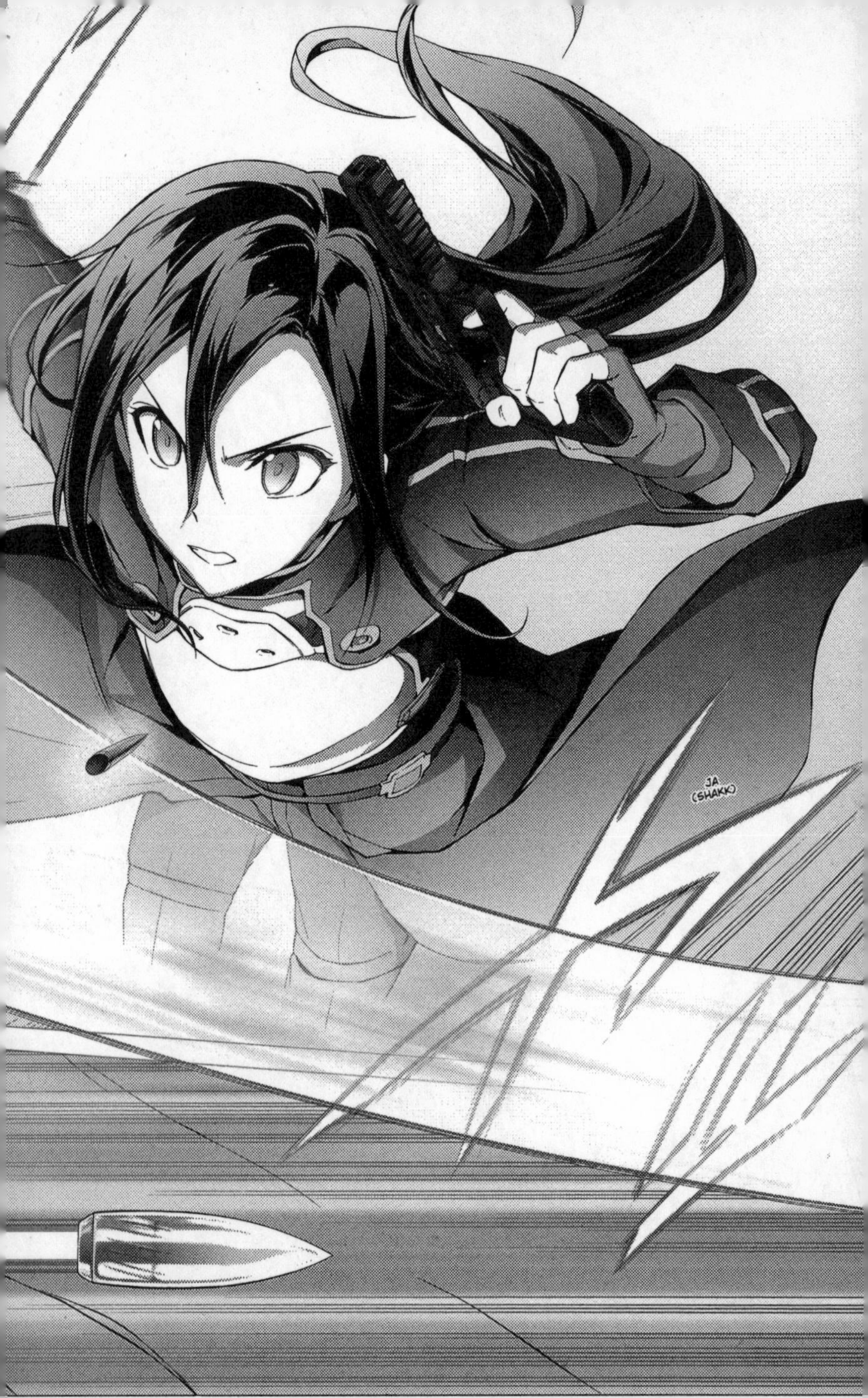
JA
(SHAKK)

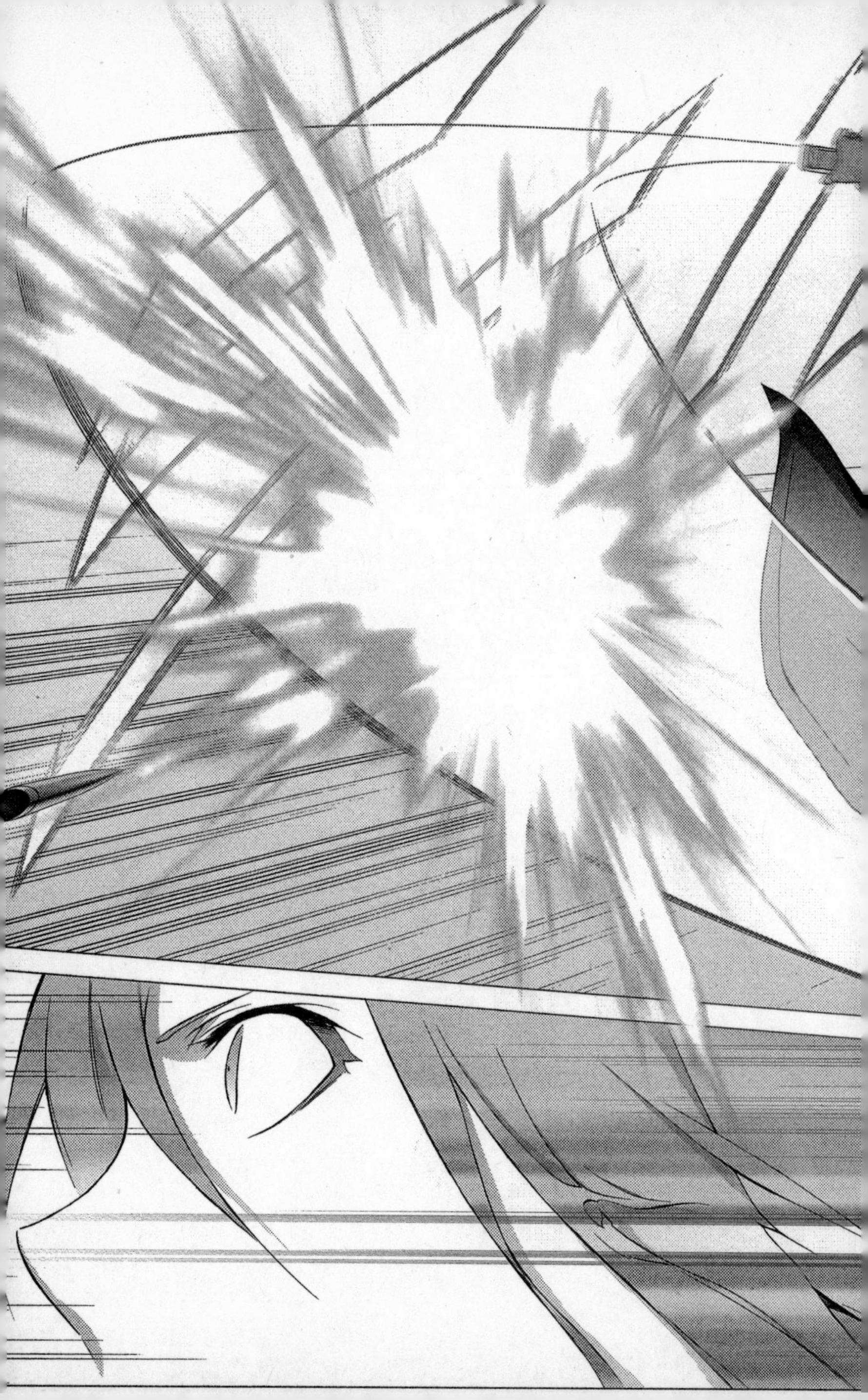

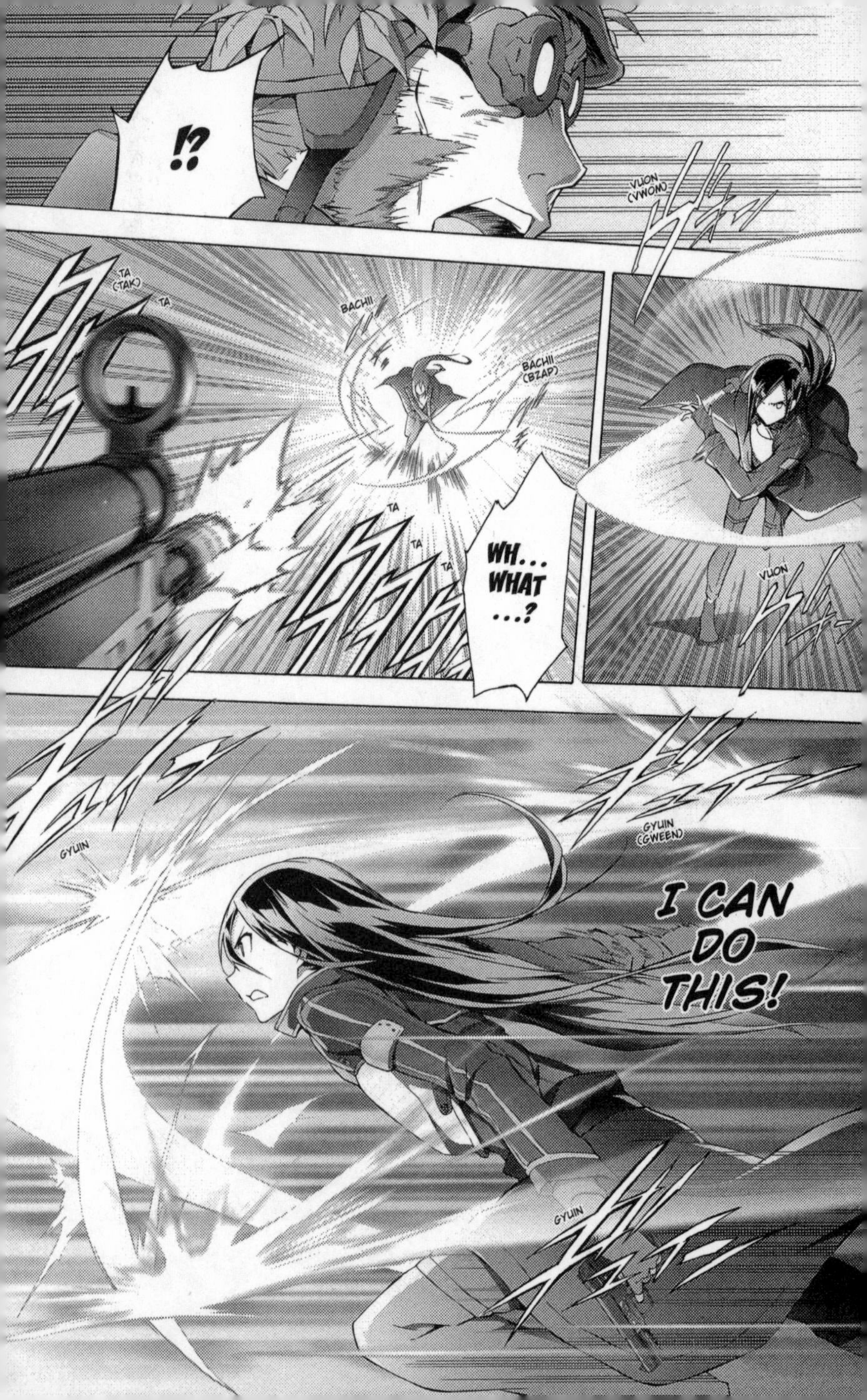
!?
VUON (VWOM)
VUON
BACHII (BZAP)
BACHII
TA (TAK)
TA
TA
TA
TA
WH... WHAT...?
GYUIN (GWEEN)
I CAN DO THIS!
GYUIN
GYUIN

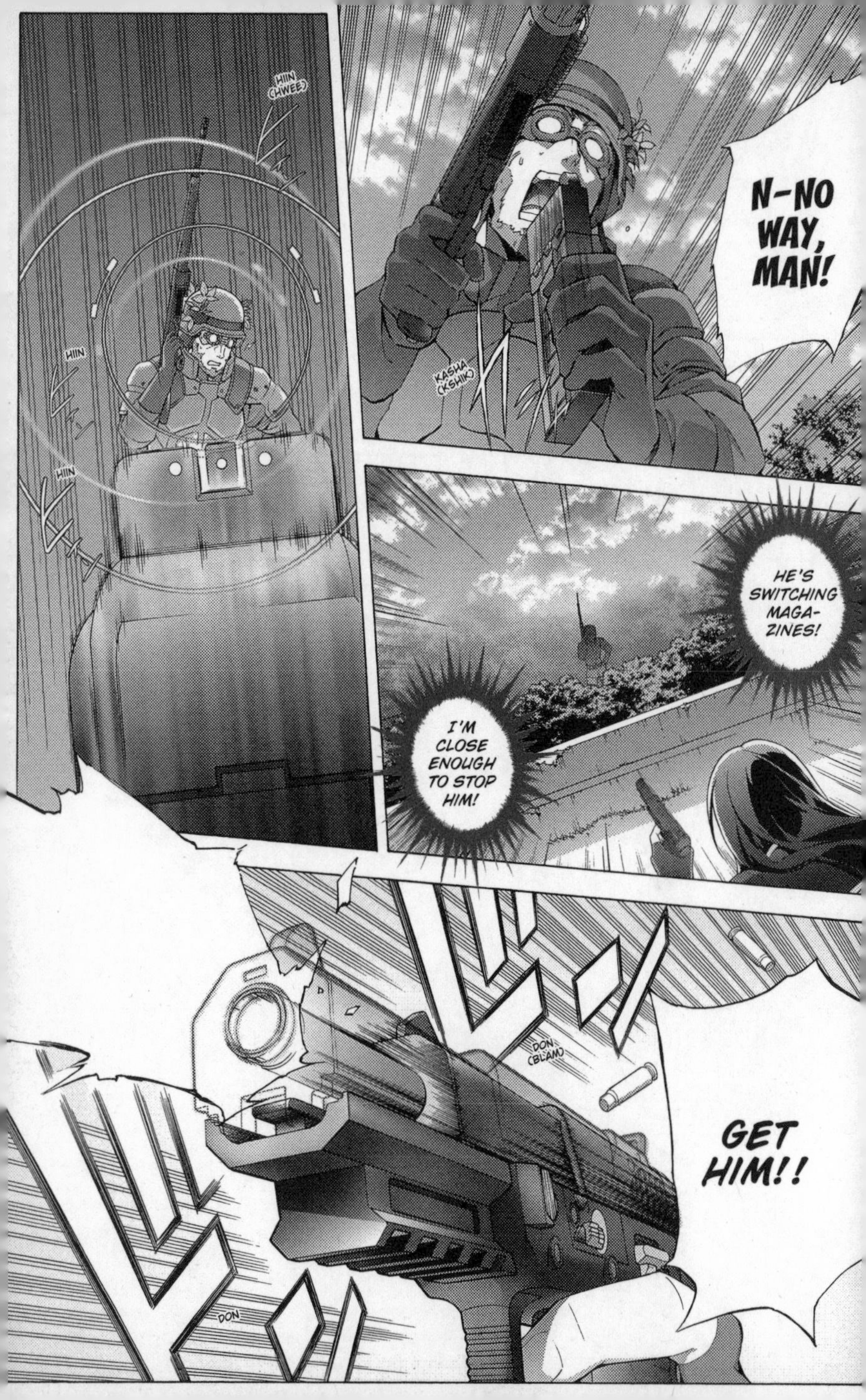
N-NO WAY, MAN!
KASHA (KSHIK)
HE'S SWITCHING MAGA-ZINES!
I'M CLOSE ENOUGH TO STOP HIM!
HIIN (HWEE)
HIIN
HIIN
GET HIM!!
DON (BLAM)
DON

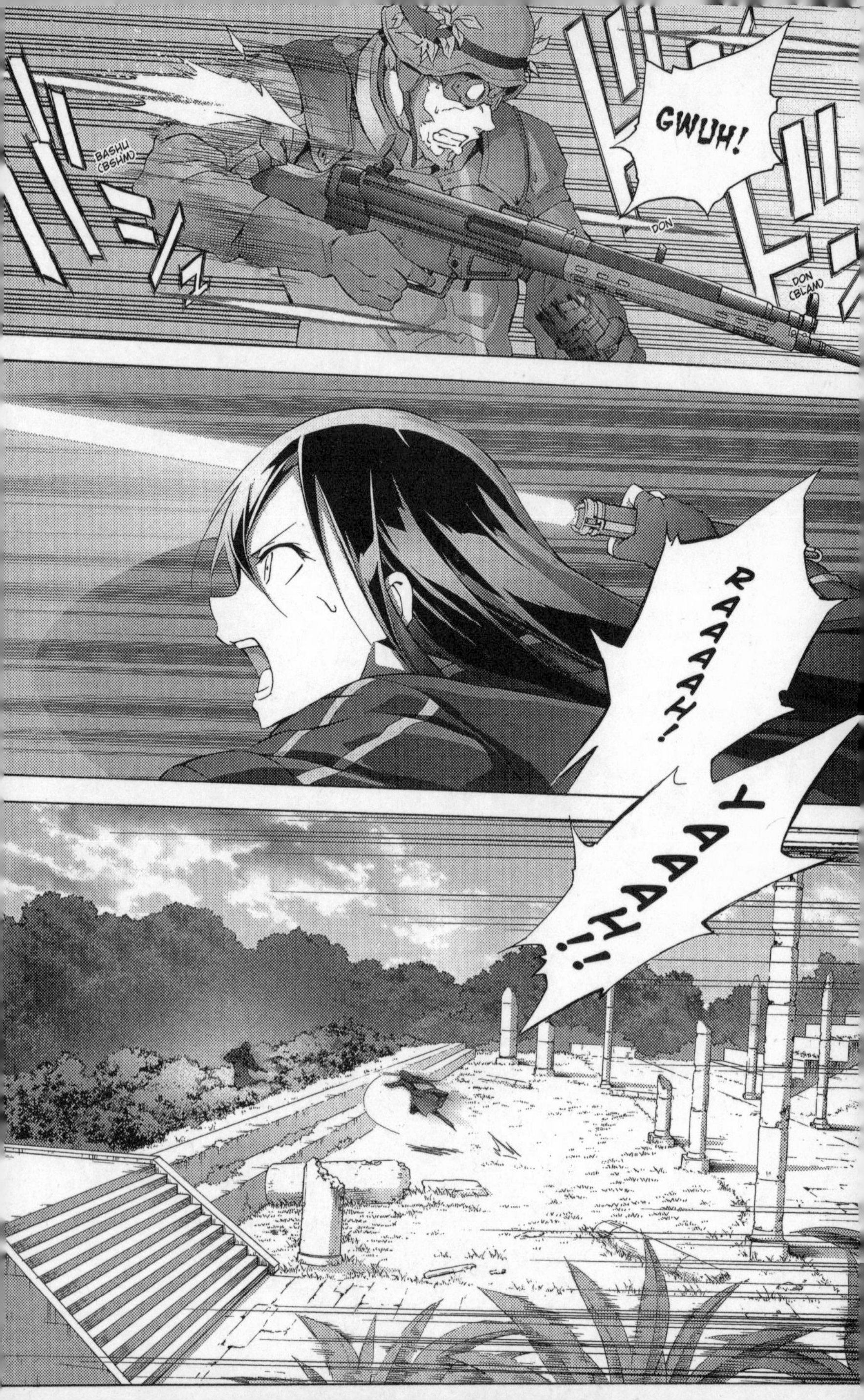
GWUH!
DON
DON (BLAM)
BASHU (BSHM)
RAAAAH!
YAAAH!!

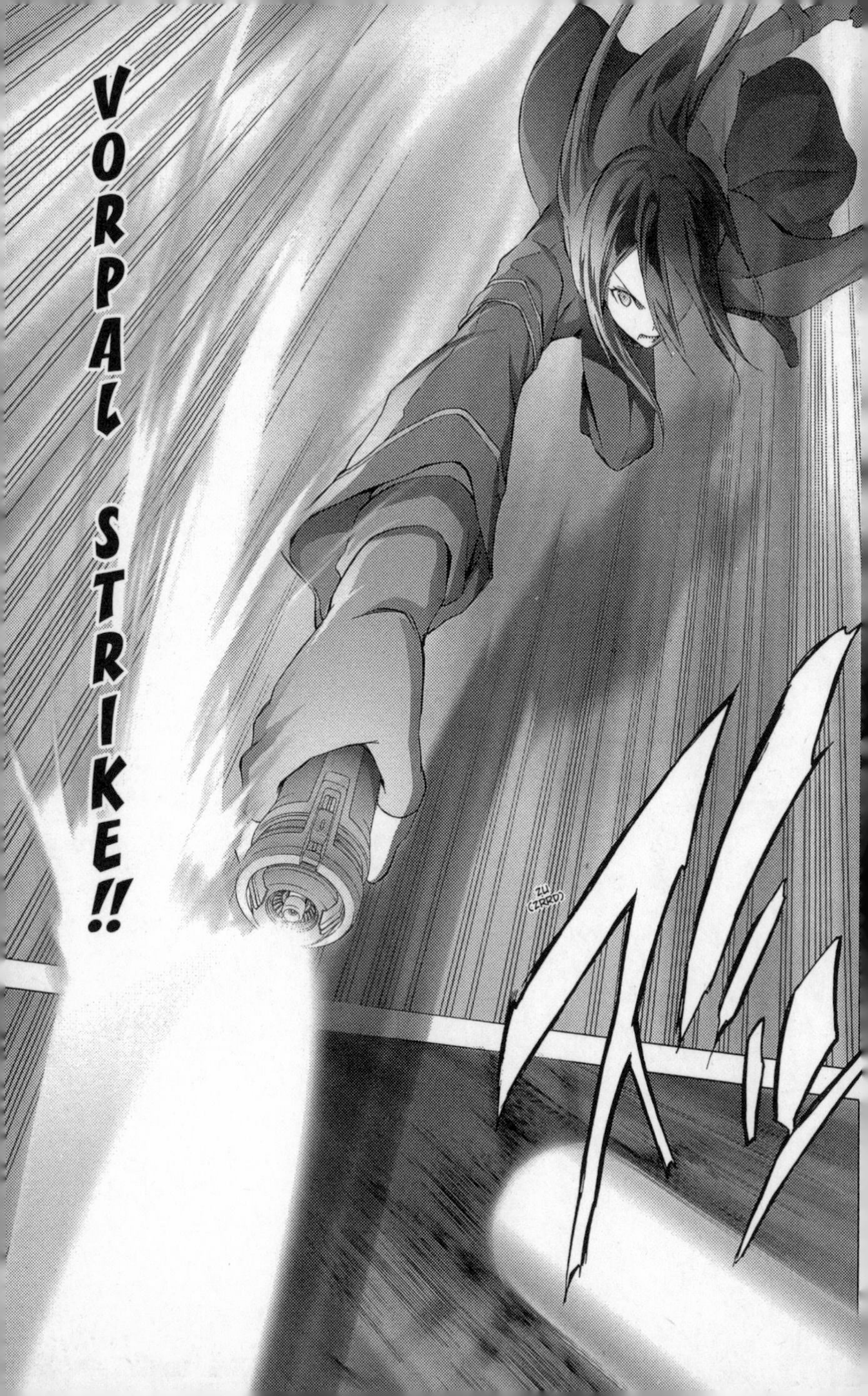
VORPAL STRIKE!!
ZU
(ZRRD)

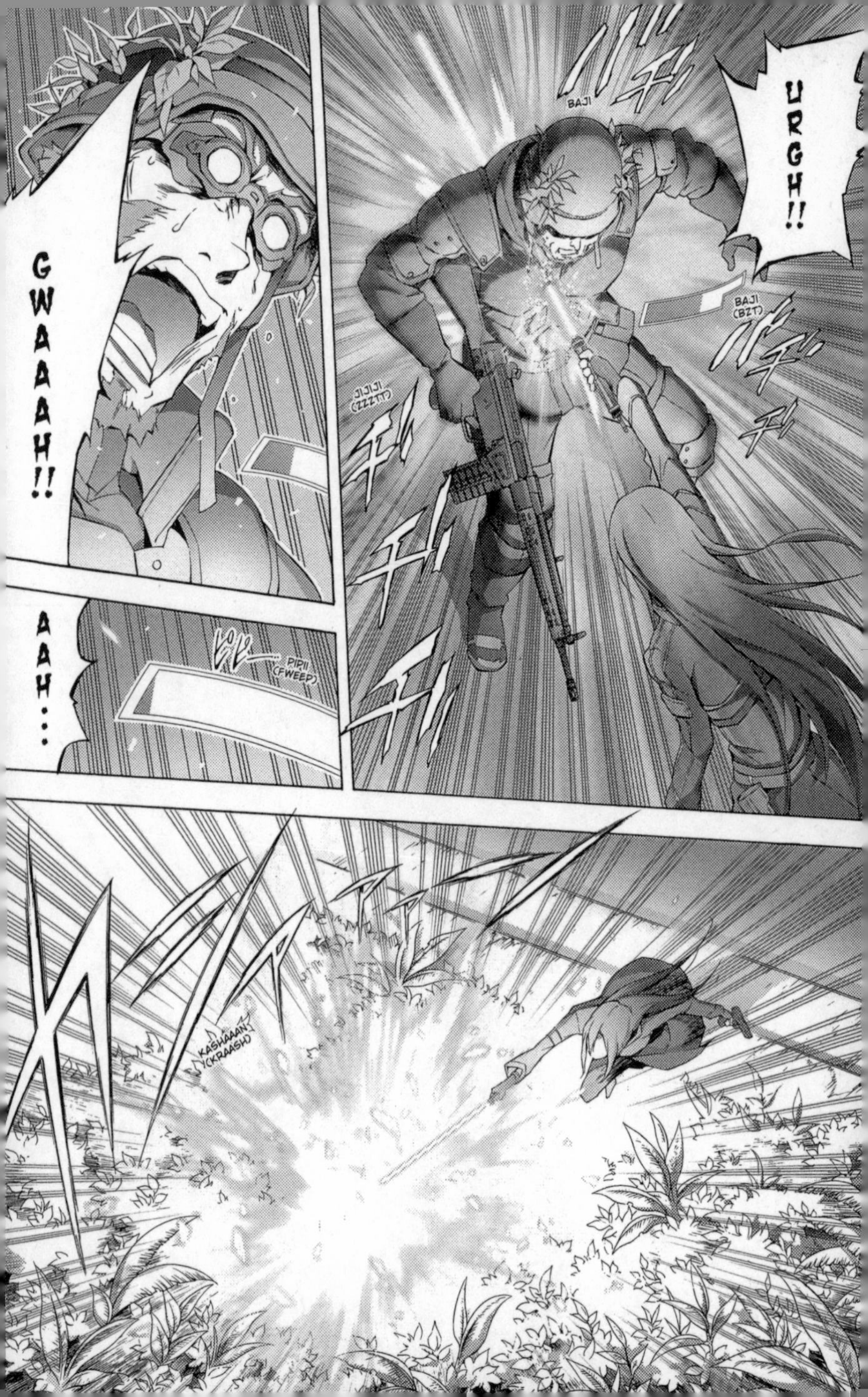
URGH!!
BAJI
BAJI (BZT)
JIJIJI (ZZZTT)
GWAAAAH!!
AAAH...
PIPII (FWEEP)
KASHAAAN (KRAASH)

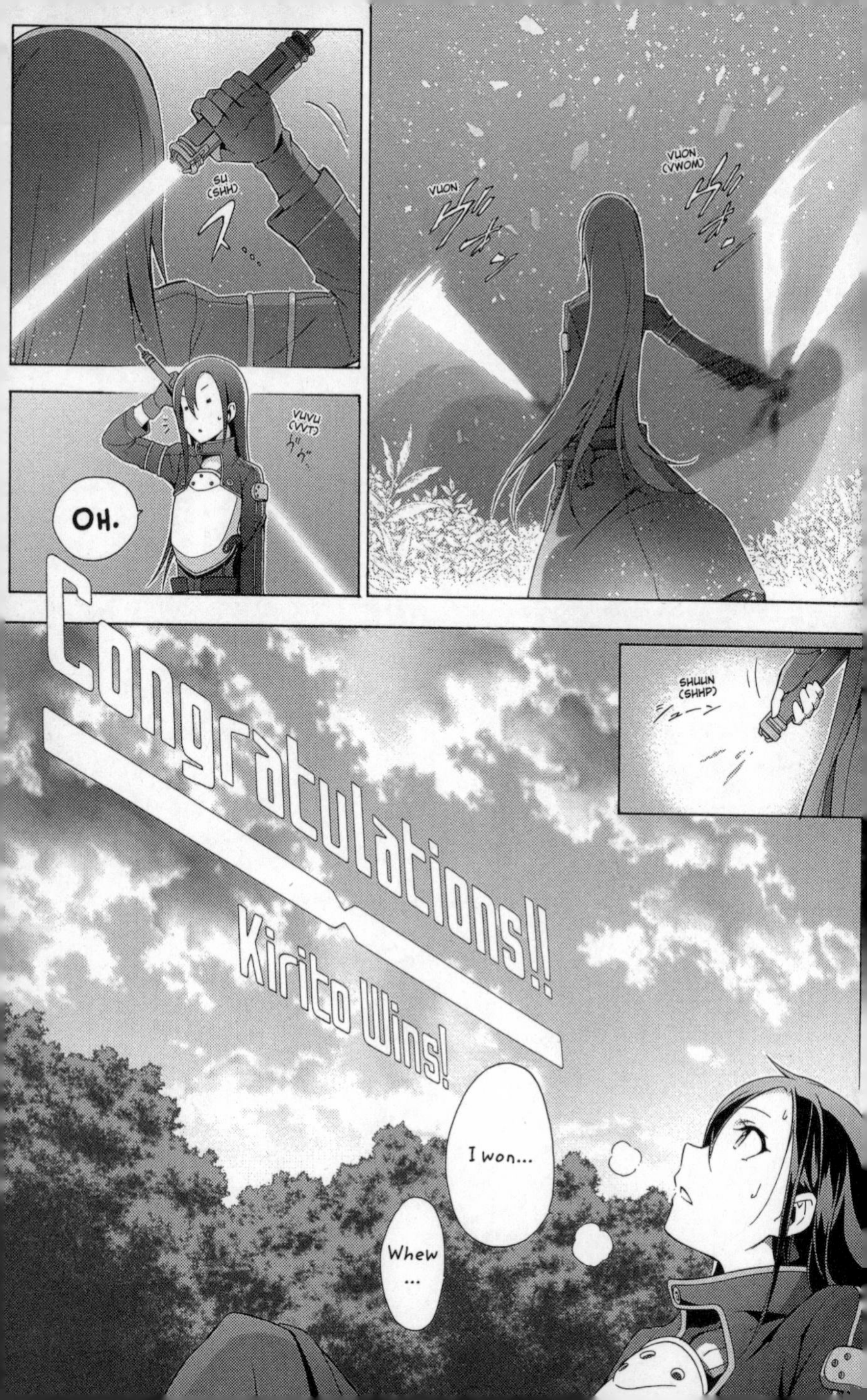

VUON
VUON
(VWOM)
SU
(SHH)
VUVU
(VVT)
OH.
SHUUN
(SHHP)
Congratulations!!
Kirito Wins!
I won...
Whew
...

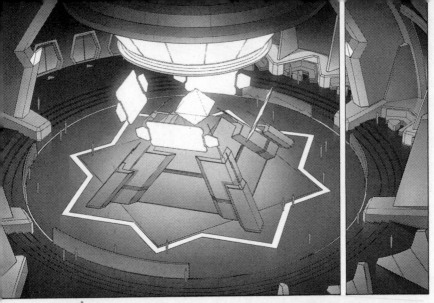

BLLIN CVMMMO

OH.

I'M BACK.

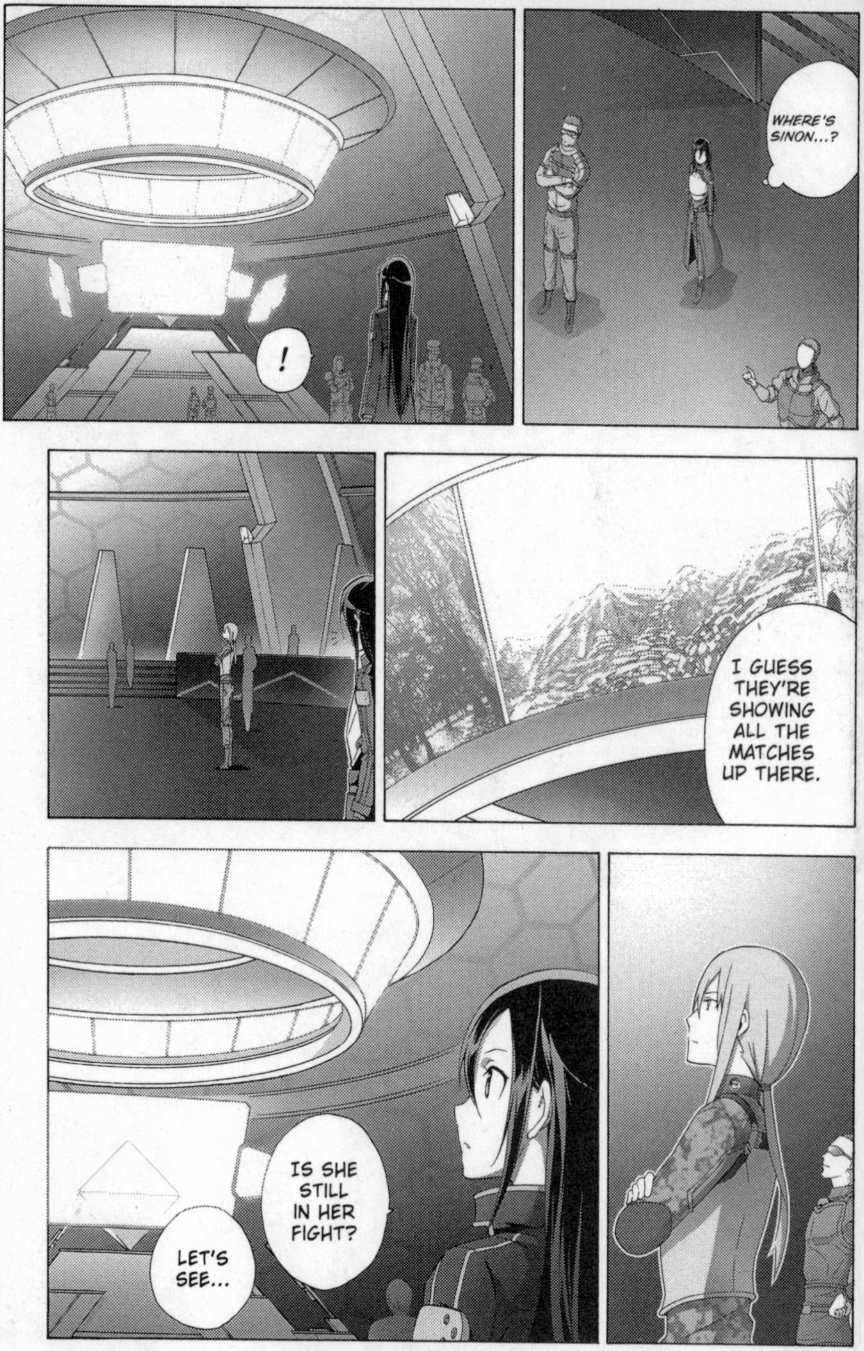
WHERE'S SINON...?
!
I GUESS THEY'RE SHOWING ALL THE MATCHES UP THERE.
IS SHE STILL IN HER FIGHT?
LET'S SEE...

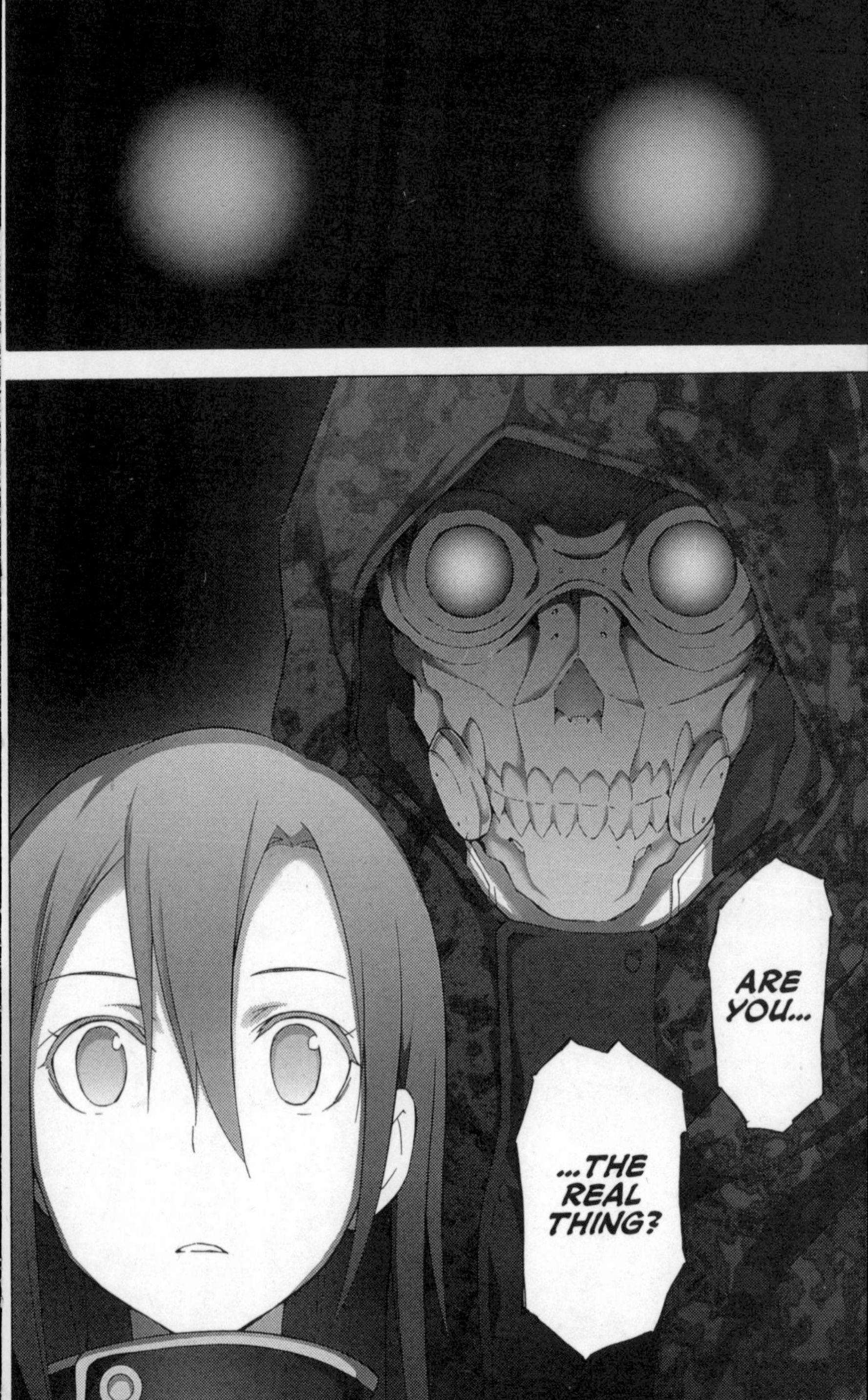
ARE YOU...
...THE REAL THING?

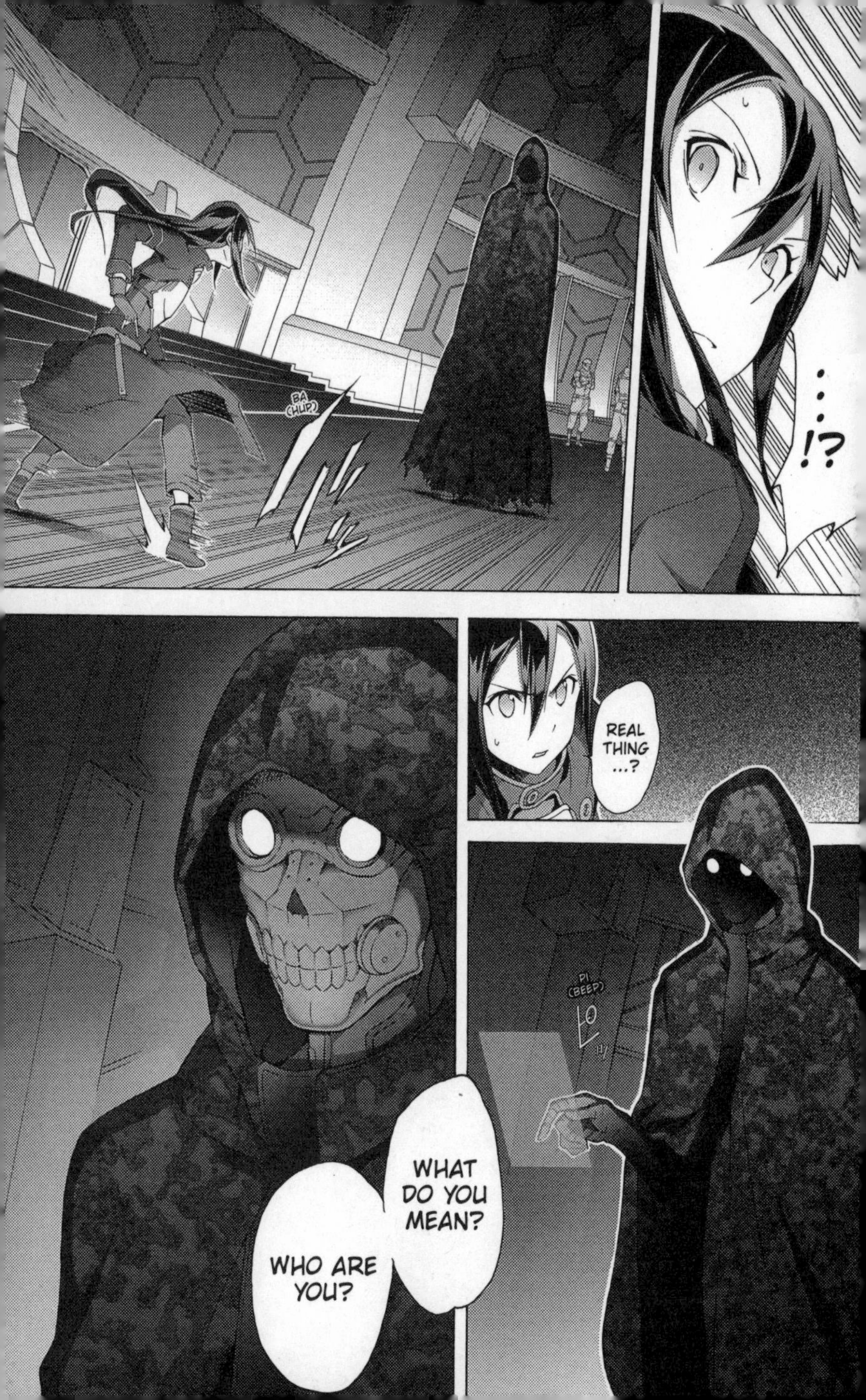
...!?
BA (HUP)
REAL THING ...?
PI (BEEP)
WHAT DO YOU MEAN?
WHO ARE YOU?

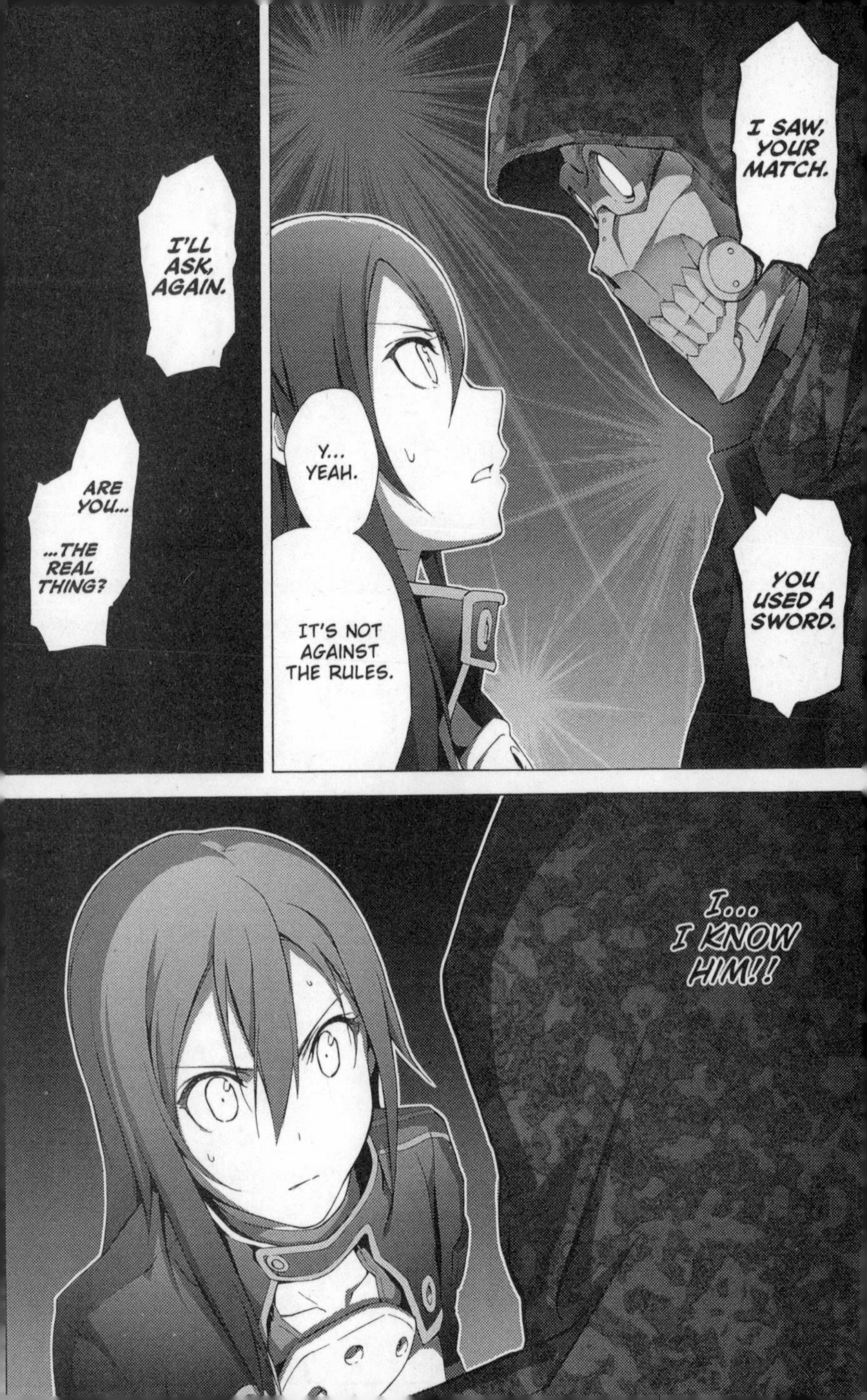
I SAW, YOUR MATCH.
YOU USED A SWORD.
Y... YEAH.
IT'S NOT AGAINST THE RULES.
I'LL ASK, AGAIN.
ARE YOU...
...THE REAL THING?
I... I KNOW HIM!!

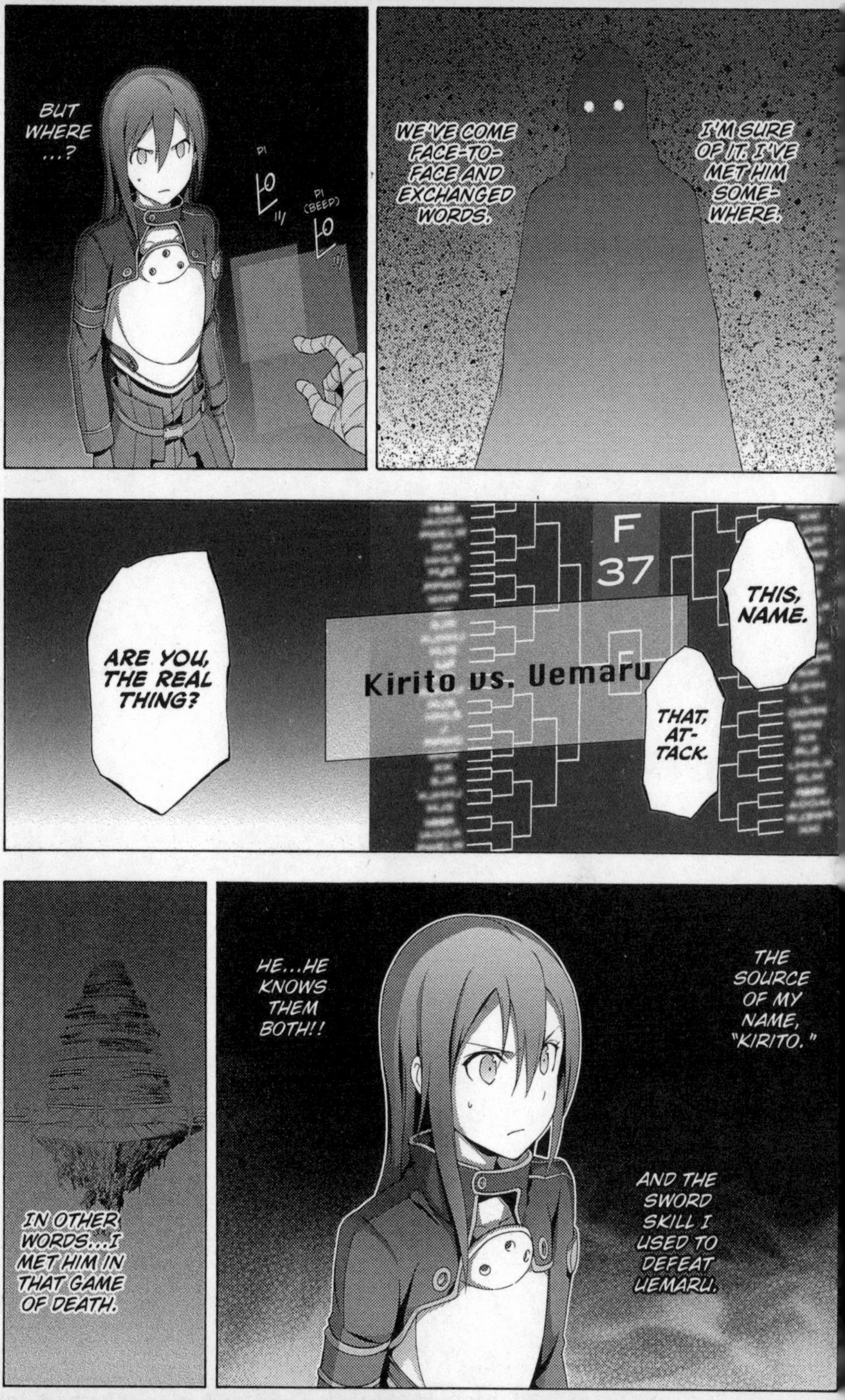
I'M SURE OF IT. I'VE MET HIM SOME-WHERE.
WE'VE COME FACE-TO-FACE AND EXCHANGED WORDS.
BUT WHERE ...?
PI
PI (BEEP)
F
37
THIS, NAME.
THAT, AT-TACK.
Kirito vs. Uemaru
ARE YOU, THE REAL THING?
THE SOURCE OF MY NAME, "KIRITO."
HE...HE KNOWS THEM BOTH!!
AND THE SWORD SKILL I USED TO DEFEAT UEMARU.
IN OTHER WORDS...I MET HIM IN THAT GAME OF DEATH.

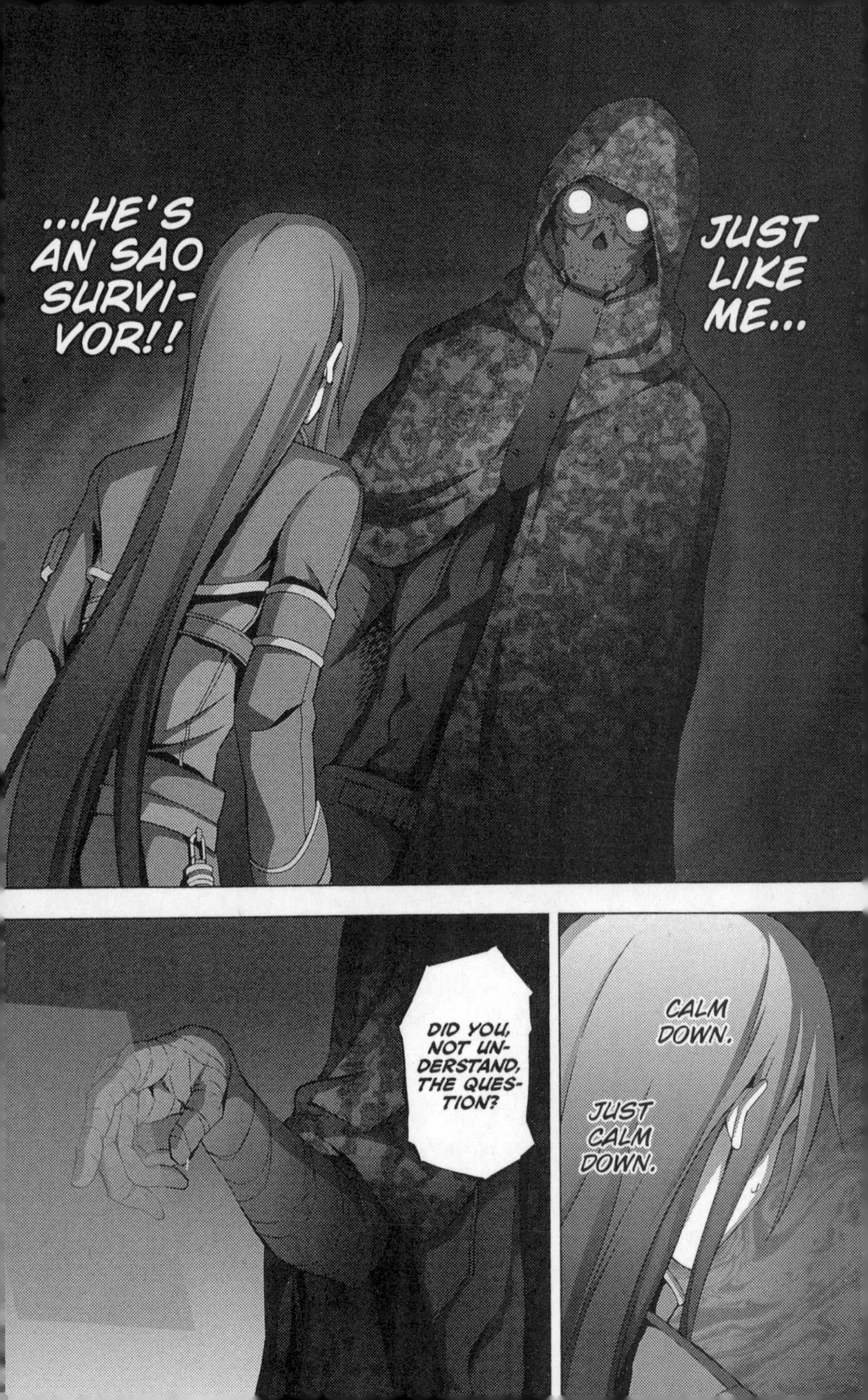
...HE'S AN SAO SURVIVOR!!
JUST LIKE ME...
CALM DOWN.
JUST CALM DOWN.
DID YOU, NOT UNDERSTAND, THE QUESTION?

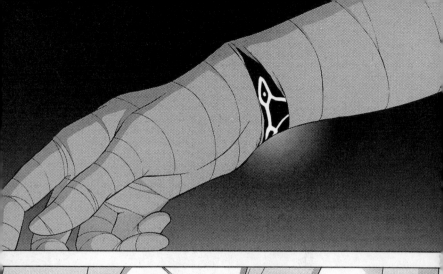

I DON'T UNDER- STAND.

WHAT DO YOU MEAN, THE REAL THING?

...

...

... YES.

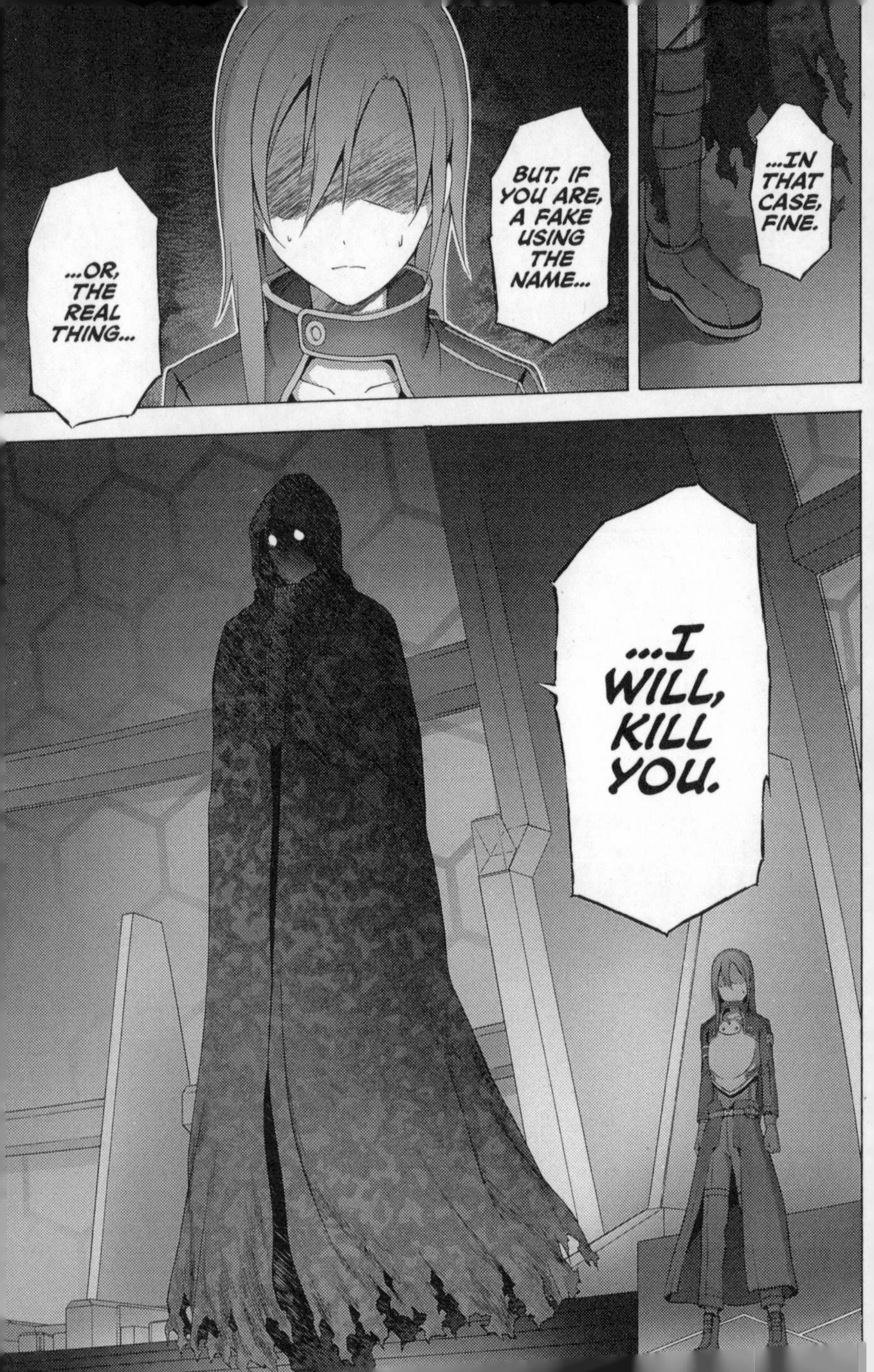
...IN THAT CASE, FINE.
BUT, IF YOU ARE, A FAKE USING THE NAME...
...OR, THE REAL THING...
...I WILL, KILL YOU.

SWORD ART ONLINE
phantom bullet

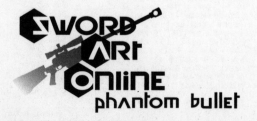

SWORD ART ONLINE
phantom bullet

check point! 003

THE REAL WORLD AND GGO: WORLD

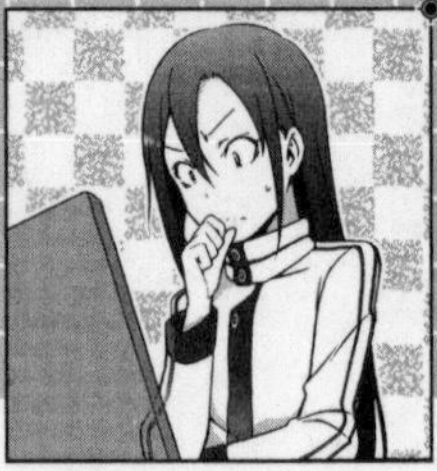

KIRITO WAS SURPRISED TO FIND THAT HE NEEDED TO ENTER PERSONAL INFORMATION TO REGISTER FOR THE BOB. ONE OF GGO'S SPECIAL FEATURES IS A SYSTEM THAT CONVERTS IN-GAME CURRENCY TO REAL-WORLD CASH, WHICH EXISTS IN A LEGAL GRAY AREA. THEREFORE, EVERYTHING THAT WOULD NORMALLY BE HANDLED OUT OF GAME, LIKE TOURNAMENT OR ACCOUNT REGISTRATION AND CASHING OUT CURRENCY, IS MANAGED THROUGH THE SECURITY OF THE GAME ITSELF. SINON CLAIMS THIS HELPS HER DIFFERENTIATE IT FROM THE REAL WORLD, BUT AS A LONGTIME GAMER, KIRITO WAS SURPRISED TO SEE HOW EXTREME THEIR BUSINESS CONFIGURATION IS.

PHOTON SWORD: ITEM

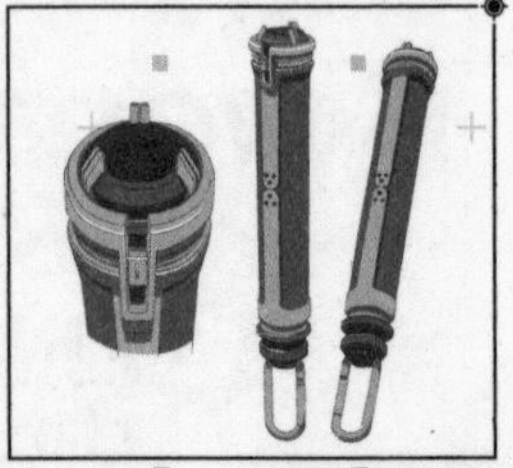

A CLOSE-COMBAT ENERGY BLADE THAT KIRITO BOUGHT ALONG WITH THE FIVE-SEVEN. ITS OFFICIAL TITLE IS A KAGEMITSU G4. IT HAS INCREDIBLE SEVERING POWER, BUT IT HAS A NATURAL DISADVANTAGE IN A WORLD OF GUNS. IT LOOKS LIKE A WEAPON STRAIGHT OUT OF A SCI-FI MOVIE OR A ROBOT ANIME, BUT UNLIKE THOSE EXAMPLES, THIS ONE HAS NO PHYSICAL FORM AT ALL. BECAUSE THERE'S NO WEIGHT, THERE IS NO AIR RESISTANCE WHEN SWINGING A PHOTON SWORD, AND CLASHING TO THE HILT IS ESSENTIALLY IMPOSSIBLE. THIS CRUCIAL DISTINCTION WILL ACTUALLY TRIP KIRITO UP IN A LATER FIGHT...

COURTESY OF: A-1 PICTURES

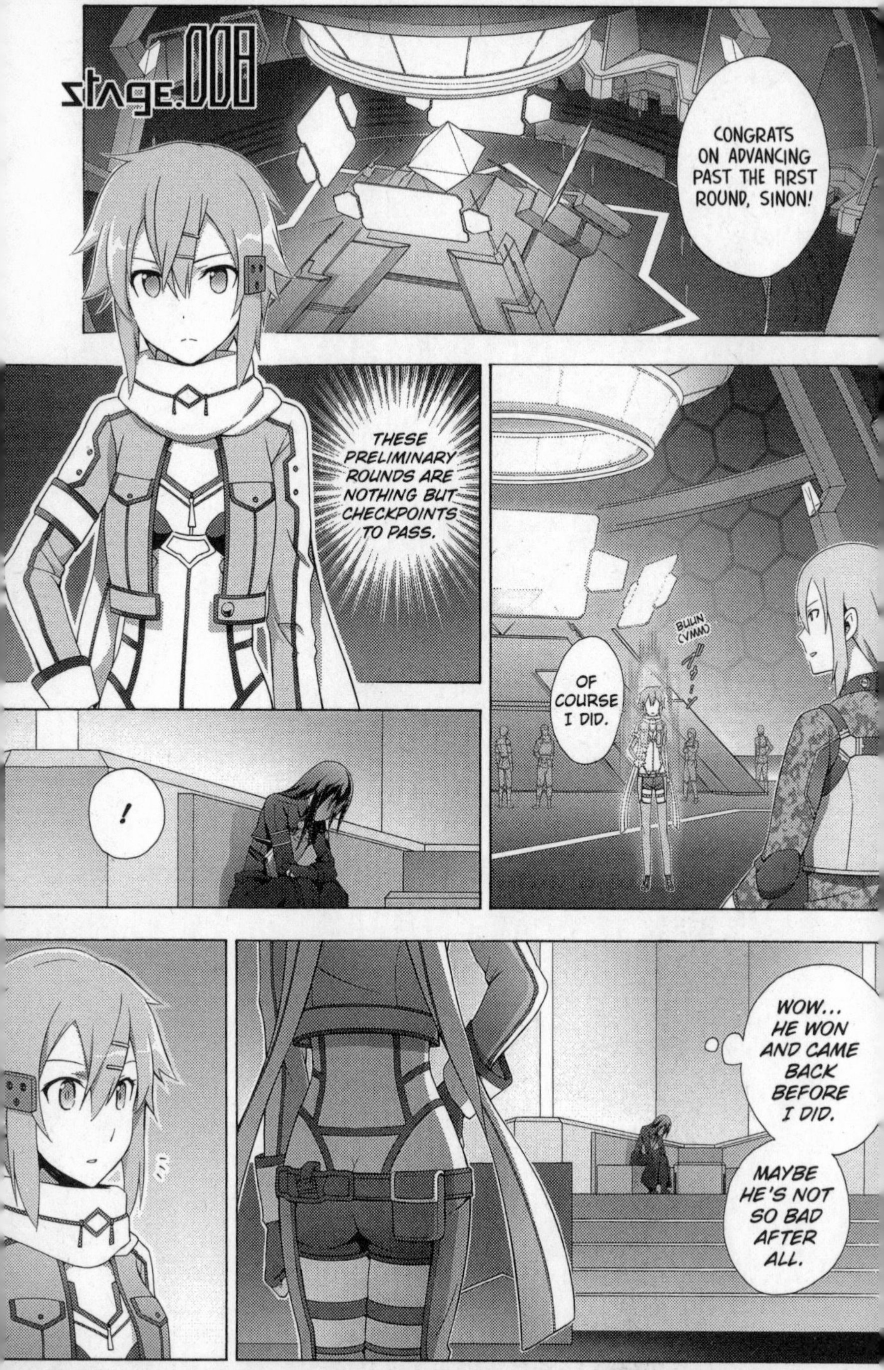
stage.008
CONGRATS ON ADVANCING PAST THE FIRST ROUND, SINON!
BULUN (VMM)
OF COURSE I DID.
THESE PRELIMINARY ROUNDS ARE NOTHING BUT CHECKPOINTS TO PASS.
!
WOW... HE WON AND CAME BACK BEFORE I DID.
MAYBE HE'S NOT SO BAD AFTER ALL.

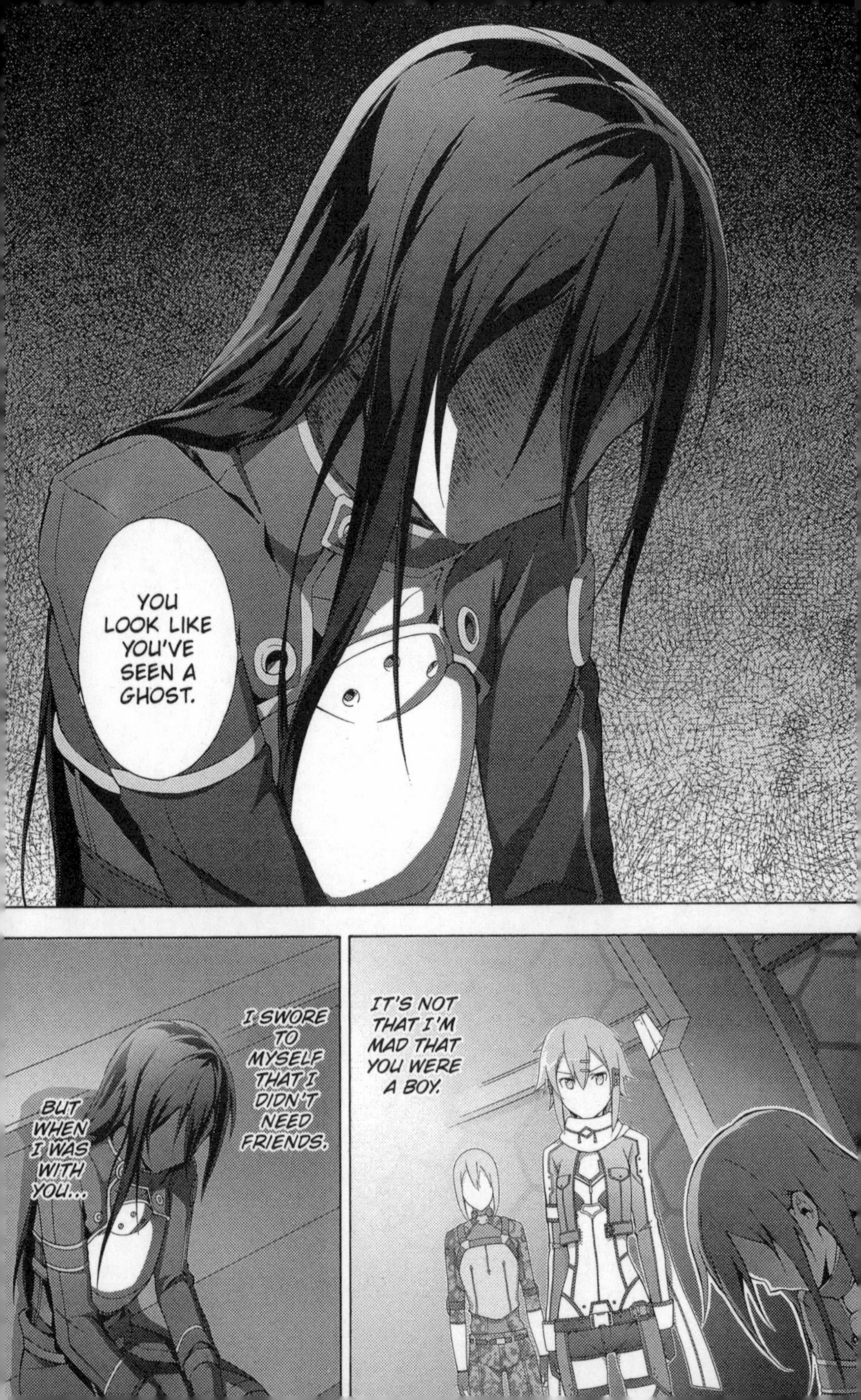
YOU LOOK LIKE YOU'VE SEEN A GHOST.
IT'S NOT THAT I'M MAD THAT YOU WERE A BOY.
I SWORE TO MYSELF THAT I DIDN'T NEED FRIENDS.
BUT WHEN I WAS WITH YOU...

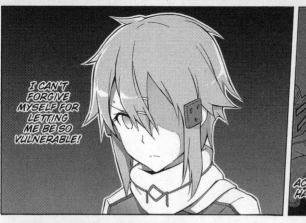

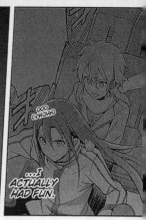

OOO (VWOHH)
...I ACTUALLY HAD FUN.
I CAN'T FORGIVE MYSELF FOR LETTING ME BE SO VULNERABLE!
SO FACING YOU IN THE FINAL AND BLOWING APART YOUR CUTE LITTLE AVATAR WITH MY HECATE...
...WILL PROVE THAT I'M STRONGER THAN WHEN I MET YOU.
GUGU (CLENCH)
I WAS LOOKING FORWARD TO THAT. BUT NOW...
YOU'RE NEVER GOING TO MAKE IT TO THE FINAL IF THAT'S HOW YOU FEEL AFTER ONE FIGHT.
DON (THUD)
GET IT TOGETHER...
SU (SHH)

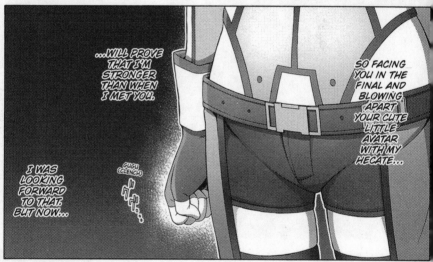

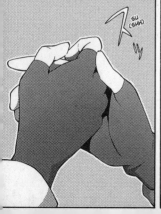

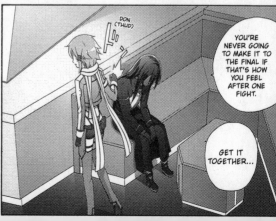

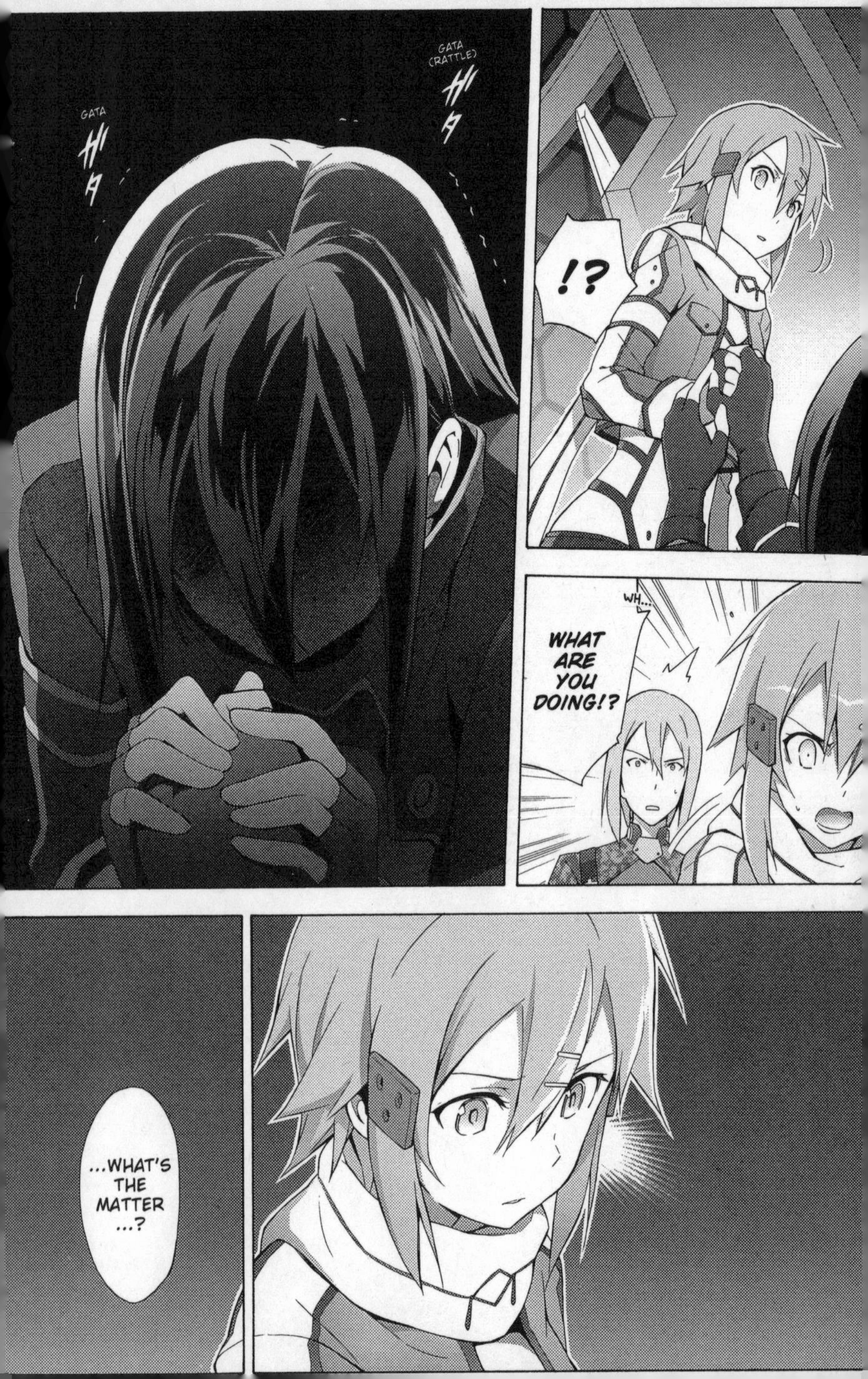
!?
WH...
WHAT ARE YOU DOING!?
GATA (RATTLE)
GATA
...WHAT'S THE MATTER ...?

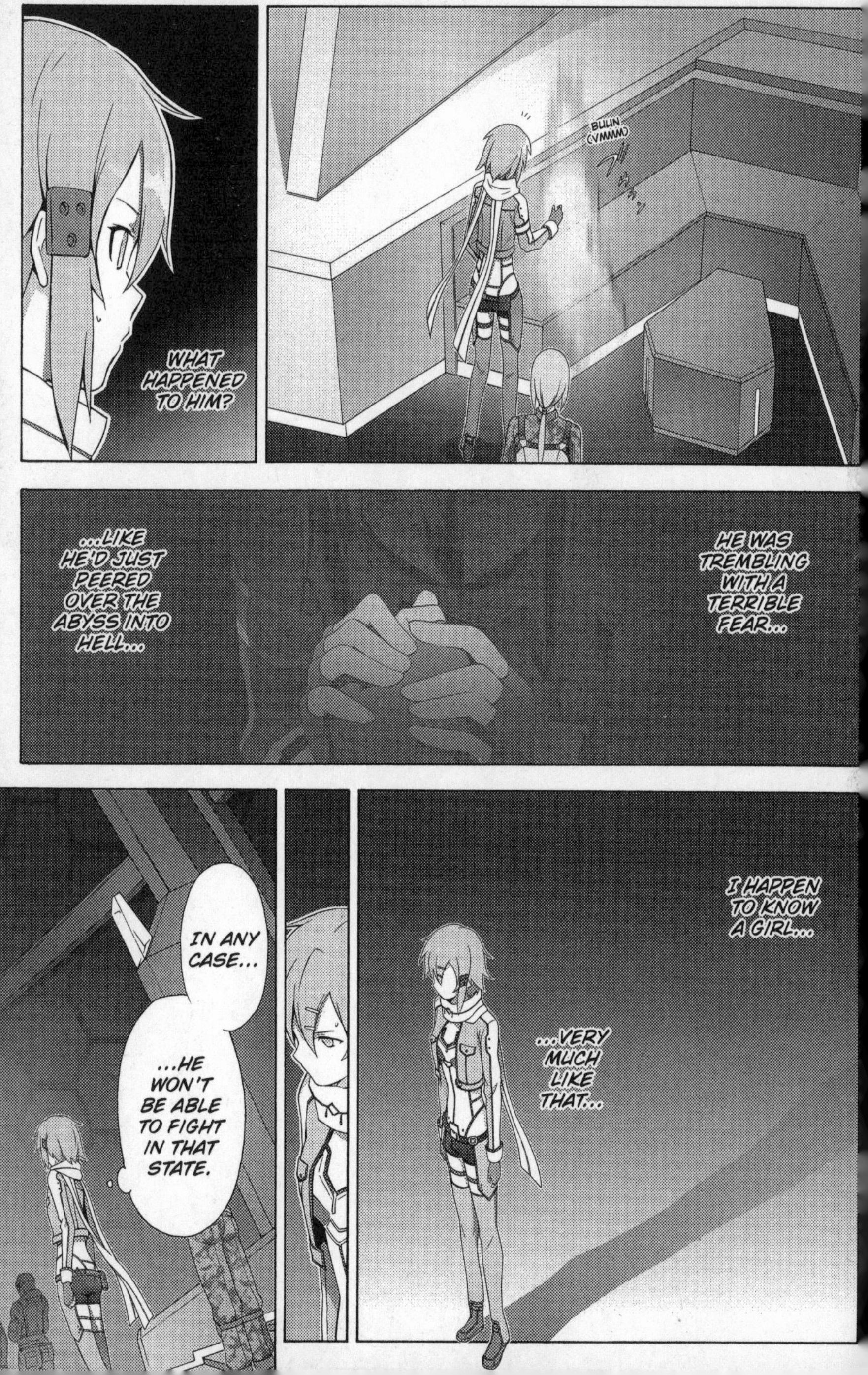
BULUN (VMMM)
WHAT HAPPENED TO HIM?
HE WAS TREMBLING WITH A TERRIBLE FEAR...
...LIKE HE'D JUST PEERED OVER THE ABYSS INTO HELL...
I HAPPEN TO KNOW A GIRL...
...VERY MUCH LIKE THAT...
IN ANY CASE...
...HE WON'T BE ABLE TO FIGHT IN THAT STATE.

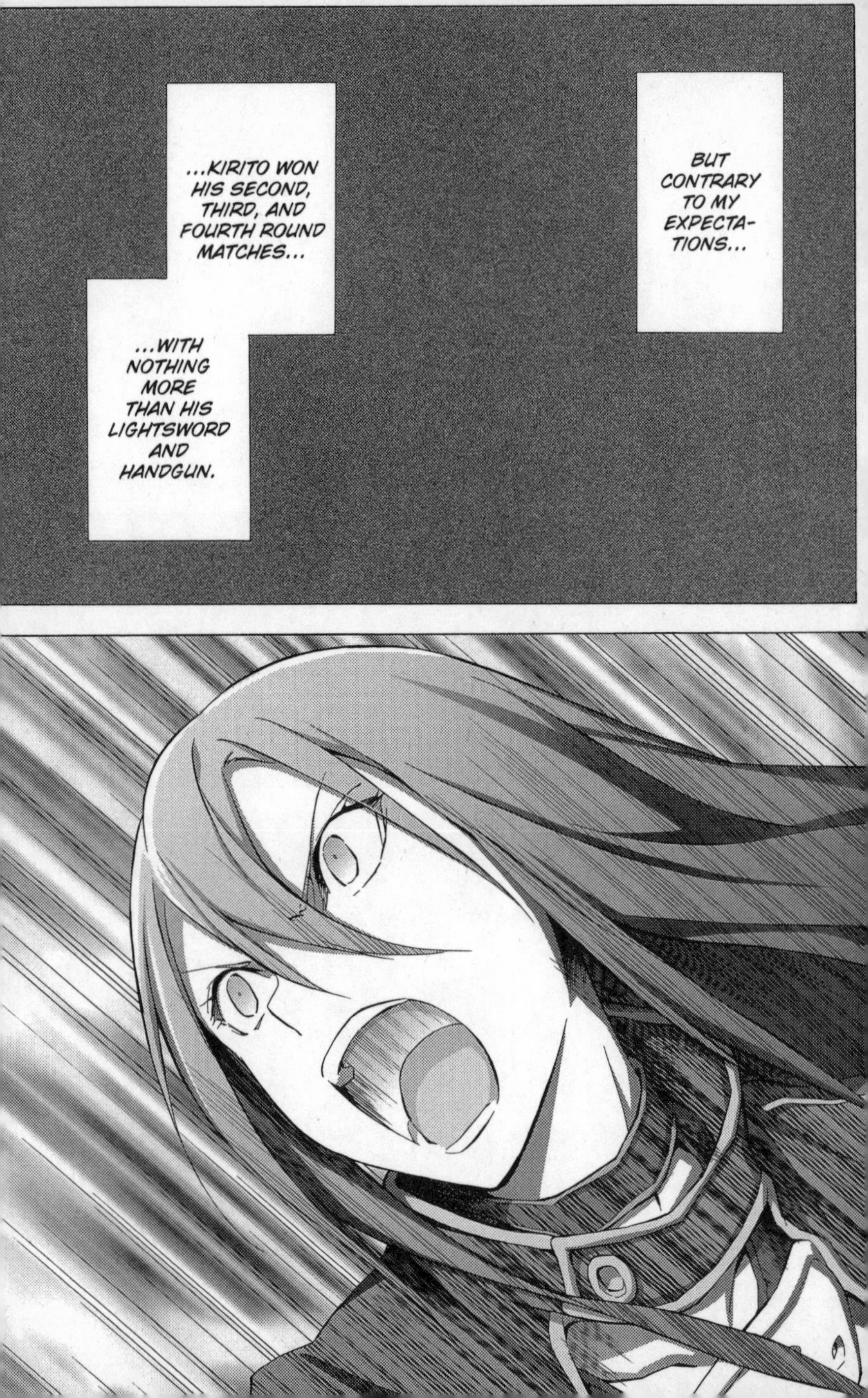
BUT CONTRARY TO MY EXPECTATIONS...
...KIRITO WON HIS SECOND, THIRD, AND FOURTH ROUND MATCHES...
...WITH NOTHING MORE THAN HIS LIGHTSWORD AND HANDGUN.

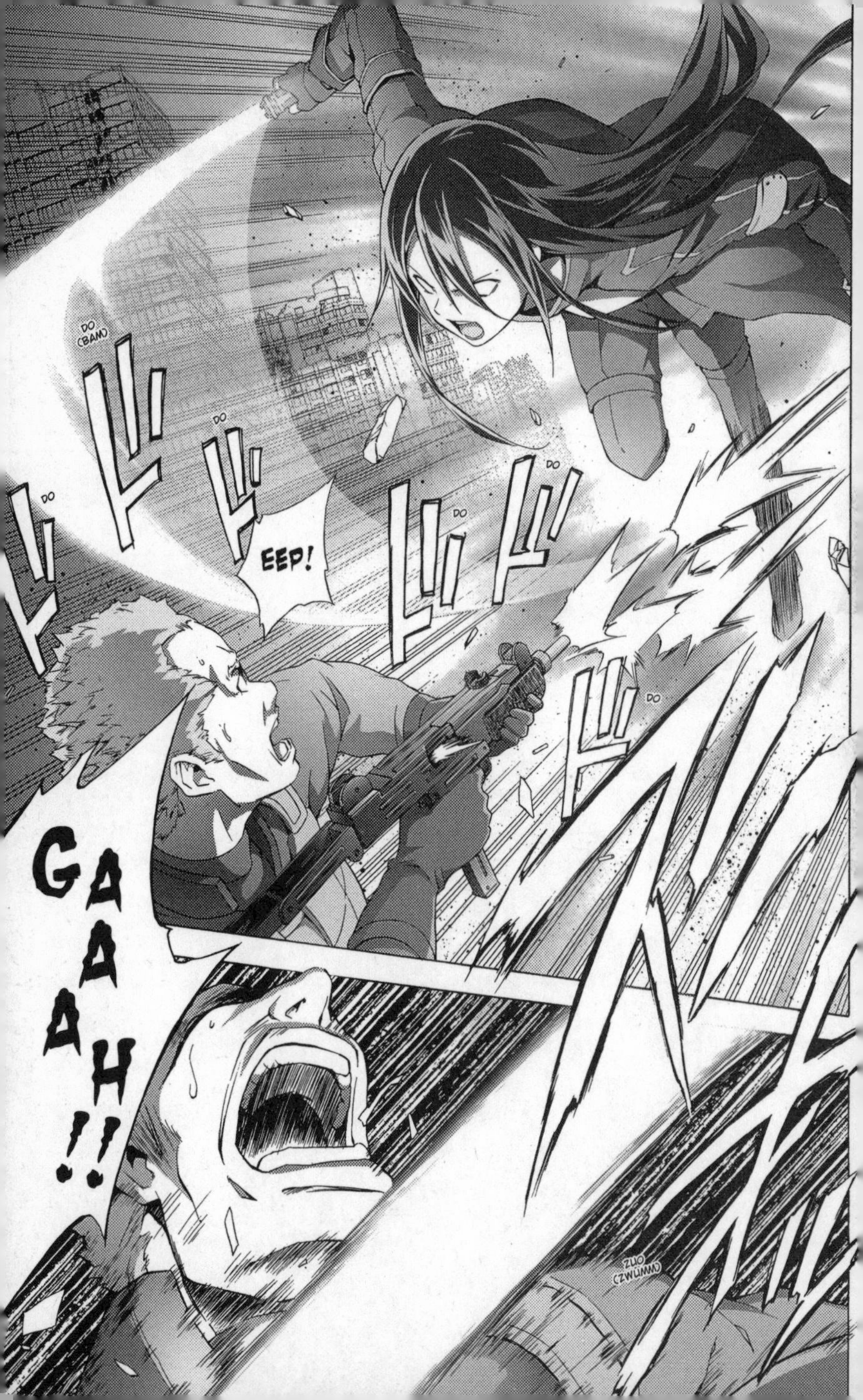
DO (BAM)
DO
DO
DO
DO
EEP!
DO
GAAAH!!
ZUO (ZWUMM)

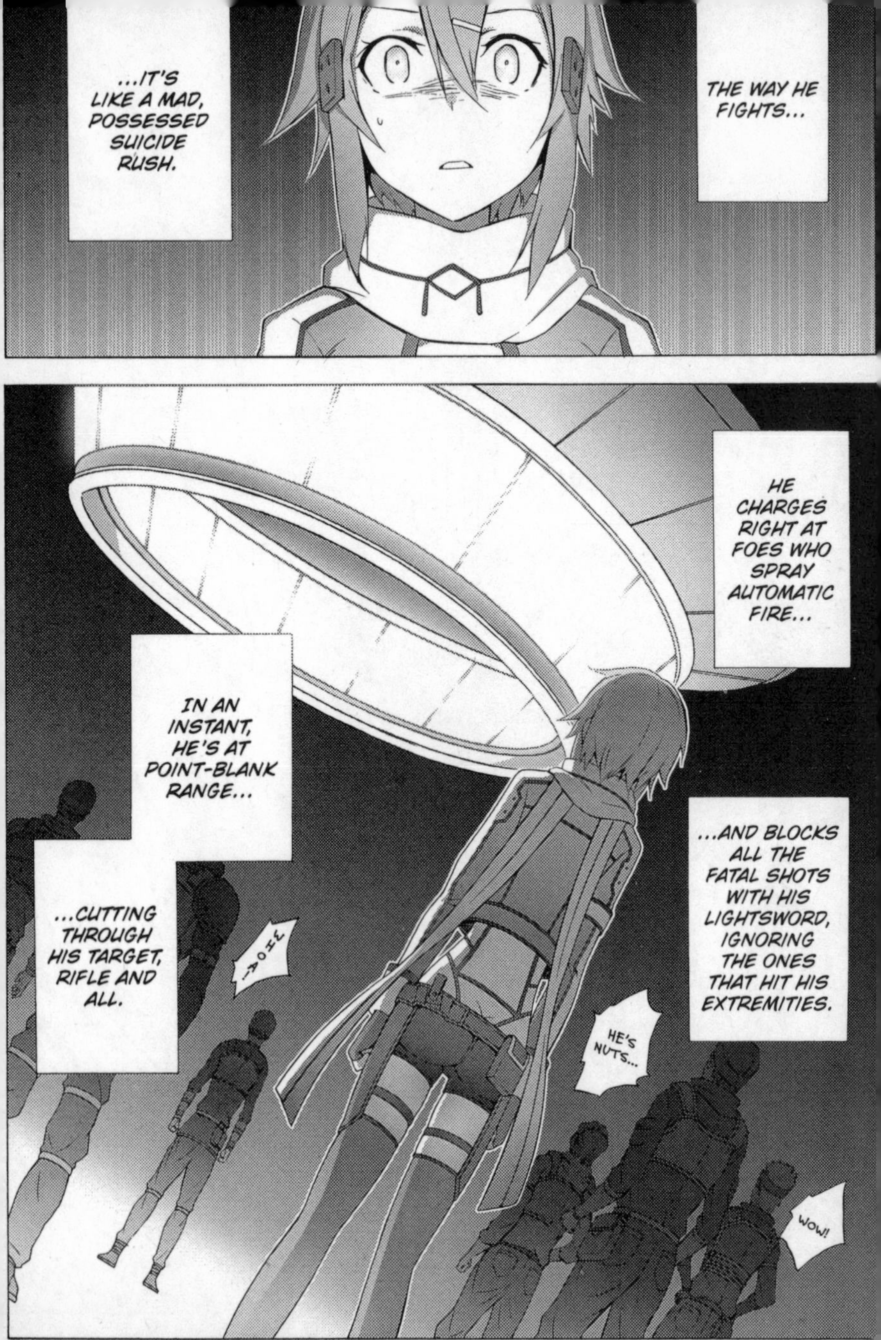
THE WAY HE FIGHTS...
...IT'S LIKE A MAD, POSSESSED SUICIDE RUSH.
HE CHARGES RIGHT AT FOES WHO SPRAY AUTOMATIC FIRE...
...AND BLOCKS ALL THE FATAL SHOTS WITH HIS LIGHTSWORD, IGNORING THE ONES THAT HIT HIS EXTREMITIES.
IN AN INSTANT, HE'S AT POINT-BLANK RANGE...
...CUTTING THROUGH HIS TARGET, RIFLE AND ALL.
HE'S NUTS...
WOW!

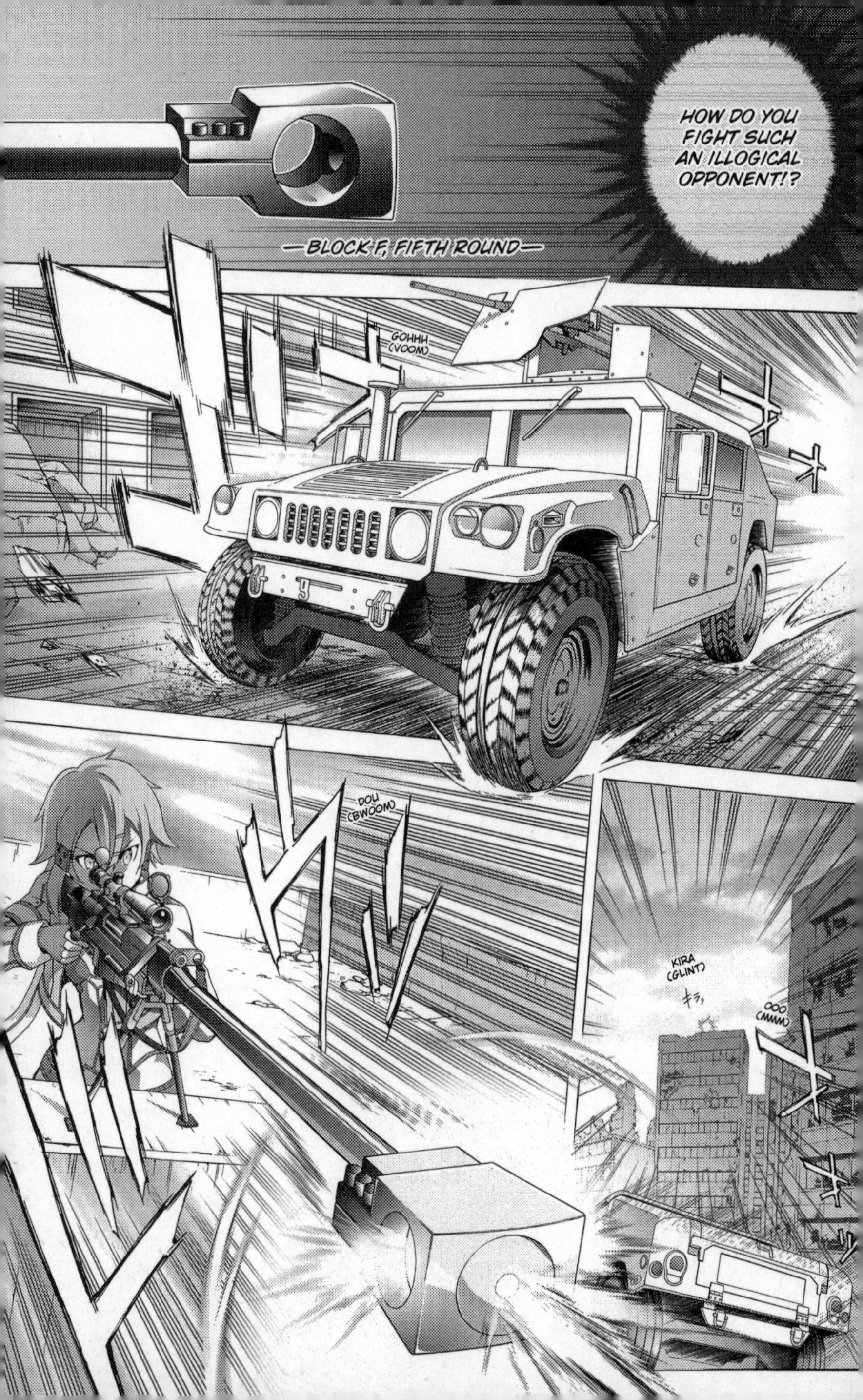
HOW DO YOU FIGHT SUCH AN ILLOGICAL OPPONENT!?
—BLOCK F, FIFTH ROUND—
GOHHH (VOOM)
KIRA (GLINT)
OOO (MMM)
DOU (BWOOM)

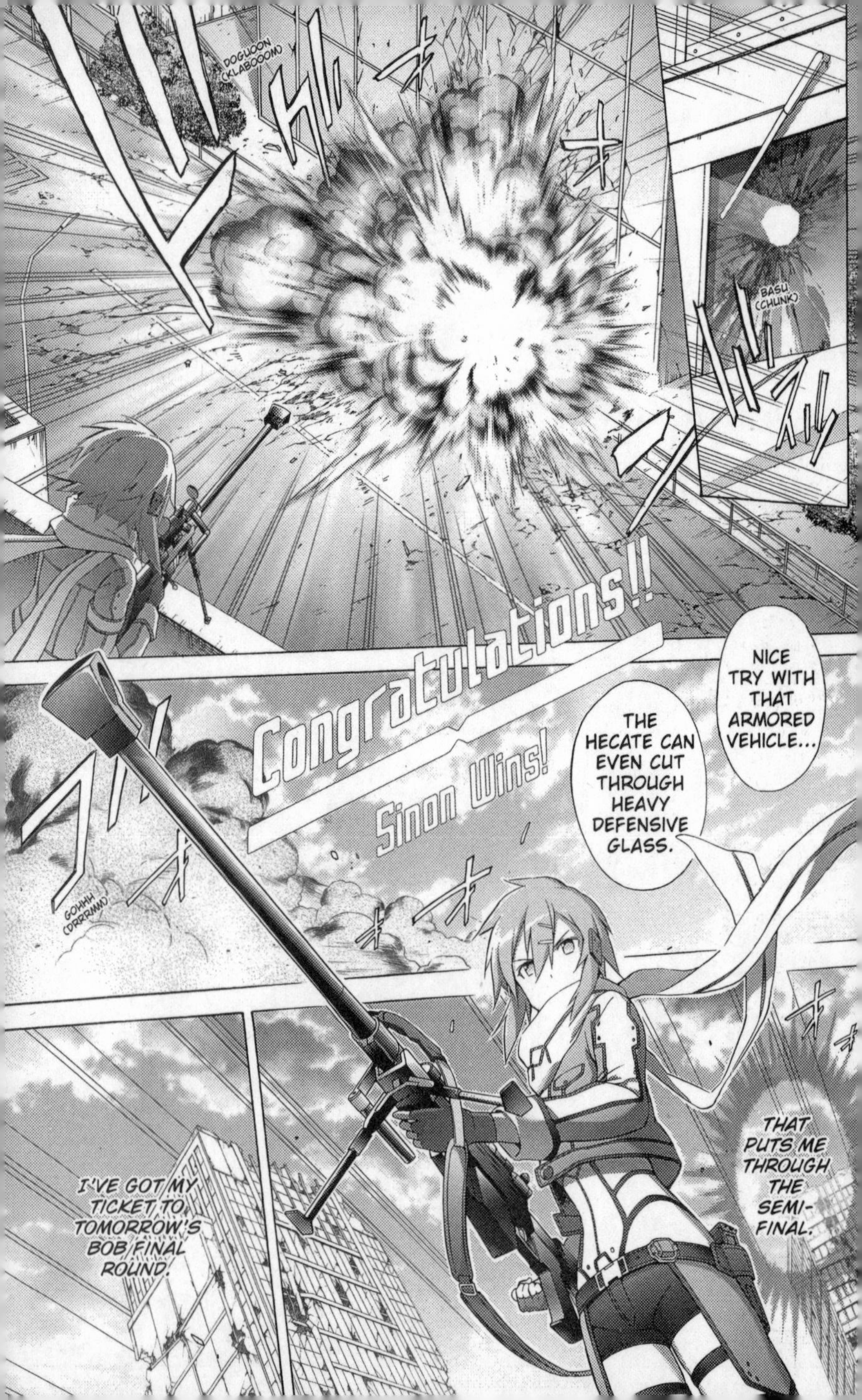
DOGUOON (KLABOOOM)
BASU (CHUNK)
NICE TRY WITH THAT ARMORED VEHICLE...
THE HECATE CAN EVEN CUT THROUGH HEAVY DEFENSIVE GLASS.
Congratulations!!
Sinon Wins!
GOHHH (GRRRMM)
THAT PUTS ME THROUGH THE SEMI-FINAL.
I'VE GOT MY TICKET TO TOMORROW'S BOB FINAL ROUND.

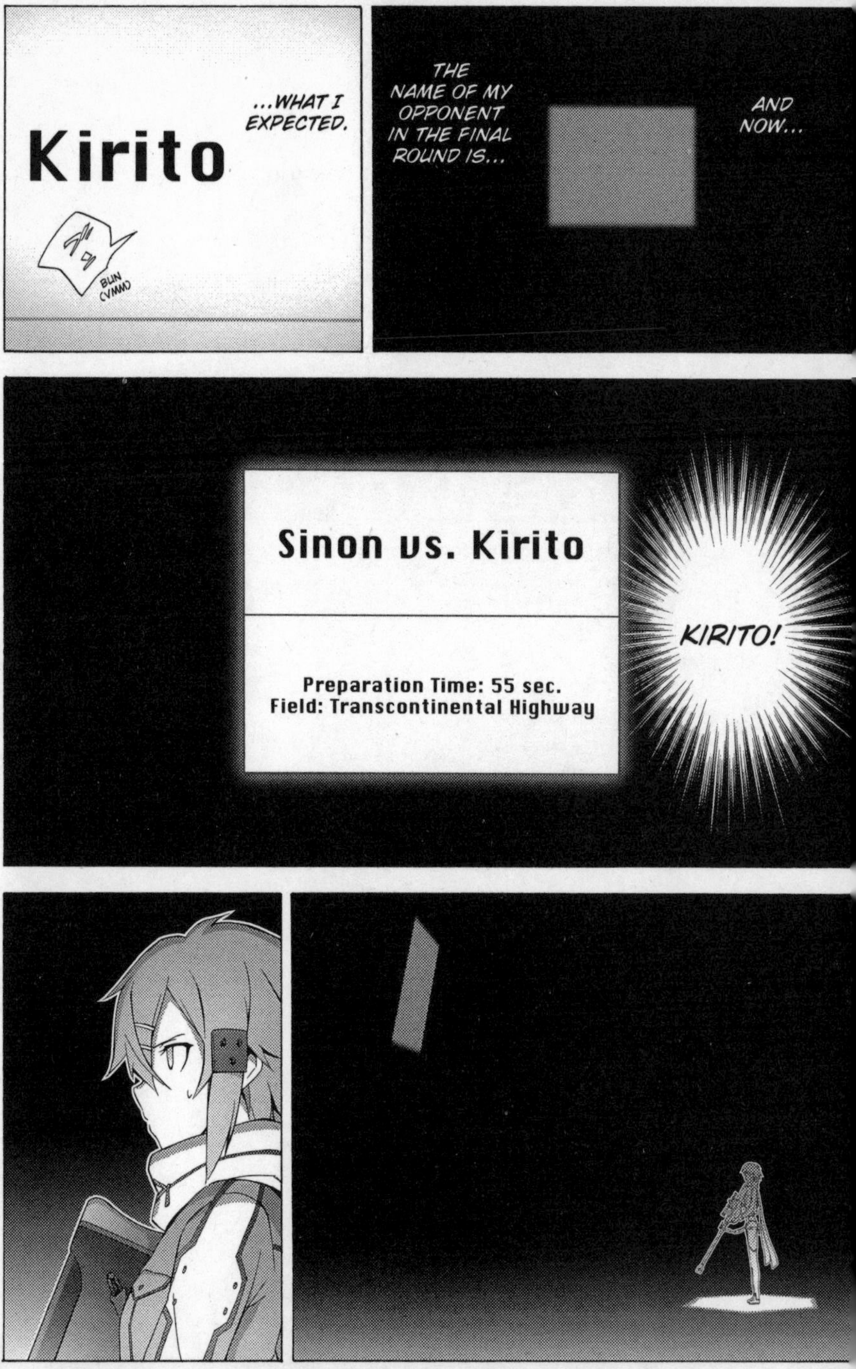
AND NOW...
THE NAME OF MY OPPONENT IN THE FINAL ROUND IS...
Kirito
...WHAT I EXPECTED.
BUN (VMM)
Sinon vs. Kirito
Preparation Time: 55 sec.
Field: Transcontinental Highway
KIRITO!

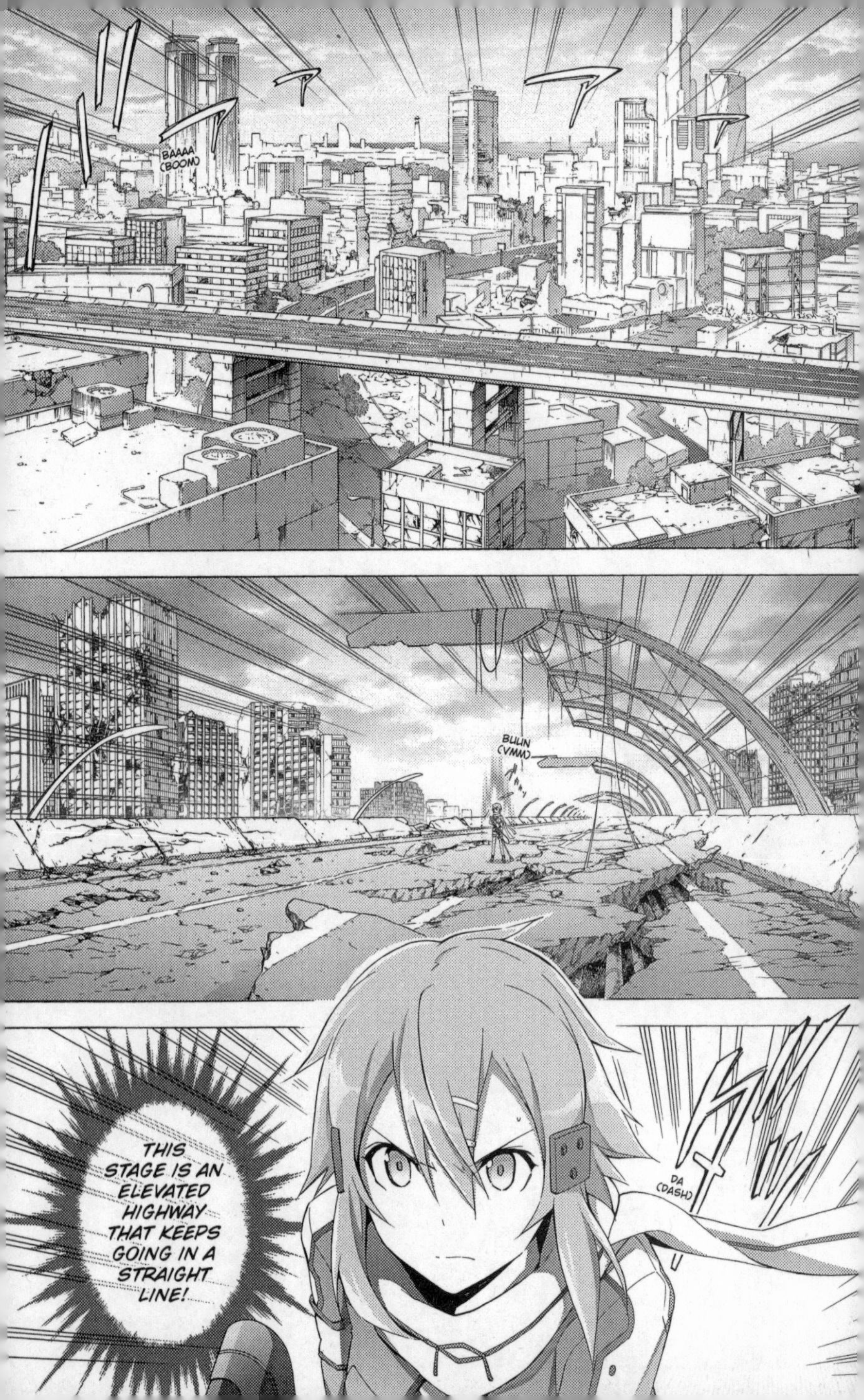
BAAAA
(BOOM)
BULIN
(VMM)
DA
(DASH)
THIS STAGE IS AN ELEVATED HIGHWAY THAT KEEPS GOING IN A STRAIGHT LINE!

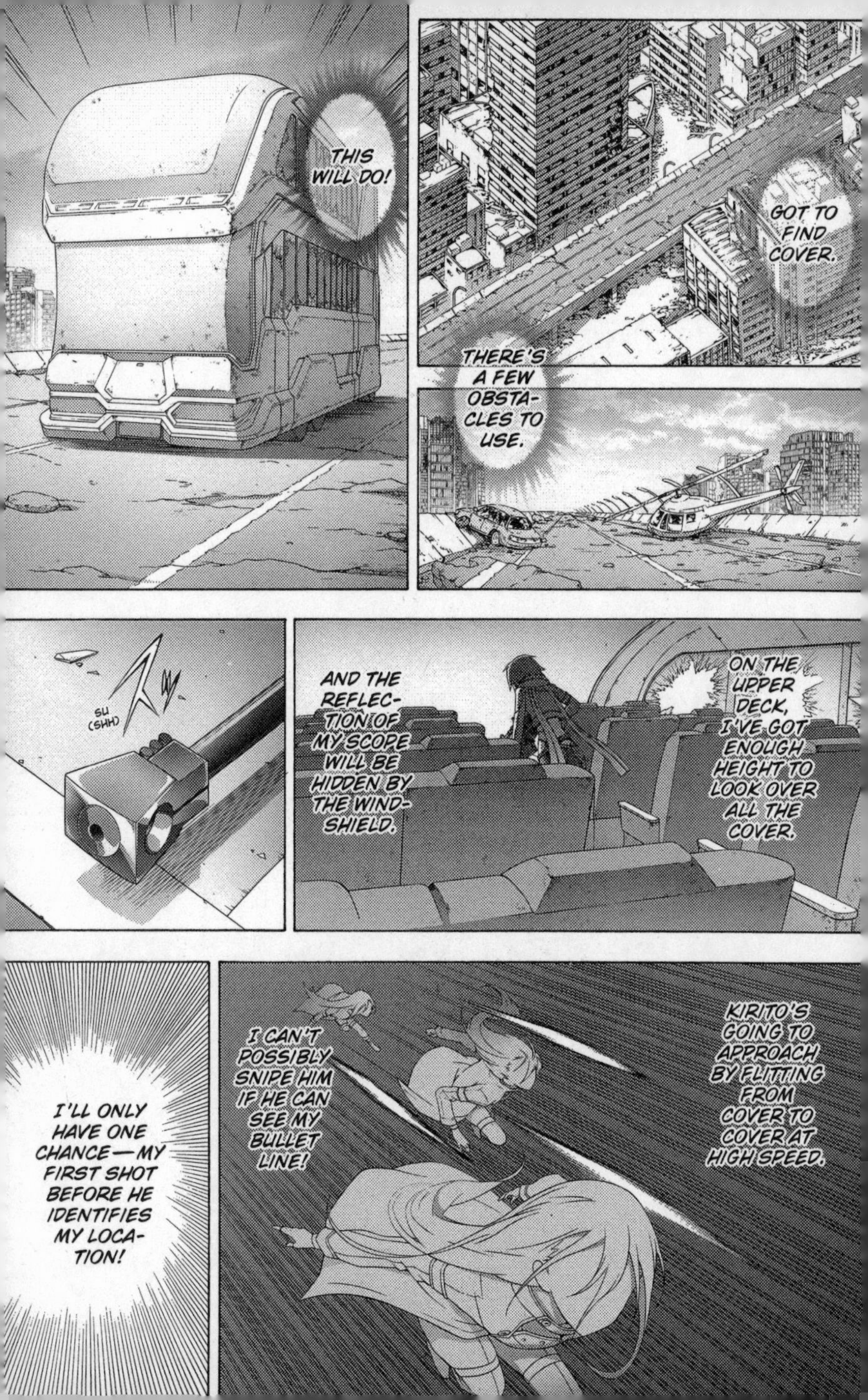
GOT TO FIND COVER.
THERE'S A FEW OBSTACLES TO USE.
THIS WILL DO!
ON THE UPPER DECK, I'VE GOT ENOUGH HEIGHT TO LOOK OVER ALL THE COVER.
AND THE REFLECTION OF MY SCOPE WILL BE HIDDEN BY THE WINDSHIELD.
SU (SHH)
KIRITO'S GOING TO APPROACH BY FLITTING FROM COVER TO COVER AT HIGH SPEED.
I CAN'T POSSIBLY SNIPE HIM IF HE CAN SEE MY BULLET LINE!
I'LL ONLY HAVE ONE CHANCE—MY FIRST SHOT BEFORE HE IDENTIFIES MY LOCATION!

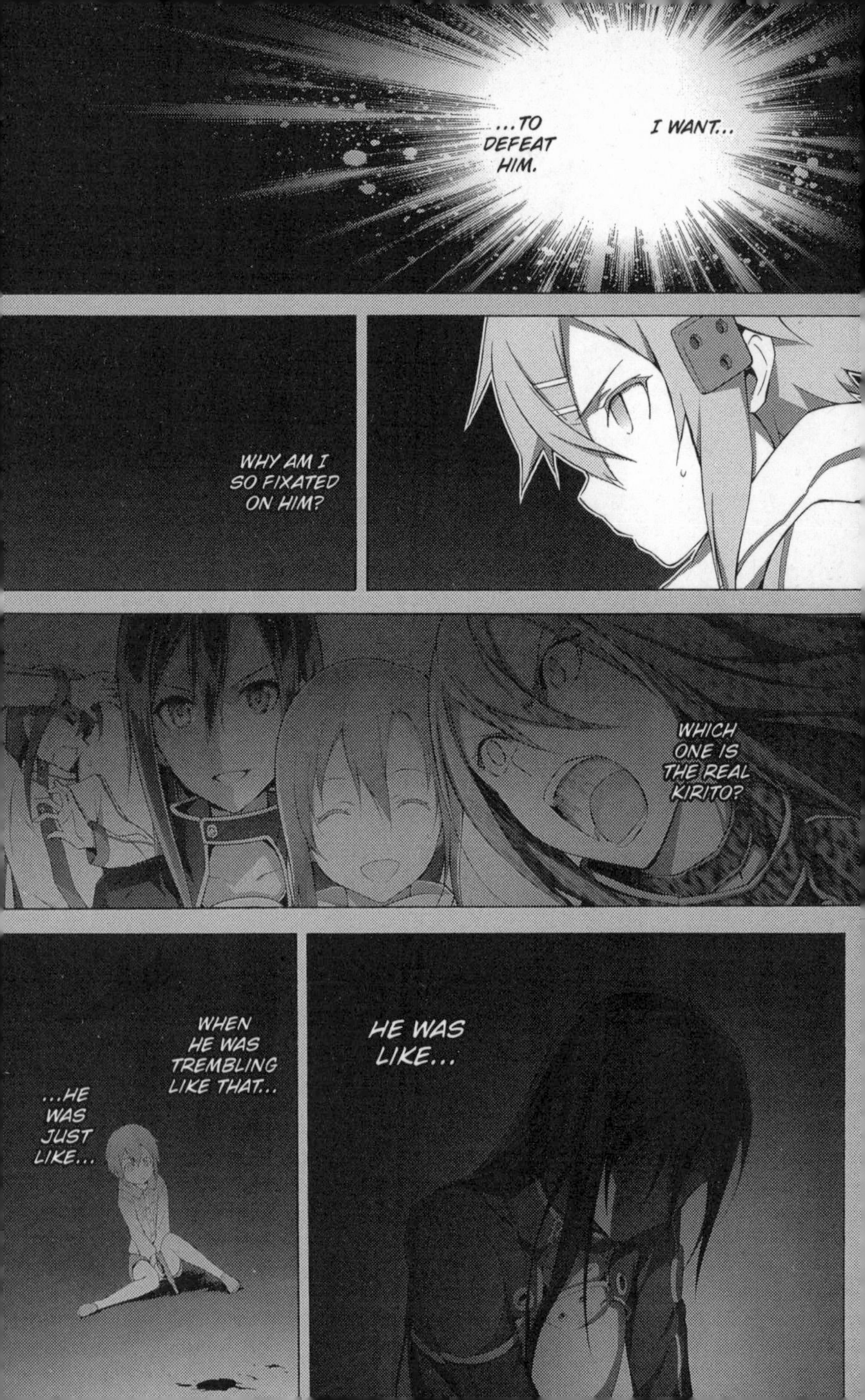
I WANT...
...TO DEFEAT HIM.
WHY AM I SO FIXATED ON HIM?
WHICH ONE IS THE REAL KIRITO?
HE WAS LIKE...
WHEN HE WAS TREMBLING LIKE THAT...
...HE WAS JUST LIKE...

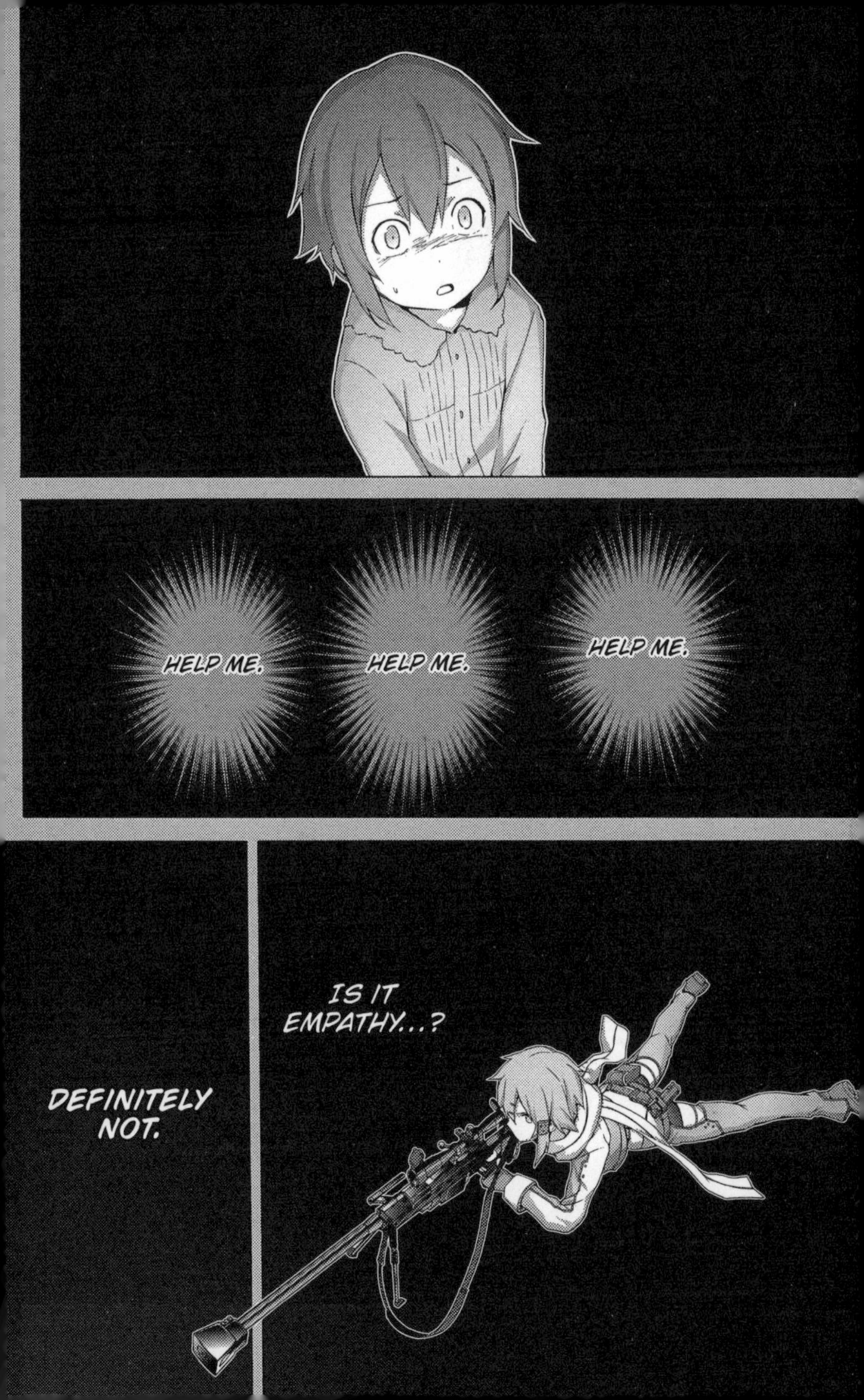
HELP ME.
HELP ME.
HELP ME.
IS IT EMPATHY...?
DEFINITELY NOT.

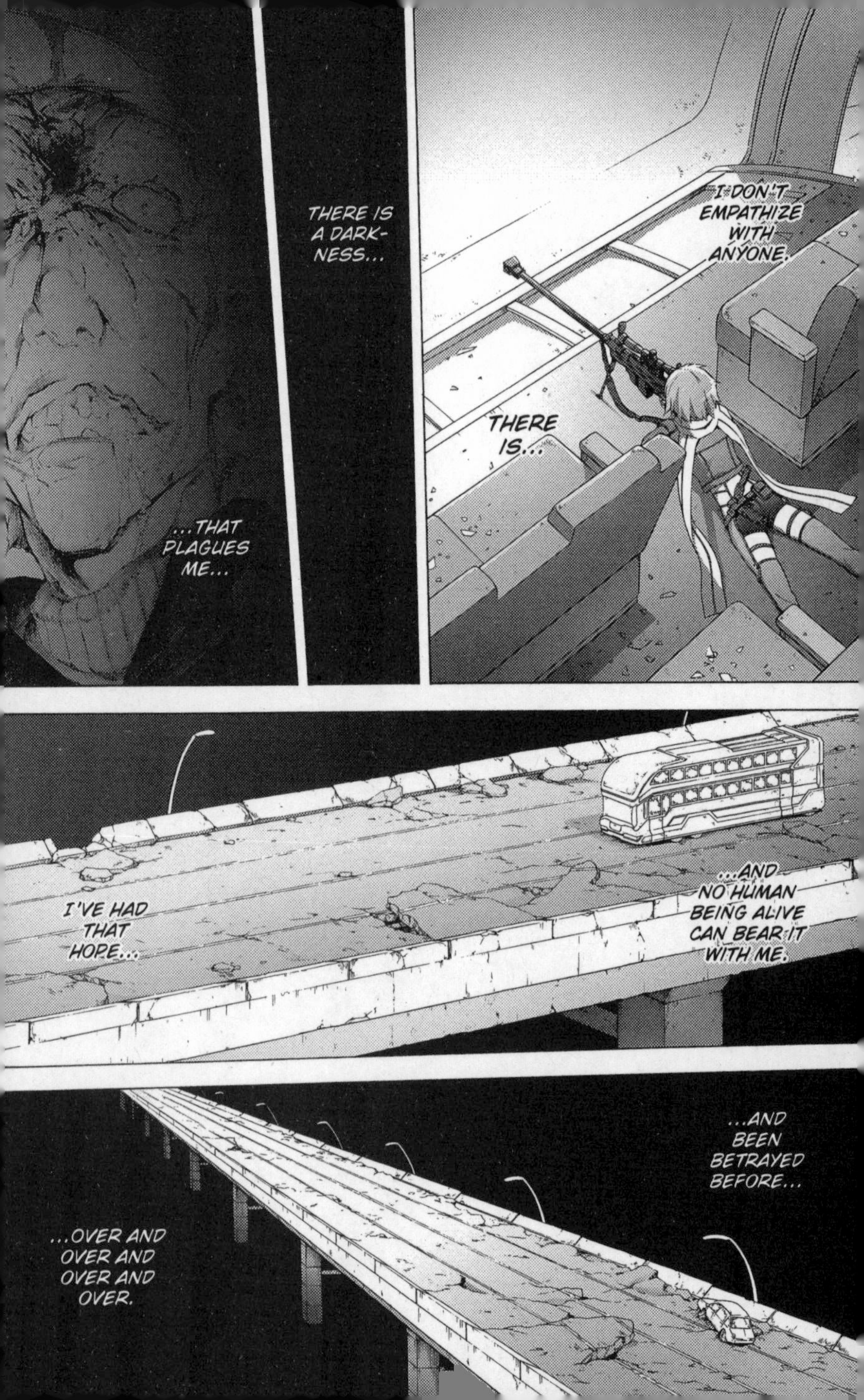
I DON'T EMPATHIZE WITH ANYONE.
THERE IS...
THERE IS A DARKNESS...
...THAT PLAGUES ME...
...AND NO HUMAN BEING ALIVE CAN BEAR IT WITH ME.
I'VE HAD THAT HOPE...
...AND BEEN BETRAYED BEFORE...
...OVER AND OVER AND OVER AND OVER.

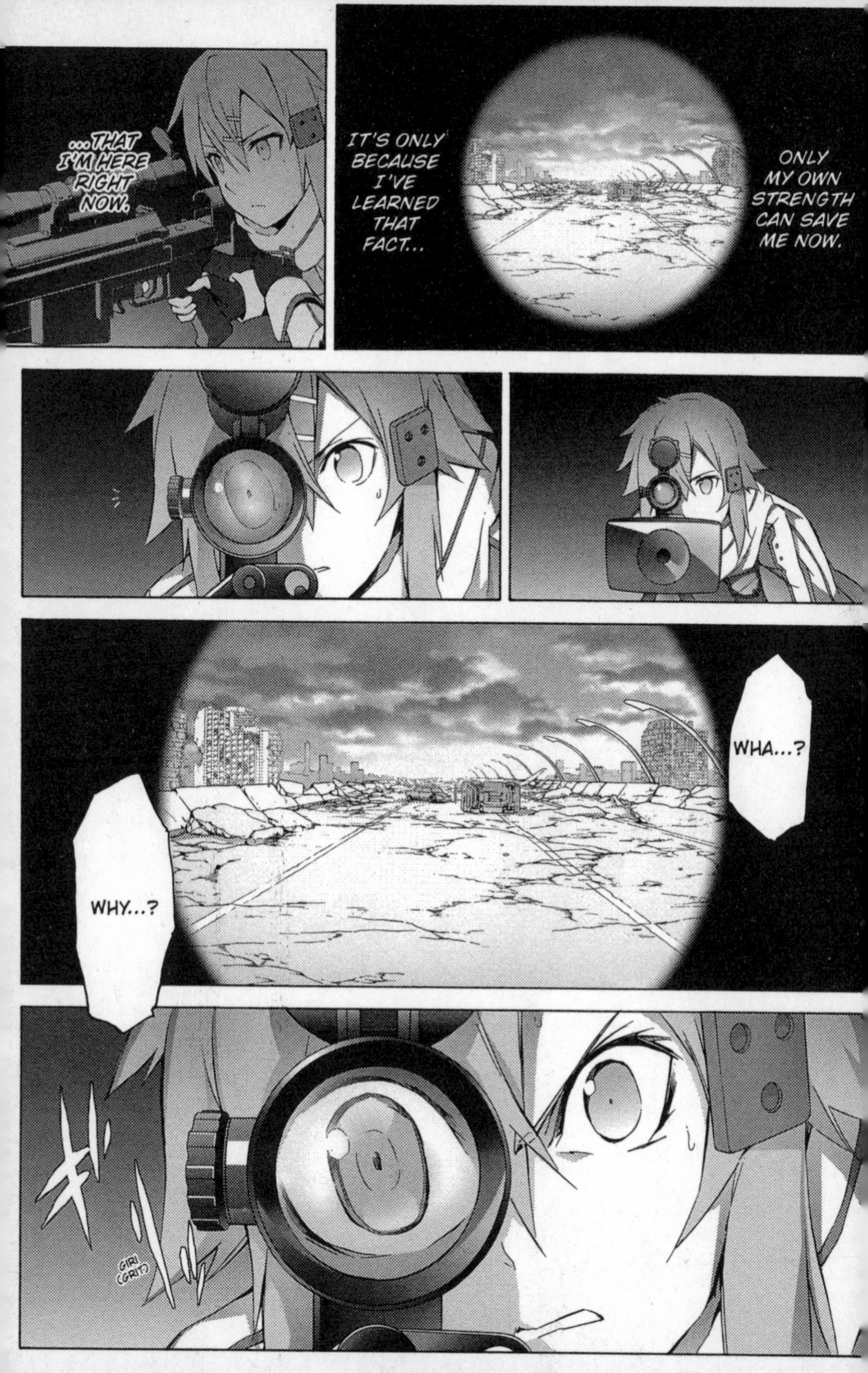
ONLY MY OWN STRENGTH CAN SAVE ME NOW.
IT'S ONLY BECAUSE I'VE LEARNED THAT FACT...
...THAT I'M HERE RIGHT NOW.
WHA...?
WHY...?
GIRI (GRIT)

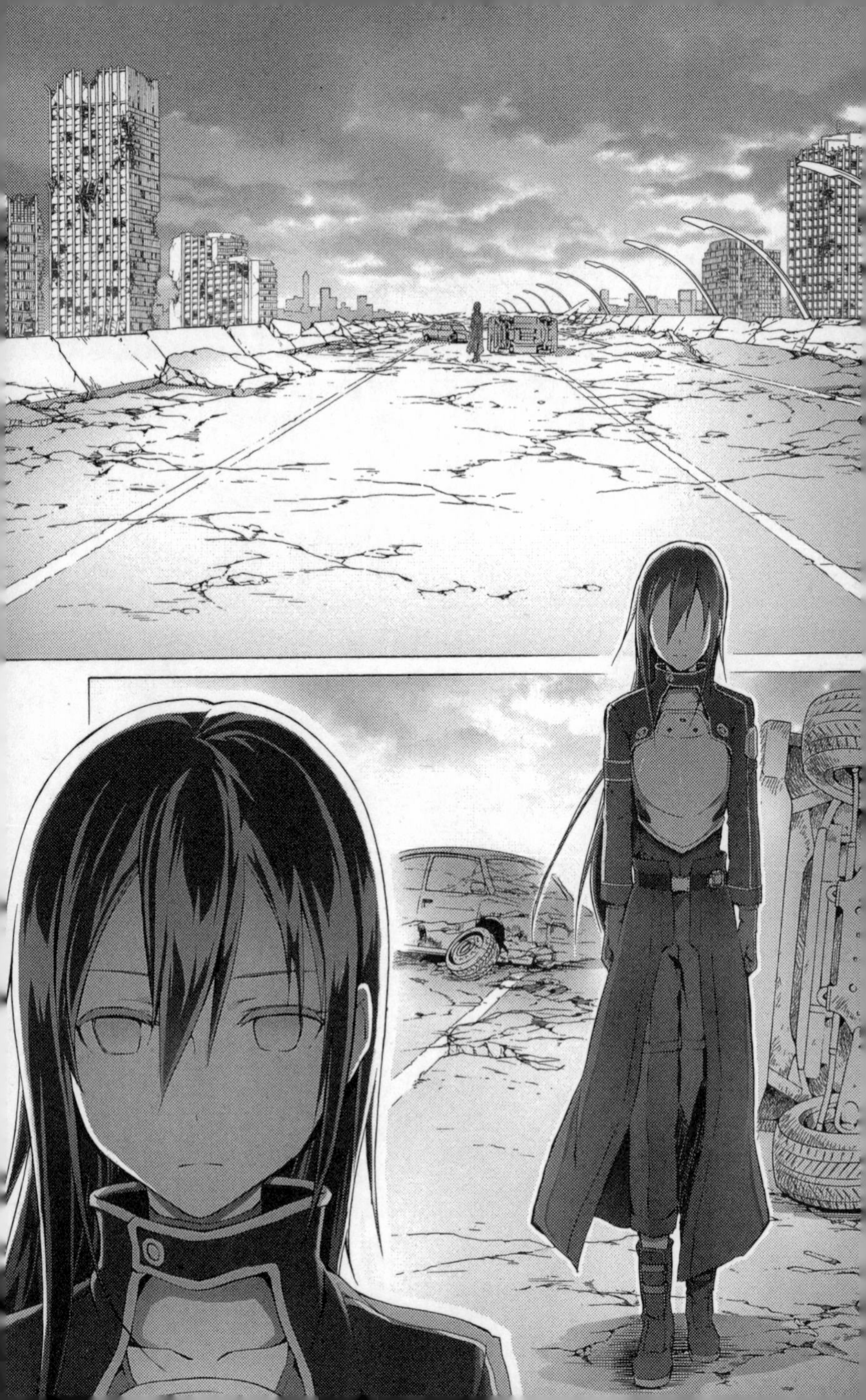

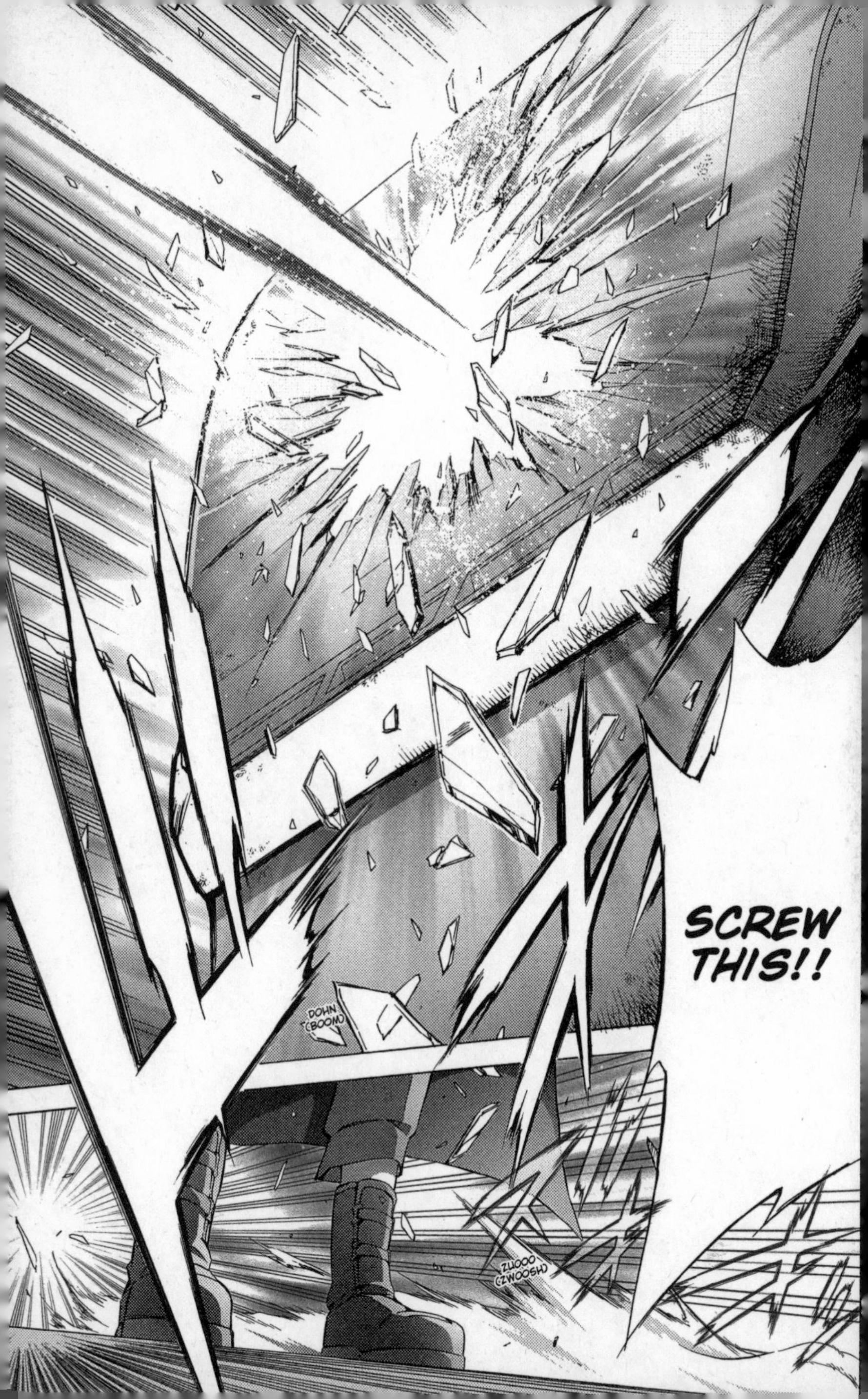
SCREW THIS!!
DOHN (BOOM)
ZUOOO (ZWOOSH)

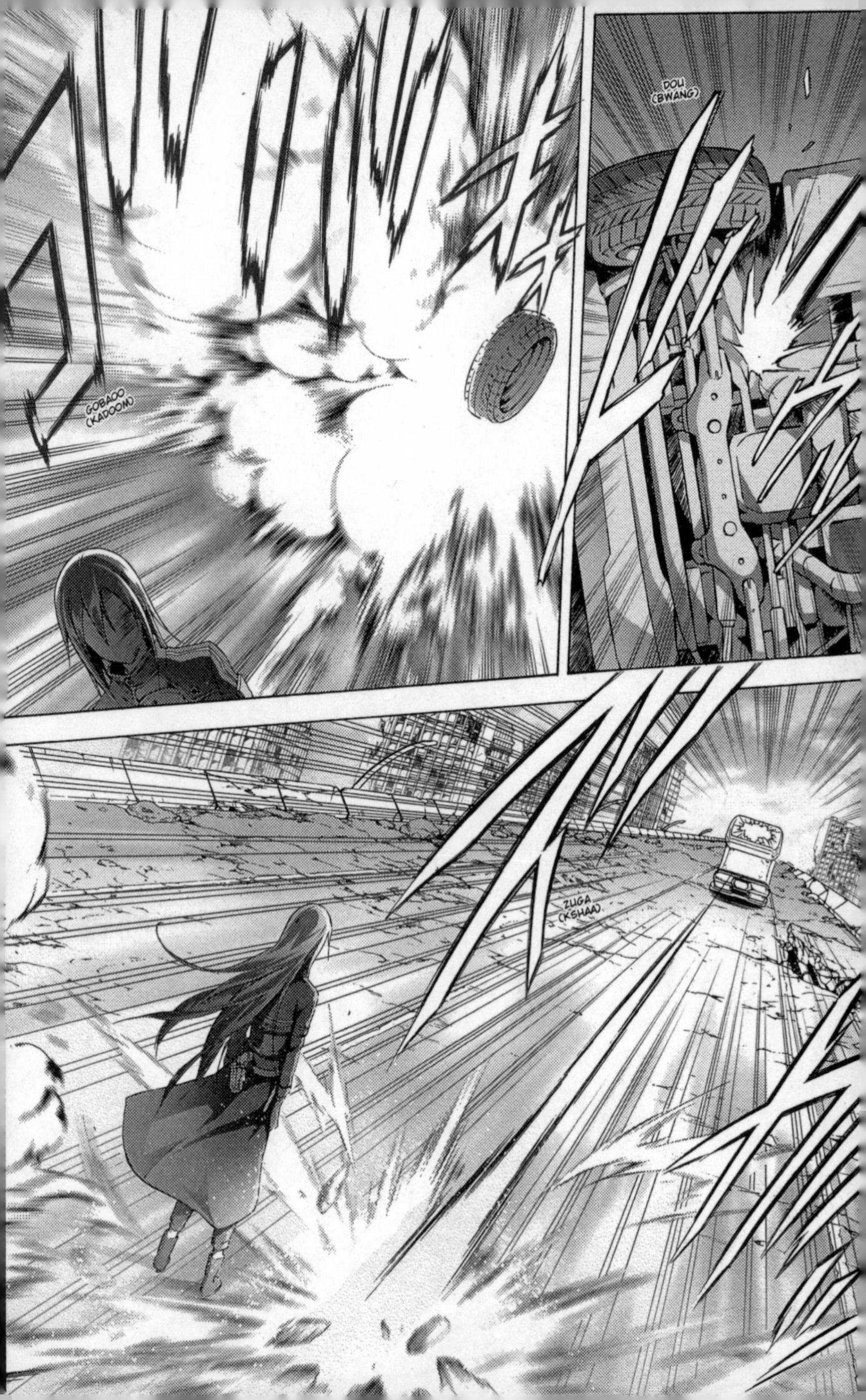
DOU (BWANG)
GOBAOO (KADOOM)
ZUGA (KSHAA)

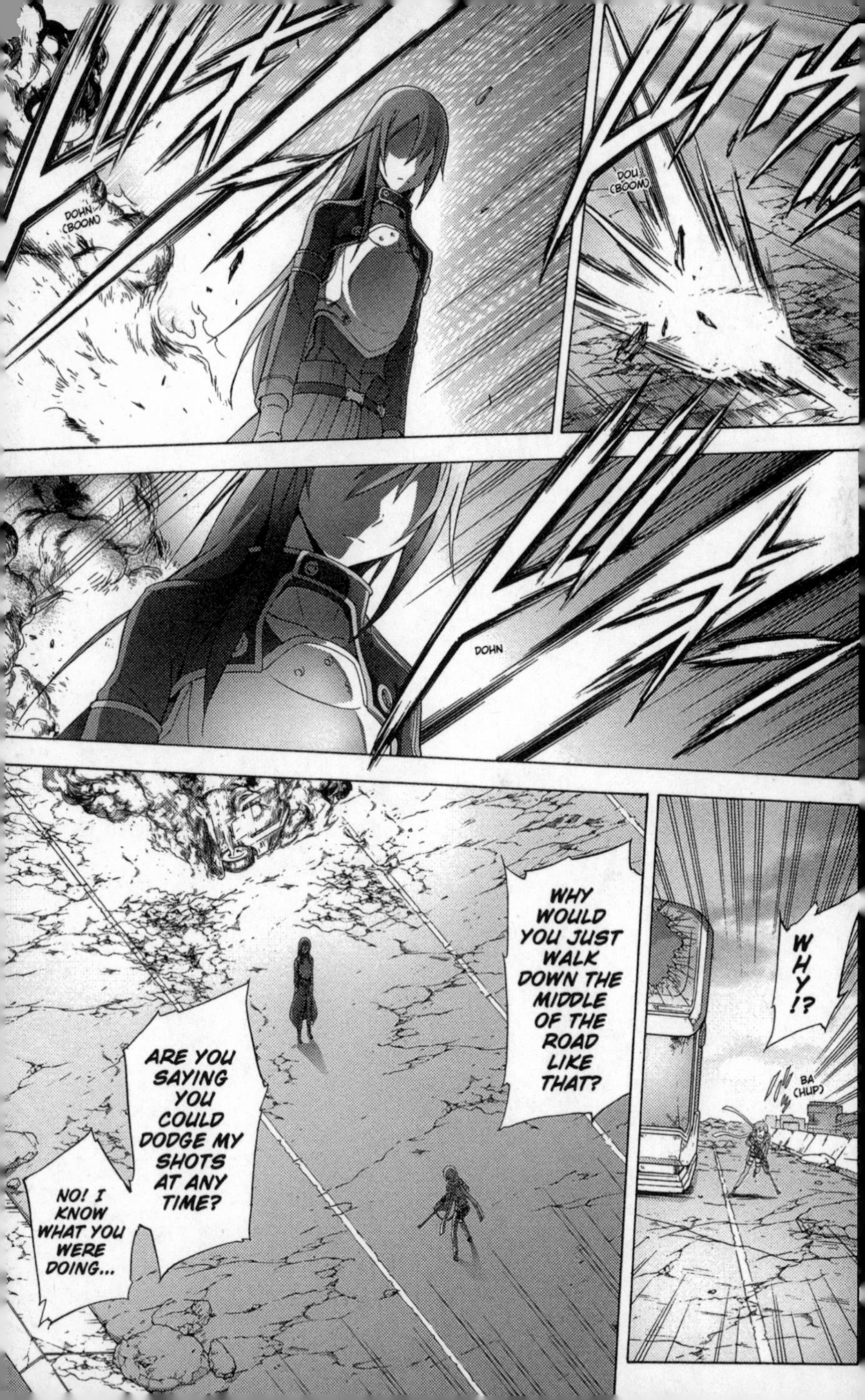
DOU (BOOM)
DOHN (BOOM)
DOHN
WHY!?
BA (HUP)
WHY WOULD YOU JUST WALK DOWN THE MIDDLE OF THE ROAD LIKE THAT?
ARE YOU SAYING YOU COULD DODGE MY SHOTS AT ANY TIME?
NO! I KNOW WHAT YOU WERE DOING...

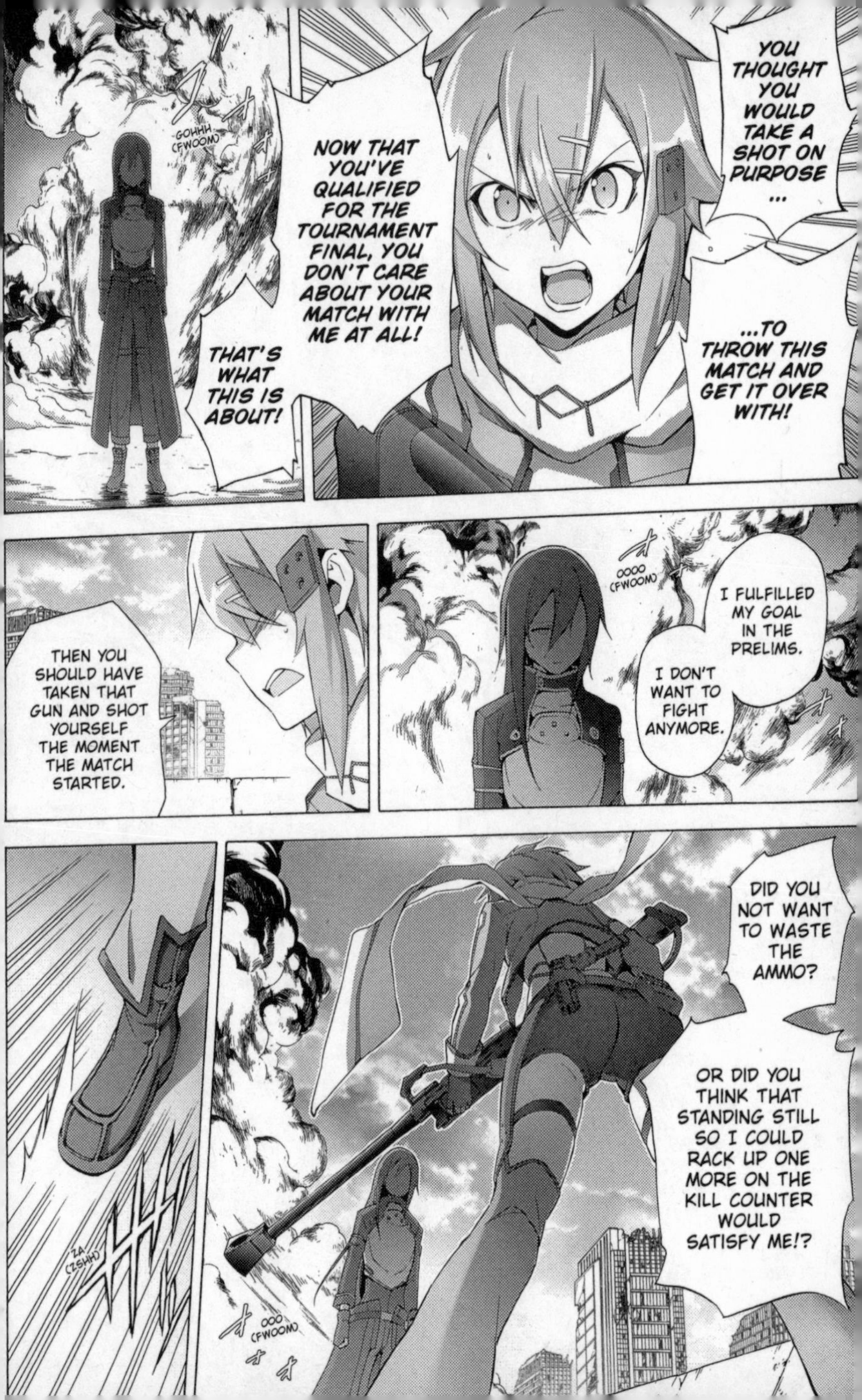
YOU THOUGHT YOU WOULD TAKE A SHOT ON PURPOSE ...
...TO THROW THIS MATCH AND GET IT OVER WITH!
NOW THAT YOU'VE QUALIFIED FOR THE TOURNAMENT FINAL, YOU DON'T CARE ABOUT YOUR MATCH WITH ME AT ALL!
THAT'S WHAT THIS IS ABOUT!
GOHHH (FWOOM)
OOOO (FWOOM)
I FULFILLED MY GOAL IN THE PRELIMS.
I DON'T WANT TO FIGHT ANYMORE.
THEN YOU SHOULD HAVE TAKEN THAT GUN AND SHOT YOURSELF THE MOMENT THE MATCH STARTED.
DID YOU NOT WANT TO WASTE THE AMMO?
OR DID YOU THINK THAT STANDING STILL SO I COULD RACK UP ONE MORE ON THE KILL COUNTER WOULD SATISFY ME!?
OOO (FWOOM)
ZA (ZSHH)

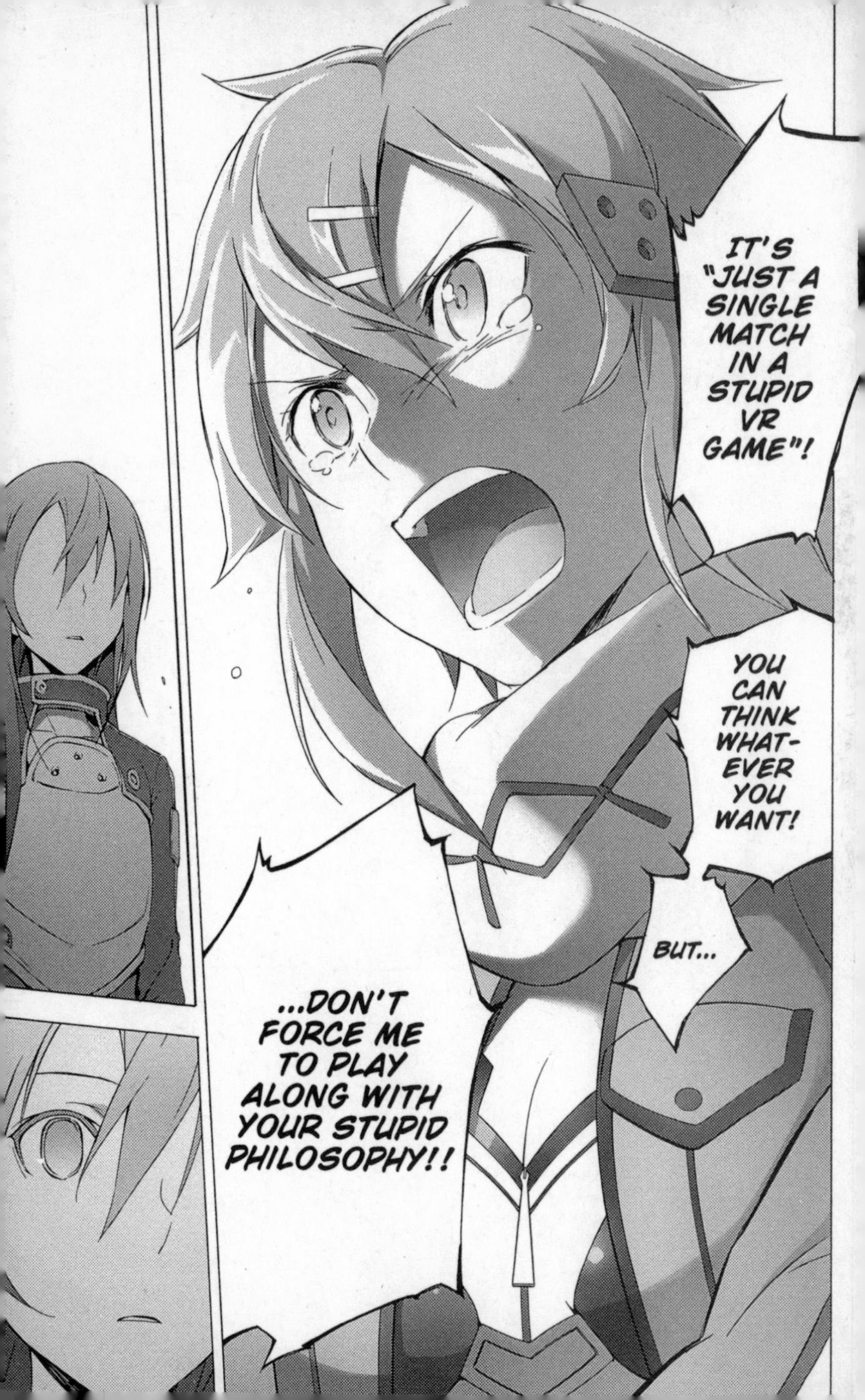
IT'S "JUST A SINGLE MATCH IN A STUPID VR GAME"!
YOU CAN THINK WHAT-EVER YOU WANT!
BUT...
...DON'T FORCE ME TO PLAY ALONG WITH YOUR STUPID PHILOSOPHY!!

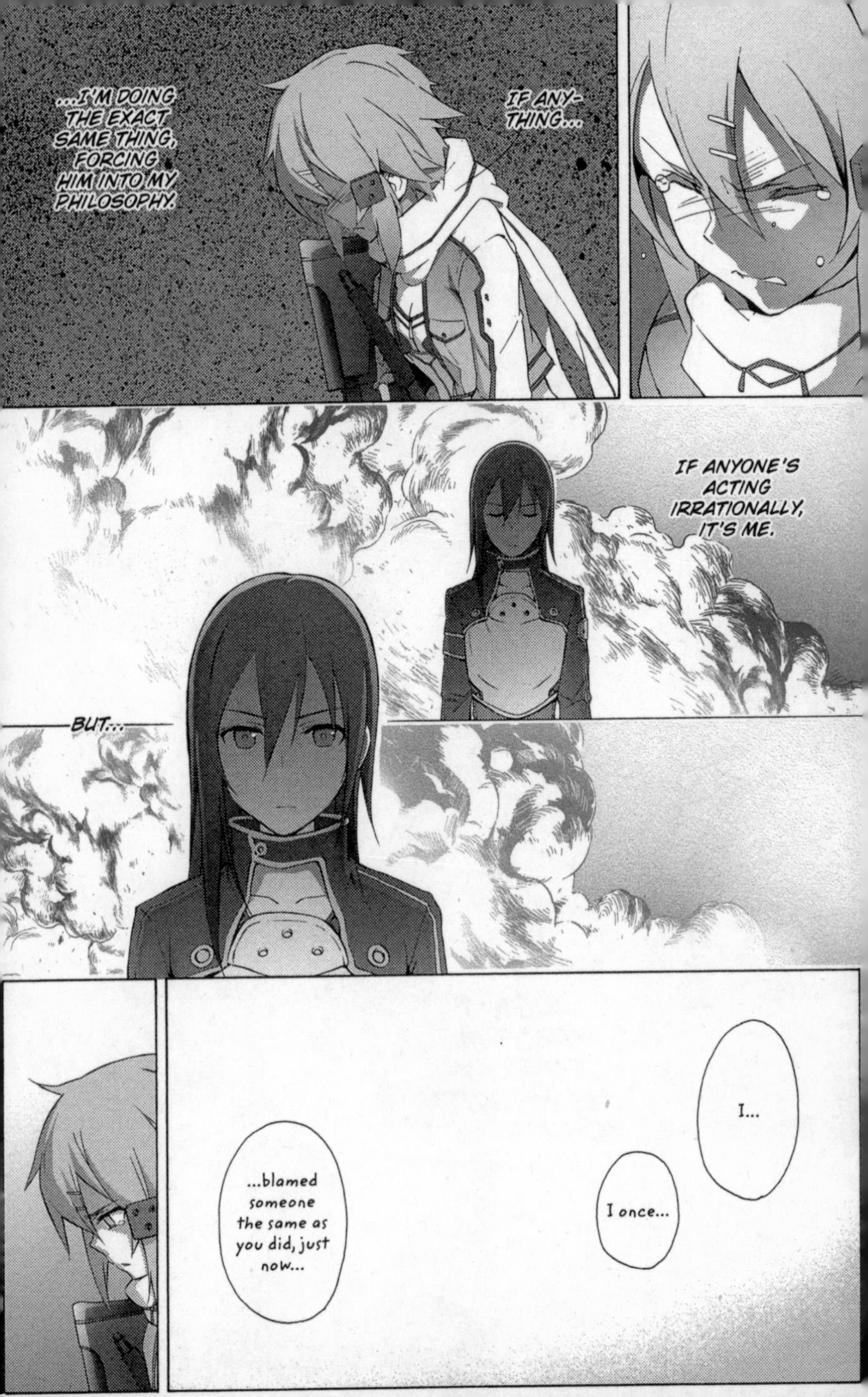
IF ANY-THING...
...I'M DOING THE EXACT SAME THING, FORCING HIM INTO MY PHILOSOPHY.
IF ANYONE'S ACTING IRRATIONALLY, IT'S ME.
BUT...
I...
I once...
...blamed someone the same as you did, just now...

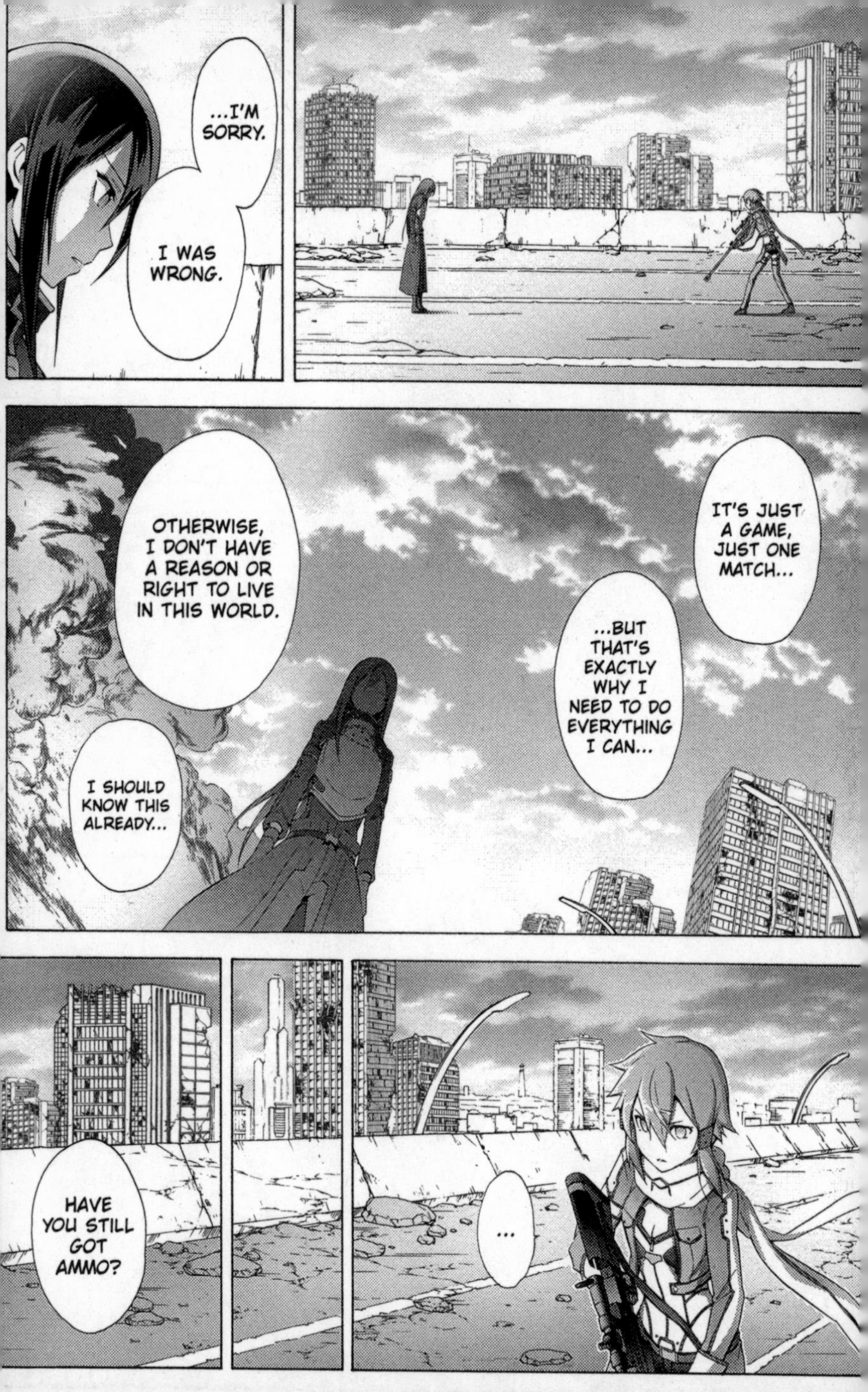
...I'M SORRY.
I WAS WRONG.
IT'S JUST A GAME, JUST ONE MATCH...
...BUT THAT'S EXACTLY WHY I NEED TO DO EVERYTHING I CAN...
OTHERWISE, I DON'T HAVE A REASON OR RIGHT TO LIVE IN THIS WORLD.
I SHOULD KNOW THIS ALREADY...
...
HAVE YOU STILL GOT AMMO?

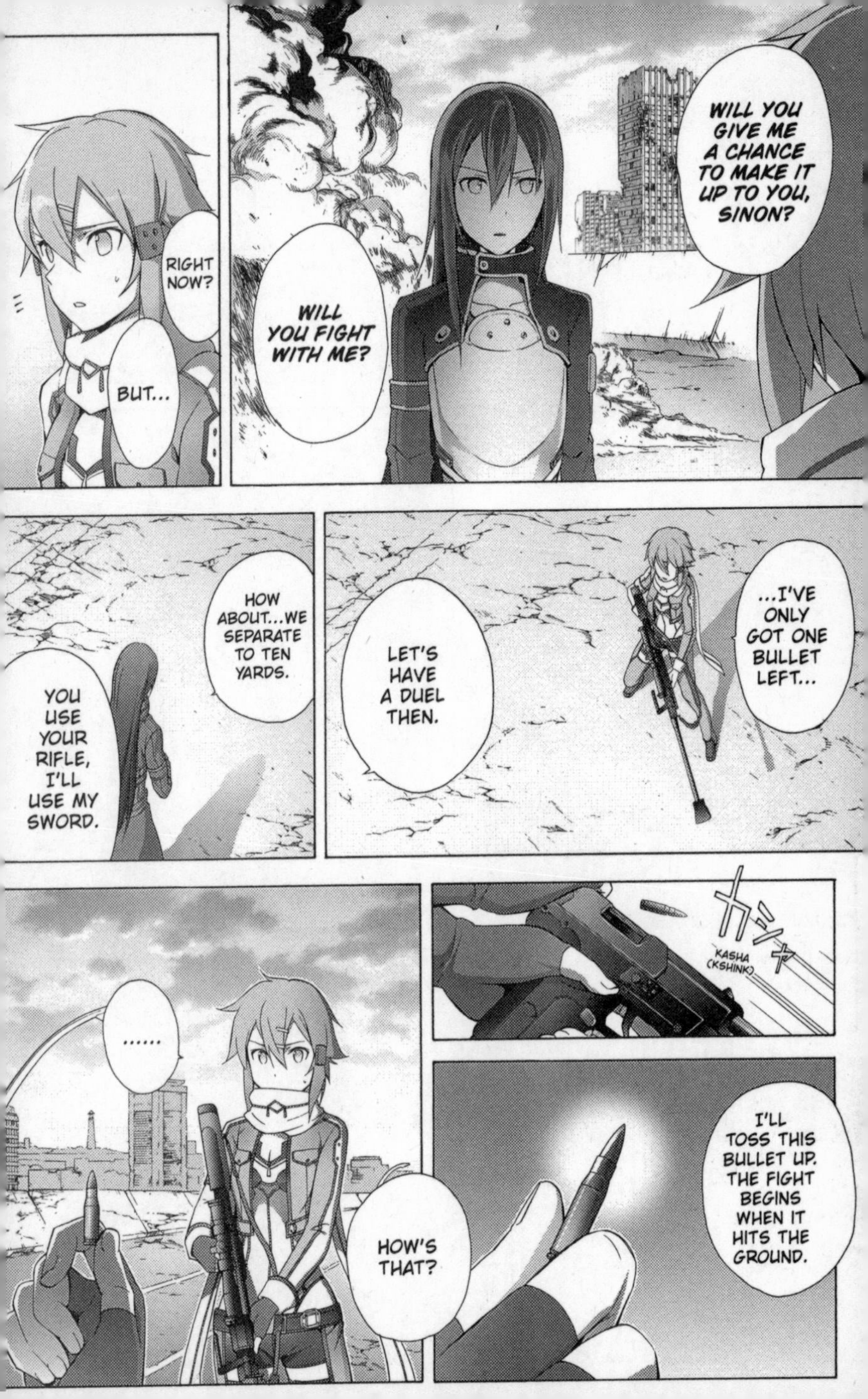
WILL YOU GIVE ME A CHANCE TO MAKE IT UP TO YOU, SINON?
WILL YOU FIGHT WITH ME?
RIGHT NOW?
BUT...
...I'VE ONLY GOT ONE BULLET LEFT...
LET'S HAVE A DUEL THEN.
HOW ABOUT...WE SEPARATE TO TEN YARDS.
YOU USE YOUR RIFLE, I'LL USE MY SWORD.
カシャ
KASHA (KSHINK)
I'LL TOSS THIS BULLET UP. THE FIGHT BEGINS WHEN IT HITS THE GROUND.
HOW'S THAT?
......

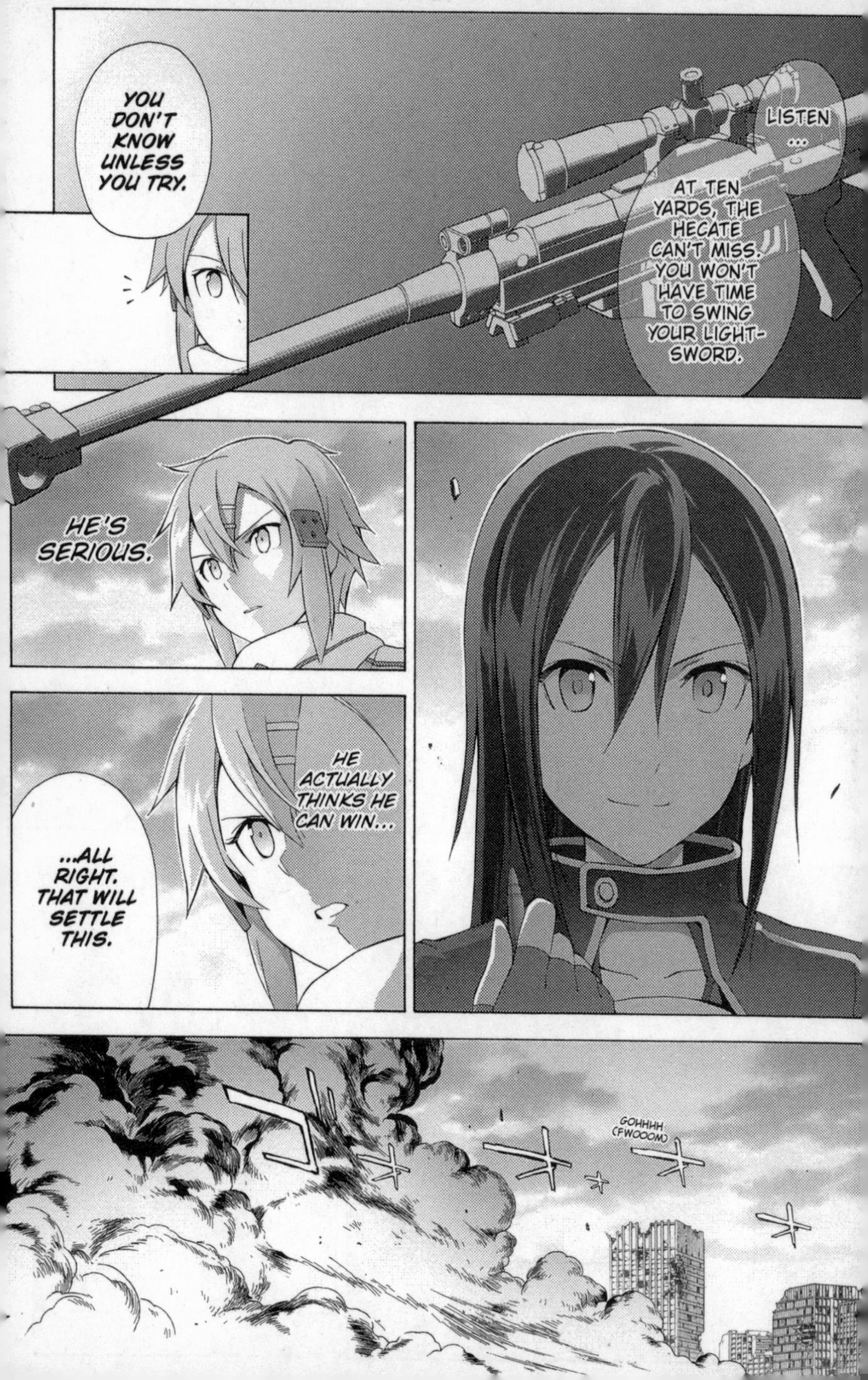
LISTEN ...
AT TEN YARDS, THE HECATE CAN'T MISS. YOU WON'T HAVE TIME TO SWING YOUR LIGHT-SWORD.
YOU DON'T KNOW UNLESS YOU TRY.
HE'S SERIOUS.
HE ACTUALLY THINKS HE CAN WIN...
...ALL RIGHT. THAT WILL SETTLE THIS.
GOHHHH (FWOOOM)

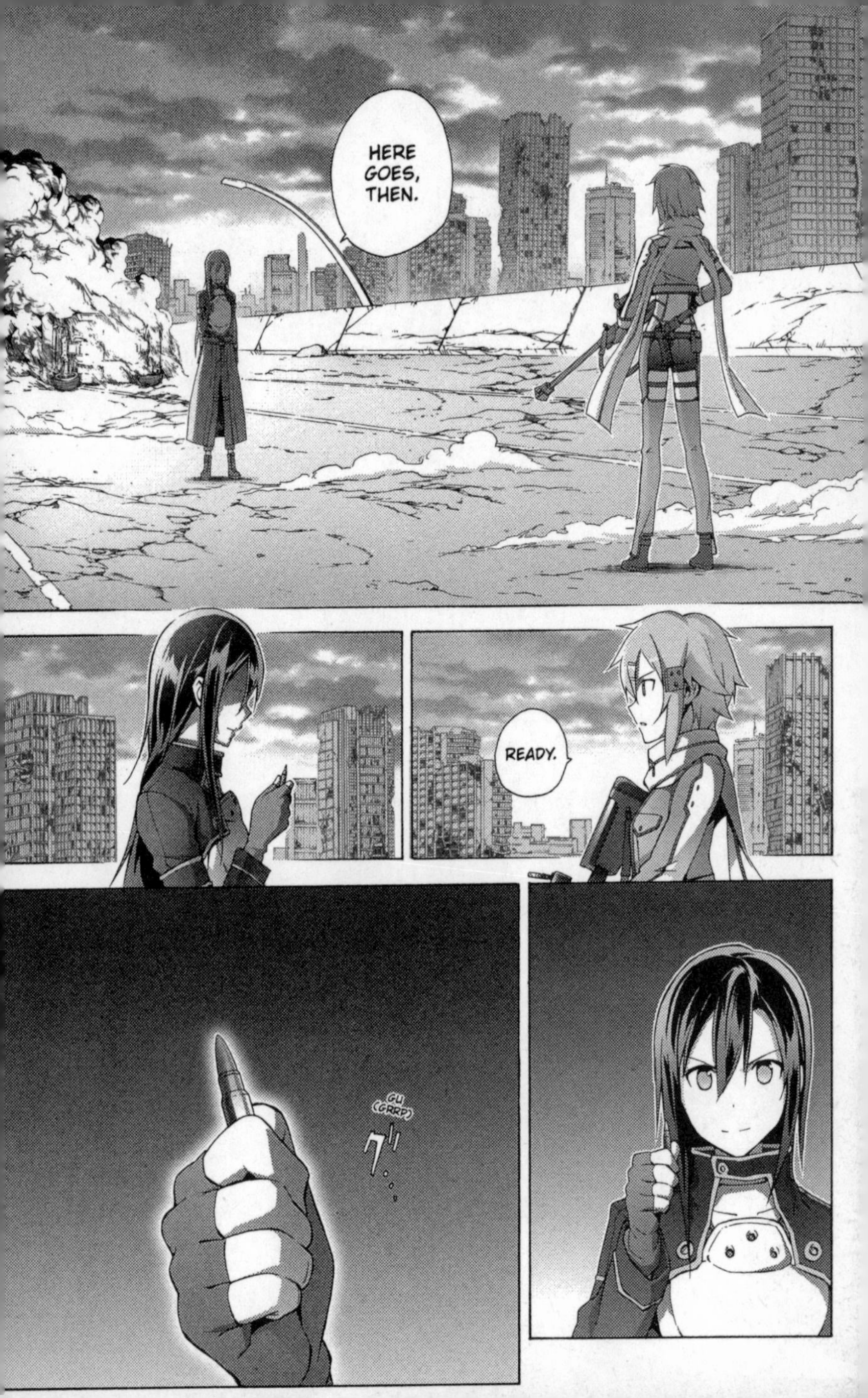
HERE GOES, THEN.
READY.
GU (GRRP)

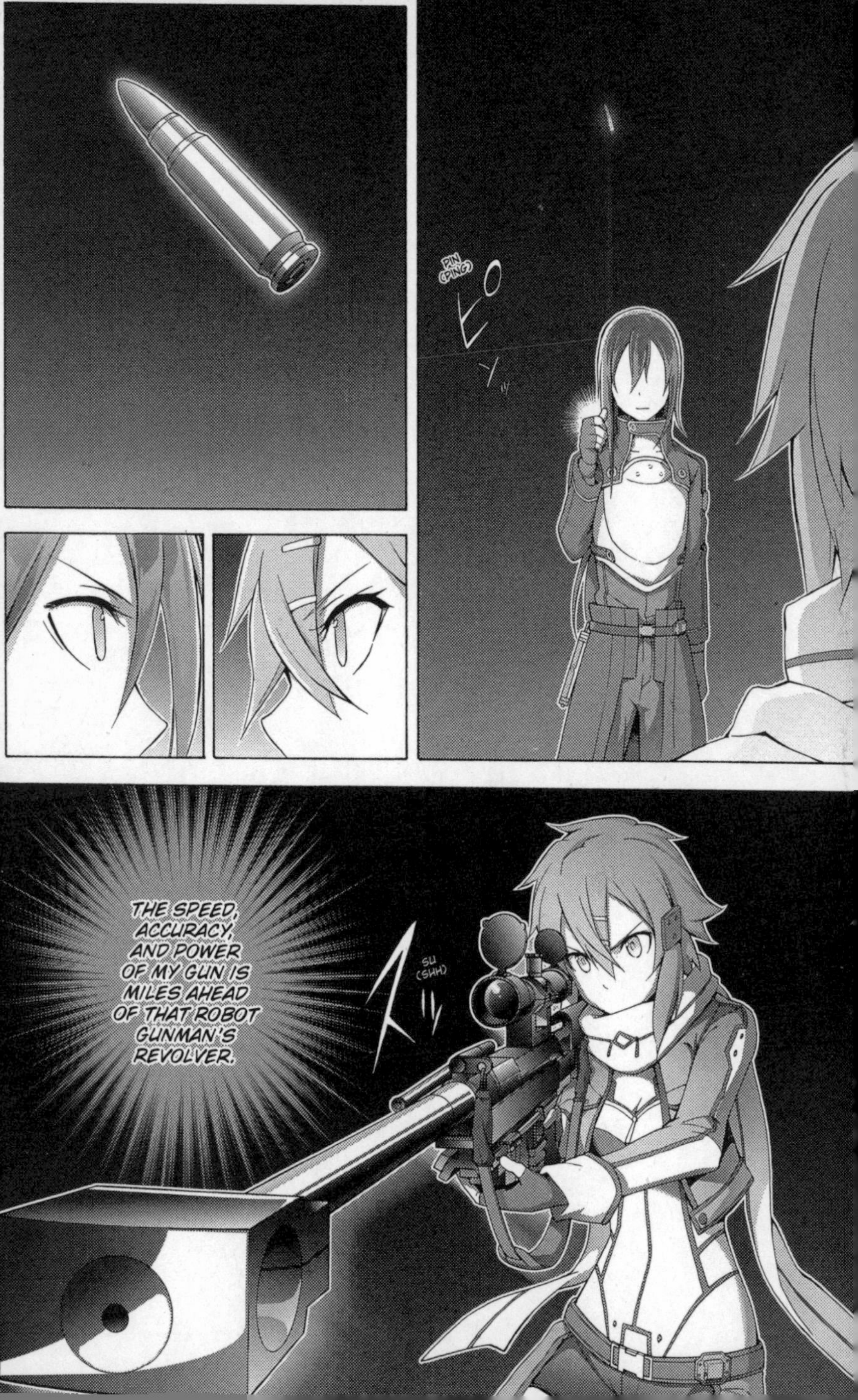
PIN (PING)
SU (SHH)
THE SPEED, ACCURACY, AND POWER OF MY GUN IS MILES AHEAD OF THAT ROBOT GUNMAN'S REVOLVER.

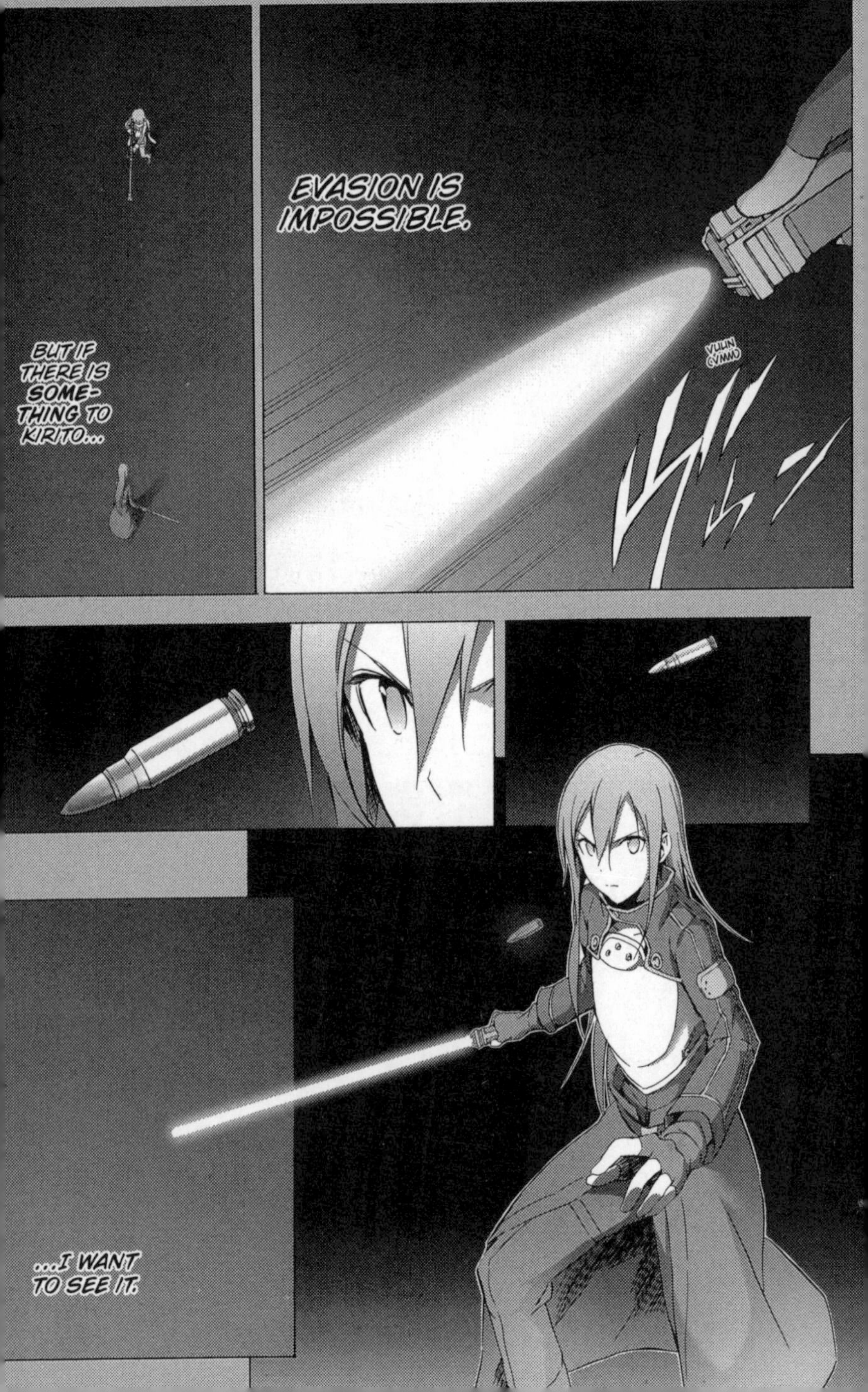
EVASION IS IMPOSSIBLE.
VUUN (VMM)
BUT IF THERE IS SOME-THING TO KIRITO...
...I WANT TO SEE IT.

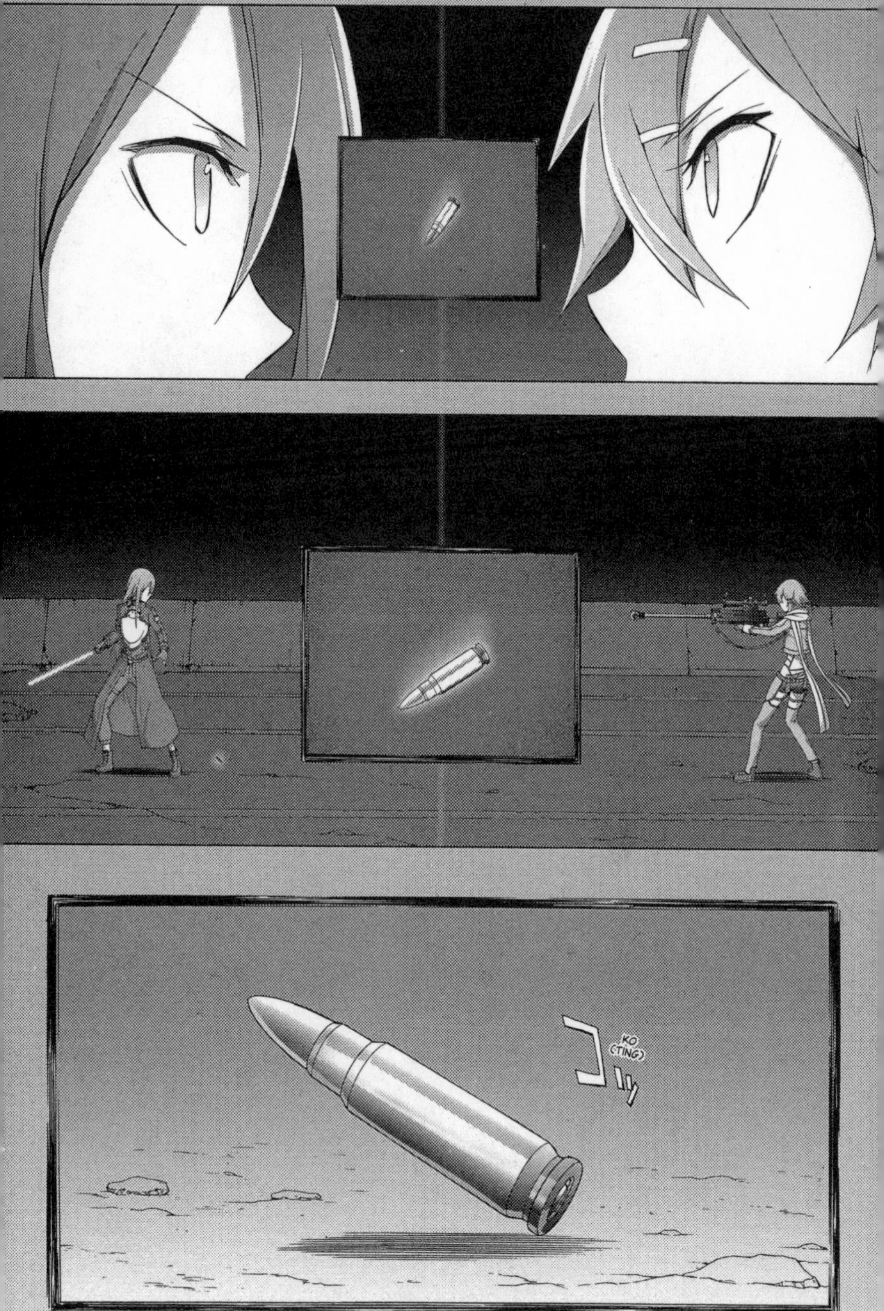
KO
(TING)

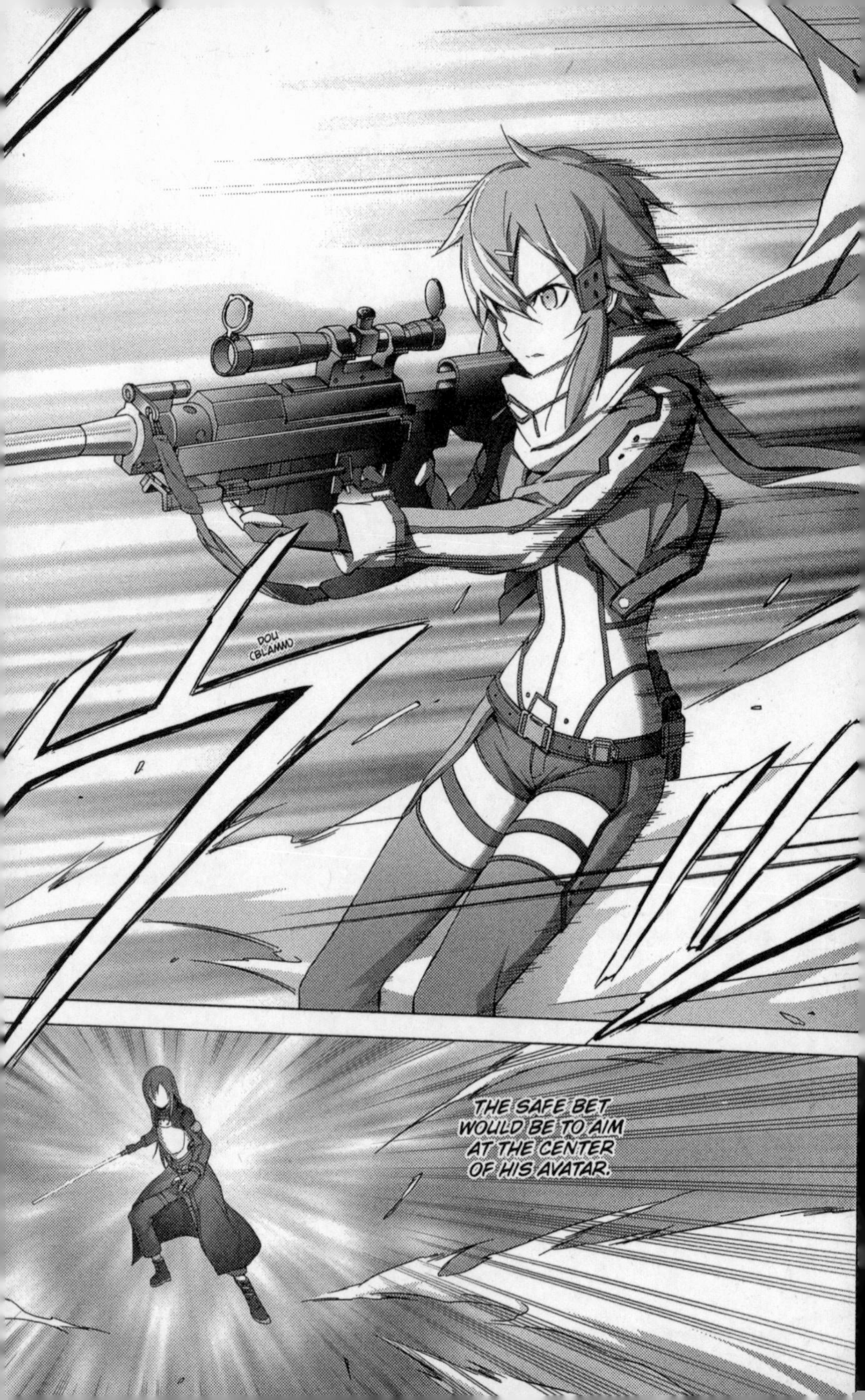
DOU (BLAMM)
THE SAFE BET WOULD BE TO AIM AT THE CENTER OF HIS AVATAR.

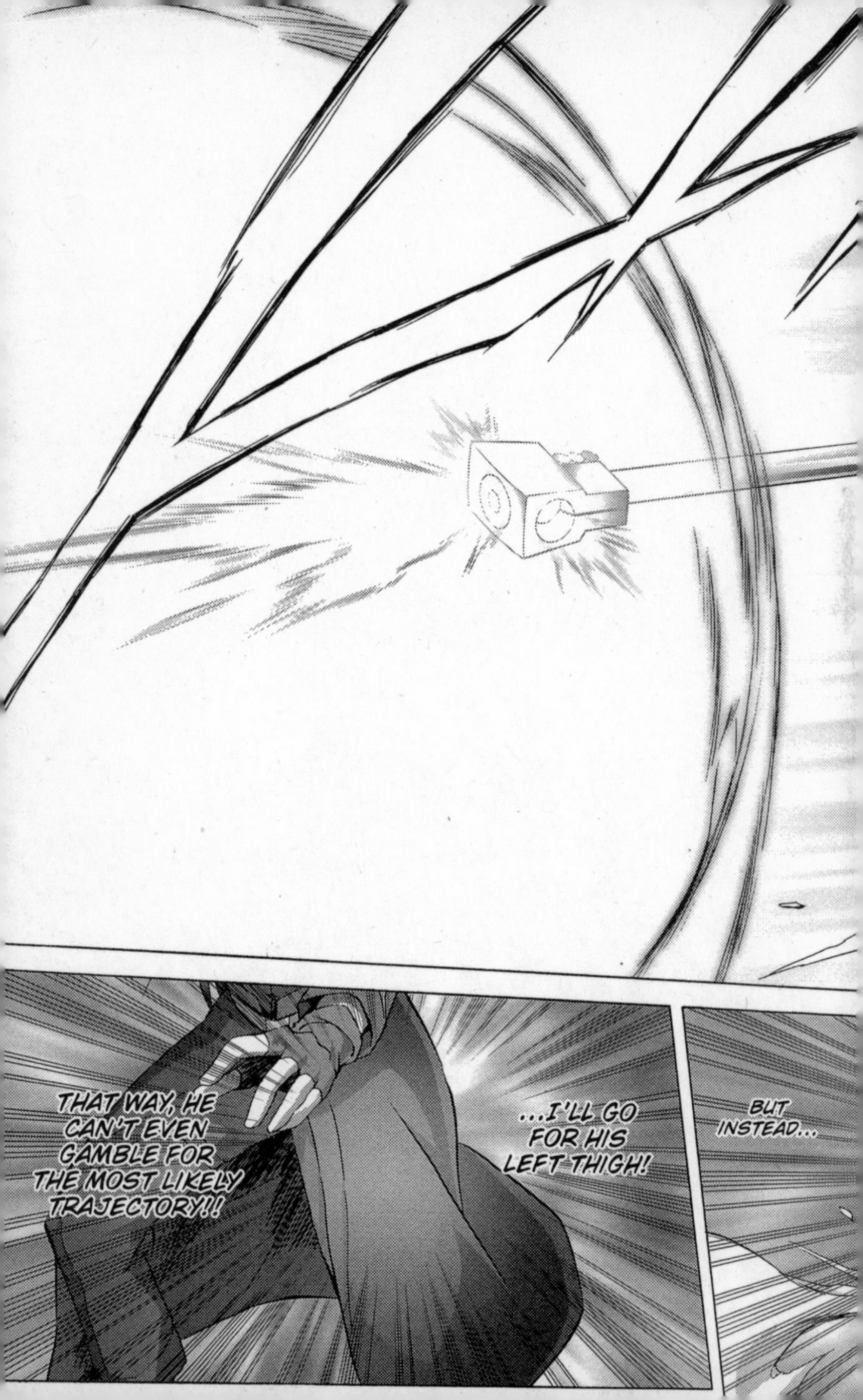
BUT INSTEAD...
...I'LL GO FOR HIS LEFT THIGH!
THAT WAY, HE CAN'T EVEN GAMBLE FOR THE MOST LIKELY TRAJECTORY!!

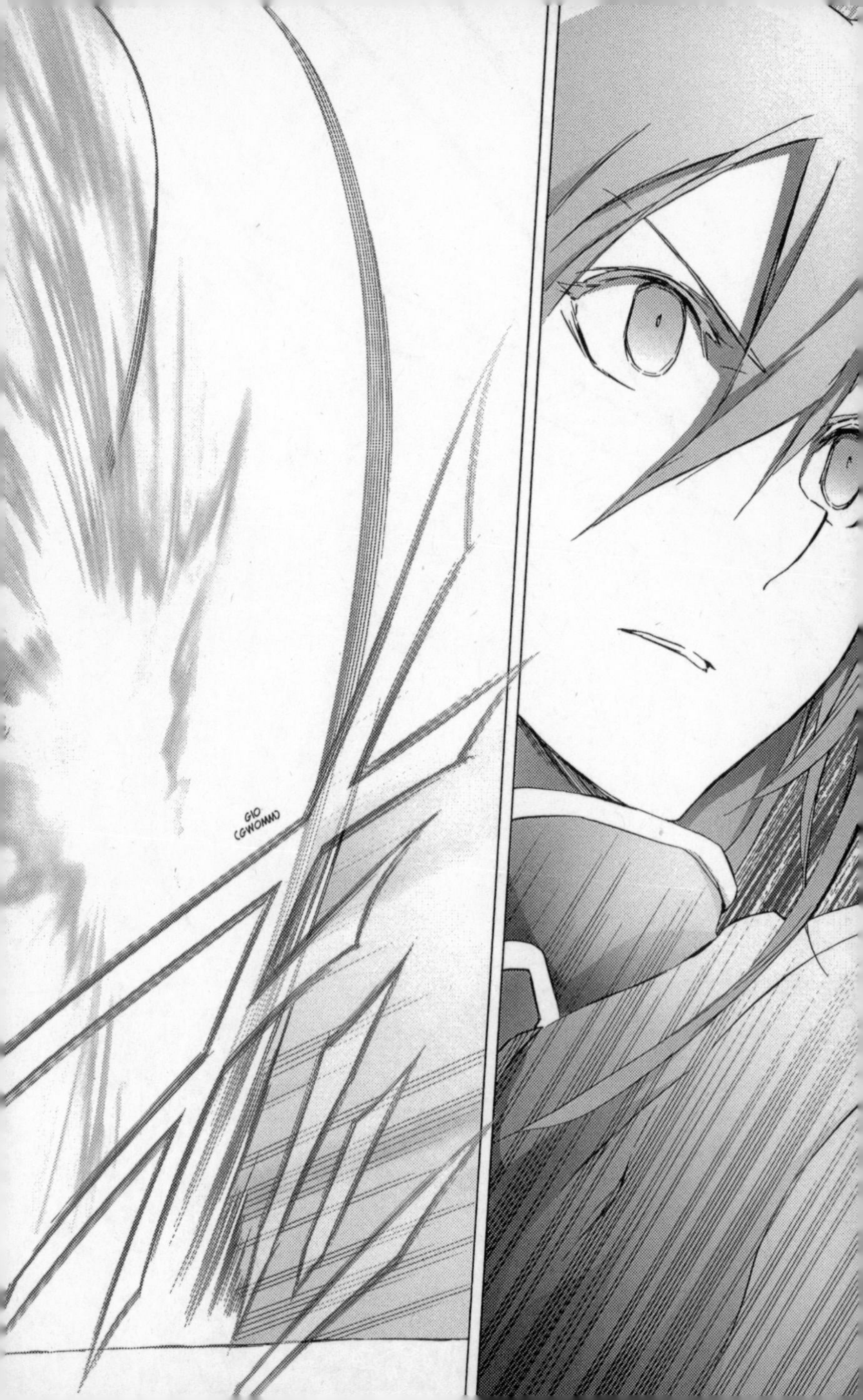
GIO
(GWOMM)

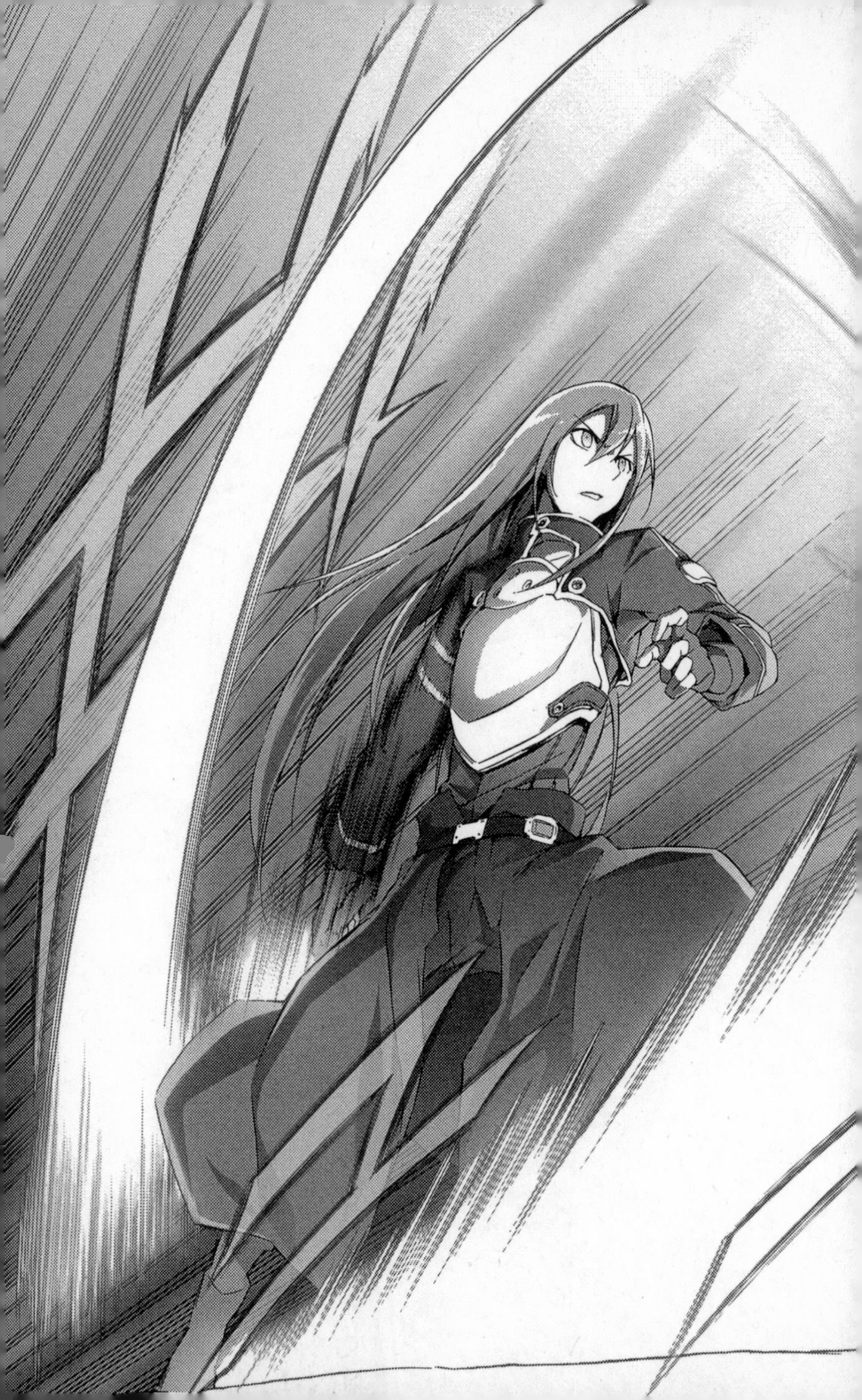

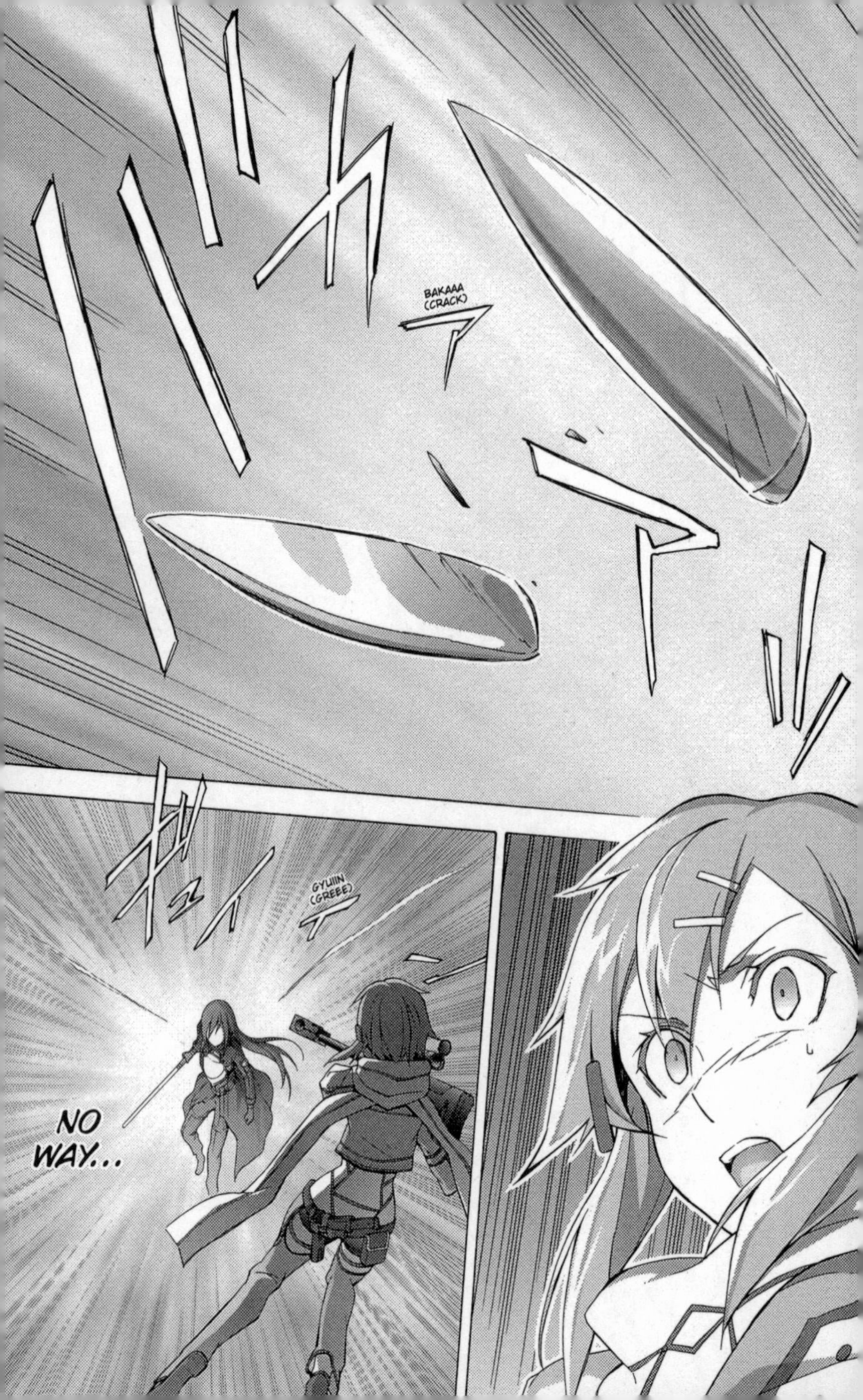
BAKAAA (CRACK)
GYUIIN (GREBE)
NO WAY...

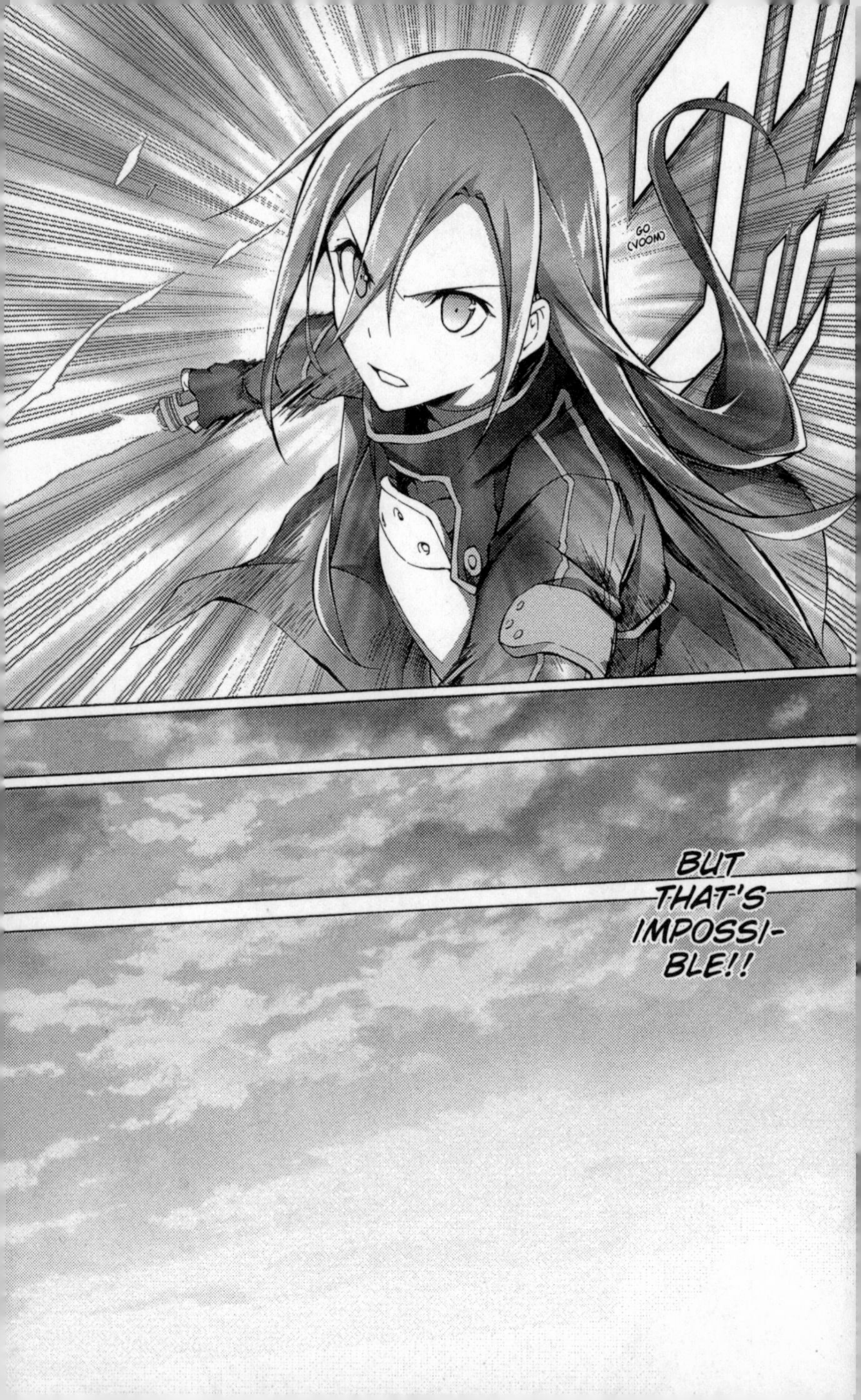
GO
(VOOM)
BUT THAT'S IMPOSSI-BLE!!

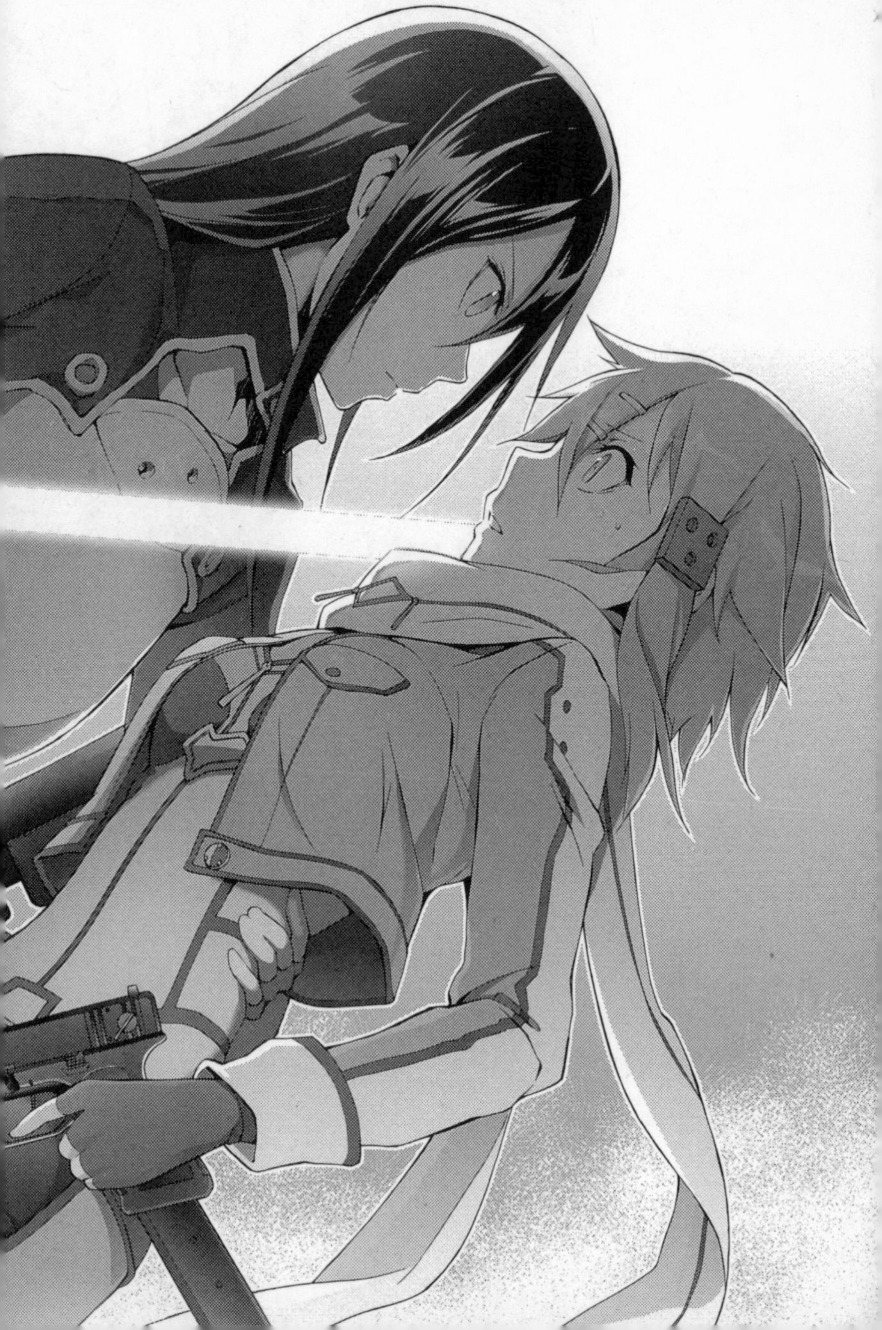

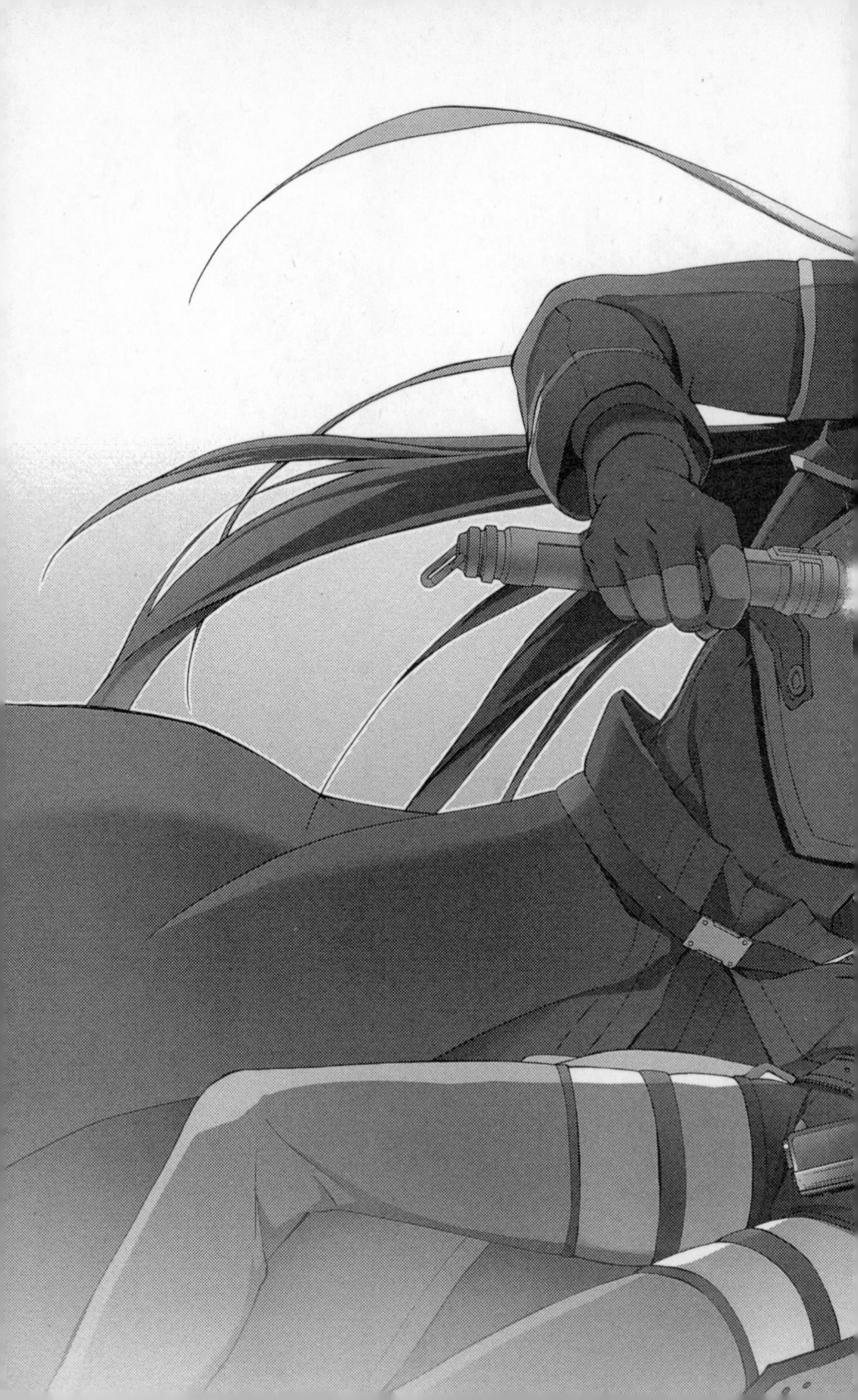

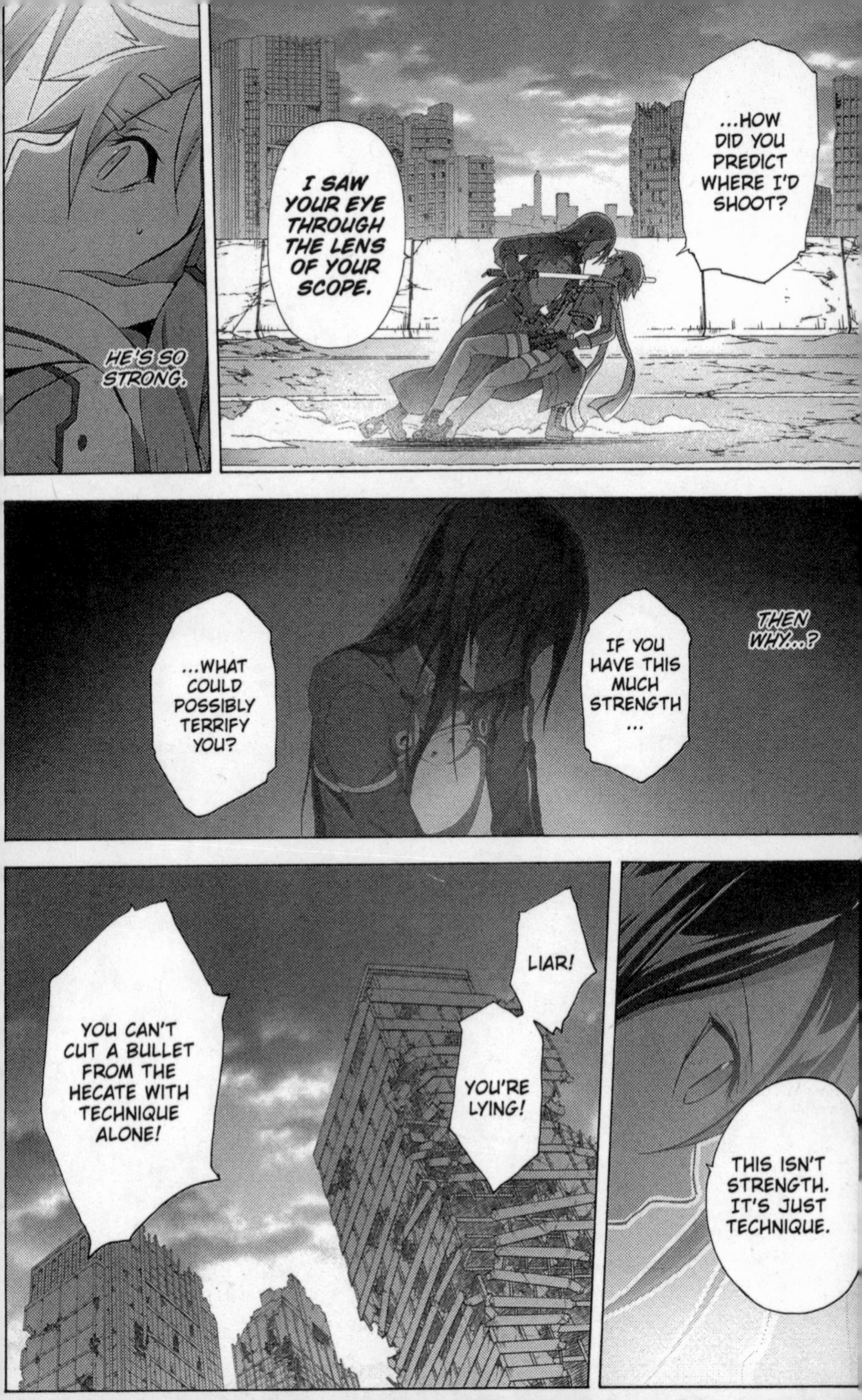
...HOW DID YOU PREDICT WHERE I'D SHOOT?
I SAW YOUR EYE THROUGH THE LENS OF YOUR SCOPE.
HE'S SO STRONG.
THEN WHY...?
IF YOU HAVE THIS MUCH STRENGTH...
...WHAT COULD POSSIBLY TERRIFY YOU?
THIS ISN'T STRENGTH. IT'S JUST TECHNIQUE.
LIAR!
YOU'RE LYING!
YOU CAN'T CUT A BULLET FROM THE HECATE WITH TECHNIQUE ALONE!

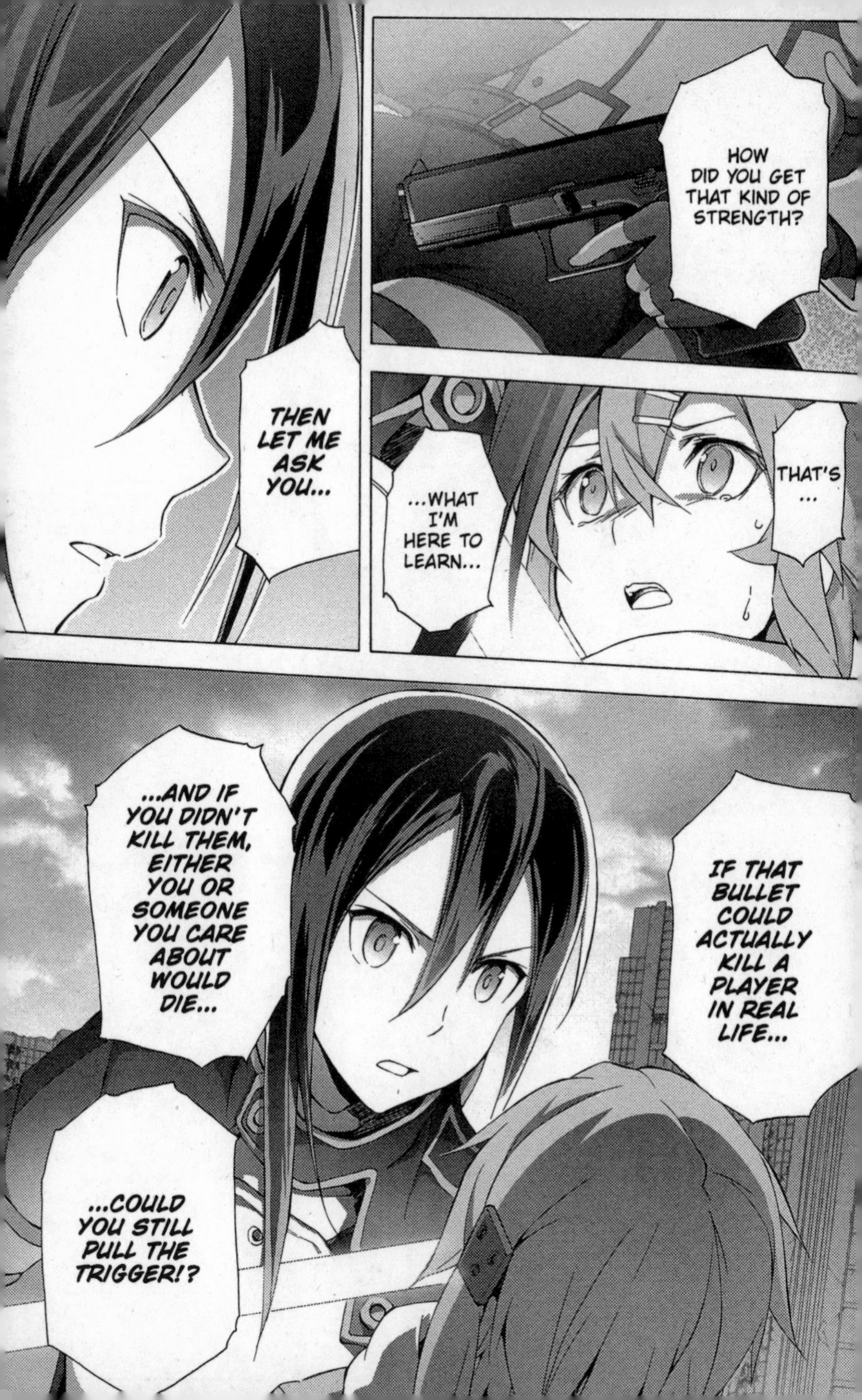
HOW DID YOU GET THAT KIND OF STRENGTH?
THAT'S ...
...WHAT I'M HERE TO LEARN...
THEN LET ME ASK YOU...
IF THAT BULLET COULD ACTUALLY KILL A PLAYER IN REAL LIFE...
...AND IF YOU DIDN'T KILL THEM, EITHER YOU OR SOMEONE YOU CARE ABOUT WOULD DIE...
...COULD YOU STILL PULL THE TRIGGER!?

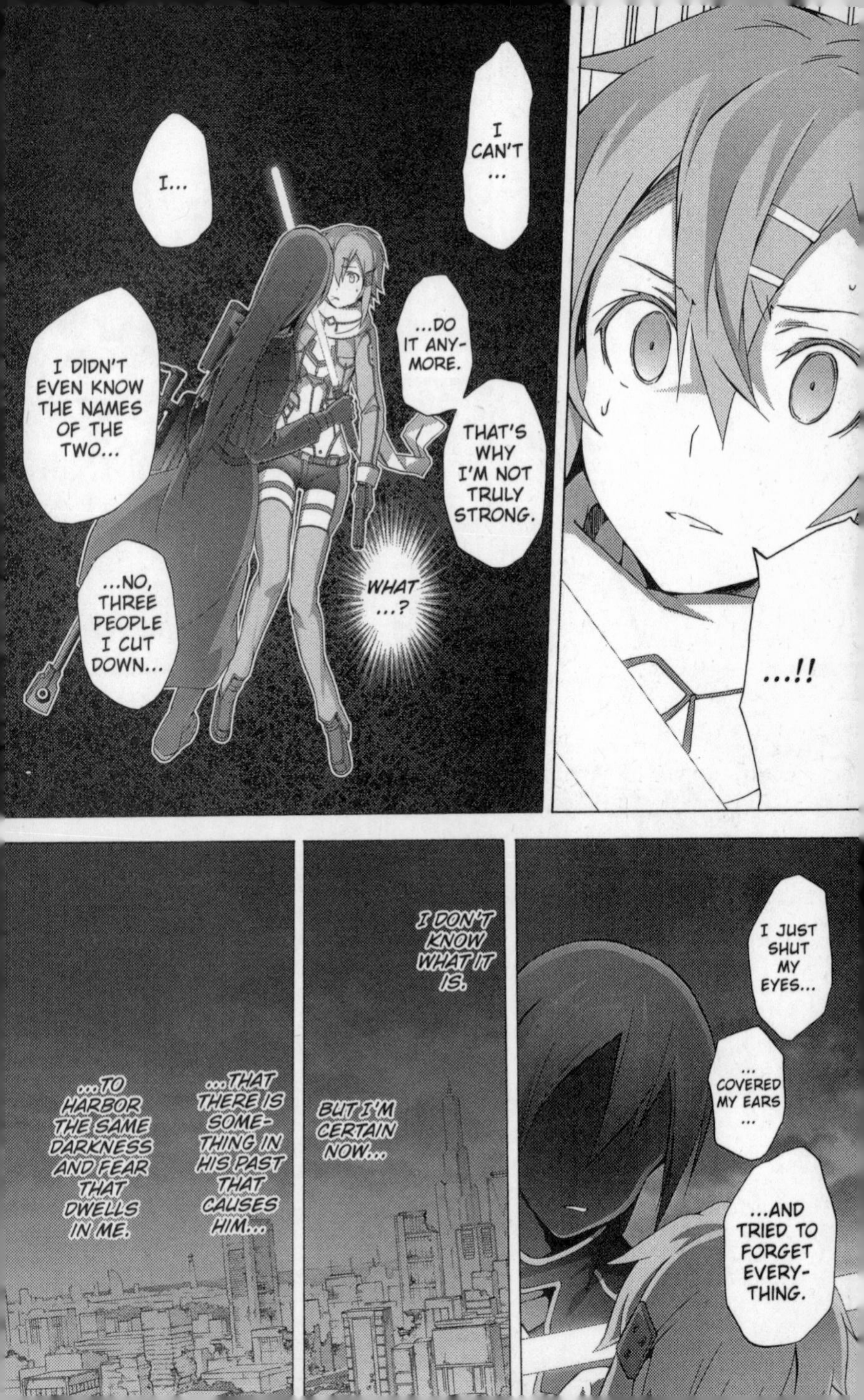
...!!
I CAN'T ...
...DO IT ANYMORE.
THAT'S WHY I'M NOT TRULY STRONG.
I...
WHAT ...?
I DIDN'T EVEN KNOW THE NAMES OF THE TWO...
...NO, THREE PEOPLE I CUT DOWN...
I JUST SHUT MY EYES...
... COVERED MY EARS ...
...AND TRIED TO FORGET EVERYTHING.
I DON'T KNOW WHAT IT IS.
BUT I'M CERTAIN NOW...
...THAT THERE IS SOMETHING IN HIS PAST THAT CAUSES HIM...
...TO HARBOR THE SAME DARKNESS AND FEAR THAT DWELLS IN ME.

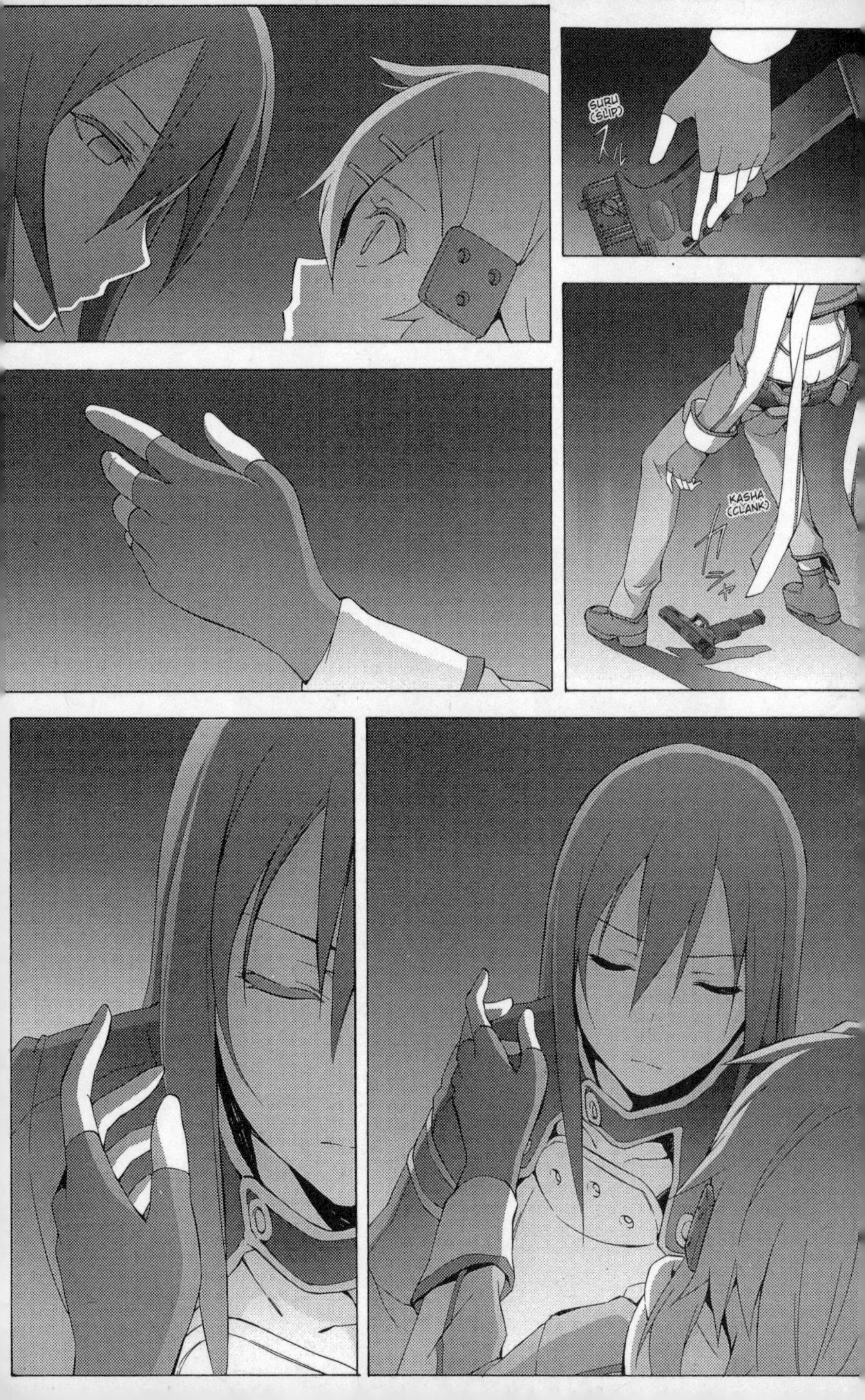
SURU (SLIP)
スル
KASHA (CLANK)
カシャ

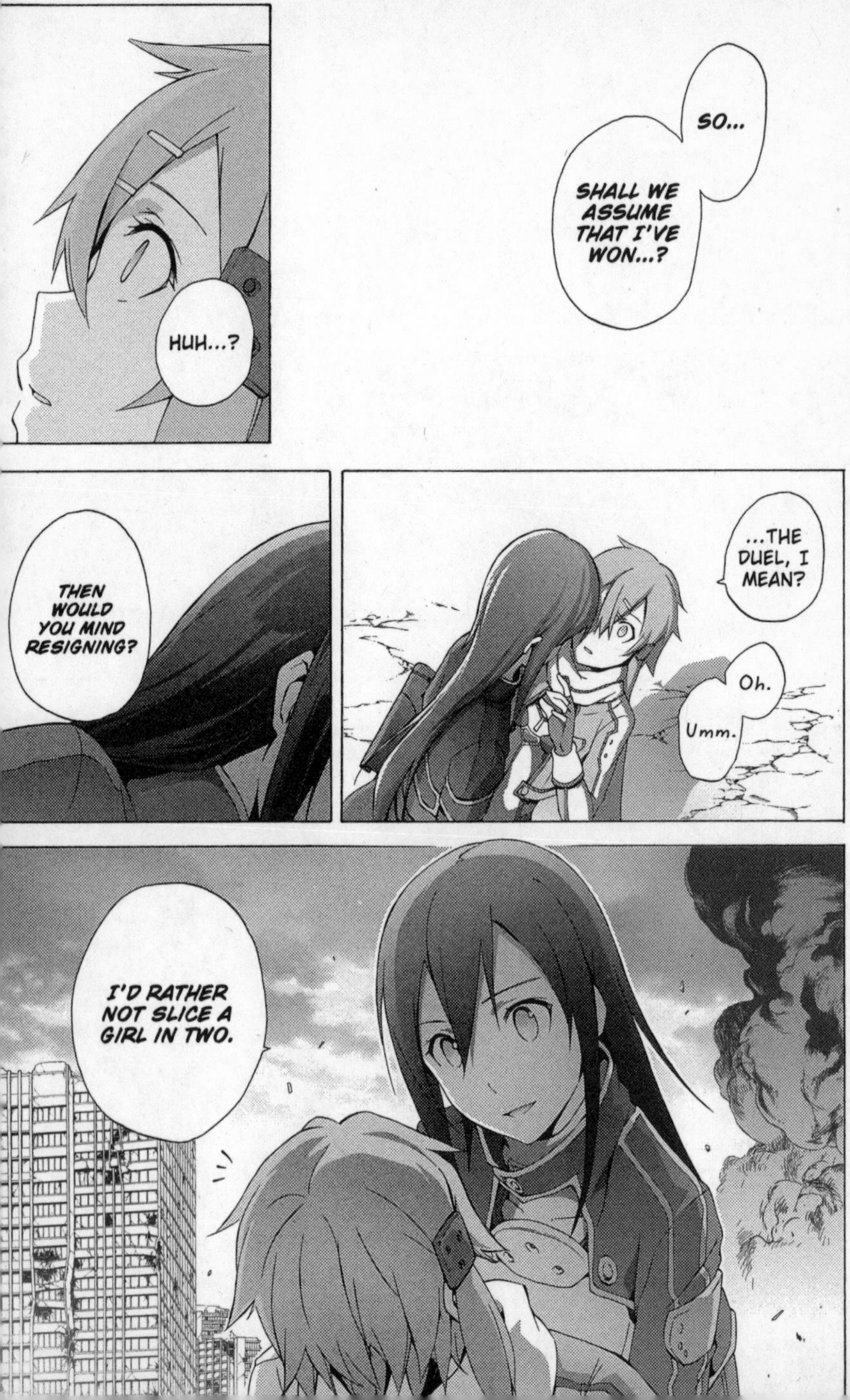
SO...
SHALL WE ASSUME THAT I'VE WON...?
HUH...?
...THE DUEL, I MEAN?
Oh.
Umm.
THEN WOULD YOU MIND RESIGNING?
I'D RATHER NOT SLICE A GIRL IN TWO.

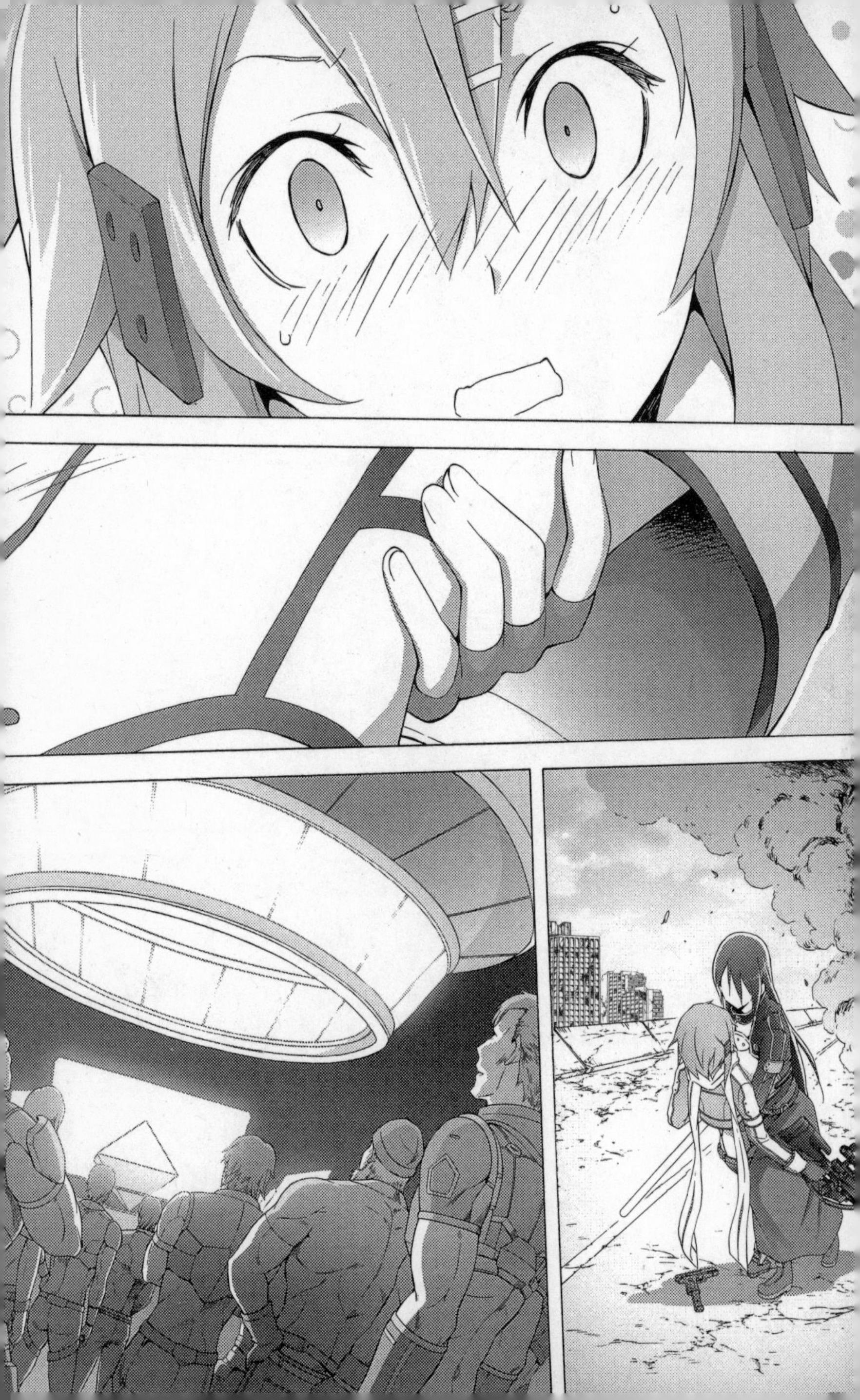

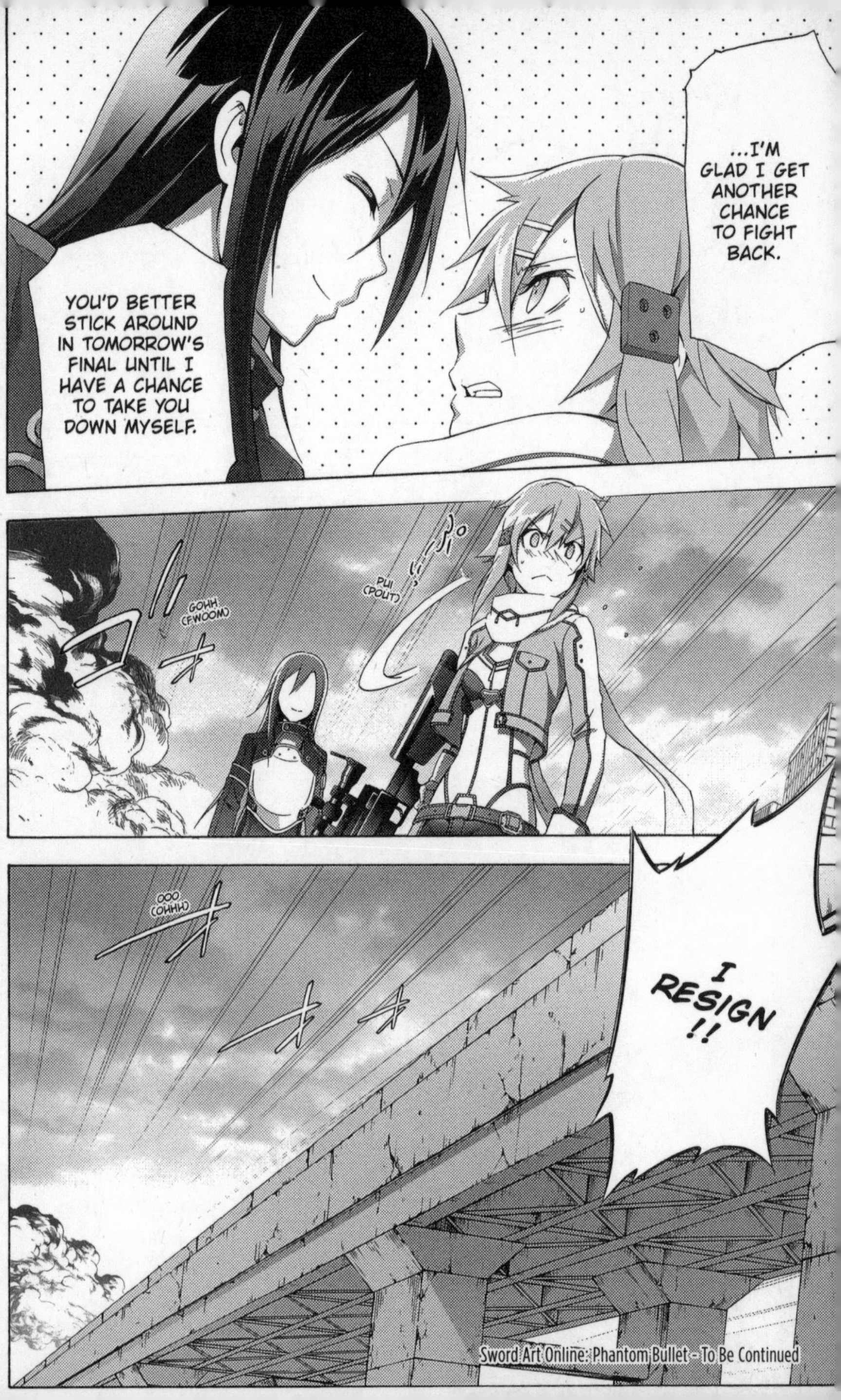
...I'M GLAD I GET ANOTHER CHANCE TO FIGHT BACK.
YOU'D BETTER STICK AROUND IN TOMORROW'S FINAL UNTIL I HAVE A CHANCE TO TAKE YOU DOWN MYSELF.
PUI (POUT)
GOHH (FWOOM)
I RESIGN!!
OOO (OHHH)
Sword Art Online: Phantom Bullet - To Be Continued

002

SWORD ART ONLINE phantom bullet

Art: Koutarou Yamada
original story: Reki Kawahara
character design: abec

SPECIAL COMMENT

original story: Reki Kawahara

CONGRATULATIONS ON THE PUBLI-
CATION OF THE SECOND VOLUME OF
PHANTOM BULLET!
YAMADA-SAN'S SINON IS SO FASCI-
NATING! BEHIND THAT COOL EXTERIOR,
SHE'S GOT THAT FRAGILE GLASS
TENSION AND FIERY EMOTION! I CAN'T
WAIT TO SEE MORE OF COOL, CUTE,
BEAUTIFUL SINON!

REKI KAWAHARA

ILLUSTRATION/REKI KAWAHARA

SWORD ART ONLINE: PHANTOM BULLET ②

ART: KOUTAROU YAMADA
ORIGINAL STORY: REKI KAWAHARA
CHARACTER DESIGN: abec

Translation: Stephen Paul
Lettering: Brndn Blakeslee

SWORD ART ONLINE: Phantom Bullet
© REKI KAWAHARA/KOUTAROU YAMADA 2015
All rights reserved.
Edited by ASCII MEDIA WORKS
First published in Japan in 2015 by KADOKAWA CORPORATION, Tokyo.
English translation rights arranged with KADOKAWA CORPORATION, Tokyo,
through Tuttle-Mori Agency, Inc., Tokyo.

English translation © 2016 by Hachette Book Group, Inc.

Yen Press
Hachette Book Group
1290 Avenue of the Americas
New York, NY 10104

www.HachetteBookGroup.com
www.YenPress.com

Yen Press is an imprint of Hachette Book Group, Inc. The Yen Press name and logo are trademarks of Hachette Book Group, Inc.

First Yen Press Edition: April 2016

Library of Congress Control Number: 2015960121

ISBN: 978-0-316-31495-4

10 9 8 7 6 5 4 3 2 1

BVG

Printed in the United States of America